PRAISE FOR
OFF THE GRID: FBI SERIES

#1 NEW YORK TIMES BESTSELLING AUTHOR
BARBARA FREETHY

"Perilous Trust is a non-stop thriller that seamlessly melds jaw-dropping suspense with sizzling romance, and I was riveted from the first page to the last...Readers will be breathless in anticipation as this fast-paced and enthralling love story evolves and goes in unforeseeable directions."

— USA Today HEA Blog

"Barbara Freethy's first book in her OFF THE GRID series is an emotional, action packed, crime drama that keeps you on the edge of your seat...I'm exhausted after reading this but in a good way. 5 Stars!"

— Booklovers Anonymous

"Getting tangled up with Perilous Trust is a rush. Barbara Freethy sets the adrenaline level so high that it takes a while to come back down to solid ground. A tortured love affair sets off a chain of events that are explosive and deadly. The suspense is killer, the danger is intense and the electricity generated between Sophie and Damon is off the charts. All come together to a create a lethally seductive thriller."

— I Love Romance Blog

"The adventure that Barbara Freethy takes us on in PERILOUS TRUST is full of twists and turns. It is a perfect suspense that will keep you guessing until the very last moment. This book definitely deserves 5 stars."

— Reading Escape Reviews

"Perilous Trust was an action packed romantic suspense novel that from the first page you are bang in the middle of the story. I liked Barbara' Freethy's writing, the story was told in duel POVs which definitely made for a good read to see both perspectives of the case developing. I also liked the side characters woven into the story. I am looking forward to seeing more of them in the series."

— Reading Away the Days Blog

"This book had a great plot, full of action and suspense. There are some great secondary characters who I can't wait to have their stories told. The plot twists are pretty awesome and even better, I couldn't figure out who the actual bad guy was. I can't wait to read the next book in this series."

— Nice Ladies Naughty Books Blog

"Perilous Trust is such a thrill ride! I love the mystery and the intense action of the characters and plot."

— Cuz I'm a Nerd Blog

"It's been a while since I have had the fun of reading a brilliant romantic suspense book – Perilous Trust gets me back into this genre with a bang!"

— For the Love of Fictional Worlds

"A uniquely seductive, gripping and exhilarating romantic suspense that is fast paced and action packed...Barbara Freethy is the ultimate seducer. She hooked me and slowly and keenly reeled me in. I was left in a trance. I just cannot wait for the next book."

— MammieBabbie.com

"This was my first time reading Barbara Freethy and I loved this story from start to finish. Right from the start the tension sets in, goodness, my heart was starting to beat a little fast by the end of the prologue! I found myself staying up late finishing this book, and that is something I don't normally do."

— My Book Filled Life Blog

"The suspense and action continued throughout the whole novel really keeping the pacing going strong and the reader engaged. I flew through this story as Sophie and Damon went from escaping one danger into having to fend off another. I'd definitely recommend this novel to anyone who like suspense romance or even contemporary romance. Its fast paced, entertaining and filled with sexually tense moments that would appeal to any romance lover!"

— PopCrunchBoomBooks.com

"This was just a well-written story with lots of twists and turns. Who's bad? Who's good? Who killed Sophie's father? There's also lots of hot and steamy romance! I'm looking forward to the next installment! 5 Sexy Stars!"

— Knottygirlreview.com

Also By Barbara Freethy

Off The Grid: FBI Series
Perilous Trust (#1)
Reckless Whisper (#2)
Desperate Play (#3)
Elusive Promise (#4), *Coming 2019!*
Dangerous Choice (#5), *Coming 2019!*

Lightning Strikes Trilogy
Beautiful Storm (#1)
Lightning Lingers (#2)
Summer Rain (#3)

The Sanders Brothers Series
Silent Run & Silent Fall

The Deception Series
Taken & Played

The Callaway Series
On A Night Like This (#1)
So This Is Love (#2)
Falling For A Stranger (#3)
Between Now and Forever (#4)
Nobody But You (Callaway Wedding Novella)
All A Heart Needs (#5)
That Summer Night (#6)
When Shadows Fall (#7)
Somewhere Only We Know (#8)

The Callaway Cousins
If I Didn't Know Better (#1)
Tender Is The Night (#2)
Take Me Home (A Callaway Novella)
Closer To You (#3)
Once You're Mine (#4)
Can't Let Go (#5)
Secrets We Keep (#6), *Coming Soon!*

Standalone Novels
Almost Home
All She Ever Wanted
Ask Mariah
Daniel's Gift
Don't Say A Word
Golden Lies
Just The Way You Are
Love Will Find A Way
One True Love
Ryan's Return
Some Kind of Wonderful
Summer Secrets
The Sweetest Thing

DESPERATE PLAY

Off The Grid: FBI Series #3

BARBARA FREETHY

HYDE
STREET
—PRESS—

HYDE STREET PRESS
Published by Hyde Street Press
1325 Howard Avenue, #321, Burlingame, California 94010

© Copyright 2018 by Hyde Street Press

Desperate Play is a work of fiction. All incidents, dialogue and all characters are products of the author's imagination and are not to be construed as real. Any resemblance to persons living or dead is entirely coincidental.

Printed in the United States of America

Cover design by Damonza.com

ISBN: 978-1-944417-41-3

One

As the sun rose over Manhattan Beach, Wyatt Tanner adjusted the baseball hat on his head and changed positions on the very uncomfortable bench upon which he'd spent the past few hours. It was a little before seven, and he was happy to see the city waking up. He was itchy to get the day going.

He pulled a granola bar out of his weathered, green seabag and downed it in two bites, then tossed the wrapper into the nearby overflowing trash can. The food did little to ease the gnawing hunger in his gut. He'd always been a big breakfast person, and right now visions of eggs, bacon, hash browns, and pancakes with powdered sugar and hot maple syrup floated through his head.

Later, he told himself, not sure that was a promise he would keep. But he'd told so many lies in his life, what was one more?

He ran a hand through his dirty, brown hair and wondered how the hell he'd gotten here. It was a thought that had been running through his head far too frequently the past several months. Of course, he knew how he'd gotten here, but sometimes the twists and turns his life had taken seemed surreal, even to him.

But he couldn't get lost in the past.

An old minivan pulled into the parking lot behind him. Three young males tumbled out of the van along with a few empty beer cans. He hoped those were from the night before.

The men pulled on wetsuits, grabbed their surfboards and headed across the sand. They were young, ripped, full of life, and cocky as hell.

He could almost remember that feeling…

Not that he was old, but this morning he was feeling every day of his thirty-two years.

As the wind picked up, he zipped up his weathered bomber jacket, and was happy he wasn't out on the ocean today. It was early December, for God's sake. This might be Southern California, and while the temp was supposed to get up into the low seventies today, it was only in the fifties now, and the sea was ice-cold. But he could understand the lure of the waves, the adrenaline rush that came from battling Mother Nature. Since he'd come to California, he'd been out on those waves more than once, impatiently waiting for the ride of his life. Usually, the ocean did not disappoint.

He sat up straighter as a black Escalade pulled into the lot a few spots away from the mini-van. The driver, a male in his mid-forties, wearing a conservative gray suit, got out from behind the wheel and moved around the front of the car to open the back door.

An older man stepped onto the pavement, his hair white, his skin tan, and his body lean in his black wetsuit. The man had probably fifty years on the three teenagers who had hit the beach before him, but there was excitement in his expression as his gaze moved toward the large waves crushing the beach. It wasn't a day for amateurs, but clearly this man did not fall into that category.

The driver handed the man his surfboard and then said, "You need anything else for now, Mr. Tremaine?"

"No, thanks, Robert. Go have your coffee. I won't be more than a half hour. Busy day today."

"Enjoy yourself," Robert replied, before heading down the strand toward a beachside café a quarter of a mile away.

The older man ran a reverent hand down his board and smiled to himself. He was clearly looking forward to riding the waves. But as he picked up the board, a dark SUV came speeding into the lot, stopping directly behind the Escalade, rather than pulling into an adjacent parking spot.

Wyatt's gut clenched. Trouble was coming.

The two men who exited the vehicle looked more like thugs than surfers, wearing jeans and dark jackets, baseball caps on their heads, dark sunglasses covering their eyes. As they moved toward the Escalade, the taller man pulled out a gun.

He jumped to his feet.

The older man suddenly realized the danger he was in as the shorter man ripped the surfboard away from him, tossing it onto the ground while his friend shoved the older gentleman up against the side of the car, pressing the gun into his side.

Wyatt wasn't about to let the man be robbed, kidnapped or carjacked. No one was paying any attention to him. He was just another homeless person on the beach.

He took a wide circle around the van, so he could creep up behind the shorter man. He grabbed him by both shoulders and bounced his head off the side of the car. The man groaned and slumped to the ground.

The taller man heard the commotion, turned toward him, gun in hand.

He rushed forward, slamming into the arm that held the gun, the weapon falling to the ground. He kicked it away as the other man threw a fist at his face.

He winced, dodging a second too late to avoid contact.

Then he reared back and landed a blow of his own. The man stumbled backward, hitting the side of the car, before racing back toward his vehicle. His fellow assailant also stumbled toward the car. They took off with a squeal of tires.

Wyatt looked down at the older man who was leaning against the side of the car, looking shocked and scared, his face as white as his hair.

"Are you all right?" he asked.

The man struggled to get out the words. "You saved my life. Those men came out of nowhere."

"Right place at the right time," he said with a shrug. "What happened to your driver?"

"Robert went to get coffee. I need to call 911. My phone. *Damn.* I don't have it with me. Do you have one?"

"Nope. I'm traveling light these days. Just me and my duffel." He tipped his head toward the bench where his duffel seemed to be drawing the interest of a homeless person, who had wandered down the beach. He jogged over and grabbed it, urging the other man to keep moving.

The older man came up next to him. "I want to thank you," he said, sincerity in his bright-blue eyes.

"Not necessary."

The man's gaze fell to the military insignia on his seabag. "You're a Marine?"

"Was," he said.

"So was I—about forty years ago." The man extended his hand. "I'm Hamilton Tremaine."

"Nice to meet you," he said, not really surprised by the firm handshake.

"And you are…"

"Wyatt Tanner."

"Do you live around here?"

"Some days," he said vaguely.

The man's gaze sharpened. "You're homeless?"

"Let's just say I'm between jobs and apartments."

"Come back to the car with me. I may have left my phone at home, but I have my wallet."

He quickly put up a hand. "No. I appreciate the offer, but I don't take charity, Mr. Tremaine."

"Call it a thank-you gift."

"I'm glad you're okay. That's all the thanks I need, especially knowing you're a fellow Marine."

"I need to give you more than my thanks. My driver usually acts as my bodyguard. But I've never had any trouble down here in the early mornings. I always send him off for coffee while I surf. I should have been more careful." His gaze darkened. "I've become predictable. If you hadn't been here...well, I don't know what would have happened."

"You should be careful, especially if you're the kind of man who needs a bodyguard."

"You haven't heard of me?" Hamilton asked, giving him a thoughtful look.

"Sorry. I've been out of touch the last few years."

"Where did you serve?"

"Afghanistan. I was in Intelligence—MCIA," he said, referring to the Marine Corps Intelligence Activity division.

"Why did you leave?"

He let out a heavy sigh. "I was injured in an ambush. Explosion took away my hearing for a while. It eventually came back but not in time to pass the physical."

"And you haven't been able to find a job since you got home?"

"It's been a rough couple of months, but I'll figure it out."

"Sure. Do you have family?"

"No, it's just me. But I'm fine with that."

"Well, I'm not fine with it. Let me help you, Mr. Tanner."

"That's very generous of you, but I can take care of myself." He grabbed his bag. "I'm going to head out."

"No. I'm not letting you leave," Hamilton said forcefully. "And I have more to offer you than charity; I run a very successful company. I'm sure we can find a job for an ex-Marine. In fact, I could use someone like you on my security team. My long-time security director just decided to retire and move to Florida with his wife, and I've been on the look-out for a replacement."

"Seriously? I am willing to work. But not if it's a job

you're just making up for charity."

"It's definitely not that. You're a soldier. You know how to fight. And I know I can trust a fellow Marine to have my back."

"Always," he said. "But I don't want to take advantage. I'm sure you have other people in your company who can do the job."

"Sometimes it's good to have an outsider's objective opinion." He paused. "You risked your life to save mine. Not many men are willing to do that. Putting you to work is the least I can do. Why don't we walk down to the café, and I'll get my—" Hamilton stopped abruptly as his driver came running down the path.

"Is this man bothering you?" the driver asked aggressively, giving him a hard look.

"He's not bothering me. He just saved my life. I was assaulted by two men, one of whom put a gun in my side, but this man ran them off. Wyatt Tanner, meet my driver, Robert Burton."

He inclined his head as Robert turned pale.

Robert gave his employer a searching look. "Are you hurt? Were you robbed?"

"No. Like I said, Mr. Tanner ran them off. I was just coming to get you. We need to call 911."

"I'm on it," Robert replied, taking out his phone.

Hamilton put his surfboard in the back of the vehicle and then grabbed Wyatt's bag from his hands and tossed it in the backseat. "I still have my seabag in a closet at home. My wife used to threaten to throw it away every other year, but I just couldn't let her do it." He paused. "I was in Vietnam. Drafted. Wasn't my idea to serve, but I'm a better man for it. What about you?"

"I enlisted at nineteen. And I'm a better man for it, too."

A gleam of understanding entered Hamilton's eyes. "Glad to hear you say that."

Two police cars pulled into the lot a moment later. After

hearing Hamilton's name, the officers became much more interested in what had happened.

They each gave their statements. Unfortunately, neither he nor Hamilton Tremaine had seen the license plate number on the car, and their descriptions of the attackers could probably match hundreds of men in the Los Angeles area.

Wyatt kept his answers as short as possible, and when the police asked for an address where they could reach him, he gave the name of a motel a few blocks away. It didn't really matter. The officers were far more interested in talking to Hamilton. One seemed particularly star struck and mentioned several times how excited he was about Hamilton's private aerospace company Nova Star.

Tremaine had pulled himself together since the attack, speaking forcefully and articulately now that the shock of what had almost happened wore off. He admitted that the attack had felt targeted and personal, and Wyatt certainly didn't disagree. But he doubted the police would come even close to finding Hamilton's attackers.

As the officers left, Hamilton insisted Wyatt get into the Escalade.

He attempted one last protest. "I appreciate the offer of a possible job, but I'd like to get cleaned up, so I don't scare your human resource people. Perhaps I could come down to your office later today."

"Do you have somewhere to go and do that?" Hamilton asked.

"There's a shelter a few blocks away."

Hamilton shook his head. "No way. We'll go to my house."

"Mr. Tremaine—can I speak to you for a moment?" Robert interrupted.

"I know what you're going to say," Hamilton replied, giving Robert a hard look. "But this man saved my life."

"You don't know anything about him," Robert said in a hushed voice that Wyatt could clearly hear.

"I know he's a Marine. That's good enough for me."

"But you can't just take him to your house."

"He's right," Wyatt said quickly. "I'll go to the shelter—"

"You'll go to a hotel," Hamilton said. "We'll check you in, drop you off, and cover any food you need. When you're ready, we'll set you up with an interview. And I'm not taking no for an answer. So, get in the car."

"All right. But the hotel doesn't have to be fancy."

Hamilton smiled. "Trust me. It will be just what you need."

———

Fifteen minutes later, Wyatt realized that *just what he needed* was a one-bedroom suite in a five-star hotel on Santa Monica Beach with a complimentary fruit basket that was apparently the precursor to a deluxe breakfast that would be on its way up shortly.

After checking out the view from his ocean-facing balcony, Wyatt went back into the living room and unzipped a pocket inside his seabag. He took out a small phone and punched in a short text.

I'm almost in.

The text that came back was filled with swear words, followed by…

You broke my nose.

He felt only marginally guilty. *You've needed a nose job for a while.*

I told you to watch the face. Where are you?

The Beaumont. Going to get cleaned up before my job interview with the very grateful Hamilton Tremaine.

Next time I get to be the bum to the rescue.

He didn't reply, just put the phone away and headed for the shower. Then he was going to have a really big breakfast.

TWO

—⇒≫✖≪⇐—

*F*our *weeks later ...*

Avery Caldwell was not a fan of funhouses or roller coasters, so she would have preferred catching up with her old friend Noelle Price at a wine bar or a nice restaurant instead of the chaotic and crowded amusement park on the Santa Monica Pier. But Noelle had insisted they do something different. She wanted to release some stress and had said there was no better place than a roller coaster to scream your guts out.

Hearing the screams on the nearby Twirling Tornado ride, Avery thought a lot of people were letting out their stress. She could understand it. It was Friday night, and she'd had a long week, too, but spinning herself upside down was not going to ease her tension. A hot bath, a glass of pinot, maybe a good book was what she needed.

Frowning, she realized she was sounding boring even to herself. Maybe Noelle was right, and she did need to change things up.

"Cotton candy," Noelle said with a squeal. "We have to get some." She grabbed Avery's hand, much the same way she'd done when they were ten years old and spending every minute together.

"It's just straight up sugar," she protested.

"Exactly. Do you want one?" Noelle asked, as they stopped in front of the stand. She let go of Avery's hand to reach into her handbag. "I'm paying."

"I'm good. Thanks."

As Noelle ordered her cotton candy, Avery couldn't help thinking how different they still were. Sometimes, it amazed her that they'd ever become friends, but the bond between them had formed when they were eight years old, and while it had sometimes bent and strained over the years, it was still there.

They'd been through a lot together over the years. Noelle had been there for her when her dad had left her mom to become a celebrity writer and motivational speaker. And she'd been there for Noelle when her dad and grandmother had died in a car crash.

They'd also been each other's wing-woman through middle school and high school and a bit into college, but that's when their differences had started to divide them. Noelle's partying had gone extreme, and Avery had been more interested in becoming an astrophysicist than hitting up the latest fraternity party.

They'd lost touch sometime their senior year and while she'd gone on to grad school, Noelle had left LA to travel and take whatever job served her wanderlust and party nature. They hadn't spoken for six or seven years. But they'd reconnected two months earlier when Noelle had reached out on social media and asked her to get a drink.

When they'd met up, it felt like no time had passed at all. Although, she had been a little disappointed when Noelle asked for her help in getting a job, thinking that perhaps that was the only reason she'd sought her out.

While she'd been a bit reluctant to recommend Noelle for a job at her employer, Nova Star Technologies, because

Noelle could be kind of flaky, she hadn't been able to say no.

Thankfully, Noelle had gotten the job and been a great employee so far.

"This is amazing," Noelle said, returning with her cotton candy, her blue eyes lighting up as she bit into the sugary web of delight. "Do you want some?"

She started to say no, but then she saw the look of resignation in Noelle's eyes and realized she was becoming quite the wet blanket. "Sure." She took a handful and popped it into her mouth.

"It's good, right?" Noelle prodded.

She laughed. "Yes, and I feel like I'm eight years old again."

"Not a bad age. It's when we met."

"I was just thinking that."

"I quickly became your bad influence."

"And I was your good influence." She met her friend's gaze with a smile.

Noelle nodded. "The first time you spoke to me was at summer camp. You gave me a hat, because my white skin was starting to freckle and burn."

"With your red hair and pale skin, I didn't know how you'd come to camp without a hat and a gallon of sunscreen."

Noelle laughed. "Later you learned I never planned ahead and forgetting a hat was probably the least of my vices."

"That's true," she said dryly. "And you learned I always planned ahead. My mother taught me to be practical."

"And she hung on to you as tightly as she could."

"She felt like she needed to hold my feet to the ground, especially since my father was always floating around like some shiny balloon about to leave one party and go to the next."

"Your father did love to chase shiny objects. Speaking of which, is he really going to marry Whitney Tremaine?"

"It looks that way," she said with a sigh. "It's ridiculous. She's twenty years younger than him."

"Men don't seem to have a problem with that age difference, especially when they're in their fifties."

"I've tried to tell both of them to go slow, but neither one is hearing me. Whitney is caught up in my dad's magnetic charm, and my father has always loved an adoring and beautiful fan."

"Maybe they'll be happy," Noelle suggested.

"I doubt it. My dad has no more substance than your cotton candy. He has built his entire life on a charade, pretending to be wise and well-traveled and self-aware, and Whitney has bought into it."

"Well, you can't do anything about it. They're both grown-ups."

"You're right. I can't change anything, so I'm trying to stay out of it. I just respect the Tremaines so much, especially Hamilton. He gave me a great job, all the freedom I could ever want to build out an incredible educational program at Nova Star, and I don't want my father to ruin my relationship with the Tremaines, which he could easily do."

"The Tremaines seem to like him."

"Hamilton was leery at first, but Whitney has been so unhappy since her mom died last year, he likes that my father puts a smile on her face."

"Well, maybe your dad will do better with Whitney than he did with your mom."

"Maybe." An odd feeling ran through her as Noelle glanced at her watch again.

Noelle was up to something. She suddenly felt like they were sixteen again, and Noelle had asked her to go to a movie. But she hadn't really wanted her company; she'd just needed a cover for meeting up with a boyfriend her mother didn't like. "What's going on?"

"Nothing."

"I've seen this act before. You invited me here for a reason, and it wasn't just to catch up."

Noelle stared back at her, an odd glint in her eyes. "You

probably know me better than anyone else, Avery."

"I used to. But we haven't been close the last couple of years."

"I'm sorry about that," Noelle said.

"Me, too. I don't really know what happened."

"I think we started judging each other."

She couldn't deny that. "We did do that."

"But we're hanging out now. We can't change the past, but we can do better in the future. I am really grateful that you got me the job at Nova Star, Avery. I know you weren't sure if I'd screw up, and I can't blame you for thinking that, because I have messed up a lot in my life, and you have often had to clean up the mess. But I am trying to change things. I'm not the person I used to be."

She was a little shocked at Noelle's surprisingly serious tone. "From what I've heard, you're doing great at work."

"I'm glad to know that." Noelle checked her watch again. "Not that it's too difficult to screw up copying, printing and filing."

"You have to start somewhere."

"I know. I actually really like Nova Star. It's inspiring to be around people who dream big, who talk about things I can't even imagine. Do you really think Hamilton Tremaine will make it to Mars one day?"

"Who knows? It makes for good press. But Nova Star is about more than a billionaire trying to get to Mars. There is important work being done on satellites and protection for those satellites."

"But none of that is as exciting as Hamilton Tremaine strapping himself into a rocket."

She smiled. "True. Hamilton is a man with a huge vision."

"And a huge bank account."

"He worked his way to money, though. His parents weren't wealthy. He made it all himself. I admire that."

"I do, too. It makes me feel like if he can do it, we can,

too. Not that you care about money—unless it's about funding some new science project," Noelle teased.

"Money is very important to science," she agreed. "But I've never wanted to live a big life—not like my dad. He loves money and fame."

"You definitely took after your mom and not your dad," Noelle agreed, sneaking another glance at her watch.

"Okay, you have to tell me why you keep looking at the time," she said.

"No reason. Just habit, I guess. Do you like my new watch? I got it the other day. It does all kinds of things—even measures my heart rate."

"I've thought about getting one of those."

"You should. It has a bunch of cool apps on it."

"Noelle, stop."

"What?"

"Are you sure you're not meeting someone else here—maybe a man?" she suggested.

"I'm dating Carter Hayes, you know that."

"I also know that Carter is a lawyer, and he's stable, and steady, and that doesn't always suit you particularly well."

"He anchors me. Like you've always done. I know I need that. I can't keep chasing bad boys, can I?"

"Isn't there something in between bad boy and boring?"

A shadow passed through Noelle's eyes. "I don't know. I make a lot of mistakes when it comes to men. You know that better than anyone. But the only excitement I'm looking for tonight is in the funhouse. Let's do that next."

She groaned. "You know I hate funhouses, Noelle."

"You're not ten years old anymore. You won't get lost again," Noelle said, reminding her of an experience she'd had a very long time ago.

"I just don't like the experience. It's creepy, and all those weird mirrors, slanted floors and odd-shaped doorways make me uncomfortable."

Noelle laughed. "That's the point. It's good for you to get

out of your comfort zone, Avery. Your head is always in the stars, but you never take your feet off the ground."

"I know you think I'm boring—"

"Not boring, just a little too cautious, careful, wary...Sometimes I think you're afraid to live. You don't want to be like your dad, so you shy away from having adventures. You dream big but it's only about space, not about somewhere you can actually go."

"Hey, if Hamilton has his way, we'll all be taking trips to space."

"Somehow, I don't think you'd be the first to sign up."

"If anything could tempt me to take a risk, it would probably be the chance to explore the universe."

"Well, until then, think about exploring a bit more here on Earth, maybe some hot guy's hard body."

She groaned. "Haven't seen too many of those lately."

"Then find one."

She frowned. "It's not that easy."

"It's easier than you make it."

"Am I really that bad?"

"You're not bad; you're just always in control, and sometimes I think you miss out on stuff. Do you ever just throw caution to the wind? Have sex because it's fun and not because it has to lead to a relationship?"

"Sex is emotional for me," she said, thinking it had been awhile since she'd gotten physically involved with anyone. "Sometimes I wish it wasn't."

Noelle smiled. "It really doesn't have to be, but I get it. You and I are different. And I don't know why I'm trying to turn you into me, because I should be the one turning into you."

She grinned back at her friend. "I have a feeling we're both going to stay exactly the same."

"Not me. I am making some changes. But first, I'm going to have a little fun."

"Well, I'm up for fun but not the funhouse."

"Come on. It will take five minutes."

"Sorry, not happening."

"If you really don't want to go, I'll go by myself." Noelle handed her the last of the cotton candy. "You can finish this. I'll be back soon."

"Really? It's that important to you?" she asked in surprise.

"I won't be long."

"And there's nothing else going on?" She couldn't shake the feeling that something was off. Not that it was that unusual for Noelle to go off on her own when Avery didn't want to do something.

"Don't worry," Noelle said. "Look, I know I haven't always been the best person, Avery. I've made some bad decisions in my life, but like I said, I'm trying to do better now. Can you trust me on that?"

"What are you talking about? You're so serious all of a sudden."

"Well, I need to shake that off right away," Noelle said lightly. "I'll see you soon."

"I'll be here."

As Noelle left, she walked over to a nearby bench and sat down, finishing off the cotton candy and tossing the empty roller into the garbage can. Then she checked her phone for texts and emails.

As the director of the educational program at Nova Star, she worked with schools, science programs and community organizations. Hamilton Tremaine was determined to bring the universe to the common man, and he'd placed a great deal of emphasis on science, creating an auditorium for shows and talks, tours for kids, and special educational opportunities for teachers, and she got to run it all. She liked it much better than teaching at the university, which was what she'd been doing before Hamilton Tremaine had approached her about a job.

As she read through the email subject headings, she

decided to put her phone away. She didn't really want to work tonight. She hoped Noelle would be back soon. She wanted to get some food. She needed something more substantial than cotton candy.

She spent the next few minutes people-watching. The pier was crowded, everyone enjoying the balmy evening. She'd grown up in Southern California, so she was used to seventy-degree weather, even in early December, and most of the time she appreciated it. But once in a while, she wondered what it would be like to have a white Christmas. That wouldn't happen this year. There was way too much going on at Nova Star to get away for the holidays.

Maybe she'd take a trip in January. New York might be fun. Perhaps Noelle would want to go with her.

Frowning, she found herself checking her own watch. It didn't have all the bells and whistles that Noelle's watch had, but it did tell the time, and at least fifteen minutes had passed since Noelle had gone into the funhouse.

What was taking her so long? There wasn't a line, so she should have gotten right in.

As another few minutes passed, uneasiness ran through her.

She tapped her fingers on the bench, crossed and uncrossed her legs, waited another five minutes and then got to her feet when she saw two teenage girls come out of the funhouse, who had clearly gone in after Noelle.

She walked over to the entrance. Debating her options for another minute, she bought a ticket and entered the attraction. The slanted floors, dark light, labyrinth of doors and rooms that often lead nowhere, the spooky noises, heavy breathing, and occasionally shrill screams made her increasingly uneasy. Her skin prickled with discomfort, goose bumps running up and down her arms, along with a cold chill.

She never should have come in here. Noelle was probably out by now, wondering where she was.

Making another turn, she faced her distorted self in the

mirror, but there was someone behind her—a shadow, a man.

She whirled around, catching a glimpse of his profile as he moved into another room. She'd seen him before...at Nova Star. Brown hair, brown eyes, really attractive...he worked in security. Noelle had said he was hot, and she had agreed.

Was he meeting Noelle here?

It had seemed weird from the beginning that Noelle had wanted to hit up the amusement park, and she'd known that Avery would never go into the funhouse. So why had she insisted on going inside?

Well, she was here now. And she couldn't go back, so she had to go forward.

Unfortunately, her imagination was spiraling in the inky darkness.

She forced herself to keep moving, turning another corner. A female scream stopped her in her tracks. It had sounded loud and close.

Her heart pounded against her chest and her lungs constricted so tightly, she could barely breathe.

She had to get out of here!

Panic flooded through her.

She bumped into a wall and banged her arm hard, then dodged under a beam that appeared to be falling. She found herself surrounded by more mirrors. She ran through thick curtains and saw a door that said *Employees Only*. She tried the knob, hoping it was a back way out, but the door was locked. She had to turn around.

She heard moaning off to her right, down another shadowy hallway.

There were footsteps to her left, behind her, in front of her, and spooky canned laughter coming out of a speaker.

It was a cacophony of terrifying sounds. She tried to talk herself through the moment.

She was fine. Everything was good.

As the noises died down, a word wafted through the sudden stillness.

"*Help!*"

Was it just another fake, terrifying plea? The word echoed through her head, the voice sounding familiar.

Was that Noelle?

She moved down the hall and darker into the shadows. The moaning grew louder. She pulled back the heavy, thick curtain in front of her and gasped in shock.

Lying on the ground was Noelle, her hands pressing against her bloody chest, her blue eyes wide open, her lips parted as she squeezed out a word. "Avery."

"Oh, my God, Noelle." She ran to her friend's side, dropping to her knees. There was so much blood seeping from Noelle's chest, through Noelle's fingers, she didn't know what to do. "What happened?"

"Trusted the wrong person," Noelle gasped.

"This is a gag," she said in disbelief. "This is a crazy funhouse gag." She put hands over Noelle's, pressing down on the gushing wound.

"Wish...it...was... Left something... apartment...you'll recognize it from when we were young. So innocent then. Get it."

"Get what?" she asked in confusion. "What are you talking about? Who did this to you?"

"Knew it was wrong...thought I could make it right...sorry." Noelle's eyes met hers. "Love you..."

"Don't," she said forcefully. "Don't give up on me, Noelle."

Noelle struggled to take in one last breath and then her eyes closed.

"No!" she screamed. "No!"

She pressed harder on Noelle's chest, knowing even as she did so that Noelle was no longer breathing.

"Help! Help! Help!" she yelled, calling out the word over and over again, until finally pounding footsteps came up behind her.

A man and then an older female came into the hall,

flooding the room with light, and then there was more screaming.

Other people came into the corridor. She didn't know if they were staff or tourists. She couldn't look away from Noelle's face. She couldn't take her hands away from Noelle's hands. *This wasn't happening. Noelle wasn't dead. It couldn't be true.*

A team of paramedics eventually pulled her away from Noelle's lifeless body. They performed CPR, then tried to shock her heart back into beating, but nothing worked.

She saw the paramedics shake their heads at each other.

Tears streamed out of her eyes.

A police officer said something about needing to talk to her, but she could barely hear him.

Noelle was dead.

Someone had killed her.

Wyatt was stopped at the exit by a uniformed police officer who wasn't letting anyone out of the funhouse until they'd been questioned.

Having just seen Noelle Price's bloody body and Avery Caldwell's horrified face, he felt a wave of anger and frustration. But he couldn't show his emotions, not now.

He was herded into a back room with a dozen other guests. He answered the expected questions, expressed great concern, and offered himself up for whatever else they might need. He acted like someone who had nothing to hide and since there were a lot of people being detained at the same time, the officers were not that interested in him. They jotted down the name he gave them, as well as a phone number and address, none of which were accurate.

Then he was allowed to leave.

Outside the funhouse, the police had set up a perimeter with yellow tape, and there were probably fifty or so people who had been drawn to that part of the pier to see what was happening.

He moved outside the tape and under the shadows of the nearby snack shack.

Several minutes later, he watched Noelle's body get placed in the ambulance. He saw the police bring out Avery and escort her to a waiting police car.

She flung a look over her shoulder, and he instinctively ducked. But there was no way she could see him now. He was behind the crowd, out of the lights.

What he wasn't so sure about was whether she'd seen him in the funhouse. He'd been shocked to see her standing in front of one of the warped mirrors and he'd dodged out of sight as quickly as possible.

Not that she would necessarily recognize him.

While he had seen her every single day of the past four weeks on the security cameras at Nova Star, he'd never actually met her.

He'd told himself that was a good thing, because he'd found his gaze settling on her far too often.

There was something about her always hopeful expression that tugged on him. He couldn't remember when he'd last felt hopeful, when he'd last put his gaze on the stars and dreamed about something impossible...but Avery did that every day in the shows she had created.

She made people look up and wonder what might be... She was a dreamer and a scientist, and—he really needed to stop thinking about her in any terms besides the immediate situation.

Pulling out his phone, he punched in a number. "Noelle Price is dead. Avery Caldwell found her body. We need to talk."

Three

After almost an hour of questioning at the police station, Avery was told to wait in the lobby, that someone would take her home.

As she sat down in a hard chair, she glanced down at her still blood-stained hands. She'd tried to wash away Noelle's blood, but she could still see traces of it on her hands. She had a feeling no matter how many times she tried to wash it away, it would still feel like it was there.

She twisted her fingers together, forcing her gaze upward, wishing this was just a terrible nightmare and that she would soon wake up.

But that wasn't happening.

And other people who loved Noelle were now experiencing the same horror, shock and sadness.

Noelle's mom had been notified and so had Noelle's boyfriend, Carter Hayes. The detective she'd spoken to had informed her of those facts as he asked her to tell him about the people who were on Noelle's contact list. She'd actually been surprised to see less than a dozen numbers. She would have expected Noelle to have hundreds of friends in her contacts; she was a very friendly person. But the few people's names she recognized were Noelle's coworkers.

The detective had also showed her that the only texts on the phone in the past week were between her and Noelle, talking about getting together and going to the amusement park.

Where were the other texts? Why wasn't there communication between Carter and Noelle on the phone?

She'd expressed surprise when the detective had asked her if she found it unusual for Noelle not to have texted her mom or her boyfriend in the last several weeks. He'd suggested that perhaps Noelle had changed phones or had a second one.

She hadn't been able to come up with a good answer to either of those questions. She didn't know why Noelle would have had more than one phone, but it was definitely possible, and it seemed like the only explanation for why there were no other texts on the phone, because Noelle had always been an avid texter.

Tapping her foot on the ground, she was about to get up and tell the officer at the desk that she would grab her own ride home, when the station door opened, and her father walked in.

Brett Caldwell was fifty-five years old, but he looked at least ten years younger. She'd gotten her dark hair from him, but she'd missed out on the charming, quirky smile and long, lean limbs that took him up over six foot two. She was barely five four, and as usual, her father's towering presence made her instinctively wary—not because he would ever physically hurt her. No, her father had only hurt her with absence and disinterest, which made her wonder why on earth he'd shown up.

But despite all the hurt and anger between them, when he opened his arms and gave her a sympathetic, worried smile, she went willingly into his embrace. For the first time in her life, her dad had actually come when she needed him.

"I can't believe you're here," she said, as they broke apart.

"How did you know?"

"It's all over the news."

"I was on the news?" she asked in dismay.

"Not you—Noelle. But when the reporter said Noelle was with a female friend, and you weren't answering your phone, I had a feeling it was you. I called around, and here I am. I'm sorry about Noelle. I know how close you were."

"I can't believe she's dead. One minute we were eating cotton candy, and the next minute she was bleeding. There was so much blood, Dad. I've never seen anything like that."

He frowned. "Let's get you out of here."

"That would be good. I just want to go home."

"I think you should come to my place. Whitney said you're welcome to spend the night."

"I really just want to go to my apartment." She could not top off this day having to make small talk with Whitney Tremaine, a woman who was her boss's daughter, her father's girlfriend, and was only five years her senior. It was too much.

The door behind her dad opened, bringing in cold air, and one frantic mother.

"Avery," Vicky Caldwell said with relief.

Unlike her dad, her mom looked every day of her fifty-five years, her brown hair laced with gray, especially at the roots, and there were heavy lines around her mouth and eyes. But then, life had not been as kind to her mom as it had been to her father.

"Are you all right?" her mother asked.

"I'm okay," she said, accepting another tight hug, this one feeling far more normal and familiar.

After her parents had divorced, she and her mom had become a very tight unit.

"Noelle?" her mom asked, searching her gaze. "Is she really dead?"

She gave a tight nod. "Someone stabbed her."

"I don't understand how this happened."

"I don't, either."

"Did you see who killed Noelle?" her father asked.

"No. It happened in the funhouse on the Santa Monica Pier. It was dark and creepy inside. I wasn't going to go in at all. But Noelle was taking forever to come out, and I just got a weird feeling. She'd been acting a little strange, so I got worried."

"How was she acting?" her dad asked.

"I don't know if I can even say," she replied with a helpless shrug. "She was checking her watch, like she was waiting for something or someone. But when I called her on it, she brushed me off. She told me I could trust her. She said she'd turned over a new leaf and was trying to be a better person." She paused. "I don't remember exactly what she said. Maybe I'm misremembering." As the adrenaline surge began to wear off, she felt overwhelmingly tired. "I want to go home."

"You're coming home with me," her mom said firmly.

"Or with me," her father put in. "The offer still stands, Avery. I know I haven't always been there for you, but I'd like to make up for that now."

"Make up for it?" her mom cut in, a scornful look on her face. "You're going to make up for splitting our family apart, for depriving Avery of a father, for choosing fame and fortune over us? You think a guest room is going to do that, Brett?"

"This is between me and Avery, Vicky. You've always tried to poison her against me."

"I didn't have to do a thing. She made her own decisions based on what she experienced.

She put up a hand as she could see the old anger simmering between them. "I can't handle this right now. Please, stop, both of you." When they fell silent, she made her decision, which was, of course, the only one she could make. "Mom, I would love to stay with you tonight."

Her mother looked mollified by her answer.

She turned to her father. "I appreciate you coming down here. Thank you. But I'll be more comfortable at Mom's. I can sleep in my old room."

"Whatever you want, Avery," he said with disappointment. "I'm only a phone call away."

"I appreciate that."

"Come on, let's get you home." Her mom put an arm around her shoulders and led her out of the police station.

She knew her mother was brimming with questions, but thankfully she didn't ask any on the way to her house, which was about fifteen minutes away.

While she'd moved out of her childhood home when she went to college and had never ever really been back for more than the occasional night at a time, when she walked into the house, she felt safe for the first time in hours.

She flopped onto the living room couch, too exhausted to even try to make it upstairs to her room.

"Can I get you something to eat or drink?" Her mother perched on the edge of the armchair across from her.

"The thought of food..." She shuddered.

"Do you want to talk about what happened?"

"Not really."

She didn't think that would satisfy her always curious mother, and she was right.

"I didn't know you and Noelle had reconnected," her mom said. "I thought you lost touch awhile ago."

"She looked me up a few months ago. She needed a job, and I gave her a referral for a position at Nova Star."

"What?" her mother asked in surprise. "You never told me this."

"I didn't think you'd like it. You haven't been a fan of Noelle's for a long time."

"Because she was always getting you into trouble. But you could have told me. I hate to think you are keeping things from me, Avery."

"It really wasn't deliberate. You've been busy, and so

have I. Where's Don tonight?"

"He's in San Diego, taking care of some family business with his sister. He'll be back tomorrow. We're leaving for Hawaii on Sunday."

"That's right."

"I don't know if I should go now."

"Of course you should go. You've been looking forward to the trip for weeks, and so has Don." Her mom had been seeing a very nice man for the last four months, and Avery had high hopes for their relationship. It was long past time for her mother to be happy.

"I know, but after what happened tonight..."

"That should not change your plans."

"I want to support you, Avery."

"You always have, Mom," she said with heartfelt sincerity. "But you can't do anything." She gave a helpless shrug. "I can't do anything. Noelle is dead, and nothing is going to change that."

"What did the police say?"

"They were more interested in asking me questions than giving me answers. They're going to do a thorough investigation, dig into every aspect of Noelle's life."

"Her mother will be heartbroken."

"I know," she said heavily. "And Noelle has been dating someone, too. I'm sure he'll be shocked and saddened. I just don't know why this happened."

"Was it random?"

"The police don't know if she just ran into some crazy person in the funhouse, or if there was more to it."

"Surely someone saw this person."

"I think there must have been cameras somewhere, but it was one dark maze inside the attraction. There were lots of people moving around in the shadows. And there were screams every other minute, coming over the speakers. I think I heard Noelle scream, but I'm not even sure. If I hadn't found her on the ground, I might have just kept going and tried to find my way out."

Her mother's lips drew into a tight line. "I kind of wish you had done that."

There was a part of her that wished that, too. But would the heartbreak be any less if she'd been outside when the cops were called, when the paramedics rolled up in the ambulance, when Noelle's body was taken away? She doubted it. And at least Noelle hadn't been alone when she died. Maybe that meant something.

"I'm surprised you called your father," her mother continued.

"I didn't. He saw the news and had this feeling I was the friend with Noelle, and I guess he must have called the police and they told him I was there."

"When I think of all the times I wanted him to be there for you, and he wasn't..."

"I know. I suspect he was only there tonight because he's been trying to get closer to me in recent months, ever since I inadvertently introduced him to the new love of his life."

Her mother blew out a breath of disillusionment. "I almost feel sorry for her. And I have to admit that I sometimes wonder if your father didn't look you up just to get closer to the Tremaines. Brett could always sniff out money and opportunity better than anyone else."

"He is successful now in his own right. It's not like he doesn't have money and he's just a gold-digger."

"Oh, sure. He's a celebrity author and a motivational speaker. But there's your father's money and then there's Tremaine money. We both know there's a huge difference."

"Believe me, the last thing I wanted was for Dad to get involved with the Tremaines, but you know how he is. He came to take me to lunch one day and suddenly he was up in the executive suite. He can be charming."

"Don't I know it." Her mother paused, giving her a concerned look. "You're very pale. Let me get you some juice or some tea."

"Tea would be nice. Something soothing."

"I have chamomile."

"That sounds good." As she said the words, she could almost hear Noelle's voice in her head, saying, *Chamomile tea? What are you—an old lady?* "Noelle would be laughing at me right now."

Her mother raised an eyebrow. "Why?"

"Because she thought tea was an old lady's drink. She always wanted coffee, as strong and as caffeinated as she could get it. Not that she needed more energy. She woke up bouncing off the walls." Her lips suddenly trembled as emotion welled up in her. "I can't believe she's dead, Mom."

Her mother immediately came to sit next to her, putting her arms around her. "I'm so sorry, Avery. I know how much you loved her."

"Even when we weren't talking, I always knew she was out there somewhere, that we'd one day be friends again."

"It's good you got back together before all this happened."

"But it wasn't enough. We were just getting to know each other again."

"It's never enough time, honey."

She drew in a shaky breath. "Noelle's mom lives in Florida now. I wonder if she'll want to bury Noelle there. But Noelle didn't like Florida. She said the mosquitos were bad. On the other hand, she'd probably want to be by her mom. Although, she does have a boyfriend. Maybe she would want to be with him. I need to talk to both of them. I need to help."

"Stop," her mom said firmly. "Breathe. You can talk to everyone tomorrow. I doubt anyone will be making decisions before then."

"I shouldn't have let her go into the funhouse alone."

"This isn't your fault, Avery."

"It feels like it." She paused, not wanting to talk anymore. "Thanks for being here, Mom, but I'm going to lie down."

"Are you sure you want to be alone?"

"Yes." She pulled out of her mother's embrace and slowly got to her feet, which seemed to take a lot more effort than it normally did.

"We'll talk about everything tomorrow, Avery. If you need help planning some kind of memorial for Noelle, you know you can count on me."

"You're leaving for Hawaii on Sunday."

"I'll change my plans."

"I don't want you to do that."

"I'm not going to leave you like this."

"There's nothing you can do to make this easier; I'm just going to have to breathe through it. A wise woman told me that once after my father left."

Her mother gave her an emotional smile. "Sometimes that is all you can do."

"But I might need to do more than breathe."

Her mom's gaze narrowed. "Like what?"

"Like try to find out who killed Noelle."

"The police will do that. You need to stay out of this, Avery. Because whoever did kill Noelle is still out there somewhere, and you don't want to be the person who knows too much. In fact, I wonder if the police shouldn't have someone watching you."

"I'm not in danger. I don't think whoever killed Noelle even saw me in the funhouse."

"But you don't know for sure."

She thought about that—the terrifying chills suddenly coming back, but she didn't want to alarm her mother. "I don't think I'm in danger. And I'm not sure Noelle's death was random. She was acting cagey. Something was off."

"Something you don't need to know anything more about. Why don't you come to Hawaii with me and Don?"

"Don would love that," she said dryly.

"He'd understand. We can get you your own room."

"I'm going to be fine. Just keep your plans."

"Only if you promise to stay out of Noelle's business."

"I wouldn't know where to start digging even if I wanted to," she said, offering her very concerned mother an answer that would pacify her. "I really don't want you to worry."

"That's my job, Avery."

"Not anymore. I'm an adult. I'll get through this."

"I know you will, but I still want you to be safe."

"Me, too." As she said good night to her mother and walked down the hall to her room, she wondered if what she'd told her mother was true—that she didn't know where to start digging into Noelle's life. Noelle had said something about her apartment right before she took her last breath.

Was there a clue there?

If there was, the police would probably find it, wouldn't they?

⸻

That question ran around and around in Avery's head as she tossed and turned all night, haunted by Noelle's face, her eyes, her last gasping breaths.

If only she'd found her a minute sooner. If only she hadn't let Noelle go into the funhouse alone. If only she'd made Noelle tell her more about what was going on in her life.

So many *if-only's* made sleep impossible.

It also didn't help that she was in her childhood bedroom. It was in this room where she and Noelle had had slumber parties, painted their nails, texted boys, gossiped about their friends, and told each other secrets in the dark of the night.

But there was no one talking now.

Noelle's voice had been silenced.

It still seemed impossible to believe that someone had murdered her in the funhouse.

Was it random?

The police had questioned her regarding the relationship

between Carter and Noelle, asking her if he was the kind of man who might hurt his girlfriend. She hadn't been able to answer the question.

Noelle had told her with her dying breath that she had trusted the wrong person, but who was that? *Was it Carter or someone else? And what was at Noelle's apartment that she wanted Avery to get?*

Throwing off the covers, she opened her eyes, relieved to see the dawn light peeking through the blinds.

Thank God it was morning. She'd never been so happy to see the sun come up. She took a quick shower, wishing she didn't have to put on the same clothes, but she no longer kept anything to wear at her mom's house. Then she went into the kitchen to find a pot of coffee ready for her as well as a note from her mom.

Early pre-Hawaii hair appointment. Eggs and bacon are in the oven. Eat something!

She smiled at her mom's thoughtfulness. She might be thirty years old, but when she was in her mom's house, her mother still continued to take care of her.

She poured herself a mug of coffee, retrieved the breakfast plate from the oven, and found herself surprisingly hungry.

Over breakfast, she pulled out her phone and forced herself to check the news. It wasn't easy to read about Noelle's death, especially since it was told in a dispassionate way, mentioning only Noelle's name, her age, her city of residence, and her employer. There was no description of the vibrant, beautiful, outgoing person, who should have had a much longer life.

To think of everything that Noelle would never have—a wedding, a husband, a child, grandchildren—it broke her heart and her eyes swelled with tears.

She put the phone down, sadness being replaced with anger. Whoever had killed Noelle needed to be brought to justice. She'd asked the police to keep her in the loop, but she wasn't sure they would. She wasn't even sure they had taken her off the person-of-interest list.

She couldn't blame them. She'd gone to the pier with Noelle, she'd conveniently stayed outside the funhouse during the murder, but then, somehow, she'd been the one to find her. It had sounded a bit odd even to her ears.

Picking up her phone again, she made the call she was dreading the most. She called Noelle's mom, Kari Price. She'd had Noelle's mom's phone number in her phone since she was sixteen years old. Both their moms had wanted their girls to have their phone numbers, just in case.

The phone rang several times before Kari's voicemail picked up the call. She sounded perky and happy. This had definitely been recorded before she'd received the worst news of her life.

"It's me, Avery," she said, her hand tightening around her phone. "I'm so, so sorry. I think you know how much I loved Noelle. I want to help you with whatever you need. Please call me back when you get a chance." She let out a breath as she ended the message. In some ways, she was relieved she hadn't connected with Noelle's mom. Her feelings were still so raw.

Getting up, she rinsed off her plate and put it in the dishwasher. As she debated her next move, she realized she didn't have her car. She'd gotten a ride to the pier, thinking that with Noelle there would be wine involved at some point. She didn't want to hang around here all day, so after leaving a short note for her mom, she called a rideshare company, then went out front to wait.

A few minutes later, she was on her way home. But halfway there, the restlessness running around inside her made her ask the driver to change her destination.

She needed to go to Noelle's apartment. It was the last thing Noelle had asked her to do. Avery needed to figure out why.

Four

Noelle lived in the Ocean Breeze Courtyard Apartments in Venice Beach. As Avery got out of the car, she couldn't help thinking that the building, while modest, was nicer than some of the places Noelle had lived in. After her father and grandmother had died, money had been scarce, and Noelle's mom had never been one to stay at the same job very long. In fact, Kari Price was probably even flakier than Noelle. But Kari had always been nice to her, and she couldn't imagine what she was going through now. Hopefully, they would have a chance to speak soon.

She walked across the street, feeling more than a little trepidation at entering Noelle's apartment. She told herself there was nothing to fear, but with so many unanswered questions, everything seemed suspicious and worrisome. She walked through the front gate into a courtyard. Twelve apartments, six on each level, surrounded the courtyard in a rectangular shape. At the back was a small pool and barbecue area.

The building and courtyard were empty and quiet at nine o'clock on a Saturday morning, and as she walked up to Noelle's second floor apartment in the back corner, she wondered if the other tenants knew what had happened to her. Probably—since there was yellow caution tape across Noelle's front door, a stark reminder of the previous evening's events. The police must have searched the apartment last night for leads into her death.

She stared at the tape for a long moment, knowing she would probably be breaking the law if she went inside. On the other hand, this seemed like the perfect opportunity to see if she could make sense of Noelle's last words.

The door had a coded lock on it, and if the police hadn't changed it, she should be able to get in. She used the four-digit code that Noelle had used for everything—6257. It was the address of her childhood home, the one that Avery had spent so much time in as a young girl.

Sure enough, the lock clicked, and she turned the knob, stepping into the apartment.

Her heart was beating a million miles a minute. She knew Noelle wasn't there, but she didn't know if the danger or trouble she was in was.

She stood just inside the door for a good minute, listening acutely for any unexpected sound. Everything was still. The room had obviously been searched, however. The pillow cushions had been pulled off the couch. The kitchen drawers and cupboards were open. It was a huge cluttered mess.

She made her way into the bedroom, finding more sad chaos. The bed was unmade and covered with clothes, probably tossed out of the upended dresser drawers. If Noelle had left something here, it was gone.

She felt overwhelmed at the idea of digging through everything to find some clue when she didn't even know what she was looking for.

And then she saw Noelle's jewelry box sitting open on the floor just inside the walk-in closet. She knelt down next to it. There wasn't much of value inside, rings, bracelets, necklaces...

Noelle had never had enough money to buy real jewelry, but there was the locket from her grandmother that she'd gotten on her sixteenth birthday and the charm bracelet Avery had given Noelle when they were ten. She'd bought one for herself at the time, too, and they'd collected fun charms over the next year. She couldn't believe Noelle had kept it all these years.

Impulsively, she grabbed both items and slipped them into her coat pocket, then she rifled through the rest of the jewelry box, finding a man's watch, that she thought might have belonged to Noelle's father, but she wasn't sure.

Standing up, she looked around the rest of the closet, wondering where Noelle would have hidden something—if she'd had something to hide. She probably would have been creative in some way. Put it where no one would expect. But where would that be?

She moved farther into the closet checking the pockets in the coats that were still on their hangers but found only a few quarters. Shoe boxes were strewn about the closet. Obviously, the police had already gone through them.

A couple of books on the floor caught her eye, and she smiled when she realized one of them was hers. She'd published a small book about space travel for kids the past year, and Noelle had bought it in the gift shop at Nova Star and made her autograph it.

She picked it up and read the inscription that Noelle had actually dictated for her: *To the smartest, most beautiful, and skinniest best friend. Love, Avery.* She closed the book and pressed it against her heart, feeling a wave of pain.

And then she heard a noise…

Her eyes flew open. Her heart sped up. *Someone else was in the apartment.*

She started toward the door, not sure if she should barricade herself in the closet or try to get by whoever was in the apartment.

Maybe it was just the police.

It wasn't!

A man came out of the bathroom dressed in dark clothes with a ski mask over his head and face, a long, black gun in his hand. She shrieked in alarm and instinctively backed up. He raised his arm, the gun pointed at her face.

"Please, don't," she begged, knowing it probably wouldn't make a difference.

But he hesitated.

She didn't know why; she was just grateful.

"Just go. I don't know who you are or why you're here," she said.

"Shut up." His voice was hard, angry, and the hand holding the gun tightened.

She drew in a quick breath, still trying to figure out an escape.

Then another man came barreling into the room, tackling the gunman to the ground. He wrestled the gun out of the guy's hand and the weapon went flying across the room.

Terrified and paralyzed, she stared in shock as the two men went after each other. It was then she realized that the man fighting her attacker was the same man from the funhouse, the one who also worked in security at Nova Star.

What the hell was he doing here?

What did it matter?

She needed to get out of the apartment while she had the chance, but the men were between her and the door.

As she hesitated, she saw the Nova Star security guy get off three quick brutal punches that sent the masked man flying against the wall.

The man quickly recovered, regaining momentum as he dodged the next blow, grabbed the security guy around the waist and knocking him off his feet.

But the security guy quickly regained his footing, bouncing back with another blow. And then in one swift motion, he ripped off the man's mask.

She saw a dark beard and tattooed Roman numerals on

the man's neck, as he picked up a drawer and hurled it at the security guy. The drawer hit her rescuer in the head, and he went down hard. As he struggled to get back up, the formerly masked man took off, and then her rescuer growled out "Stay here," and ran after him.

She let out a breath of relief. But staying in the apartment didn't seem like a good idea. Still clutching the book in her hand, she left the bedroom.

The living room was empty. The front door was open. She saw a woman across the courtyard staring at her, and she was talking on her phone, probably calling the police.

She should stay and wait for them to arrive, tell them what happened, but the yellow tape on the front door made her realize that she'd tampered with a crime scene, and no one was going to be happy about that.

As she stepped into the exterior hallway, her rescuer came jogging back to her, a grim, angry expression on his face. She backed up a step.

"Come on," he said. "You need to get out of here."

"I'm not going anywhere with you."

"Look, I work in security for Nova Star. You can trust me."

"Can I?" she countered. "I saw you at the funhouse last night—right before Noelle was killed."

Dark shadows filled his brown eyes. "I didn't kill Noelle."

"I don't know if I can believe you."

"You were the one kneeling over her. Maybe you killed her. Maybe you came to her apartment to find something you didn't want anyone else to know about."

She gasped at the suggestion. "Noelle was one of my best friends."

"Good. Then you'll want to stay alive long enough to find out what happened to her. Move, Avery. There will be more coming."

"You know my name?" she asked in surprise.

"It's my job to know who you are."

She didn't want to go with him, but she also didn't want to stay here and wait for whoever else might show up, so she followed him out of the building. "I think the neighbor called the police," she said as they hit the sidewalk. "We should wait for them."

"It's too dangerous to stay here. You can talk to the police later. Where's your car?"

"I don't have one."

"Then you'll come with me."

"Why would I trust you?"

"I just saved your life."

"Did you? Why were you there?"

"We're not having this conversation here." He opened the door to a nearby silver SUV. "Get in."

As a car came speeding down the street, all thought of resisting him fled. She didn't know who he was, but he had saved her from a gunman, so she jumped into the vehicle.

He slid behind the wheel as the other car passed by without incident.

Then he started the car and peeled down the street in the opposite direction.

"Where are we going?" she asked.

"Somewhere that isn't here."

It wasn't much of an answer, but, somehow, she'd made the impulsive decision to trust him.

And then Noelle's last words came back to haunt her...*I trusted the wrong person.*

She hoped she hadn't done the same.

Wyatt drove quickly away from Noelle's apartment building, pissed off at what had just gone down. But right now, his only focus was on getting Avery to safety. She was damn lucky he'd gotten there when he did, or she might be in the same condition as Noelle. He knew she didn't trust him, but that didn't matter. She was shaken up, but she was alive.

She was wearing the same clothes she'd been in last night: skinny dark jeans, a cream-colored knit top, and a short black leather coat. Her brown hair fell loose around her shoulders, her face was pale, and her brown eyes appeared shocked and weary, but she was still a very attractive woman. Normally, there was a warm, inviting, exciting air about her. He'd been drawn to her every time he'd seen her on the security monitor.

He'd told himself he needed to get closer to her because she was tight with Hamilton Tremaine, but he'd never had the chance…until now.

This wasn't the opportunity he'd expected, but he'd take it.

Avery and Hamilton shared a love of the stars, and Hamilton spoke of her with great fondness. Avery had gotten even deeper into the family when her father Brett Caldwell had become romantically involved with Whitney Tremaine, the youngest of Hamilton's three offspring.

She'd been on his radar to check out, but she'd moved higher up the list when he'd seen her at the pier on Friday night. Avery had been the one to get Noelle her job at the company. While he'd never seen them spend much time together at work, clearly, they'd gotten together after business hours.

But Noelle was dead, stabbed with deliberate violence, and Avery had watched her friend bleed out. Now, she was running for her life. He couldn't imagine what she was thinking—probably wondering what kind of hell she'd walked into.

He wished he could tell her it was going to be okay, but he had no idea if that was true. He needed to find out what she knew and then figure out how much danger she was in. It was bad enough she'd been in the funhouse last night, but this morning she'd seen a man's face—the same man who might have killed Noelle. That could be a big problem.

As he glanced at her, he noticed the book clenched in her hand. She'd brought it from Noelle's apartment. Maybe it was a clue. "Why are you holding that book?"

At first, she gave him a blank look and then she glanced down at the book in her hands. "Oh, it's mine." She held it up, so he could see the cover and her name. "I wrote this about space for kids, and we sell it in the Nova Star gift shop. Noelle bought it and had me sign it for her. I saw it on the floor of her room, and I just grabbed it. Then the man came out of the bathroom with a gun." She paused. "I don't know why I didn't leave it there. Noelle bought it as a joke. She dictated what she wanted me to write when I autographed it."

"What did you write?"

She opened the book and read the inscription: "*To the smartest, most beautiful, and skinniest best friend. Love Avery.*" She gave him a sad look. "Noelle was one of a kind. She was the brightest star, the life of the party, the girl who did things no one else dared to do. She could be crazy and funny and generous..."

As her voice trailed away, he wondered what she was leaving out. "And..." he prodded.

"She could be flaky at times. She was almost always late. She sometimes ditched me for a better offer, but I couldn't really blame her, because I was usually nowhere near as much fun as she was." She let out a sigh. "But I shouldn't say any of that, because she's dead."

"Say whatever you want. Dying doesn't turn anyone into a saint."

"She didn't deserve to die. It still feels unreal, like it's a horrific nightmare. I want to wake up, but I can't."

He nodded, knowing there was nothing he could say to make her feel better. She was going to have to live through the grief.

As he reached the Pacific Coast Highway, he sped up, not stopping until he saw a small parking lot near a public beach. He pulled off the road and into an open spot.

"Why are you stopping here?" Avery asked, shooting him a wary look.

"Seems as good a place as any. We need to talk. Let's take a walk on the beach. I could use some fresh air. I'm betting you could, too."

He could see she was torn between going with him or staying in the car. Probably in her mind, neither option was a good one. But, finally, she nodded and got out, leaving the book on the seat as she did so.

He wondered if there was more to that book than she'd said; it was interesting that she'd taken it from Noelle's apartment, especially since he didn't know why she'd gone there in the first place.

They walked across the sand to the edge of the water and just stood there for a moment.

It was a cool, sunny December morning, with only a few people on the beach: a couple walking their dog, a family with a couple of kids digging sandcastles, and a lone woman sitting on a towel, reading a book.

"Why does everything look normal when it's not?" Avery questioned.

He doubted she really wanted an answer, so he didn't give her one. He was just happy that her breath had slowed down. He needed her thinking clearly.

"What's your name?" she asked abruptly, turning to look at him.

"Wyatt Tanner."

She waited a moment, then said, "You already know my name."

"I do. You're Avery Caldwell, an astrophysicist, and an employee of Nova Star. You created and currently manage the educational outreach program at the company. And I know that because I work in security, as I mentioned before. I've gone over the personnel files for everyone at the company."

"That's a lot of people."

"Well, I'm not the only one on the team," he said, meeting her brown-eyed gaze, and thinking irrelevantly that she was even prettier in person. Clearing his throat, he added, "I hope my position at Nova Star makes you feel more comfortable."

"Why would it?"

"It's my job to protect the employees of Nova Star, and Noelle was one of them. I didn't hurt her, Avery."

"But I saw you in the funhouse, and even though I was freaked out, I recognized you."

"Why were you freaked out? You saw me before you found Noelle."

She frowned. "Yes, but I hate funhouses. I got lost in one when I was a little kid."

"Then why did you go in last night?"

"Because Noelle never came out. I was watching the door, and I kept seeing people come out who had gone in after her. I got worried."

"You didn't think she was just having fun?"

"I had a bad feeling. She was acting weird."

"How so?"

"She was checking her watch a lot, like she was waiting for something or was going to meet someone."

"But she was with you. Why would she be meeting someone else?"

"Obviously, I don't know the answer to that question. When I thought I saw you in the mirror, I wondered if she was meeting you." She paused, a question in her eyes. "Was it you? Were you supposed to meet Noelle in the funhouse?"

"No."

"It seems like the oddest coincidence that you were there."

"I was supposed to meet a friend at the pier. She was late, so I thought I'd check out the funhouse while I was waiting."

"When did you know that Noelle got stabbed?"

"I was almost at the exit when I heard screams. One of the employees told us to wait, that something had happened."

"Us?"

"There were about a dozen of us."

"Did you see Noelle?"

"No. They put us in a back room."

"Why?"

"To question us on what we'd seen. Unfortunately, I hadn't seen anything." He paused. "I understand you found her."

"Yes, and it was awful. She was covered in blood. I wanted to save her, but I could see that she was slipping away."

"Slipping away?" he echoed, his gut tightening. "She was alive when you found her? Did she say anything?"

Avery hesitated, the suspicion back in her eyes. "It feels like you're asking all the questions and I'm giving all the answers."

"I investigate crimes. Asking questions is what I do."

"But the crime didn't happen at work. Why did you come to Noelle's apartment this morning?"

He hesitated and wondered why. He lied every single day of his life. It was second nature. And it rarely bothered him. He could pass lie detector tests. He could face down a team of interrogators without giving anything up, but there was something about Avery's haunted expression that made him wish he could tell her something that would help her make sense of things. But that was impossible. More information would only put her in more danger.

"Well?" Avery demanded. "Are you going to answer me?"

"Hamilton called me last night after he heard the news. He asked me to make sure that Noelle's death wasn't tied to her job at Nova Star."

"Why would it be?"

"I don't know, but he asked me to see what I could find

out."

"At her apartment?"

"Yes. Now, do you want to tell me why you went there?"

"I'm not really sure. Noelle muttered a few cryptic words before she died. She said she'd trusted the wrong person and she said something about me going to her apartment, but she didn't say why. I thought about it all night and decided I should go there and see if anything stood out to me. Unfortunately, when I got there, the place was a mess. I don't know if the police turned things upside down or if someone else did. I walked into the closet and then that man came out of the bathroom with a gun. I froze. And then you came in."

"Did he say anything to you? Did you recognize him when I got the mask off?"

"No. I'm absolutely certain I never saw him before. What about you?"

"Same."

"He was looking for something in Noelle's apartment. Do you think he found it?"

"My guess is you interrupted his search."

"I wish I knew what he was after, why Noelle implied I should go there." Her gaze turned toward the ocean. "Noelle often trusted the wrong people. She liked men who were exciting and daring and sometimes walked a fine line between right and wrong. And it wasn't just the men in her life who led her down the wrong path; it was also her female friends. That's why we stopped hanging out together. I felt like she changed into someone else." Avery looked back at him. "Sorry, I'm rambling."

"You're entitled. You've suffered a huge personal loss." He paused. "Although, it sounds like there was a break in your friendship."

"We barely spoke over the last six, seven years. It wasn't until she looked me up two months ago and asked me to help her get a job that we became friends again. And, before you say it, yes, I did think she was probably using me, but she was

still my friend and I had the ability to help her, so I did."
Avery took a breath and let it out, folding her arms in front of
her. "What's going to happen now? Noelle's neighbor called
the police. She saw us. I'm thinking we should go down to the
station and talk to the detectives I spoke to last night and tell
them what happened."

"We could do that," he said slowly. "But we broke into a
crime scene."

"I knew the code," she protested.

"But you crossed the police tape."

She frowned. "How did you get in?"

"You didn't lock the door behind you."

"What about the other guy? He was there before me.
How did he know the code?"

"No idea." He paused, as he considered his options. He
didn't want to go to the police, but he could see she was
already working up a lot of steam for that course of action.

"Why don't you want me to go to the police?" she asked,
giving him a suspicious look.

"I'm trying to protect you." That wasn't even close to the
truth, but hopefully she'd buy it.

"Or protect yourself."

So much for her buying it.

"This isn't about me. If I'm reluctant for you to go to the
police, it's because Hamilton asked me to look into this.
He's concerned about Noelle's death. If it's tied in any way
to Nova Star, it will bring negative press and intense
scrutiny to the company, and with the satellite defense
launch scheduled for Tuesday, that's the last thing he wants."

She paled. "I don't care about any of that. I love Nova
Star, and I am a big fan of Hamilton's, but I want justice for
Noelle. If every employee at the company has to be
questioned, then that's what has to happen."

He liked that she wasn't intimidated by Hamilton. "I want
justice for her, too. Why don't we work together on that?"

"If you want to work together, then come with me to the

police station."

"Is this a test?"

"It's a suggestion."

He'd have to make a quick call, but he could probably make it work. "All right."

She looked surprised. "Really? Why the change of heart?"

"No change of heart. You're clearly determined to speak to the police, so I'll go with you. Before we do that, tell me about Noelle's boyfriend."

"Carter? I don't know a lot about him. We had dinner together once. He seems nice enough. He's a lawyer and works in patents at Nova Star. Noelle told me he was steady, and she liked that about him. He kept her feet on the ground the way I used to." She sniffed as emotion came back into her eyes. "Maybe it was good Noelle had a chance to really fly, knowing now how little time she had." She cleared her throat. "Anyway, I don't know much about Carter except that he works a lot."

"You haven't spoken to him since last night?"

"No. I know the police were going to call him. I did try to reach Noelle's mother, but she didn't answer. I left her a message."

"Is Noelle's family local?"

"Not anymore. Her father is deceased. Her mom moved to Florida seven or eight years ago. I don't think there's anyone left here in Los Angeles. They didn't have the biggest family to start with. Noelle and I had that in common. Although my father didn't die, he did leave, so by the time Noelle and I were in high school, we were both basically fatherless."

"I've seen your father in your office. He must have come back at some point."

"Yes, but he was gone for a long time before that. And even when he was around, he wasn't really around. Although, he did come to the police station last night; I guess he's trying to show that he's changed."

"Your father came to the station?" he echoed, making a mental note of that fact.

"Yes, and then my mom showed up, and suddenly I felt like I was thirteen again, watching them fight over who was going to take me home from soccer practice. Only it wasn't soccer, and I wasn't a kid, and Noelle had just died." She drew in a shaky breath. "Oh, God...I don't know how to deal with all this emotion. I'm angry and sad, scared and confused. It's too much."

"It won't get easier for a while."

She stared back at him. "You know I actually appreciate you saying that instead of trying to tell me I'll feel better soon."

He shrugged. "I know what it's like to lose a friend. It's very difficult, especially when the circumstances are sudden and violent."

"I never could have prepared myself for what happened last night."

"No."

"All right. So, I guess we should go to the police station. And then hopefully I can go home, change my clothes and catch my breath."

"I'll take you there."

"Thanks."

As they walked back to the car, he hoped he was making the right decision. He didn't particularly want to talk to the police again. He needed to make a play...something that would continue to allow him to build trust with Avery but not get him in deeper with the cops, who would only make his assignment more difficult.

After opening the car door for Avery, he walked slowly around the back of the vehicle, pulling out his phone and texting a quick message to his team leader. He needed the FBI to pull some strings, and they had to do it fast.

As he slid behind the wheel, he got a text that they were

on it.

Relieved, he started the car and pulled back onto the highway.

"You haven't been at Nova Star that long, have you?" Avery asked.

"About a month."

"And before that? Where did you work?"

"I was in the Marines—intelligence."

"That's where you saw friends die."

"Unfortunately."

A gleam entered her eyes. "Hamilton was a Marine. I'm sure that made you a good candidate for the job. Always faithful, right?"

"Semper fi," he murmured, thinking that faithfulness did not describe him at all. He came and left in the dark of the night. He lived his life in the shadows, under different names, different disguises. He was a chauffeur one day, a trucker the next—a gambler, a hustler, an importer, an exporter. He'd lost track of all the different roles he'd been required to play.

Sometimes, he thought he was losing track of himself.

But now wasn't the time to think about that.

He had a job to do, and it wasn't security for Nova Star. It was high-stakes industrial espionage by a possible foreign power into the aerospace industry, and Noelle's death had just raised the stakes. He needed more access, more information, and as he glanced over at Avery, he realized she might be valuable on a lot of levels. If anyone could get him deeper into the inner circle of Nova Star, it was her.

But that meant he would have to play her...and for the first time in a long time, he felt a reluctance to do that.

He would have to get over it.

Five

W yatt took his time getting them to the police station, wanting to give his contact a chance to get there ahead of him and smooth the way. Fortunately, there was a fair amount of Saturday morning beach traffic, so he didn't have to try that hard to go slow.

When they arrived at the station, almost forty-five minutes had passed since his text. Hopefully that was enough time.

As Avery got out of the car, she looked grimly determined but not very happy.

"Still want to do this?" he asked.

"I feel like I should."

He had a feeling this was a woman who always did what she thought she *should* do. "Then let's do it."

When they checked in at the counter in the lobby, he made sure to give his name as well as Avery's. A moment later, a uniformed officer came into the room. The man asked Avery to wait and then escorted him down a hall and into a conference room.

When he stepped inside the room, he was surprised to see a friendly and familiar face. The beautiful brunette with the sharp, always insightful, green eyes, was one of his closest friends, not just at the bureau but in life. He'd met Bree Adams at Quantico, and through the years, they'd saved each other's life more than once.

"Bree, what are you doing here?" He looked around, making note of the fact that they were not in an interrogation room. "Where's Flynn?"

"Don't worry. We're cool," Bree said, reading his expression. "As far as the police know, I'm meeting with you to find out what happened at Noelle Price's apartment this morning. Flynn contacted Special Agent Joanna Davis, who gave me a brief read-in on your situation. She's meeting with the homicide detectives now to inform them we'll be handling the investigation going forward."

"Good." He was pleased that Flynn had brought Joanna in. She could be the public face of the investigation. Since Joanna had already spoken to Hamilton months ago, it would make sense for her to be involved again. "It's the right move. Nova Star is aware that the bureau is concerned about a spy in their ranks. With Noelle Price's murder, the company won't be surprised that they're back on the hot seat, but as long as they don't know I'm working from the inside, we're good."

"Joanna said you're on a specialized task force run by Flynn MacKenzie. That shocked me. You and Flynn were intense rivals at Quantico."

He saw the speculation in her eyes and shrugged. "Things change. I liked the job he was offering, so I took it."

"How's the investigation going?"

"Not as quickly as I would like. We haven't had a lot to go on until now."

Bree nodded. "I've been wondering ever since I saw you at the beach before Thanksgiving if I would run into you again, or if you would try to contact me, but it's been very quiet the last month."

"I was about to go under with Nova Star when I saw you there, and you weren't alone."

"No. I was with Nathan, and I figured you were undercover. You look better than you did then. You got rid of the beard."

"I had to clean up my act for my job in security. I'm a suit and tie guy now, at least during the week. What about you? You're working for Joanna?"

"Yes. After everything that went down in Chicago, I needed a change, and I've always wanted to live at the beach. I'm not sure I love the work yet; it's been more administrative than I like, but on the other hand, it's a nice break from the emotionally intense drama of working with missing children."

"I know you had a rough time in Chicago. I'm glad things worked out." He paused. "Or did they? The kid...*your* kid..." He let his words slip away. He might be friends with Bree, but he didn't know how much she wanted him to know.

"She doesn't know anything yet," Bree said quickly. "Someday, but not now. It's easier being here in California. I keep in touch, but I'm not right there wondering what she's doing every second. Plus, I'm with Nathan, and I get to run by the sea every morning. It's not bad."

He smiled, noting the genuine happiness in her eyes. "It sounds good, and Joanna is lucky to have you."

"I'm not sure she feels that way. She didn't recruit me, and she still remembers me as being on the Quantico team that screwed up and got Jamie Rowland killed. Not that she says that out loud, but I feel her judgment."

"That had nothing to do with you."

"I know. Hopefully, she'll eventually get past all that old history, and realize I'm a seasoned agent now. Anyway, what can you tell me about this morning?" Bree asked. "You went to the homicide victim's apartment?"

"Yes, and I ran in to her best friend there—Avery Caldwell. I also ran into a masked gunman. Fortunately, I got a look at his face. Unfortunately, he got away."

"What can you tell me about him?"

"Caucasian male, mid-thirties, beard, brown hair and eyes, scar over the right eyebrow and the Roman numerals MMX—2010 tattooed on his neck—could be a gang initiation date."

"Why was Ms. Caldwell at the apartment? Does she know something about the murder?"

"No, but she's trying to figure out who killed her friend."

"You need to get her out of this, Wyatt."

"Too late for that. I'm concerned that not only was she at Noelle's side when she died, she also got a look at the guy in the apartment this morning. She could be in danger. I'm going to stay close. I have this feeling she's the key to something—I just don't know what. She's also tight with the Tremaines, and while I've developed a relationship with Hamilton, I've had little access to his sons, his daughter, or their spouses. Since Avery's father is living with Whitney Tremaine, Avery is in the immediate family circle. She might be able to help me."

"Or she could turn them against you."

"It's a risk, but I'm not worried about that right now."

"What does Hamilton Tremaine think about Ms. Price's murder?"

"He'd like to believe her death has nothing to do with his company. In fact, he'd like me to prove that. I've managed to become a valuable confidant. We share Marine stories."

Bree smiled. "Are you making those up?"

"I actually used one Jamie and Damon told me about from their Army days."

"Always thinking on your feet."

"It's what keeps me alive."

"I heard about the sting you set up to get into Nova Star. Jim Abrams is pissed you broke his nose."

He gave a faint smile. "Not intentional. I thought he was better at ducking."

She smiled back at him. "I'm glad we're going to work together, even if it's from afar. One of these days, I want you to meet Nathan. He's very important to me."

"I'd like to meet him sometime."

"Before you go..." She jotted a number on the back of her card. "I know you're working through Flynn, but in case you ever need anything unofficially...I just got this number."

"Thanks." As he put her card into his wallet, the conference room door opened.

Joanna Davis walked into the room. Dressed in a slim black skirt and black blazer over a silky blouse, her short, straight blonde hair framing her face, she looked both sophisticated and professional. Joanna was in her early forties, a divorcee who had been at the bureau for fifteen years.

He respected Joanna, but she was one of only a handful of people who could make him uncomfortable. She was too flirtatious and a bit of a man-eater, both on the job and in her personal life, and he preferred to spend as little time as possible with her.

Fortunately, he worked for Flynn, not for Joanna, so while she might be Flynn's boss, they had little contact with each other, and that's the way he preferred it.

"Wyatt, you look good," she said, her gaze raking his body. "I've been wondering when we'd run into each other. I didn't think it would be here."

"What happened with Detective Larimer?"

"He's standing down. We're in charge now. I'll inform Mr. Tremaine of that fact as well."

"That will simplify matters."

"Well, I live to simplify things for you," she drawled, sarcasm in her tone. "I understand Mr. Tremaine is giving you more responsibility and access. Is that true?"

"It is. He has even asked me to keep an eye on his sons' activities."

"So, while he tells the FBI there's nothing to see where his sons are concerned, you're hearing a different song?"

"Yes. Hamilton is an idealist, a dreamer, but he's also a smart man. While he doesn't want to believe anyone close to him would sell him out, he's not stupid. He may not want to work with the bureau, but he's determined to find out if someone in his company is a mole."

"Good."

"I need to go. I don't want to leave Avery alone in the lobby too long. She might try to talk to the cops and confuse things. Thanks again for the help here."

"Once this is over, we'll catch up," Joanna said. "I'd like to hear about what else you've been doing the past several years."

"Sounds good," he said, seeing a teasing light lurking in Bree's eyes. Bree and his other friends had been well aware of Joanna's interest in him at Quantico.

After leaving the conference room, he found Avery pacing around the lobby, a worried look on her face.

"Did you tell them what happened?" she asked immediately.

"Yes. We can go." He put his hand against the small of her back and pushed her gently toward the door.

"What do you mean?" she asked in surprise. "I don't need to answer any questions?"

"Nope. We're good."

"They don't want to talk to me?"

"I told them everything we knew."

"And that's it?"

"That's it."

She gave him a suspicious look as they left the station, but she kept walking until they got to his car. Then she stopped.

"Okay, seriously, what's going on, Wyatt? Why did they want to speak to you alone? Why wasn't I questioned? I'm Noelle's friend."

"And I run security for Nova Star, where Noelle was employed. I knew the information they needed to proceed, and I gave it to them."

"And they didn't care that neither one of us was supposed

to be in the apartment?"

"I wouldn't say they didn't care, but we're not under suspicion." He opened the door for her, and she reluctantly got in.

He walked around the car and slid behind the wheel. "I'll take you home now."

"I still don't get it," she said a few moments later. "Something is off." She shot him a suspicious look. "I think you're lying to me, Wyatt."

"What do you think I'm lying about? If the police wanted to talk to you, don't you think they would have called you in? I wasn't stopping anyone from doing that. You were sitting in the lobby."

"You also weren't gone that long."

"There wasn't a lot to say. I know you're on edge—"

"On edge does not begin to describe how I feel. You may be looking into this on behalf of Nova Star, but Noelle was my friend. She meant something to me. This isn't just a case to me. She was an important person in my life."

"I understand, which is why I told the police what we both knew so you wouldn't have to go through it again."

"And Detective Larimer was really okay with that?"

"It wasn't his choice. There was a special agent from the FBI there."

"Wait a second—the FBI was there? Why?"

"They didn't say; they just informed me that they're taking over the case."

"But that doesn't make sense."

He shrugged. "Like I said, they didn't feel it necessary to explain their actions to me. But the good news is that we have more people looking for answers and for justice for Noelle."

"Well, that's true. I'm sure the FBI will have more resources than the local police."

"Exactly. Now, you can go home and catch your breath, the way you wanted to."

"I would like to do that," she admitted. "I need a minute

or two to regroup. And then I have to start making calls."

"Do you want to give me your address?" He actually already knew where she lived, but realized he was about to give that away.

She started. "Oh, sorry. Yes. You're actually going in the right direction. I live in Hermosa Beach. 312 Taylor Avenue. It's right off the 405." She paused. "What do you think will happen next, Wyatt? Will the FBI be able to find the man in Noelle's apartment based on his tattoo? You did tell them about the tattoo, didn't you?"

"Yes, and it will hopefully give them a good lead."

"Do you think that man is the same person who killed Noelle?"

"It's possible."

She let out a breath. "I was thinking that, too. The FBI has to find him."

"If anyone can, they can."

Several minutes later, he pulled up in front of a three-story apartment building, grabbing a parking spot not too far from the front door. He scanned the area for anything out of the ordinary, but all looked peaceful and quiet. It was possible the man from Noelle's apartment did not know who Avery was, but he didn't want to underestimate anyone.

"I'll walk you up," he said, as he turned off the engine.

"That's not necessary."

He ignored her comment, meeting her on the sidewalk. "After what happened at Noelle's, I'm not letting you go in alone. You're very important to my boss."

"Why do you say that?" she asked curiously.

"He speaks very highly of you, Avery. He loves your passion for space. He says you're one of the few people who really understands his vision. He also told me how you have helped him bring Nova Star to the masses with your educational outreach programs. He's quite impressed with you."

Wyatt had to admit he was fairly impressed with the

beautiful astrophysicist as well, which seemed crazy, because geeky science girls were not usually his type. *But there was something about Avery...* He refused to let himself finish that thought. Avery was part of his job. He couldn't forget that.

"Well, I'm impressed with Hamilton, too," Avery said, as they entered her building and headed up the stairs. "He has never met a barrier he didn't want to break down, or a challenge he couldn't overcome, and I like that kind of bulldog tenacity. I also respect his brilliance and his big dreams. He's the kind of person who changes the world. It's inspiring to be around him."

"How did you come to take the job with him?"

"Hamilton came to a lecture I gave at UCLA three years ago. He waited around afterward to speak to me and insisted I have coffee with him. He wanted to tell me about his company and how he needed someone like me to share his passionate love of space with the outside world. I was intrigued. He basically offered me a blank check to do whatever I wanted to do. I couldn't turn that down, so, I said yes. I've never regretted it." She paused in front of her door. "This is me."

"Let me go in first," he said, as she unlocked the door.

She waved him inside, and he made a quick scan of the small living room and adjacent kitchen area and then headed down the short hall to check out the bedroom and bath. Avery dogged his every step, staying close behind him as he opened the last remaining closet door.

Then she let out a heavy breath. "No one has been in here."

"It doesn't look like it. Everything is very neat."

"I don't like clutter. When I get stressed, I clean."

"You must have cleaned this morning."

"Actually, I didn't stay here last night. I went to my mom's house. But the last few weeks have been tense. With the upcoming satellite defense launch, there have been a lot more requests for educational information, which get siphoned through my department."

He nodded, following her back into the living room.

While everything was very organized, the apartment was still warm and interesting and smart, he thought with a smile, noting the shelves laden with hardcover science books, the photographs of space on the walls, the colorful blanket tossed over the back of the couch, and the extremely old telescope by the window.

"Do you take this up on the roof?" he asked.

"Occasionally, but I don't use that one very often. I got it when I was twelve. I have access to much better telescopes at work. Have you ever been out to Nova Star's test facility in the desert?"

"Not yet."

"The rooftop there affords some of the best viewing I've ever experienced. Are you interested in the stars?"

"Not really. When I look up for too long, I tend to trip over reality."

"That can happen. I've been accused of having my head in the clouds, but space also gives me perspective. When I get too caught up in my day, I look up, and I realize how very, very small my life and my problems are. Although, today, they seem rather huge. Do you want something to drink?"

"I'd love some water," he said, happy that she wasn't eager to kick him out. He wasn't ready to walk away yet—for multiple reasons, some that went beyond Noelle's murder.

Avery took out two glasses, popped in some ice, and then filled them with water from a filtered spout on the outside of her refrigerator.

He took a seat at her small kitchen table, noting the organized pile of bills next to her checkbook. "I bet you actually balance this thing," he said, as she handed him a glass.

She made a face at him. "I used to. I've gotten busy, and so much is direct deposit and online bill pay now but keeping track of my finances was a lesson my mother taught me early on. Money was tight when I was growing up. Before my father became a celebrity writer, he was fairly unsuccessful, and we were living off my mom's teacher's salary. My mother always had to make sure that we had our bills covered while my dad chased his big dreams."

He heard the note of bitterness in her voice. "It seems like your father succeeded in achieving some of those dreams. From what I understand, he's quite famous now."

"Yes, because he created a male self-help bestseller called *Meat, Sex, Sports—A Man's Guide to Happiness.*"

"That's all it takes, huh?"

"Men are apparently fairly simple creatures," she said dryly.

"And that book sold well?"

"Over five million copies. It also spawned a series of webinars and motivational talks, first for men, then spreading into the general public how to find happiness, peace, and success. My father has since written three other books on variations of that theme." She took a sip of her water. "I'm happy that he found the success he wanted; I'm just not that impressed with his work. I'm an academic. I like substance, and my dad is all style and talk and not a lot else. He changes with the wind. You never really know who you're going to get when he shows up." She sighed. "I don't know why we're talking about him."

"How do you feel about your father's relationship with Whitney?"

"I hate it, but I can't do anything about it."

"Did you introduce them?"

"Yes, of course. He came to have lunch with me, and the next thing I know, we're up in the executive suite. Now he has become entrenched with the Tremaines. He bought a big house in Calabasas, and Whitney moved in with him. I'm really afraid he's going to mess things up for me. I know that sounds selfish, but I like my job, and I care a lot about the Tremaines. As Hamilton told you, he and I are kindred spirits when it comes to our interest in space."

"What do you think about the upcoming launch on Tuesday? Is the satellite ready to defend itself? Or is Hamilton rushing under the pressure of his rivals?"

"I honestly don't know. He could be pushing too hard. But that's understandable since there are several companies hot on our heels. Do you have any idea how much activity on Earth is controlled and aided by satellites?"

"I've been getting a crash course on that subject the past month," he said. "Hamilton likes to talk."

"That he does—to anyone who will listen. Space is the new frontier; it's the next battleground, Wyatt. Being able to defend our satellites is going to be hugely important. And being able to take down other weaponized satellites, missiles, rockets, etc., without creating space debris will also be a significant advancement." She smiled. "But the general public is not as interested in the satellite as they are in the idea of Hamilton getting in the *Star Gazer* rocket ship one day and making a trip to Mars with some of his best friends. That's the story that captures the imagination."

"He tells me that could happen within the next five years. Do you agree?"

"We're getting closer to the possibility of interplanetary travel. But five years is overly optimistic. I'd say fifteen is a better guess, but who knows?"

"Would you go to Mars?" he asked curiously.

"Get in a rocket and soar into the universe? I wish I could say yes," she said with a yearning sigh. "I would love to be part of that, but I don't have the guts."

"Not even to see what you've spent your whole life learning about?"

"Big old coward," she admitted. "I wish I wasn't. I wish I was brave."

"You were brave this morning."

"No, that's not true. I froze. I didn't even try to help you when you were fighting with that man. I could have gone for the gun. I just stood there—paralyzed. I was lucky he didn't go after me when he hit you with that drawer."

"I should have seen that coming," he said with a frown. "But don't sell yourself short. You stood up to danger, and you've held it together since then."

"Barely, but I probably shouldn't admit that. I have a feeling an adrenaline crash is coming my way soon. You might want to get ready for that."

He smiled at her endearing self-deprecation. "I will buckle up."

"I just want answers, Wyatt. I want to know why Noelle is dead. I want to make sure someone pays for killing her. And while I understand why Hamilton wants to protect the company, Nova Star's work is not more important than Noelle's life. I hope you're really trying to get to the truth and not cover it up."

"That is what I'm trying to do," he reassured her.

She didn't look entirely convinced. "But your loyalty is to Hamilton."

"Not at the expense of someone's life." He paused, thinking that he needed to give her a bit more information in order to get her to trust him. "I'll let you in on a little secret; Hamilton doesn't just want to protect his company, he's also worried about his son, Jonathan."

"Jonathan?" she echoed. "What does he have to do with any of this?"

"Jonathan had a drink with Noelle three nights ago at Steamers, a bar in the Pelican Point Hotel in Palos Verdes."

"What?" she asked in surprise. "How do you know that?"

"I saw them."

"You saw them together—just by chance?"

He ignored that question, going for one of his own. "Do you think Noelle and Jonathan could have been having an affair?"

"Jonathan is married, and Noelle has a boyfriend. I didn't think they even knew each other. Are you sure it was her?"

"I am sure. It doesn't seem like they would have business to discuss since they don't work together."

"No, they don't." She gave him an unhappy look. "What happened after this drink? Did they stay at the hotel?"

"They left in separate cars."

"And you saw that, too? Were you following Noelle? Or Jonathan?"

"That's not a question I can answer."

"Why not?"

"Because it involves other issues at Nova Star I'm not cleared to speak about."

"If those issues have to do with Noelle's death—"

"I don't know that they do," he said quickly.

"But they might." She pressed her fingers to her temples. "I'm getting a headache."

"I realize this is tough, Avery. You don't know me, and I'm asking you a lot of questions, but I am trying to help. Did Noelle ever say anything about Jonathan to you?"

She lifted her gaze to his. "She said he was attractive and funny. She admired him from afar. But that's true of a lot of the women at Nova Star. Jonathan is personable and friendly. Everyone likes him."

"Okay. But somehow Noelle, who was a Level 1 admin got close enough to the owner's son to have a drink with him. How do you think that happened?"

"I don't know, but Noelle's job or educational level has never deterred her from getting a date. She has always been very attractive to men. Trust me, I went to enough bars with her to know that when she was in the room, it was like there was a spotlight on her. Men were drawn to her, and she didn't even have to say a word. She just had this gleam in her eyes, this secret smile, that everyone wanted to explore."

There wasn't any jealousy in Avery's tone, but he couldn't help wondering what it would have felt like for Avery to have a friend who was always in the sun, while she was in the shadows. *Although, maybe Avery had preferred that.* Despite her proficiency at her job and her ability to speak to hundreds of people in a group, there was an innate sense of shyness about her, as if stepping into the light was no more in her comfort zone than going to Mars.

"I'm sure Jonathan just ran into her somewhere at the company," Avery continued. "Maybe she told him she needed career advice or something. Or maybe he hit on her. I don't know."

"Would she go out with a married man?"

Avery hesitated. "She wasn't a slut, Wyatt, but she did like men, and she didn't consider sex to be that big of a deal."

"I'm going to take that as a yes."

She let out a heavy sigh. "Even if they were having an affair, what does that mean?" She paused. "Are you suggesting that Jonathan Tremaine could have something to do with this?"

"I don't know. I'm looking for a motive. This wasn't random. Someone wanted to kill Noelle."

"If she was having an affair, Jonathan could have been afraid she'd tell his wife," Avery said slowly.

"That's one scenario," he said, happy to let her throw out her theories first.

"Or her boyfriend could have found out she was cheating on him. But Carter doesn't seem the angry type, and the person who killed Noelle..." She shook her head, biting down on her lip whatever she was remembering. "It was violent, Wyatt. It was personal. It felt like Noelle had betrayed someone." She took a breath. "But if she and Jonathan weren't personally involved, then their meeting had to have been about something else. You were following Jonathan for a reason that you don't care to explain, so Noelle's death might not have anything to do with an affair." She rolled her head around her shoulders. "I feel like we're going in circles. Nothing makes sense."

"Not yet. But one thing is clear to me, and it should be clear to you. You're in the middle of a very dangerous situation. You can identify the man in the apartment this morning. You were with Noelle last night. You heard her dying words." He paused, seeing her face pale. "I know you're a smart woman. You understand what I'm saying."

"Yes, I do."

Avery's phone buzzed, and she jumped. As she looked at the number, the lines of tension around her eyes deepened. "It's Noelle's mom. I have to take this."

He nodded. "Of course. But I'm not leaving you alone in this apartment, so I'll be here."

Avery didn't reply as she took the phone with her into the bedroom. "I'm so sorry, Mrs. Price," she said, and then she closed the door.

Wyatt let out a breath, hoping he'd played his cards correctly. He usually didn't share information, but Avery was sharp, and she was in danger, and his gut told him that the only way to gain her trust was to bring her into the problem— at least part of the problem.

Feeling restless, he got up and paced around the living room. The book Avery had taken out of Noelle's apartment was on the coffee table. He picked it up, wondering if it was a clue. He read the inscription again, remembering what Avery had said earlier—that Noelle had dictated the words to her.

He'd never spoken to Noelle, but Avery's deep affection for the woman had brought her alive in a way he had never expected. Even though his heart had iced over years ago, he felt a pang of sadness that such a bright woman was gone. He would find out who had killed her. He didn't know if Avery would like the answer or if Noelle's activities might hurt the people who loved her, but at least they'd get to the truth.

Flipping through the pages of the book, he wondered if by some small chance Noelle had jotted something down inside the book, but it was pristine. Nothing appeared altered in any way.

Taking a seat on the couch, he read through the introduction and then into the first few chapters. The book was for kids, but Avery had not dumbed anything down. Her passion for science and space rang through on every page, and he could only imagine how many children would be inspired to go into astrophysics or become astronauts after reading her story.

A few minutes later, he heard the shower go on. Avery must have finished her call. Maybe when she was done freshening up, he could encourage her to pack a bag and find another place to stay.

She'd probably fight him on that. She might think she was a coward, but when he looked at her, he saw a strong, capable, beautiful woman with a really big heart.

He would have liked to have met her away from the job. But that would have never happened. He was almost always on assignment, living a life that was not his own. That's why he rarely had relationships with women. He had nights, the occasional weekend. But no one ever knew the real him, and he never really knew them. It had worked well for the most part. *But every now and then...*

He shrugged off that wayward thought and tried not to think about Avery's beautiful curves under a spray of hot water.

Thankfully, his phone rang, and he was relieved by the distraction. When he saw Hamilton Tremaine's private number flash across his screen, he got his head back in the game.

"Tanner," he said briskly.

"How is Avery?" Hamilton asked, genuine concern in his voice. "I was just informed by Special Agent Davis at the FBI that she was attacked this morning at Ms. Price's apartment. Why didn't you call me, Wyatt?"

"I haven't had a second. Avery is fine. Unfortunately, the person involved got away. What else did Agent Davis have to say?"

"That the FBI is taking over the case because of Ms. Price's employment at my company and the other incidents we've previously discussed. I don't see how this woman could have been involved in any kind of sabotage or theft. From what I understand, her job was barely more than an administrative clerk. She didn't have access to anything, and she only worked for us for a few months. In fact, I suspect, based on the resume I read, that she was only hired because of Avery's influence. Unless...there's something I don't know?"

"I'm just beginning to dig into Ms. Price's life. She did have a boyfriend at the company—Carter Hayes."

"Yes. Mr. Hayes is a junior attorney in the patent department. Have you spoken to him?"

"Not yet. I'm most concerned about Avery right now. She can identify the man who almost shot her this morning, and I'm worried about her safety."

"So am I," Hamilton said with alarm. "You need to stay with her. I don't want anything to happen to Avery. She's very important to me. She's not just an employee; she's practically family."

"I understand. And I intend to keep a close eye on her."

"Good. Keep me updated. I want to know anything and everything as soon as you know it. I don't like what's going on. This break-in following the murder...disturbs me. Especially since you told me last night that Jonathan had a drink with Ms. Price several days ago. The FBI are going to jump on that like bees to honey, the same way they did with the death of that Chinese woman."

"Did you ask him about his meeting with Ms. Price?"

"I haven't been able to reach him. I've left several messages with his wife. But I'll see him at dinner tomorrow night."

"I know you've been reluctant to have me speak to Jonathan, but I think it's important."

"Not before I do," Hamilton said firmly. "Once I hear what he has to say, we'll discuss it."

Hamilton was still protecting his son.

"But I know Jonathan," Hamilton continued. "He didn't kill that woman, whatever else he might have been doing with her. Someone is either continuing to frame him or he was just in the wrong place, wrong time. You need to find the real killer. Get the job done. I'm counting on you."

"I will do my best," he promised.

As he was about to put down his phone, a text appeared from Flynn MacKenzie. They rarely communicated, but apparently this was important.

There were only three words. *Fire Courtyard Apartments.*

A chill ran down his spine. He immediately got on the internet for more details, quickly coming across a breaking news story about a four-alarm fire at an apartment complex in Venice Beach. The entire building was engulfed in flames. Residents said it started quickly, some sort of explosion in a corner apartment.

His gut twisted. He knew exactly which apartment that was. Whatever hadn't been found this morning was forever gone.

Avery came out of the bedroom a moment later, wearing tan jeans frayed at the hem, a pair of flats and a soft green sweater that hugged her breasts. Her long brown hair was still damp and curling at the ends, her gold-flecked brown eyes bright and beguiling, her face showing a lot more color than she'd had before. But that wasn't going to last long.

"I've been thinking," she said. "I know you're worried about me, but I'll be fine here. I'll keep the doors locked." She stopped abruptly as he got to his feet.

"No," he said flatly.

"Look, I appreciate your concern, Wyatt, but I'm not involved in anything remotely classified at Nova Star. I don't know secrets. I run shows for kids and teachers and tourists."

"You're not staying here, Avery." He turned his phone around, so she could see the screen. "Look."

"What?" she asked, taking his phone. "Is that a fire

burning? Is it close by?"

"It's in Venice Beach—an apartment building."

"Oh, my God! Is that Noelle's building?"

He met her suddenly terrified gaze. "Yes. Pack a bag, Avery. And do it fast."

"Why? This doesn't have anything to do with me. Maybe it's all over now. Noelle is dead, and her apartment is destroyed. There's nothing left to find."

"Except you were there. You had a book in your hands. And they don't know that it was just your own book autographed to your friend."

She stared back at him, her gaze sharpening as she took in his words. "It's possible they think I have whatever they were looking for?"

"And that's why we're getting you out of here. Pack for several days and bring that book."

"Why?"

"I don't know, but just bring it."

Six

---》》《《---

"Where are we going?" Avery asked twenty minutes later, as Wyatt drove away from her apartment building. She'd thrown a pile of clothes into a suitcase, without putting much thought into what she was bringing, grabbed what little cash she had stashed in her place for when the cleaners came, and then jumped into Wyatt's car.

The fire at Noelle's apartment building had definitely brought home to her the fact that this was not over and that she might really be in danger.

For a brief moment in the shower, she'd tried to talk herself out of that idea, rationalizing that whoever was interested in Noelle's place was not interested in her. But with Noelle's apartment gutted by fire and Wyatt's reminder that she had been seen there, it made sense to get away. Although she didn't think her book was important in any way, she'd put it in her bag at his request. Maybe they'd go through it together later.

"Wyatt?" she pressed, realizing he hadn't answered her.

There was a hard set to his jaw, a simmering tension in his movements, and that didn't make her feel better at all. Wyatt had jumped in front of a gun for her. He was an ex-soldier. He was clearly someone who ran into dicey situations when everyone else was running out, so if he said they needed to run, she had to trust his instincts.

"Sorry. Thinking," he said in clipped tones, shooting her a quick look, his dark eyes filled with shadows. "What about your mother's house?"

"No. My mom will have a million questions. Plus, she's leaving for Hawaii tomorrow, and I don't want her to change her plans."

"What about your dad then?"

"And bring danger to him? Or to any of my friends? I need to stay somewhere that isn't attached to me, where no one would expect me to be. Why don't you just drop me at the nearest hotel?"

"I'm not dropping you anywhere."

"We can't stay together," she protested.

"Why not?"

"Because...we can't," she said, floundering for a good reason that wouldn't make her sound like an idiot.

"We'll get separate but connecting rooms. However, I'd like to stop at my apartment and pick up a few things before we do that."

"I'm very capable of taking care of myself, Wyatt," she said, trying to infuse as much confidence into those words as she could. But the truth was she didn't feel at all optimistic that she could take care of herself, not after what had happened to Noelle and what happened to her at Noelle's apartment.

"In ordinary situations, I'm sure you are," Wyatt returned. "But this is not ordinary, Avery. If what I've told you isn't enough for you to realize the need to be careful—"

"I recognize the need. I'm not stupid."

"I know you're not stupid; I just don't think you've ever had to deal with the kind of danger that you might be in."

He was right about that. "Fine. We'll stay at the same hotel, but I can't just hide out there. I have to go on living. I told Noelle's mom that I would meet her at the mortuary at four o'clock today to discuss plans. I'm not going to let her deal with that alone."

"I'll go with you."

"To the mortuary? To discuss funeral plans? To listen to Noelle's mother sob with grief?" she asked with surprise.

"If that's what you're doing, that's what I'm doing."

"Why do you care what happens to me? You don't know me. We're not friends. I'm not your problem. Why go out of your way to make sure I'm safe?"

"I told you before; it's my job to look out for Nova Star employees, and that includes you. Especially you, actually. I spoke to Hamilton while you were in the shower. He's concerned about you, and he asked me to stay close. He's the boss."

"I doubt he made a point of that."

"He said you're practically family. Why don't you call him and ask him if you can trust me?" Wyatt suggested.

Her gaze narrowed on his confident expression. "You know he'll say yes."

"I do. But I want you to feel as comfortable as you can with me."

She debated for a moment and then pulled out her phone and called Hamilton. She rarely used the personal number he'd given her, but these circumstances were extraordinary. And as much as Wyatt seemed trustworthy, there were bits and pieces of his story that bothered her, like the fact that he'd been at the funhouse the night before, that he'd seen Noelle with Jonathan Tremaine but couldn't explain how that came to be.

Hamilton answered a moment later. "Avery—are you all right?"

She heard real concern in his voice, and it touched her deeply. In truth, Hamilton sometimes felt more like a father to her than her own dad. "I'm hanging in there."

"I am so sorry about your friend. Your father told me

how close you were—ever since you were children."

Emotion knotted her throat at his caring words. "Noelle and I were best friends for a long time. I really hope they catch the person who killed her."

"You need to leave that to the police," he said. "Wyatt told me what happened this morning. Why were you at your friend's apartment?"

So, Wyatt had talked to Hamilton. At least, he hadn't lied about that. "I just needed to go there," she said vaguely, not wanting to get into any more details.

"I'm worried about you, Avery. Wyatt says the intruder got a look at your face."

"Well, Wyatt was certainly chatty," she said. "While the situation isn't ideal, I'm being careful; I don't want you to worry."

"It's too late for that. I didn't know your friend, but she was an employee, and the manner of her death disturbs me. The fact that you could be in danger makes the situation even worse. I want Wyatt to protect you until we can hire additional security."

"I don't think that's necessary."

"I do. Now, will I see you tomorrow at your father's birthday dinner? With everything that's going on, I'm sure it's the last thing you want to do, but I know Whitney has gone to a lot of trouble, and I'm quite certain your father would appreciate you being there."

She'd completely forgotten about the birthday party. "I haven't given it any thought."

"Completely understandable. But please make it happen. I'd like to talk to you in person, Avery. I know you're going through a difficult time, but there are also some things I need to know about your friend. With the launch coming up on Tuesday, I have to know if there is any break in my security."

"I understand. I'll see you tomorrow then, but I have one request. Please don't say anything to my dad about what happened at Noelle's apartment this morning. It will only upset him."

"He's your father; he has a right to know."

"But there's nothing he can do about it. I'd really appreciate it if you wouldn't say anything."

There was a hesitation on the other end of the line, but finally Hamilton said, "All right. I will respect your wishes."

"Thank you."

"Take care."

"I will."

"Well?" Wyatt asked, as she disconnected the call.

"You weren't lying. Hamilton asked you to look out for me."

"And…you'll let me be your shadow for a while longer?"

"Yes." She turned her head to meet his gaze. "But I'm pretty sure you're going to be bored out of your mind."

For the first time since she'd met him, a smile curved his lips.

"Bored, huh? So far hanging out with you has been anything but boring."

"But this isn't my normal life. That is usually quite uneventful."

"Well, hopefully we can get you back to that."

"Hopefully," she echoed, although a tiny part of her wondered if that was really what she wanted.

Not that she needed to live in a world where her friends were dying, but Noelle had just ranted to her the night before about being too complacent, unwilling to take risks, always playing it safe.

Well, she wasn't doing any of that anymore. She was not playing it safe and she was taking a risk by trusting Wyatt, because as much as Hamilton seemed to like him, he'd only known Wyatt for a month. Maybe she needed to find out more about Hamilton's favorite new security guy.

--→➤➤◄◄←--

Despite her interest in getting to know what Wyatt Tanner was all about, his studio apartment gave her few clues. It was very small, utilitarian, no real signs of any kind of personality. He had a couch and a chair in front of a large TV and a queen-sized bed in a sleeping alcove, but there were no pictures or photos anywhere in the apartment.

"It doesn't feel like you've lived here long," she said, as he threw some clothes into what appeared to be an old Marine duffel bag.

"Why do you say that?"

"There's nothing here that feels personal. Where are your photos?"

"On my phone."

Somehow, she doubted that. "Really?"

He shrugged. "I don't take a lot of photos. I keep memories here," he said, tapping the side of his head. "And I don't need my space to be personal. It's just a place to crash."

"Exactly. It's not a place to live. And I can't help but feel that your salary at Nova Star would allow you to live a richer life."

"I'm not into material things. I've spent a lot of my life moving around. It's easier to leave when you don't have to pack and unpack."

She stared back at him, studying his expression. Wyatt certainly didn't give much away, his gaze unreadable, his thoughts masked, and his emotions hidden away. He was over six-feet tall, with a powerful stance, a commanding presence. He was definitely the kind of man anyone would follow—the kind of man a woman would look at twice, or three times...

She drew in a quick breath at that distracting thought, trying not to notice his full, sexy lips, the strong jaw, the thick wavy brown hair that fell over his forehead.

"What?" he asked, his brows furrowing at her continued stare. "Something in my teeth?"

"No," she said. "Sorry for staring. I was just...thinking." She licked her lips. "So, you said it's easier to leave if you don't unpack. Does that mean you're not planning to stay here or at Nova Star?"

"I have no plans to leave, but life can be temporary. This weekend is proof of that. I've seen a lot of people plan for a future that never came. It seems pointless."

"That's cynical and depressing."

"Or realistic and pragmatic," he returned, as he moved toward his closet.

She couldn't help but notice that he didn't have much more in there than a few suit jackets, dress shirts and slacks. He grabbed several of those items and put them in a green duffel bag that looked like it had seen better days.

"Is that from the service?" she asked.

"It is."

"Why did you leave the Marines?"

"You're very curious," he said, zipping his bag.

"I'm a scientist. I question things. And you didn't give me an answer."

"I lost my hearing in a bomb blast. It came back about two weeks after they booted me out of the Corps."

"I'm sorry you were injured. Do you miss being a soldier?"

"I still fight, just on a different battlefield."

There was a steel gleam in his eyes, cockiness in his tone, and a core of strength that she found very, very appealing. She had no real reason to trust him, but she did. She hoped she wouldn't regret that.

"We should get going," he said. "I want to get us checked in somewhere before we go to the mortuary. We can talk later."

She nodded, but she wasn't sure if they would talk later, at least not about personal matters, and maybe it was better that way. She needed to think of Wyatt like a bodyguard, keep a good solid emotional wall between them.

After leaving his apartment, Wyatt drove them to a hotel in Marina Del Rey. It was big, impersonal, with lots of people around, and she suspected his choice was deliberate. After Wyatt checked them in, they took the elevator to the seventh floor. They had two connecting rooms and the first thing Wyatt did was open the door between the rooms and do a thorough check of both.

"What are you looking for?" she asked as he opened up her closet and the dresser drawers.

"Just looking."

"No one knows we're here or that we'd be assigned these rooms."

"No, but I'd like to know if anyone comes in when we're not here." He pulled a piece of paper off a notepad by the phone, slipping it between two drawers. If anyone opened the drawer, the paper would fall.

"Very clever. I'm starting to feel like I'm in a spy movie," she said.

"But this isn't a movie, Avery, and you can't forget that," he said somberly, drawing her gaze to his.

"I know that, believe me."

He nodded. "Okay." He set up a few other simple traps in their rooms, and then they went back downstairs and headed to the mortuary.

The Sweet Peace Mortuary was housed in a two-story building about three blocks from a very large cemetery. Avery's nerves tightened as she entered the building. It was the first time she'd ever been in a funeral home and she didn't care for it. It was quiet and dark and had an odd smell, probably a mix of formaldehyde and something else. She did not want to think about what went on in the back rooms, so she tried to focus on the woman standing behind a tall counter.

The receptionist, who appeared to be in her sixties or seventies, gave her a sympathetic smile and asked if they were all present.

"We're waiting on one more," she said.

"Let me know when you're all here, and Director Stanyan will see you in his office," the reception replied. "Please have a seat."

"Thanks."

As she moved away from the counter and took a seat on one of the lobby sofas, she saw brochures on the coffee table in front of her for caskets, as well as pamphlets about burial rights and cremations. The people used as models for the promotional materials were all older, white-haired, having lived long and full lives, and a wave of anger ran through her.

"It isn't fair," she said to Wyatt, who had taken a seat next to her, picking up one of the brochures and waving it at him. "It's too soon for Noelle to be gone. She doesn't belong here. Can this be real? Can my best friend, a woman who is only thirty years old, be dead? This is a place for really old people."

Wyatt's brown eyes filled with compassion. "I wish it wasn't real, Avery."

"Me, too." She put down the brochure and hugged her arms around her waist, feeling ice-cold, but she doubted any amount of heat would make her feel warm again.

"Tell me how you met," Wyatt said.

"What?" she asked blankly.

"How you and Noelle first met."

"I—I don't know if I can talk about it."

"You can." He gave her an encouraging smile.

She thought for a moment. "It was at summer camp. We were eight years old and in the same cabin. We were going to the lake, and I saw that she had left without sunscreen or a hat, so I grabbed both items and told her she couldn't be out all day in the sun without them. She looked at me like I was crazy. But that was me. I was the worrier, the girl who looked before she leapt. Noelle just dove in, headfirst, unafraid, ready for any adventure." She paused. "I guess I should be glad she had so many adventures. She lived life. It was just too short." She drew in a breath, trying to rein in her emotions, not wanting to break down in front of Wyatt. Plus, Noelle's mom would be here soon, and she had a feeling Kari Price was going to be a mess. "I need to keep it together, especially with Noelle's mom coming."

"What's her mother like?"

"Kari is a lot like Noelle—red hair, blue eyes, big personality. She can also be emotional and kind of flaky and sometimes a little too caught up in herself. At least, that's the way I remember her. I haven't seen her since college graduation." She twisted her hands together in her lap. "Kari was a young mom. She had Noelle when she was eighteen. Noelle's dad was eight years older, and he was a good influence on Kari, according to Noelle, but he died when Noelle was eleven. After that Kari went off the rails. She was depressed. She drank too much. She brought home different men, some who weren't so great. She was always late picking us up when it was her turn to drive us somewhere. It used to make my mom crazy. Eventually, she stopped letting Kari do any of the pick-ups or drop-offs. She just didn't trust her."

"That must have been rough on Noelle."

"It was hard at times, but on the flip side, Noelle had no restrictions whatsoever. Kari looked at Noelle like she was a friend, not a daughter, so Noelle had no curfew, no mom worrying about where she was or asking too many questions. Noelle got into a lot of trouble in high school."

"Did she take you down with her?"

"No. I tended to bail when things got dicey. She usually had other friends who were willing to keep up with her."

"It sounds like you were complete opposites."

"We were. But despite how different we were, we really had a bond. We told each other everything when we were kids. We were like sisters." She paused. "When Noelle came back into my life this year, I was wary, but I was also happy, because I'd really missed her. I don't think I've ever been as honest with anyone as I was with her. She knew all my bad stuff, all my quirks, and I knew all of hers—or I used to. Now, it feels like I didn't know anything about her. I want to find out what happened, Wyatt. I want to get justice for her. But I'm also a little afraid of what we're going to learn."

Wyatt gave her an understanding nod. "I get that. The truth is we never really know anyone, even when we think we do. Everyone has a secret, something no one else knows."

"I don't think that's true."

"Isn't it?" he challenged.

"Well, I know you have secrets, and you're very private, but I feel like my life is pretty open."

"But you're not involved with anyone. You live alone. Who's to know if you eat a pint of mocha almond fudge out of the carton after midnight?"

"It would not be mocha almond fudge, probably strawberry swirl or cookie dough," she said, knowing Wyatt was trying to lighten the mood. "But I wouldn't worry about hiding that from someone. I'm not single because I have an ice cream addiction; I just haven't met the right person."

"Maybe you're too busy looking up at the stars," he suggested.

She rolled her eyes at that comment. "Have you been talking to my mother? That's her favorite thing to say. I've been building a career. There's nothing wrong with that."

"No, there's not."

"What about you? Are you single because you have some secret fetish?"

"No, I'm single because I'm a terrible boyfriend."

"Did someone tell you that?"

"More than one someone. I'm not good at relationships."

"Maybe because you look at everything as being temporary. No woman wants to think she's just good for the next few minutes or days or weeks."

"Unfortunately, my past career didn't allow me much time to build anything longer than that."

"You're not a Marine now. You can put down roots. You can hang a picture—if you want to."

"I knew you were judging my apartment décor," he said with a gleam in his eyes.

"Décor? You had nothing in your apartment, Wyatt. Certainly nothing that would count as décor."

"Well, I might consider hanging a picture, once this is all over."

"Maybe something from the Nova Star gift shop—with the stars, the moon, Mars—they sell some amazing and wonderful photos."

He gave her a smile that sent a little shiver down her spine, and some of the cold in her heart seeped away.

But as their gaze clung for seconds too long, she felt uneasy, wondering what she was doing. *How could she even be thinking of Wyatt as a man when she was sitting in a mortuary about to figure out funeral arrangements for her best friend?*

Although, she could almost hear Noelle saying, *I get it— he's hot—and you're still alive. Don't waste your life.*

But was that Noelle? Or was it her own voice?

The door opened, and she stood up as Kari Price walked in. Her hair was a darker red than she remembered, and Kari was very thin, wearing a loose sweater over black leggings. Dark glasses covered her eyes, but as she stepped forward, she removed them, revealing red-rimmed eyes. She held out her arms, and Avery ran into her embrace as they exchanged a long, sad hug.

"I'm sorry," she said, gazing into Kari's eyes.

"Our girl is gone. I can hardly believe it. All the way here, I kept telling myself it was a dream."

"I know the feeling." She felt tears well up within her, but she needed to keep them at bay.

"Are you Noelle's boyfriend?" Kari asked Wyatt, who had gotten to his feet.

"No," he said quickly. "I'm Wyatt Tanner. I worked with

your daughter."

"He's trying to help me find out what happened to Noelle," Avery added.

"Thank God someone is looking for my daughter's killer. The police just told me the FBI has taken over the case but no one from the bureau is calling me back," Kari said, anger in her eyes. "Shouldn't someone have some answers for me by now?"

"I'm sure they'll be in touch," she replied. "But let's worry about that later. Are you ready to discuss arrangements?"

"I don't know. I'm not sure what to do. I don't have any idea if Noelle would want to be buried or cremated, and where she would want any of that to take place. I'm hoping you might know, Avery."

She shook her head. "We didn't talk about any of that."

"Of course not. Why would you? My baby shouldn't be dead," Kari said, sobs taking over the last part of her sentence.

Avery put her arm around Kari's shoulders as the director, a serious-looking man in his mid to late fifties came out of a back room and suggested they move into his office.

"I'm going to wait for you here," Wyatt said quickly, a pained expression on his face.

She nodded, thinking it would be better to do this with Kari on her own. But it wasn't going to be easy, and there was a part of her that wished she could stay in the reception area, too.

But she needed to be there for Noelle's mom. Noelle had always hated when her mom was unhappy. She'd often felt personally responsible for it, as if it was up to her to make up for her dad dying. If Noelle was looking down on them now, at least she'd know that Avery was taking care of her mother. It was the last thing she could do for her friend.

Seven

$\rightarrow\!\!\!\rightarrow\!\!\!\Longleftarrow\!\!\!\Longleftarrow$

Wyatt was happy to wait in the reception area while Noelle and Kari discussed funeral arrangements. Just being close to their raw emotion had made him feel uneasy. It had also made him realize how little emotion he'd let into his life the past few years.

Everything was about work, and in order to do his job well, he couldn't let emotion into it. Most of the time he had no problem staying on track, but talking to Avery about her friendship with Noelle, her childhood, her life, had reminded him that once upon a time he'd had friendships too, real friendships. He'd also had a family and a home.

Frowning at the direction of his thoughts, he pulled out his phone and checked the time. He could hardly believe It was almost five. The day had passed in a blur, and it wasn't over yet.

He felt a restless urge to connect with someone, but it couldn't be someone from his distant past. He walked outside, drawing in several deep gulps of fresh air before punching in the number Bree had given him.

"Just wanted to check in," he said. "I saw the news about the fire in Venice Beach. Are you at work? Can you talk?"

"I am in the office. Hold on one second," she said.

He perched on the edge of a brick planter outside the mortuary and watched the traffic for a few moments until Bree came back on the line.

"Sorry about that," she said.

"No problem. I probably shouldn't be calling you, but I thought you might have more up-to-date information than Flynn."

"It's fine. I just got off the phone with the fire investigator. The blaze was set in Noelle Price's apartment. Witnesses at the scene mentioned an earlier fight involving you, Ms. Caldwell, and the man with the tattoo on his neck."

"No one else was seen at the apartment after we left?"

"Not that anyone remembers, but it was a chaotic scene. The fire spread quickly. People were focused on getting out of the building with a few personal items and their lives. The only thing we know for sure is that whatever was in that apartment is gone. The fire investigation is just beginning. I'm sure we'll know more in a few days."

"I'm not sure we have a few days. With the satellite launch coming up on Tuesday, Noelle's murder, and now the fire, everything is ratcheting up."

"Which should make Nova Star more interested in cooperating with us, but Joanna said while your boss expressed concern about Ms. Price's death, he didn't believe it was connected to the company. He said his security is also looking into the matter, which I guess is you and your team at Nova Star."

"Yes. But Hamilton is not quite as confident as he would have you believe. He is determined to protect his family, and he thinks Jonathan is being set up for a fall."

"Then he needs to help us prove that."

"Well, he's got me to do that. Are you spending the whole weekend at work?"

"Maybe. Nathan went back to Chicago for a few days, so I figured I might as well keep busy. By the way, Vincent

Rowland showed up in the office a few minutes ago and whisked Joanna off for a drink."

He was surprised. Vincent Rowland was retired FBI and the father of a former friend. "What is he doing in LA?"

"He's here for his daughter Cassie's engagement party."

"That's good. I'm glad the Rowlands have a happy event to celebrate. That memorial a few months back was kind of rough."

"I really wanted to be there for that."

"Work comes first."

"Yes. But I'm not sure Vincent would agree with you. He was very short with me. I think he's still angry that I wasn't there."

"You had a good reason. You were looking for a missing child. Vincent understood that. He's just a reserved man. I wouldn't take it personally."

"I just wish sometimes I could talk to him about Jamie. I cared so much for his son, but sometimes I think he blames me for Jamie's death. He once told me that Jamie's penchant for falling in love distracted him from what should have been his true priority."

"Jamie's death was an unfortunate accident. Everyone agrees on that."

"I know," she said with a sigh. "Sorry to bring all that up. I just got rattled when I saw Vincent. Anyway, let's get back to you. What's going on? Where are you now?"

"I'm at the mortuary with Avery Caldwell. She and Noelle Price's mother are making funeral arrangements."

"That's depressing."

"Very. Have you been able to ID the man at Noelle's apartment this morning?"

"Not yet, but we're working on it."

"All right. I've moved Avery to a safer location just in case anyone is interested in going after her. I'm going to stay close to her this weekend, which will actually work in my favor. There's a dinner party tomorrow night for her father's birthday, and the entire Tremaine family will be there. I'm going to get myself on the guest list."

"That should be an interesting party. I saw Ms. Caldwell's photograph. She's very pretty."

"Which has nothing to do with anything," he said bluntly, hearing the teasing note in her voice.

"I know you're always professional on the job."

"Exactly."

"And she's definitely not your type."

"I don't have a type."

"Well, you don't usually date rocket scientists, do you?"

"Maybe I would if they looked like Avery."

"So, you are intrigued," she said knowingly.

"I'm not blind, but I'm not going to do anything about it. She's terrified and grief-stricken, and I would never take advantage of that. Plus, she has no idea who I really am."

"Do you ever get tired of the undercover life, Wyatt?"

He would have normally answered that question very easily, very quickly. Going undercover was what he did best. But today, all he could see were a hundred shades of gray. "I am a little tired," he admitted. "But I'll be fine."

"Sometimes changing your job isn't a bad thing. I did it."

"I change my job all the time—every assignment."

"I mean change your real job."

"I don't think I could go back into an office at this point." He paused as a car turned in to the lot and a man got out. "I have to go. Looks like Noelle Price's boyfriend just showed up."

He stood up, slipping his phone into his pocket as Carter Hayes hurried across the lot, wearing jeans and a button-down shirt instead of the suit he usually wore to work.

In his early thirties, Carter had sandy-brown hair, fair skin, and a boyish look that was strained and frazzled today.

"Mr. Hayes," he said, stepping in front of him.

Carter gave him a surprised and blank look. That was understandable. While he had seen Carter numerous times on the security cameras at Nova Star and had also begun to look into his life since Noelle had shown up at a restaurant with Jonathan Tremaine, Carter had no idea who he was.

"Yes?" Carter said. "Who are you?"

"Wyatt Tanner. I'm in security at Nova Star."

"Oh. You're here with Avery?"

"Yes. She's inside with Noelle's mother. I'm very sorry for your loss. Avery told me that you've been seeing Noelle for several months."

"I have," Carter admitted. "And I can't believe any of this. It's a nightmare. I spoke to Noelle just a few hours before she went to the pier with Avery and then she's killed, stabbed by some crazy person? How does that happen?"

"I don't know," he said somberly, seeing what appeared to be genuine horror in Carter's face.

"Do the police have any idea who killed her?"

"Not that they've told me."

"They won't tell me anything. I think they consider me a suspect. I spent half the night at the police station answering questions and an hour ago, I got a call from some FBI agent who wants to talk to me next, but I have no answers. All I know is that Noelle went to meet Avery and ended up dead."

He nodded. "That's rough."

Carter hesitated, giving him an odd look. "Is there any chance you can turn down the heat on me? You said you're in security, right?"

"Yes, but there's nothing I can do to stop the FBI from investigating, and I'm sure you want to find who killed Noelle."

"Of course. But it wasn't me. And I'm up for a promotion at Nova Star. I've been working really hard for it. If the Tremaines get wind that I'm a suspect...well, I don't want to be fired. I've been at the company for three years. I'm a loyal employee."

"I doubt anyone is looking to fire you," he said, although it seemed like Carter's concerns at the moment were very self-centered for a man who had just lost his girlfriend.

Carter shifted back and forth, digging his hands in his pockets. "I'm sorry. I'm wound up. Too much coffee, not enough sleep."

"I can understand that."

"I don't want to be here, but when Noelle's mother called me, I couldn't say no. Is she inside?"

"She's with Avery. They're meeting with the director now."

Carter hesitated. "What's her mother like?"

"You haven't met her?"

"No. I've just heard Noelle argue with her on the phone. Her mom has been having money problems, and she has been asking Noelle for help. But Noelle hasn't been on the job long, and she doesn't have extra cash." Carter paused. "I'm a little afraid Noelle's mom is going to hit me up for money, and that's why she wants me here."

Now Carter was worried about money as well as his job? Noelle was getting pushed further and further down his list of concerns.

"You think she'd do that now?" he asked.

"Maybe. Noelle says her mom is terrible with money, that she always has to bail her out. On the other hand, I know how much Noelle loved her mother. I feel like she'd want me to help her."

Carter's words echoed what Avery had said earlier. Maybe he needed to look more closely at Kari Price. *If Kari had had money problems, had Noelle done something to get the cash her mother needed?*

He stepped back and opened the door for Carter. "After you." For a split second, he thought Carter might bolt, but the man drew in a breath and stepped inside the lobby.

Wyatt had no sooner followed him inside when Avery joined them.

Relief flashed through her brown eyes as she saw Carter.

"Carter." She gave him an emotional hug. "Kari said you

were coming down."

"Sorry I'm late. It's been...a lot." Carter ran a hand through his tousled hair.

"I know. I feel the same way."

"Where's her mom?"

"Kari is still meeting with the director. If you want to join her, I'm sure she'd be okay with that."

Carter swallowed hard. "Maybe I should just wait."

"All right. She's almost done."

Carter nodded. "Is, uh, is Noelle's body...is it back there?"

"No," Avery said quickly. "Her body hasn't been released by the medical examiner yet, but Kari doesn't know how long she can stay in town, so she wanted to start making arrangements."

"Is she taking Noelle back to Florida?"

"I think she wants to talk to you about it."

Carter appeared panicked by Avery's words. "Me? I don't know what to do. I mean, I loved Noelle. I did. But we haven't been together that long."

"It's okay, Carter," Avery said, putting a hand on his arm. "I know how shocked and upset you are, because I feel the same way."

"I am shocked," Carter echoed. "I don't know how we got here."

"I don't, either."

"The police said you found Noelle, but why weren't you with her? Why was she alone?" Carter asked.

"She wanted to go into the funhouse, and I didn't, so she went without me. When she was taking too long, I decided to look for her. I'm so sorry, Carter," she said, her eyes filling with tears.

"You're not to blame, Avery. I know you cared a lot for Noelle. She was happy the two of you were friends again."

"I was happy, too." Avery took a breath. "So, getting back to what needs to be done now...Kari is very concerned about the financial burden of a funeral. I don't think she has much money."

"From what Noelle said, she doesn't," Carter said, his lips drawing into a tight line. "She was always calling, asking Noelle to send her some cash. She was sending her a check almost every other week, but it never seemed to be enough."

"I didn't realize things were that bad," Avery murmured.

"Look, I can contribute something toward this funeral," Carter said. "But I don't want to talk to her mother. I have to go. If you need help, call me." He pulled out his wallet and handed Avery a business card.

"Please, don't go, Carter," Avery said. "I know Kari would like to see you."

"She doesn't know me; I don't know her. I've just said hello over the phone. It's better this way." Carter whirled around and dashed out the door, leaving Avery with a stunned look on her face.

"Well, I didn't expect that," she said, turning back to him. "What did I say?"

"Nothing. Carter was amped up before he walked in here. He said the police gave him a grilling last night. He's worried he's going to be accused of Noelle's murder."

Avery stared back at him. "Really? He's worried about that? I know boyfriends and husbands are often people of interest, but that can usually be cleared up pretty quickly."

"Maybe Carter is overreacting to whatever the police asked him."

"He has to be. I don't believe Carter had anything to do with Noelle's death." She paused, frowning. "Do you?"

"I wouldn't think so, but I've learned never to count anyone out. So, what's going on back there? Is Kari planning a funeral?"

"No. I don't really know what she's going to do. She kept bursting into tears every few minutes, especially when she heard what things might cost. The director asked me to let him speak to her alone, and I was fine with that."

As she finished speaking, Kari returned to the lobby, her cheeks wet with tears, her eyes bloodshot. "I'm sorry, Avery."

"What?" she asked. "What's wrong now?"

"I don't have the money to do any of this. I thought maybe I could swing it, but the truth is I can't. I don't have the funds to bury my own daughter or to give her a memorial. I'm a horrible mother." She collapsed into Avery's arms, sobbing her heart out.

He knew Kari's grief was real and raw, but he also thought some of the drama was part of her play to get Avery to step up to the financial plate.

Avery gave him a helpless look and then helped Kari over to the couch. "It's going to be fine. I'll help. Carter said he would contribute, too."

"He was here? Where did he go?"

"He just left. He's very upset."

"But I wanted to speak to him. Why didn't he wait?"

"I don't know. He's exhausted and sad and angry—like we all are. I think we should take a minute or a day and just let things ride. We don't have to decide anything right now."

Kari looked a bit more encouraged. "That's true. We can take a little time. She just died last night."

"Exactly. We can talk later or tomorrow," Avery said. "How did you get here? Did you drive? Do you need a ride somewhere?"

"No, my friend Connie is picking me up. I just called her. She's only a few minutes away. I'm staying with her for a few days."

"I'm glad you won't be alone. I'll wait with you until she comes."

"No. I'm okay," Kari said, wiping her eyes. "You go ahead, Avery. This is a dreary place to wait in."

"We can go outside."

"I'll be all right. I'm sorry about my meltdown. I'm just so overwhelmed."

"Completely understandable. We'll talk later."

"I'll call you." Kari turned her gaze toward him. "It's Wyatt, right?"

He nodded. "Yes."

"Please help Avery find out who killed my daughter. She was my only child, my baby, and she deserves justice."

"Believe me, I'm going to do everything I can."

"Are you sure you don't want me to stay?" Avery asked.

"No, thank you. You were always a good girl, Avery, such a positive influence on Noelle. When you were around, I trusted she'd be okay, she wouldn't go too crazy. When you stopped being friends, I was very sad. I'm glad you got back together before...before all this. I know how much you meant to her."

"She meant a lot to me, too. I'm never going to forget her."

"I know you won't."

Avery gave Kari another hug and then got to her feet. He opened the door for her and followed her outside. Afternoon shadows were falling, and the temperature had dropped ten degrees, but the crisp air felt great after the stifling atmosphere in the mortuary, and he could see Avery drawing in deep, calming breaths as they walked to the car.

As they got into the vehicle, he said, "You handled both Kari and Carter quite well."

"I have to admit they surprised me in different ways. Carter bailed out on everything. Kari apparently can't afford even the cheapest funeral. Which leaves me."

"It sure looks that way."

"I didn't realize Kari's problems were so bad or that Noelle was supporting her. She never said anything about that, although she might have thought I'd say something judgmental. I always liked Kari, but I did have a front row seat to a lot of her screw-ups." She paused. "I guess I now know why Noelle was so desperate to get a corporate job instead of pursuing her acting ambitions, the way she had before. It makes sense."

"Does it also make sense that she picked a lawyer to date, someone who could probably take care of her, if she needed it?"

"Maybe. He wasn't her usual type, but people change. But if she did think she could count on him, she was probably wrong. Today, he seemed like the least likely person anyone should count on. I don't care if he thinks he's on the hot seat with the police. His girlfriend is dead. He should have manned up and helped out."

He liked Avery's passionate, angry response to Carter. "I thought the exact same thing."

She met his gaze. "Right? Who acts like that?"

"Something in his behavior was off," he agreed, wondering if it was just grief and shock or something more sinister. Avery let out a heavy sigh, drawing his attention back to her. "What are you thinking now?"

"I feel guilty for saying it."

"You need to stop feeling guilty. It's a waste of emotion. You can't change the past. You have to move forward. Focus on finding Noelle's killer, getting to the truth, instead of blaming yourself for what happened to her."

"I wasn't actually feeling guilty about that."

"Oh, then what?" he asked with surprise.

"I'm hungry. I'd like to get something to eat."

The conflict in her eyes curved his mouth into a smile. "It's not wrong to be hungry. It's almost dinner time."

"I know, but it feels like getting something to eat means I'm just going on with my life, like nothing ever happened."

"Which is what you have to do. But it will never ever be like nothing happened. Noelle was important to you. You're going to miss her. You're going to carry her with you through your life. It won't be enough, but it will be something. And what choice do you have?"

"None. But I do like the idea of carrying her with me through my life. Thanks for those words of wisdom."

"I have my moments," he said lightly. "Now, let's get

something to eat. What do you like?"

"Pretty much everything. You choose. I don't think I can make any more decisions today."

He heard the weary note in her voice and wanted to make that decision for her. In fact, he wanted to make a lot of things easier for her.

A voice inside his head reminded him that making things easier for Avery was not his job; he was just supposed to keep her safe. *Maybe he could do both...*

Eight

—➤➤✦◀◀◄—

He took Avery to a Mexican restaurant he'd found a few weeks ago. It was a hole-in-the-wall café, a dozen blocks off the beach, tucked between a dry cleaner and a thrift shop. There were only eight tables in the small space, but the delicious food was cooked by Carlos Ortiz, an amazing chef in his early fifties. Carlos's wife, Magdalena, ran the front of the house, his son, Felipe, was his sous chef, and his three daughters, who looked so much alike Wyatt could never remember their names, provided excellent service.

He'd eaten there a dozen times already, which went against his usual practice of never being too predictable or settling into too much of a routine. But the food was that good.

"*Hola*, Wyatt," Magdalena said with a cheerful smile.

"*Hola*." He pointed at an empty table at the back of the room, away from the windows and the front door. "That one okay?"

"All yours," she said. "Katerina will be right with you."

"They know your name?" Avery asked as they settled in at the table.

"I guess I have become a regular."

"Then you must know what's good."

"Everything. I like the burritos. They are huge, though."

"Good, because I'm starving." She set the paper menu down. "And I'm thinking a margarita would taste really good."

"Did I hear someone say margaritas?" Katerina asked, giving them a smile as she dropped off two glasses of water. "How are you, Wyatt?"

"I'm hungry," he said with a smile. "And we're ready to order."

"That was fast. What can I get you?"

"I'm going to have the loaded chicken burrito."

"And I will have the same," Avery said. "As well as a margarita."

"You're not going to let her drink alone, are you?" Katerina asked him.

"Sure. I'll take a margarita."

"Great." Katerina picked up their menus and headed toward the kitchen.

"It smells good in here," Avery commented as she glanced around the room. "How did you find this place?"

"I stumbled in one day, and I was amazed. I've had good Mexican food in California, but this is at the top of the list."

"So, is this your home away from home?"

"I suppose, but…" He paused, thinking this restaurant was really nothing like any home he'd actually lived in.

"But," she pressed.

"I did not grow up in a house like this, so it does not remind me of home."

"Where did you grow up?" she asked curiously. "We've been talking so much about me and my family and my relationship with Noelle, I know very little about you, except that you were a Marine."

"There's no big story," he murmured, wishing he hadn't opened that door.

"Come on, give me a few details." She rested her

forearms on the table, leaning forward with curiosity in her sparkling, gold-flecked brown eyes. She was looking for a distraction, and he was it.

"What do you want to know?" he asked warily.

"Are your parents alive? Where do they live? Where did you grow up? Are you from California or somewhere else?"

He inwardly flinched at the barrage of questions, knowing he should have expected them at some point, because clearly Avery had a mind that was wired to want to know everything. He decided to stick as close to the truth as possible, while, of course, leaving out big chunks of the story.

"My parents are alive. I grew up in New York. I have an older brother. What else?"

"What else?" she echoed. "That's barely more than I'd see on your driver's license."

He waved his hand around the warm, happy, colorful restaurant. "See all this? Well, the house I grew up in was nothing like this. It was professionally decorated, filled with expensive, luxury furniture, paintings, and art, but there was no personality."

"Interesting. Much like your current apartment, which is not professionally decorated but still has no personality," she said with a bit of sarcasm.

He grinned. "Maybe that's why I'm comfortable there; it feels familiar in an opposite sort of way."

"Why was your parents' home so sterile? What are they like? What's your relationship with them?"

He waited to answer until Katerina had dropped off their margaritas. Then he said, "My parents entertained a lot, for both my father's work, and also because they had a country club lifestyle. Our home wasn't supposed to reflect a normal, messy family life, it was a stage for events. As for my relationship with them—it was good enough for a long time, and then it was really bad."

"Well, that's about as cryptic an answer as anyone could give," she said, sipping her drink. "Talking to you is like playing twenty questions. Why so reserved, Wyatt?"

"I'm a private person."

"Well, you're not making a public speech; you're just talking to me. And I've been pretty honest with you."

"That was your choice."

"What made things go from good enough to really bad?" she pressed.

Now they were getting into territory he never talked about. On the other hand, what he had to say would probably not affect his cover in any way, so what did it matter?

It mattered, because then she'd know more about him than most people did. That could make him vulnerable. And he never put himself in that position.

"You're having quite a long argument with yourself," Avery said, a perceptive gleam in her eyes. "Are we back to everyone has a secret, especially you?"

"We are back to that." He sipped his drink and then said, "I thought my parents were average, a little snobby, a little highhanded, maybe, but I grew up with money. It was all I knew. We had a nice house in a neighborhood where everyone had a beautiful home. My dad played golf. My mom played tennis. They had parties every weekend, and they were very popular. My father could charm anyone."

"Sounds like my dad," she muttered. "Go on."

He ran his finger around the base of his margarita glass as he neared the edge of a personal cliff. *What the hell—he might as well jump*. It was too late to backtrack now.

"My father had a big secret. He was a financial wizard, someone everyone trusted, but they shouldn't have. He moved money around, played games, borrowed from Peter to pay Paul. He was always looking to score, get a huge payout, and he often got it—until he didn't. Then his house of cards started to fall apart. He not only lost a lot of money, everyone came after him, the SEC, the banks, it was a colossal mess. The worst thing was that by the time that happened, my brother was already working for him, and he went down, too.

My family lost everything. My mom was ostracized from her friends. My brother had to defend himself in court for so long that his wife left him, taking their baby with her."

"I'm so sorry," she said with concern in her eye. "And you? How did you fare?"

"I was the youngest. I was the least involved in anything, so I walked away from it all. I took myself out of the spotlight, away from the press, the accusations, the trials. I distanced myself from everything and everyone."

She stared back at him. "That sounds lonely, Wyatt."

He shrugged. "It wasn't like the kids I grew up with wanted to be friends anymore. A few did, but their parents immediately squashed that. It didn't matter. It was time to move on. The life I had led was gone. I had to accept it."

"So, you joined the Marines."

"I knew I had to change my life," he said, playing with the truth.

"What happened to your mom and dad and your brother?"

"My father went to jail. My mom divorced my father and moved in with her sister but recently remarried. My brother served some time but got out last year. He changed his name and started over. He has some contact with his daughter, but he missed out on some very formative years. I don't think he will ever live the life he imagined or planned for."

"That's terrible. And that's why you said earlier that you'd seen people plan for futures they never got. I thought you were talking about friends who lost their lives, but you were talking about your family."

"I was talking about both," he admitted.

"I'm sorry you had to go through all that. It must have been incredibly painful, especially you seemed to end up on the outside of the circle."

"The circle broke. We were like a chain of beads that fell off a string and scattered to different corners."

"And you don't talk to anyone anymore?"

"I don't. We all had to find a way to make our lives work, and we couldn't do that together."

"I don't see why you couldn't, but I suspect there is more you haven't told me."

"I've told you enough. Anyway, my life is what it is. I don't look back. I don't worry about tomorrow. I just live."

She nodded, then let out a sigh. "I get it, but I am the complete opposite. I look back, I look ahead, and I look sideways. I don't know how to stop planning and trying to control things I can't control."

"That must be exhausting."

"So tiring," she agreed. "I wish I didn't worry everything to death. I know it doesn't affect anything, but I just don't know how to stop. However, if I've learned anything over the past two days, it's that any belief I have that I'm in control is just an illusion."

He was impressed by her self-deprecating honesty. He didn't know if Avery was always so forthcoming or if the stress of Noelle's death had put her over the edge, but he had to admit he liked talking to her. She was a good listener, and she didn't judge. It had felt surprisingly good to tell her about his parents, and that wasn't a subject he shared with just anyone. But instinctively he knew he could trust her with the information.

"Thank you for telling me about your family, Wyatt," she added. "I'm beginning to understand why you have so many walls up. I also have a feeling that if I looked you up on the internet, I wouldn't find anything about you. You said your brother changed his name and started over. Did you do the same?"

Avery's brain certainly worked at an incredible speed. She put facts together and read between lines more quickly than most anyone he'd met. He decided to give her a truthful answer. "Yes, I did."

She raised a brow. "Wow. I wasn't sure you'd admit to that. Are you going to tell me your real name?"

"No."

"Okay then." She sat back in her seat. "I guess I pushed one button too many."

"The person I was doesn't exist anymore." He hoped she had enough on her plate right now to prevent her from looking for more information. Although, if she did, she wouldn't find anything. He'd buried his past more deeply than she could ever dig up, even if she did put parts of his story together. But considering how many other issues were occupying her brain right now, he didn't think it would be a problem. By the time she got back to thinking about who he was, he'd probably be gone.

He took a long drink, that sobering thought annoying him more than it should have.

"I can relate to part of your story," Avery continued. "My dad didn't go to jail, but I think he's a bit of a con artist. He wouldn't admit to that, but his moral code is built on shifting sand. He makes people believe he holds the secret to the perfect life, and they pay him large sums of money to hear him spout quotes made famous by other people. I guess none of it is technically illegal, but it always feels a little wrong to me." She cleared her throat. "My dad thinks my mother poisoned me against him, but she didn't. I was there. I lived with him until I was fourteen. I saw who he was then, and I see who he is now. He's charming and funny, and he's someone who can become whoever you want him to be, but only for a little while. If you look at him too hard or stay too long, you realize he has no more substance than a puff of smoke. I just wish..." Her voice fell away.

"Wish what?" he asked curiously.

"That I didn't love him so much," she confessed. "Even with all the disappointments, I still remember the good times. My dad was fun. When I would hang out with him, it was like being with the most entertaining person you could meet. We would do crazy things. We once hopped a fence and went swimming at a pool in a gated community after midnight, because it was hot, and our air conditioning wasn't working. Being with him was an adventure."

He could hear the love and the conflict in her voice. "But you felt that you were betraying your mom when you liked being with him."

"Especially in the year right before they divorced and immediately afterward. Of course, as the years passed, and my dad let me down numerous times, those adventures became a distant memory."

"But you're not distant anymore."

"I know. And it feels weird that he's back in my life again."

"How does your mother feel about it?"

"She hates it. But, fortunately, she has someone new in her life, too. Don is a great guy. He's taking her to Hawaii tomorrow, which I am really grateful about now that there is so much going on."

He was glad her mother was leaving, too. Anyone connected to Avery could be used as a bargaining chip, and while her dad had security because of his celebrity and his relationship with the Tremaines, he doubted her mother had any protection.

"Oh, wow," Avery said, as Katerina set down their burritos. "You weren't kidding. These are huge. But I think I'm up to the challenge."

He smiled. "Me, too."

She picked up her fork, then hesitated. "There's something I should have said earlier, Wyatt."

"What's that?"

"Thank you. You saved my life this morning. You've been by my side every second since then, even when that meant sitting through a sob fest at a mortuary. I know you'll say it's part of your job, but I think you're going above and beyond."

"You're welcome. Now eat."

"You don't have to say that twice."

Avery dug into the delicious flavors of her spicy burrito stuffed with chicken, rice, beans, onions, salsa, and topped with guacamole and sour cream. Wyatt was right; it was probably the best burrito she'd ever had. And Wyatt was surprisingly easy to have dinner with.

He'd started out the day as a mysterious and somewhat alarming stranger. But now he felt more like a friend. She was happy he'd opened up about his family. His dad and her dad shared some bad traits in common, and for some reason that made her feel closer to Wyatt. She'd read between the lines of his story and had seen the loneliness and disappointment in his eyes as he talked about the decimation of his family. She'd felt similar emotions, even though their situations had been different.

She'd also isolated herself a bit, diving into her studies with perhaps more intensity than she might have if she hadn't been so shattered by her parents' divorce. Wyatt had done the same and taken it to another level by changing his name.

As she ate, she teased him with suggestions of what his name might really be, enjoying a conversation that for a brief moment in time felt almost normal.

Wyatt, of course, did not confess to his true identity, although he'd told her she was getting closer when she'd suggested his real name was George. She doubted that was true, seeing the gleam in his brown eyes, but it amused her to think of him as a *George*.

The staid, formal, somewhat old-fashioned name didn't suit him at all. He really felt more like a Wyatt—a man of action, intensity, purpose, and fearless courage. She felt safe with him.

But there were other feelings, too, and those she should probably set aside for another day—a day far away from now.

As she managed to get down the last bite of her burrito, her phone rang. "It's my mom," she said. "I need to take this."

"Go ahead. I'm going to pay the bill, give you some privacy. Don't go outside without me."

She frowned at the warning reminder but was glad when he moved over to the counter to speak to Magdalena.

"Hi, Mom. How are you?"

"I'm fine. It's you I'm worried about. I just saw some disturbing news on the TV. There was a fire in Venice Beach at Noelle's apartment."

"Yes, I heard about that, too."

"What happened? Why would someone burn down Noelle's apartment? What was she involved in?"

"I really don't know, Mom."

"This is getting worse and worse. I just told Don I think I should skip the trip."

"You are absolutely not going to do that."

"I'm worried about you, Avery."

"You don't need to be. I'm okay."

"You'd say that even if you weren't."

"But I am all right," she reiterated. She really needed her mother to go to Hawaii, so she didn't have to worry about her.

"Are you at home? Maybe I should come by and we can talk. Or you can come here?"

"I'm actually out with someone."

"You're out? With who?"

"A friend from work," she said vaguely. "I'm not alone. And I really want you to go on your trip and have a good time. There's nothing for you to do here."

"What about the funeral arrangements?"

"I spent some time at the mortuary with Kari today. Nothing is going to happen immediately. In the end, we'll probably just have a very small service or some kind of memorial celebration."

"How is Kari holding up?"

"Not very well. She spent a lot of time crying today. She also said that she doesn't have enough money to pay for anything."

"Of course she doesn't," her mother said, an edge to her voice. "Kari never saved a dime and lived beyond her means. Now she wants you to pay, doesn't she?"

"I said I'd contribute; so did Noelle's boyfriend."

"Well, you know I'll help. I didn't like Kari, but I liked Noelle very much. She was like a second daughter to me."

"I know she felt that way about you, too. Anyway, you and Don have fun, take pictures."

"If anything happens, Avery, promise you'll call me. I don't care how small or unimportant you think it is."

"Don't worry," she said, deliberately avoiding that promise. "It's all going to be fine."

"I really hope so."

"Everything all right?" Wyatt asked, as he returned to the table.

She slipped her phone into her bag. "My mom heard about the fire, but I convinced her to go to Hawaii tomorrow anyway."

"Good. Then neither of you will have to worry about the other."

"Exactly." She got to her feet. "Shall we go?"

As they walked outside, she couldn't help noticing the change in Wyatt's demeanor. He'd gone from relaxed and easy to hypervigilant, keeping his hand on her arm, his gaze darting in every direction, sweeping the street for any sign of danger.

After they got in the car and Wyatt pulled out of the parking spot, she asked, "How long are we going to do this?"

"It's a short drive to the hotel."

"I don't mean that. I mean *this*—you and me, hiding out. I have a dinner tomorrow. I have to go to work on Monday. I have a life."

"And I want you to keep living that life, which means you're going to have to bear with me a little longer."

"I just don't know what's going to change that will suddenly make my life safer."

"The FBI could find the person who was at Noelle's apartment this morning. That would be a start. The investigation into the fire could also provide clues."

"Do you really think so?" she asked doubtfully.

"I don't know, but something will break. It always does."

"You've been involved in situations like this before?"

"Not exactly like this, but I've worked in security and intelligence long enough to know that the clues will come as long as we keep looking."

"Okay, but we're not exactly doing anything proactive at the moment."

"We took a short break. We'll get back to it."

"Do you have a specific plan in mind?" she asked, not seeing any possible way for them to figure out what happened to Noelle. "We're not the police or the FBI. What can we do on our own?"

"We can focus on the personal. You knew Noelle better than anyone."

"But she didn't tell me anything."

"Maybe you just don't remember. It could have been something that sounded like nothing at the time, but in retrospect..."

"I've already been racking my brain wondering if I missed some clue, but I don't think so. Since Noelle started working at Nova Star, we saw each other fairly often. We had lunch at least twice a week. We went out a few times on the weekends, saw a couple of movies, went to brunch with some old high school friends..." She shrugged. "Nothing stands out."

"These old high school friends—who were they?"

"Jenny Fordham and Lindsay Swanson. Lindsay is getting married, so we went out to toast her engagement."

"Do they work in the aerospace industry?"

She almost laughed at that question. "No. Jenny is an assistant manager at a clothing boutique and Lindsay is a dental hygienist. We went to the Montage Hotel, gossiped about old times, and had a few glasses of champagne. That was it. Nothing mysterious about it."

"What about Carter?"

"What about him?" she countered. "You met him today. What did you think?"

"That he was self-absorbed, more concerned about his reputation and the police's interest in him, than his girlfriend's death."

"I felt the same way, but he did seem genuinely upset. Maybe he's just processing everything. I hate to judge him on a day like today. I'm probably not acting exactly right, either." She tapped her fingers on her legs, feeling restless and impatient. "I want to do more than wait around for something else to happen. I know I should be feeling calmer after my margarita, but I'm amped up. I don't know what to do with all the emotion."

"We could go for a run."

"After that really excellent but huge burrito? No thanks. But I have to say going back to the hotel and staring at the walls doesn't sound appealing, either."

"I have an idea," he said slowly.

"Oh, yeah?" she asked, a fluttery feeling in her stomach. "What's that?"

"It's better if I show you."

Her nerves tightened, and her lips went dry.

If Wyatt made a move on her, she'd say no. He was very attractive. He stirred her senses, but that was just because her senses were already stirred up. And she didn't do hook-ups. That was Noelle. That wasn't her. She was careful, cautious, boring.

So, she'd definitely say no—wouldn't she?

Nine

—➤ ➤➤ ➤➤ ➤—

"You want me to scream?" Avery asked doubtfully, as Wyatt parked the car at a vista point overlooking a beach, just north of Malibu. "Here?"

"Not exactly here. Come on." He got out of the car, pulled out his phone and turned on the flashlight to show a dirt path going down the bluff to the sand. Then he extended his hand.

"This seems like a bad idea," she said, but still she slipped her hand into his.

"Well, you can tell me later if it was."

He led her down the path, helping her over some boulders as they reached the bottom. The tide was out, and they had at least fifty yards of sandy beach. With the bright moon overhead and thousands of stars in the night sky providing just enough light, Wyatt put his phone in his pocket.

"It's cold," she said, as the wind whipped her hair. "But I like it." She also liked the fact that he was still holding her hand, even though she knew she should let go.

"Me, too," he said, squeezing her fingers. "Perfect weather for screaming. There's no one around for miles—no houses, no people, no one to judge you."

"Except for you. I can't believe you have ever come out here and just screamed into the wind. That does not sound like a Wyatt Tanner move. You're very calm, cool and collected. You let frustration go, because tomorrow is another day, right?"

"That is my usual mantra. But screaming into the wind worked really well for someone else I know, someone who was bottling things up, afraid to show how scared and unhappy and sad she was, because she was terrified of giving up control, letting loose of her emotions."

"Who was that?" she asked, curious to hear the answer.

"My sister-in-law. When my brother went to jail, she had a three-month-old baby at home. She was trying to hold everything together, but their assets were frozen, her friends were deserting her, her parents were embarrassed, my parents had their own problems, and she was trying to be a good soldier. But inside she was raging. One day, I put her in the car, and we drove to the beach—not this one, but another one. And I told her to scream. She was reluctant at first, but after the first half-hearted effort, she got into it."

"Did you scream with her? Because you must have shared some of her feelings of frustration and anger. Your dad ripped your family apart."

"I was angry, and on that day, at that beach, I let out the loudest yell of my life. It was the first time in my life I just let it rip. I felt better. So did my sister-in-law. I think you will, too."

She frowned. "I'm just not a screamer."

"Never? Not even…"

At his laugh, her cheeks warmed with embarrassment. "I wasn't talking about that."

"I know. You're easy to tease. You have a sweet quality about you."

She wasn't thrilled with that adjective. "Sweet doesn't sound awesome. In fact, it sounds close to boring. Noelle told me many, many times how boring I was."

"I don't think you're boring at all. I also don't think you see yourself the way others see you."

"I see myself just fine, thank you. And Noelle wasn't the only one to suggest I could lead a more exciting life."

"Excitement is a relative thing. You have a passion for what you do."

"I do," she agreed, waving her free hand toward the night sky. "Look at all those stars. There's so much out there we know nothing about. How can anyone not be fascinated by the universe?"

He smiled. "I don't know. You're certainly making me more interested."

As his fingers tightened around hers, and the moonlight played across the strong planes of his face, she had a feeling he was far more interested in her than the stars, and she sucked in a quick breath of nerves and anticipation. She didn't know exactly what he saw when he looked at her, but she knew what she saw when she looked at him: a man of power, drive, strength, courage, compassion, and remarkable kindness. He was rough around the edges, guarded and cryptic at times, but there was something about him that encouraged her trust. Maybe it was the personal story he'd shared over dinner, the fact that he'd opened himself up, revealed a side of himself that she doubted he showed many people. Maybe that's why she couldn't let go of his hand. Or maybe it was the incredible physical pull she felt toward him.

As his gaze clung to hers, the air seemed to sizzle between them. "I don't know what you want from me," she said finally. Even though what she should have said was that she didn't know what she wanted from herself.

"I want you to let go of the emotions that are making your head spin. I want you to be whoever you want to be— the woman who holds it all in, who hangs onto control with utter desperation, or the woman who lets it all go. There's no judgement here."

"Are you sure no one can hear us? Because I really don't want the cops to come running."

"There's no one around for miles. And this doesn't have to be about yelling. Just talk it out. Say what you're feeling."

"I'm numb."

"You *were* numb. You're not anymore."

That was true. "I'm angry."

"Louder," he encouraged.

"I'm angry," she yelled, feeling a bit ridiculous and yet liking the sound of her voice on the wind. The waves crashed on to the beach in front of her, almost in answer to her statement, as if the ocean was in turmoil, too.

"Why are you angry?" Wyatt challenged.

"Because it's not fair. Noelle was too young to die."

"Say it again," he ordered.

"She was too young to die. It's not fair," she said more loudly.

"And what's happening to you—is that fair?" he asked. "Should you have to hide out? Should you be afraid to go home? Should you be planning the funeral of your best friend? Is that fair?"

"No, it's not fair." She let go of his hand and turned toward the sea, screaming into the wind, into the onrushing waves. "It's not fair! It's not fair! It's not fair!"

The words ripped through her again and again, louder and louder, and then she felt the last bit of her control snap like a branch in a storm.

The tears she'd been holding back streamed down her face. Sobs erupted from deep in her chest. She could barely breathe. A moment of panic hit her. This was why she didn't like losing control, because now she was floundering, breathing too fast, not able to rein anything in. She was drowning in a sea of feelings, and she didn't know how she could get through it.

But then Wyatt turned her around and pulled her against his chest. He wrapped his strong arms around her, tucking her head under his chin, and she held on to him like he was a lifeboat in a stormy sea.

He wasn't going to let her drown, and as his strength surrounded her with warmth and courage, she started to feel the ground beneath her feet again. The fear receded.

Her sobs slowed down, as did her tears. She was able to breathe again.

"You did good," Wyatt whispered in her ear.

She lifted her head, wiping the tears from her face as she stepped away from him. "I feel like a fool."

"A less stressed fool?" he asked with a hopeful smile.

She couldn't help but smile back. "Maybe the screaming did help. I bet you weren't expecting the waterworks show, though. That took me by surprise. I'm not really a crier."

"I know. You hold everything in."

"I had to after my dad left. My mom was so sad. My tears only made things worse, so I stopped crying."

He nodded in understanding. "When my father's crimes became publicly known, my mother was also a basket case. She wasn't just worried about my dad, but also about my brother."

"And you had to be the strong one."

"I did. But my relationship with my mother didn't get better because of that."

"Really? I would have thought she would have leaned on you, that you would have been the good, shining light in her life."

"She didn't think I helped enough. She thought I could have been more outspoken, more loyal, especially with the press. She basically wanted me to help her hide the crimes, but there was no way to do that."

"It wasn't your job to make their mistakes seem better."

"She didn't see it that way. We weren't that close before it all went down, and we became strangers afterwards. She was much tighter with my brother."

"Do you see her at all anymore?"

"No."

"Not ever?"

"Not in a long time. And it's fine. You don't need to suggest I look her up," he warned.

"I wasn't going to," she said. "I wouldn't want someone to tell me what to do about my family, either."

"Exactly. We're two of a kind."

"I don't know if I'd go that far but, thank you. Not just for making me let go, but for sharing something so personal with me. I'm not sure why you did."

"I'm not sure, either," he admitted. "I don't usually share, but there's something about you, Avery."

"There's something about you, too, Wyatt. I don't know how we went so fast from not trusting each other to telling our secrets. I've gone out with men for months who know less about me than you do right now. I don't understand it. It doesn't make sense, but we're connected."

"Not everything makes sense."

"I prefer it when it does."

He gave her a small smile. "I know you do. But there's no set time period to connect with someone. And not all moves are thought out in advance, Avery. Sometimes you've just got to go with the current."

He moved closer, his hands settling on her waist, and the heat of his gaze triggered a new set of emotions that had nothing to do with sadness and anger and everything to do with desire and recklessness.

"What is your next move?" she asked, feeling like that current might turn into a riptide.

"I know what I want it to be."

"So do I." Throwing her innate sense of caution into the same wind that had heard her screams and released her anger, she put her arms around Wyatt's neck, pressed her body back against his and touched her lips to his mouth.

She'd never felt so hungry for a man, and kissing Wyatt touched off an explosion of heat and desire, of real, honest, soul-stirring passion. There was no holding back, no tentative exploration. It was everything all at once. She wasn't on the sidelines. She wasn't hiding in dark corner while everyone else had fun. She was in the arms of an attractive and sexy man, whose hard body was sending tingles of desire to every part of her body.

Wyatt ran his hands up under her jacket, and she could feel the heat through her light-weight sweater, sending all sorts of ideas through her head of the two of them tearing off each other's clothes, lying down in the soft sand, and making love in the moonlight, under the stars…

But Wyatt was pulling away. His ragged breath curled up in a cloud of heat that she wanted to throw herself back into.

As she took a step forward, Wyatt grabbed both of her arms.

"Hang on," he said tightly. "We need to stop."

"Do we?" she asked. "Aren't you the one who said I should live in the moment?"

"Yes," he conceded. "But not…not tonight. You've had a long day."

"You're really saying no?" she asked in surprise. "Okay. I guess I misread—"

"You didn't misread anything," he said quickly, his fingers biting into her arms. "What happened just now—that was crazy good."

"It was, wasn't it? So why…"

"Because you're running on emotion. And I cannot take advantage of that."

"You're not taking advantage, Wyatt. I know what I want. And I want you."

"A man you met earlier today? A man you're not sure you can trust?"

She didn't appreciate the reminders. They were making her think again, when all she wanted to do was feel.

"I want you, too, Avery, but not like this. I want you to choose, not just fall into something… You'd regret it. And I don't want you to have any regrets."

"You don't have to protect me from myself. I'm a grown woman. If I get hurt or have regrets, that's on me."

"Okay. Then maybe I'm protecting myself."

She didn't know quite how to take that. *Was he implying she could hurt him? She could break his heart?* That seemed unlikely.

"It's been a rough day," he continued. "Let's go back to the hotel."

"To our separate but connected rooms?"

His jaw tightened. "It could be a long night."

"I don't know what to make of you, Wyatt."

"I know. There have been some mixed signals tonight. I'm not happy about that. Chalk it up to your extreme attractiveness."

"You do realize this might have been your only chance, and you just said no."

"God, I hope not," he said with so much sincerity, she couldn't help but smile, the tension breaking inside of her.

"I guess we'll see."

"Let's walk back to the car."

As she followed him up the path, she decided to torment him just a little more. "You know when we were talking about secrets? There is one secret I haven't shared with you yet."

"What's that?" he asked warily.

"I don't like pajamas, so I don't always wear them."

He groaned. "You're going to kill me, aren't you?"

She shrugged. "Just saying…"

Was he a complete and utter fool?

That question plagued Wyatt all the way back to the hotel in Marina Del Rey.

He couldn't remember the last time he'd said no to a

beautiful and willing woman who'd stated quite bluntly that she wanted him. In fact, he didn't think that had ever happened before.

But something about Avery's sweet sexiness had sent off warning bells in his head. She might think he'd opened up to her with the story of his family, but he was still holding back a lot—a hell of a lot. He was living a lie, and she didn't deserve anything but the truth.

He needed to remember that in the upcoming days— make that hours, since he'd now have to spend the night wondering if she was really sleeping in the nude or had just said that to pay him back for calling a halt to things.

As they neared the hotel, he forced his brain back on the job at hand, which was keeping Avery safe, not taking her to bed. Fortunately, they were able to park and make their way up to their rooms without incident.

He checked the small traps he'd set up around the room and everything was exactly as he'd left it. He was very happy about that.

"Everything okay?" Avery asked, as she tucked strands of her wind-blown dark hair behind her ears. Her dark eyes stood out against her pale skin, and there was noticeable red around her eyes and nose from her breakdown at the beach. Her haunted beauty made him glad he'd ended things before they'd really started. She had enough emotion to deal with. While some sweet release could go a long way in situations like these, there was always a morning after.

"It's all good," he said briskly. "But I would like to leave the door open. I promise not to peek."

She gave him a tired smile, and he had a feeling the adrenaline was wearing off.

"Get some sleep, Avery."

"I think I will sleep. I'm suddenly exhausted."

He nodded and moved toward the door to his room.

"Wait, Wyatt."

He looked back at her. "Yes?"

"I'm glad you took me to the beach. You were right. I needed to scream, to let out my emotions. I'd been holding everything in since Noelle died. I'm just sorry I cried all over you."

"Don't worry about it. Now you know what to do when you feel like you're about to snap."

"Yes. But there's one more thing." She paused, giving him a serious look. "Kissing you was separate from that. I feel like you should know that. Anyway, goodnight."

"Good-night."

Walking into his room took a lot of willpower. He'd crossed a line that he shouldn't have crossed. He couldn't let it happen again. Not until this job was over.

Hell, who was he kidding?

Once this job was over, he'd disappear like he always did. He'd move on to the next assignment.

Avery didn't need another man in her life who would turn into a ghost.

So, he needed to keep her close—*but not that close.*

Ten

–→→»«←–

Avery thought she might have fallen asleep before her head hit the pillow, and when she woke up, the sun was streaming through the sheer drapes. She got up, smiling to herself as she pulled her T-shirt down over her PJ bottoms and walked to the window. She hadn't actually lied to Wyatt about sleeping in the nude, but last night she'd felt cold, and had wanted the extra warmth when she'd gotten into bed. But hopefully, she'd given him something to think about.

It was a sunny day, not a cloud in the sky, the ocean sparkling in the distance several blocks away. The beautiful view made her feel a little sad that Noelle wasn't alive to see it. She'd always loved the beach, whether it was in the hot summer or the windy spring or the cold winter.

She wondered how many days it would take before she would wake up and Noelle would not be the first thing on her mind—probably too many to count.

Looking at the ocean also reminded her of the night before, letting out her grief, lowering her guard, and experiencing one of the most amazing kisses of her life. She put her fingers to her lips, remembering how it had felt to have Wyatt's hot mouth on hers.

Noelle would have been proud.

"I got out of my comfort zone," she whispered, thinking of the last conversation she'd had with her friend. "I just wish I could tell you about it."

Even as she said the words, she realized last night wouldn't have happened if Noelle hadn't died. She might have never said two words to Wyatt, even if she had seen him at Nova Star. They worked in very separate departments, and she didn't spend much time trying to create a social life for herself. It was just easier...and safer...to bury herself in work.

Her phone buzzed on the nightstand, bringing her back to reality. She hurried across the room to answer it. It was Noelle's mother.

"Good morning, Kari," she said, frowning as she heard what sounded like a public announcement in the background. "Where are you?"

"I'm at the airport, Avery."

"What do you mean? You're leaving?" she asked in surprise. "We haven't made any decisions."

"I'm sorry, but I have to go home. If I don't go to work tomorrow, I'll lose my job."

"But what about Noelle? What about the arrangements? There is so much to do."

"You know what Noelle would want better than me. I'll send you money as soon as I get my paycheck. Carter said he would help out, too. She finally met a good, solid man. I wish they could have had more time together."

"Are you coming back?"

"No. I don't think so. I can't afford it, Avery."

"Well, do you want the memorial to be in Florida? Do you want Noelle to be buried there?"

"Noelle didn't like Florida. I think she'd want to be here—near her friends, the places she loved most. And she wasn't a fan of formal funerals. Maybe something simple..." Kari's voice broke. "I know you must think I'm a terrible person to dump all this on you. And you're not wrong. Your mother will probably say, what did you expect—I've always been a flake. But I just don't have the money to stay here, and I feel so ashamed and embarrassed that I can't bury my own daughter."

"You don't have to be ashamed. I will take care of everything. And when I have time to figure out the details, I'll make sure to let you know what I have in mind. Hopefully you can be a part of something."

"Don't wait on me, Avery. Do what's best for Noelle. You were like sisters. I trust you, and I know she did, too. Good-bye."

"Good-bye." She barely got the word out before Kari hung up.

"Avery? What's going on?"

Wyatt's concerned voice drew her head around. "That was Kari. She's leaving town. She says she can't do it. I'm in charge."

Anger flashed through his eyes. "That's ridiculous."

"She doesn't have any money. She's embarrassed."

"She's Noelle's mother. She could at least stay and help you."

"Hopefully, Carter will help." She ran a hand through her tangled hair, noting that Wyatt looked good, having already taken a shower, his dark hair damp, his face cleanly shaven, a hint of cologne wafting around him. He wore dark jeans and a long-sleeved gray sweater that clung to his broad shoulders. She really wished they were having this conversation after she'd had a chance to clean up, too.

"Well, you have time to figure all this out," he said.

"I don't know how much time. I should at least organize something at work this week to honor her."

"That would be nice. It doesn't have to be too complicated. You can save that for the bigger service."

"If there is one. Kari just reminded me that Noelle hated funerals." She let out a sigh. "There's so much to think about."

"I'm here if you need to bounce off ideas."

"Right now, I just need a shower."

"Good idea. I thought I'd go downstairs and grab us some coffees from the café down the street. How does that sound?"

"Like heaven. If you run into some bagels and cream cheese, that would be good, too."

"You got it." He smiled, his gaze running down her body with an appreciative gleam. "By the way, I like the PJs, although I would have liked your usual sleeping attire better."

She flushed. "I was cold last night."

"And you wanted to torture me."

"That, too."

He cleared his throat. "Right. Okay. I'll be back shortly. Keep the door locked. Don't open it for anyone."

His words reminded her of why they were in the hotel. "I won't. You be safe, too," she added on a more serious note. "I wasn't the only one who saw that man's face yesterday."

Wyatt headed downstairs and got into his car, wishing he could have kept Avery warm last night. But deep down, sleepless night aside, he knew he'd made the right decision. He had gotten too personally involved with her last night, and he needed to get things back on track.

He was going to pick up coffee and bagels but first he had a quick stop to make. While he was in deep cover, he kept contact with his colleagues to a minimum, but with everything that was happening, he needed a check-in.

He took a circuitous route to his destination, making sure no one was on his tail before he parked near a secondhand bookstore.

He waited another moment in his car and then headed down the block. Next to the store was a door leading up to an apartment. He pressed three numbers on the intercom and saw a small security camera click over his face before he was buzzed inside.

Jogging up the stairs, he opened what appeared to be an electrical box but was in fact a retinal scanner. Once he was cleared to enter, the door clicked open.

The two-bedroom apartment had been turned into a command post six weeks ago when Flynn had formed the task force to look into foreign espionage in the aerospace industry, specifically at Nova Star.

A bank of computers sat on a long table, with two guys tapping away on their keyboards. Mark and Connor were young agents, barely out of Quantico, but they were equipped with the latest cyber hacking skills. He'd been siphoning out footage from Nova Star's security cameras for the past month, and they were in charge of pointing out any anomalies or people to look into.

With his input, they'd also compiled reams of data on the Tremaines and other personnel at Nova Star who had access to secure data. Unfortunately, none of that data had given them a clear lead on who had leaked information to the Chinese.

At the kitchen table sat Flynn MacKenzie, the leader of their team. Flynn had blondish hair, a scruffy beard, and compelling blue eyes. He also had a British accent that seemed to drive women crazy and was one of his best skills for getting what he wanted.

He almost hadn't taken the job Flynn had offered him because they'd gone through Quantico together as rivals in every way. He'd thought at the time that Flynn had played fast and loose with some of the rules of their training missions just to get a win. In fact, at one point he'd wondered if Flynn's antics hadn't been part of why his good friend Jamie had died during a training incident. Not that he had any proof, and certainly Flynn had seemed to be just as upset about Jamie's death as anyone, but something had clearly gone wrong, and no one had ever been able to figure out what that was.

That incident aside, Flynn had proven himself to be a good agent in the intervening years. He pushed the boundaries, and he'd managed to use his skill at politics to build connections in the bureau that had put him into the position of running his own task force at a very young age.

Wyatt could hardly blame him for climbing the bureaucratic ladder faster than him, since he hadn't tried to climb it at all. He just wanted to do a job that made a difference. As long as Flynn had the same goal he did, he was on board.

"What do you have for me?" Wyatt asked.

"We found the man you ran into at Noelle Price's apartment yesterday." Flynn held out a photo. "Unfortunately, we can't question him."

He sat down across from Flynn and took the picture from his hand. The man who had pulled a gun on Avery was on the ground, dead from a single bullet to the head—execution style. "He pissed off his boss. Do we have an ID?"

"Anton Bogdan. Thirty-two years old. Came to the US from the Ukraine fifteen years ago with his family. Father and uncle are roofers. He works part-time for them and lives in El Segundo. He has a record of assault, theft, DUI, etc. but no major felonies. He runs with a Russian gang, led by this guy, Stash Ivanov." Flynn pulled out another photo, this one of a square, stocky man, dressed in an ill-fitting suit. "Stash runs a private investment firm. He moves money around for rich people."

He nodded, knowing that whatever break that they got in whatever case they were working almost always led back to whoever was moving the money around. "What do these guys have to do with Noelle Price?" He set the photos down on the table. "Any evidence either one was at the Santa Monica Pier Friday night?"

"No. We haven't found them on any security footage, but we're still going through the video obtained from cameras on the pier and adjacent streets. Medical examiner didn't find any

DNA on her body, so nothing to go on there. But if the Russians are involved...it's doubtful they're working with China. So, Ms. Price's murder could be unrelated to the death of Jia Lin."

"Or both China and Russia are in play. Someone wants to steal or sabotage Nova Star's new satellite defense system technology."

"Joanna is working Nova Star from an official bureau position, but we need you to put more pressure on Jonathan Tremaine. With the launch Tuesday, we're running out of time."

"I know. I'm going to do that tonight. I'm going to make sure I'm at Brett Caldwell's birthday party. All the Tremaines will be there. I'll pull Jonathan aside and show him the photos I have of him and Noelle together. I'll tell him his father asked me to follow him after what happened with Jia Lin in San Francisco. Hopefully, if he thinks my intent is to protect him from being fingered in Noelle's death, he'll be more forthcoming. At any rate, I will handle the Tremaines, but what I need your help on is Noelle's boyfriend, Carter Hayes. I only had time to run a cursory check on him before Noelle was killed, since she'd only been on my radar for a few days."

"We're already on it."

The apartment buzzer went off, and he glanced at the security monitors in the room, one showing the front door, the other positioned behind the building. He was surprised to see Bree's pretty face at the front door. "What's Bree doing here?"

"She's joining the team."

"Since when?"

"Since I decided we need more help, and Joanna is wasting Bree's talents, having her run data checks like she's fresh out of Quantico. She's better than that, but Joanna doesn't like having competition."

"Whereas you don't see anyone as competition."

Flynn raised a questioning brow. "You have a problem, Tanner? I thought you and Bree were tight."

"We are tight, and I don't have a problem. I just didn't think she was a big fan of yours."

"We both want to get the job done." Flynn buzzed Bree in. "I heard she's living with some dude now."

"Yes, and she's happy. Don't screw with that."

"Wouldn't go down that road again," Flynn said. "She already shot me down once."

A moment later, Bree walked in the door, her smile brightening when she saw Wyatt. "I didn't expect to see you here, Wyatt."

"Likewise. You're joining the team?"

"Didn't want you to have all the fun."

"Bree is going to the media event at Nova Star tomorrow. She'll interview whichever Tremaines make themselves available to the press," Flynn said. "The reporter who was going to do the interview got reassigned. Her editor owed me a favor."

He was constantly amazed at how many cards Flynn seemed able to call in when he needed them. "Sounds good."

"Joanna had me dive into Noelle's financials," Bree said. "There was a cash deposit of $5000 made last Thursday."

"The night after she met with Jonathan and the day before she was killed," he muttered. "It's not a lot of money, though."

"But a significant anomaly in her bank account which ran close to zero quite often."

"She was allegedly supporting her mother."

"She did send Kari Price money on a regular basis. But we didn't see any other unrecognizable deposits besides that one."

"Okay. Thanks." He stood up. "I need to get back to Avery before she gets suspicious. I'll be in touch."

Eleven

—➤➤❥❦❧—

Avery felt like a new person after her shower and much more prepared to take on the day. After changing clothes, she repacked her suitcase just in case they had to make another quick exit, and checked her watch a few times, wondering why it would take Wyatt an hour to pick up coffee and bagels.

Wandering over to the window, she looked out at the water again, hoping it would calm her, but a feeling of uneasiness ran down her spine, making her nerves tingle uncomfortably. In the brief time she'd known Wyatt, she'd come to count on him. It was crazy how fast she'd gone from not trusting him to literally putting her life in his hands. She'd told him last night that there was an incredible pull between them, an unexpected and inexplicable connection, and it was just as strong now as it had been yesterday.

As the minutes passed, she grew more worried, not just for herself, but also for him. While Wyatt acted as if all the danger was about her, that wasn't true. He'd been at Noelle's apartment. Heck, he'd been in the funhouse, too, a fact which still didn't quite make sense to her. He'd told her he was there to meet a friend, but that was before they'd gotten to know each other, before he'd told her that Noelle had met Jonathan earlier that week and that Wyatt had been following at least one of them. Maybe he'd been following Noelle on Friday night. In fact, that seemed to be the best explanation. He'd clearly lied to her about his presence on the pier, although that was before they'd gotten to know each other. He had also stated quite clearly that he was taking orders from Hamilton Tremaine, and there were some things he couldn't disclose; perhaps that was one of them.

But they were too deep in this to have secrets between them.

She'd ask him to explain when he got back. Trust had to work both ways.

Her phone buzzed, and she walked over to pick it up from the nightstand. The call was from Kimberly Walton, head of media relations at Nova Star. They worked closely together when it came to public events, and the upcoming week was going to be full of those events. In all the craziness surrounding Noelle's death, she'd almost forgotten just how much needed to be done tomorrow.

"Hi, Kim," she said.

"Avery, I'm so very sorry," Kim said. "I've been thinking about you since I heard the terrible news about Noelle. I kept picking up the phone to call you yesterday, but I just didn't know what to say. This is such a horrible situation."

"It really is," she said, sitting down on the edge of the bed.

"Noelle was a great girl. We had drinks together on Thursday. I was thinking then that we could be really good friends."

"I didn't know you had drinks," she said, thinking Noelle had been out every night last week with various people. "Or that you even knew each other," she added.

"Noelle was assigned to our department for a few days last month. We bonded over press releases and brochures. She was really helpful. I had her running all over the building, trying to get statements from our key leaders. You know how difficult it is to get Kyle and Jonathan Tremaine to stand still long enough to give us more than a soundbite."

"Was Noelle able to get anything from either of them?" Maybe this explained why Noelle had met with Jonathan a few days ago. It might have been completely innocent. She could have tracked him down, trying to get a quote from him.

"She did, thank goodness, so we're all set. But here I am talking about work when poor Noelle..."

Her hand tightened on the phone. "I know. It's surreal."

"Are you going to take some time off, Avery? It would be completely understandable. I just need to know what should be taken off your plate, so nothing falls through the cracks."

"Right." She hadn't given one thought to her job the last twenty-four hours, which was odd, since most days her life was consumed with work.

"You were going to edit the show for the press tomorrow morning. You said you wanted to combine two of your videos to make it more pertinent to the launch, so that they would have more educational information to base their upcoming articles on."

"I did most of that on Friday. I just have to finish the last piece. I'll do that today. I was planning to come in anyway."

"Are you sure? Maybe we don't need it."

"No, it's important. I'll take care of it, Kim."

"Is there anything I can do for you? A lot of people are asking where they can send flowers or donations, or if there will be a service. I'm not sure what to tell them."

"I'm not sure, either," she murmured, feeling the weight of the world on her shoulders.

"How's Carter doing?"

"Do you know Carter, too?"

"Not really, just what Noelle told me about him."

"What did she tell you about him?"

"Well, not a lot. I commented that he's kind of quiet, and

she said I'd probably be surprised at how ambitious he is. She said he wasn't going to be a junior lawyer for long. I got the feeling she liked his drive. I don't know him well enough to reach out, but I hope he's okay."

"He's hanging in there." She paused, as she heard the door open behind her. Her tension eased when she saw Wyatt. "I need to go. I'll talk to you tomorrow."

"Thanks, Avery. Call if I can help in any way."

"I will." She put down the phone and got to her feet as Wyatt deposited two coffees on the table as well as a large brown paper bag. "You were gone a long time."

"I stood in line at the first place and then their coffee machine broke right when I was about to order. So, I had to go somewhere else. Good news, though—the second place had more food items. I got bagels and cream cheese as well as some breakfast sandwiches and fruit.

She sat down at the table and unwrapped a croissant filled with scrambled eggs, ham and cheese. "This looks good. I'll start here."

He took the seat across from her. "Who was on the phone?"

"Kim Walton. She's director of media relations. She reminded me that I need to finish a few things before tomorrow's press tour, which includes a show that I'm putting together."

"Can't someone else take care of that?"

"It's my job, and it's almost done. I just need to add one piece. I have to go by the office at some point today."

He nodded agreeably. "We can make that happen. I actually want to check in at the office, too. We were already amping up our security for this week, but we need to double it now."

"That seems like a good idea." She took another bite of her croissant. As she swallowed, she added, "Kim told me that Noelle has been helping out in her department, that she'd tasked Noelle with the job of getting quotes from all the top people at the company to be used in this week's press materials." As Wyatt's gaze met hers, she continued. "I think that's why Noelle met with Jonathan last week. I don't think they were having an affair. It was business."

Wyatt's gaze gave little away. She couldn't tell if he was convinced or thought she was crazy.

"What do you think?" she asked when he remained silent.

"It's something to consider. Maybe you can ask Jonathan and Kyle about it tonight."

"That's true. They'll both be at my father's party."

"I'd like to be there, too."

She wiped her mouth with her napkin. "I don't know if that's a good idea."

"Where you go, I go—remember?"

"I'll be safe at my father's house in Calabasas. He lives in a gated community. It's very safe."

"I'd still like to go. Hamilton asked me to stay close to you, and I'd like to meet your father."

"And I would like you *not* to meet my father."

"Why? Do you think I'm going to embarrass you?"

"I think my father will ask questions about why you're with me, who you are, what you are to me. I don't need that right now, Wyatt."

"Just tell him I'm your bodyguard. He'll appreciate that someone is watching out for you."

She let out a sigh. "Is it really that important?"

"It is, Avery."

She sensed there was more behind his desire to come to dinner than to just watch out for her. "It's not just me you want to get close to, is it?"

"I wouldn't mind having a conversation with Jonathan. Even if Noelle's conversation with Jonathan was completely innocent, it could factor into the FBI investigation. They'll be going through her life—every detail, every phone call, everyone she spoke to. Jonathan needs to know that his meeting with her could come up and put both him and Nova

Star in an awkward situation."

"That's true. You're very persuasive, Wyatt."

"Does that mean you're taking me to dinner?"

"Yes."

"Good. Now that we have that out of the way, I want to ask you for another favor."

"What's that?" she asked warily.

"I want you to call Carter Hayes and set up a meeting. Tell him you need to talk about funeral arrangements. See if we can meet him at his place. If Noelle spent time there, maybe whatever she was trying to protect is there."

Her pulse quickened. "You're right. She just said apartment. She didn't say *her* apartment. I just assumed it was hers that she was referring to. Carter might be in danger, too."

"It's possible."

"I'll call him. I just hope he'll agree to see us. Yesterday, he couldn't get away from us fast enough."

While Avery spoke to Carter on the phone, Wyatt considered telling her that the man who had pulled a gun on her yesterday was dead, but then he'd have to explain where he got the information, which would lead him down a path he didn't want to go. She couldn't do anything with the information; so, for the moment, he would keep it to himself.

Listening to Avery's side of the conversation, it was apparent that Noelle's boyfriend was not too thrilled with the idea of getting together with them, but when she told him that he might be in danger, he agreed to hear her out.

Wyatt didn't know what he thought about Carter Hayes, but he definitely needed more information. Hopefully, Flynn would come up with something on his background as well.

"Carter said to come by in a half hour," Avery said. "I think he's afraid I'm going to hit him up for money, but I told him quite frankly we needed a conversation about much more than that. However, I don't know what we're going to learn from him."

"We'll find out."

She sat back in her chair. "Wyatt, we need to talk about a few things."

His senses went on high alert at those words. There was a very serious expression in her brown eyes now, and he could almost feel the fire at his feet. "What do you want to discuss?"

"The funhouse on Friday night. You told me yesterday that it was a coincidence you were there, that you went to meet a friend. That wasn't true, was it?"

"No," he admitted, happy that her first question was one he might be able to get past with a little truth-telling and an apology.

"Why did you lie to me?"

"Because I didn't trust you then. You were the person kneeling next to Noelle when her body was found."

Her eyes widened. "You thought I had killed her?"

"I wasn't sure what to think, especially when I found you at her apartment."

"So, why were you there?"

"I was following Noelle."

"Because she'd met with Jonathan?"

"Yes."

She frowned, her smart brain computing what he'd told her, and obviously things weren't adding up. "What aren't you telling me?"

That was a loaded question. There was so much he wasn't telling her he didn't know where to start. But he could see the glint of determination in her eyes. She was much more clear-headed today, and she wanted some answers. He would have to give her something.

"Nova Star has a security leak, Avery. Hamilton has tasked me with finding the mole. Noelle's unusual meeting with Jonathan sparked my interest."

"You think Noelle was leaking information?" she asked slowly. "But how is that possible? She didn't have access to anything. She didn't work in engineering or any of the labs."

"She might have been working with someone else. She could have been the middleman."

"Someone like Jonathan Tremaine?"

"Or someone else. That's why I followed her to the pier. I saw Noelle go into the funhouse alone, while you waited outside. It seemed to be taking a long time, and I could see you were getting nervous, too. After you entered, I went in, too. I saw you in the mirror, but I did not see Noelle. I was almost out when I heard screams and I was held by the exit. You know the rest."

Her face paled, his words obviously taking her back to that horrible night. "When you saw me in the funhouse, did you think I might be the leak?"

"I actually didn't think that until I saw you at her apartment the next day."

"Really?" she asked, shocked etched across her face. "That's what you thought?"

"It didn't make sense to me that her friend would go into her apartment so early the next morning and break through the police tape in order to do so."

"When did you decide I wasn't the leak?" She paused, her gaze narrowing. "Or maybe you haven't decided that?"

"I knew you were not the mole as soon as we started talking. Your grief for your friend was completely genuine. It was obvious you weren't involved in her death. Everything since then has been about keeping you safe and trying to figure out who did kill Noelle."

Avery got up and paced restlessly around the room. "I don't want to believe Noelle was passing classified information to someone. Do you have anything to go on besides this meeting with Jonathan?"

"Yes. Noelle had a cash deposit of $5000 put into her bank account the day before she was killed. It broke the pattern of her usual banking behavior, and there was no indication of where or who the money came from."

"How do you know that?"

"The FBI told me that when I met with them at the police station yesterday."

"What? Why didn't you tell me that then?"

"There was a lot going on. And I didn't think you were in the frame of mind to hear it."

She ran a hand through her hair. "This just gets worse and worse. Why did the FBI give you that information?"

"Because of my position in security at Nova Star. They've been in touch with Hamilton, too. They know that I am working on the inside while they do their thing. Obviously, Noelle's death raised the stakes. And with the upcoming launch on Tuesday, we need answers fast."

"Maybe Hamilton should scrub the launch."

"I've suggested that more than once. He doesn't want to do that. He doesn't want to lose his advantage."

"But people are dying..." She sat back down at the table. "I knew something was off with Noelle. She was rambling on about trying to be a better person. That doesn't sound like someone who is stealing secrets."

"It's possible she had a change of heart about whatever she was doing and was looking for a way out. Someone killed Noelle for a reason, Avery. Based on what we know so far, that someone also thought she left something behind at her apartment. It's possible she reneged on a deal she'd made and paid for it with her life. But we're not going to know which side Noelle was on until we find out who killed her."

"I just don't know why she would do it."

"Her mom was broke. She was supporting her, right? Money and desperation are good motivators."

"But she could have just asked me for money, for help. I'm not rich, but I make a good living. I could have given her $5000. That doesn't seem like enough money to lose your life over."

"I'm sure there was more promised."

"Do you think Jonathan could be the mole—the person passing information through Noelle to a third party? Does Hamilton believe his oldest son, his heir to his fortune, to his company, would be selling him and the company out?"

"He doesn't want to believe that. He thinks Jonathan is being framed."

"For Noelle's murder?"

"Among other things."

"What other things?"

"I can't tell you."

"You've told me this much, Wyatt. Tell me the rest."

"Knowing more is only going to put you in more danger."

She did not like his answer, an angry light entering her eyes. "I'm already in danger. I'm hiding out in a hotel room with you. I have a right to know what else is going on. And if you don't tell me, I'm not taking you to dinner tonight. I'm not giving you access to Jonathan or Kyle or anyone else you want to talk to."

Despite his dislike of her words, he actually admired the ruthless note in her voice. Apparently, sweet Avery also had a stubborn side.

He would tell her just enough to get her back on his side.

"Fine. I can say this much. A Chinese female aerospace engineer by the name of Jia Lin was killed three months ago in San Francisco. She worked for a state-funded aerospace company in Beijing that's in competition with Nova Star. She met with Jonathan for dinner the night before she lost her life in a single-vehicle accident. In her possession were classified specs for Nova Star's *Star Gazer Rocket II*."

"What? She met with Jonathan, too?"

"Yes."

"But that rocket won't go into production for another year. How are there even specs?"

"Apparently, they are preliminary but still highly

proprietary."

"What did Jonathan say? I assume someone talked to him about it."

"Both the police and the FBI spoke to him. This happened before I came on board. Hamilton told me that Jonathan took the meeting because Jia Lin is a top-level engineer, and she was looking for a job. While he doesn't ordinarily talk to recruits, he was going to be in San Francisco for other meetings, so he agreed to see her. He denies handing her any information or having anything to do with her death."

"I assume there was no real evidence tying Jonathan to the accident, or he would have been arrested."

"That's correct. But the FBI were concerned that Nova Star's security had been breached by a Chinese national. They wanted Hamilton's cooperation, but when it became clear the bureau was a little too interested in making Jonathan a scapegoat, Hamilton shut them down and told them his security team would take care of it. He hired me shortly thereafter because I have more experience in gathering foreign intelligence than his previous director of security, who had also decided to take an early retirement."

"Hamilton is very loyal to family, and I can understand why he would have trouble seeing any kind of motivation on Jonathan's part to sabotage the company he will one day inherit. Plus, Hamilton and Jonathan are very close. Frankly, if you'd told me that Kyle was the suspect, I'd have more doubt in my mind."

"Why is that?"

"Because Kyle and Hamilton often butt heads over the direction of the company, the priorities, the focus. Kyle is less interested in sending his father and friends to Mars and more interested in how space technology can benefit people on Earth. He fought Hamilton to get the funds to develop this satellite defense system. That's really his baby." She paused. "Which, now that I've said all that, reminds me that Kyle wouldn't sabotage the company, either, not when he's about to get everything that he has wanted for a very long time."

"Perhaps someone doesn't want Kyle to get everything."

She met his gaze. "If you're talking about sibling rivalry, I think you're going down the wrong road. Jonathan and Kyle are opposites in personality, but I've always felt there was a strong bond between them."

"What about Whitney? She doesn't seem to have much to do with the company. Is that by choice?"

"Definitely. She has no interest in science or the universe. She's into clothes and art and decorating. Although, apparently, she's now very much into bettering her spiritual mindset and becoming at peace with her soul."

He raised a brow at her words. "You sound like you read that on a brochure."

"I did. My father gives a class on that; it's in his course description. Shortly after he met Whitney, she took his seminar, and she said it changed her life. She now does yoga and drinks a lot of green juice and treats my father like he's a god. It works great. She adores him, and he needs someone to adore him."

"Interesting. Now I'm really looking forward to tonight, although, I hope we don't have green juice for dinner."

"You never know. You haven't met Whitney?"

"No, not yet. Hamilton said he used to worry about her until she met your father. At first, he was uncomfortable with the age gap, but he soon realized that Whitney was very happy, and she deserved that. I guess she wasn't always a happy person."

"I think she has struggled with depression, especially after her mother died last year. She had much more in common with her mom than she does with her father and her brothers." She paused. "I know I should probably try harder to like her, but despite her sudden interest in peace and love, she has a high-handed, snobbish attitude that I don't really care for."

"And it's weird for your dad to sleep with someone who

is only a few years older than you."

She grimaced at his words. "Please, don't talk about that."

"Sorry. So, can I go to dinner now?"

She nodded. "I wish you would have told me some of this earlier."

"A lot has happened really fast, Avery."

"Well, that's true." She glanced at her watch. "And the world isn't done spinning yet. Time to meet Carter. I'm almost afraid to find out what he has to say." She stood up, then gave him a worried look. "Wait a second."

"What?" he asked, as he got to his feet.

"Is it possible that Carter is the one who made Noelle the middleman?"

"The thought has crossed my mind."

"You haven't done any research on him?"

"Very minimal. As I said, Noelle just appeared on the radar a few days ago. We need to be careful what we say to Carter, Avery. You can't discuss what I just told you." He hoped he hadn't made a mistake in telling her so much right before they met with Carter.

"I understand. You can trust me, Wyatt. I won't blow this. I want to know what happened to Noelle. And if Carter got her into trouble, if he's the reason she's dead, then he's going to pay."

"I agree. But until we know that for sure, we need to treat him like he's a devoted, loving, and grieving boyfriend."

"I can do that. Thanks for being honest with me, Wyatt. We'll get further if we work together."

He nodded, knowing he wasn't even close to being honest with her. But he couldn't think about that now. The stakes were bigger than one person, and he couldn't forget that.

Twelve

—➤➤❰❰❮—

Wyatt had certainly given her a lot to think about, and his revelations occupied her thoughts as they drove across town to meet with Carter.

The idea that Noelle could have been a spy was just mind-boggling. She didn't even think Noelle had been particularly good at keeping secrets. When she heard something interesting, she had to talk about it. She lived for gossip and drama. How could she possibly have kept something so big, so important, from everyone in her life?

And if she had been involved in the leaking of proprietary material, then she'd betrayed not only Nova Star but her—her best friend, the woman who had put her own job and reputation on the line to get Noelle into the company.

Had she been completely blind when it came to Noelle?

She'd always known Noelle could be flaky, that she was often late, that she didn't always work that hard, and that she'd choose fun over responsibility just about any day of the week. But breaking the law, conspiring with a foreign government—that seemed too ridiculous to be true.

On the other hand, Noelle had been acting strangely. She had needed money to support her mom, and there had been cash in her account that hadn't come from her paycheck. The facts were adding up in a very bad way, and she desperately wanted to prove the facts wrong. She wanted there to be another reason for everything, a reason that would show that Noelle was a good person and not a criminal, not a traitor.

"You okay?" Wyatt asked, giving her a concerned look.

"I don't think I'm going to be okay for a long time. I'm just thinking about everything you told me, trying to figure out if any of it makes sense. It doesn't. The Noelle I knew wouldn't, *couldn't*, have done what you're suggesting."

"Well, maybe she didn't."

"You're just saying that to make me feel better. You don't believe it."

"I actually haven't made a decision about Noelle. And you shouldn't, either. We need more information. Hopefully Carter can give us something else to go on."

"Hopefully," she echoed, but she wasn't feeling overly optimistic.

Carter hadn't even been helpful when it came to talking about funeral arrangements; she doubted he was going to tell them anything that would help them find Noelle's killer. But she was eager to hear what he had to say. He'd been the person closest to Noelle. If anyone could shed light on her life outside of work the past few months, it would be him.

Fifteen minutes later, they pulled up in front of a series of townhouses in Hermosa Beach, a city just a few miles south of Venice Beach where Noelle had lived. When Carter opened the door to let them in, he didn't look any better than he had the day before. In fact, he looked worse. He wore black track pants and a gray T-shirt and had two-day's growth of beard on his jaw. His face was pale, and his eyes were a little too bright, as if he'd had a lot of caffeine.

"Hi, Carter." She felt like she should give him a hug, but he wasn't the kind of person who looked like he wanted that kind of connection. "Thanks for meeting with us. You remember Wyatt."

Carter nodded, as he waved them into his home. "I can't believe Noelle's mother just left town the way she did. How could she just abandon her daughter, after everything Noelle did to try to help her get back on her feet?"

"It shocked me, too," she said, following Carter into the living room.

His townhome felt new, with sleek hardwood floors in the entry and a plush rug under the couch and chairs in the living room. The kitchen boasted cherry cabinets and black appliances and the adjacent dining room offered a glass table and a view of the palm trees lining the nearby beach. There was also a balcony with a grouping of cozy chairs and a barbecue. That felt more like Noelle.

She looked around for more signs of her friend and found a few: the bright yellow coffee mug on the counter, the now wilting flowers in a vase by the couch, the fashion magazines on the coffee table. Noelle might not have put her stamp on the masculine brown leather couch and matching recliner, the golf photos on the walls, or the law books in the bookcase, but she'd definitely left pieces of herself in Carter's home. Those pieces seemed jarring, though, as if they didn't really belong, as if Noelle had not really belonged here.

Carter was certainly different from the long-haired, hard-drinking, musicians Noelle had often dated. Frowning, Avery couldn't help wondering what she was missing, why Noelle and Carter's relationship just felt so...*off*.

She wandered over to the vase filled with flowers, emotion putting a knot in her throat as her gaze came to rest on the sunflower.

"This was her favorite flower," she said, fingering the petals. "Noelle liked to lift her face to the sun, feel the heat on her skin. She felt like the sunflower did the same thing. It opened itself up to the light."

Silence followed her words. When she looked up, both men were staring at her with varying expressions of alarm and concern. She dropped her hand. "Could I have some coffee?"

"Uh, sure," Carter said, relieved by the unemotional question. "I actually just made another pot. Wyatt?"

"I'm good," Wyatt said. "Can I use your bathroom?"

"Yeah, down the hall on the left," Carter replied, as he moved into the kitchen.

As Wyatt left the room, she suddenly realized the bathroom was just an excuse. He wanted to take a look around Carter's apartment. And she could help by providing a distraction.

She moved into the kitchen and slid onto a stool in front of the island. Carter set a mug of coffee in front of her.

"You want anything in it?" he asked. "Although, I think I'm out of cream."

"Black is good. How are you doing today, Carter?"

He leaned against the opposite counter, crossing his arms. "Not so great. I'm sorry I ran out on you yesterday. When I was in the mortuary, I couldn't breathe."

"It was difficult for me, too."

He gave her a sad smile. "But you did it anyway. Noelle always told me that you were the strong one. You were her anchor. Like the weight on the end of a balloon string. You stopped her from flying away."

His words hit her hard, because she could hear Noelle's voice saying those same exact things. Her eyes watered, but she blinked back tears. There was no more time for crying. "I used to think that we stopped being friends because I held her back, because she wanted to soar, and she couldn't do that with me."

"She told me she was a wild child. Frankly, I didn't know why she went out with me in the first place. I knew I wasn't her usual type, but she was so attractive, so bright and appealing. When she was in the room, I couldn't look away. Somehow, I found the courage to ask her out. And she said yes. I have to say I was stunned. I didn't think we'd make it past the first date, but we did. We had more in common than we thought."

"What did you have in common?" she couldn't help asking, then saw him flinch. "I'm just trying to understand. I'm sorry if that was insensitive."

"No, I get it. Most people wouldn't see us together. But when we were alone, we were in sync. Noelle loved her job. She said it was the first time she'd ever felt like she was really contributing to the greater good. And I felt the same way. We talked about work all the time. She supported my ambitions. In fact, she gave me the courage to ask for a promotion, more responsibility, greater access to the key players in the company. Without her, I probably wouldn't have gone for it."

"That's great. Did you get it?"

"I'm supposed to find out tomorrow. I don't know what's going to happen now. The FBI stopped by this morning. They had a lot of questions for me. They think I had something to do with her death, but I didn't. I loved Noelle. She loved me."

"Did the FBI tell you that her apartment was burned down yesterday?"

He nodded. "I couldn't believe it."

"Did they also tell you that someone was looking for something in Noelle's apartment before that happened?"

"They mentioned that. They asked me a lot of questions about her life—who she spent time with, who she talked to on the phone, whether she kept anything here. They wanted to search the place, but I had to draw the line somewhere. I'm all for cooperating, but I'm a lawyer; I know when someone is putting a case together, and I'm a target." He stopped talking. "Where's Wyatt?"

"He's just using the restroom."

"Is he? Or is he looking around?"

As Carter straightened, ready to investigate, Wyatt came around the corner.

"You know, I think I'll have that coffee after all," Wyatt said. Taking in the tension in the room, he added, "What did I miss?"

"Carter said the FBI came by this morning," she replied. "He's afraid they are going to try to pin Noelle's death on him."

"And I am innocent," Carter proclaimed. "I would never kill anyone and certainly not the woman I loved."

"They're just going down the checklist of usual suspects," Wyatt said. "If they had any real evidence, you'd have been arrested."

"What is your involvement in all this?" Carter asked, giving Wyatt a suspicious look. "Isn't your job just to sit behind a monitor and check for intruders at Nova Star?"

"It's a bit more complicated than that," Wyatt said, not taking offense at Carter's rude comment.

"Wyatt is trying to help me figure out who killed Noelle," she interrupted. "He's also protecting Nova Star and its employees, one of whom is you. He suggested we come over here today so that we could alert you to the fact that you might be in danger because Noelle spent time here, and whoever was looking for something at her apartment might come here next. So, you might not want to attack him for doing his job and being concerned about you."

Carter frowned. "Sorry. I'm not myself today. I appreciate your concern. I can't imagine what Noelle could have left behind that someone would be looking for. I thought the attack was random. Now it sounds like something else was going on."

"Did you notice Noelle talking to anyone new, being on her phone a lot, acting out of the ordinary?" Wyatt asked.

"No. But the last week or so, I was working late, because the upcoming launch had tripled our workload, and I wanted to show I was ready to take on a bigger role. Noelle and I were missing each other a lot. But she was fine with it. She told me she wanted to spend more time with you, Avery, so she was going to ask you to go to the pier with her Friday night. I told her to have fun." His voice broke. "That's the last thing I said to her."

She bit down on her lip as emotions threatened to swamp her once again. "She was having fun. She had cotton candy, and she looked like a little kid, eating that pink, sugary confection."

"I can't imagine why she would have wanted to eat that," Carter said, wrinkling his nose in distaste.

No, he couldn't have imagined it, she thought. No matter what Carter had said about him and Noelle being in sync and having a lot in common, she still wondered if Carter had really known Noelle at all.

But maybe that wasn't his fault. Maybe Noelle hadn't let him see the real her. Perhaps she'd had other reasons for spending time with Carter.

Shaking her head, she realized she was going down a path she didn't want to go, but she couldn't turn around just yet. "You said Noelle really liked her job and that she also wanted to move up. Do you know if she was talking to anyone about a transfer?"

"She spent a lot of time with Kim in media relations. I know she was doing some work for her, but she never said what it was. Press stuff, I guess. She'd have been good at that. She was great with people. Her phone was always going off with texts and calls."

"Really? Because I saw her phone at the police station, and she didn't have any texts on there, none with you, and only a couple with me, setting up our plan for Friday night. Did she have another phone, Carter?"

"I—I don't know. I don't think so. It had that yellow polka-dot case."

"That's right, it did," she said, realizing the phone she'd seen at the station had been in a simple black case, but she'd seen the other phone numerous times before. "She must have had two phones. Maybe whoever searched her apartment was looking for her other phone."

"Can we look around for it here?" Wyatt asked.

"No," Carter said sharply, shaking his head. "I don't

know what's going on, but I know you two have more information than I do, and I don't like it. I will look for the phone, and if I find it, I'll turn it over to the FBI."

"What are you afraid of?" Wyatt challenged.

"Nothing. But this is my apartment. Noelle was my girlfriend, and this is my call. You both need to go."

"Hang on," she said, sliding off the stool. "We're on the same side, Carter."

"It doesn't feel that way."

"Well, it's the truth. And we still need to talk about a memorial for Noelle. Her friends at work are going to want to say good-bye, to celebrate her life, and you need to be a part of that."

"I told you I'd give you some money. How much do you want?"

"I don't want money; I want your input. You just said you loved Noelle. Don't you want to give her an appropriate send-off?"

"An appropriate send-off?" he asked in bewilderment. "I don't even know what that is. She's gone, Avery. She's not coming back. There's no chance to say good-bye. It's done. Do whatever you want. And if you need money, I'll chip in. But I can't plan anything. I can't."

She heard desperation in his voice and saw anger and sadness in his eyes, but there was some other emotion at play, and she didn't know what it was.

"I'll show you out," Carter added, waving them toward the door.

"Carter—"

"I'm sorry, Avery. I know I'm being an ass, but I can't do this right now. I will look through Noelle's things. I'll tell you if I find anything."

"Okay, thanks." As they stepped outside, he slammed the door behind them. "That was weird," she said, looking at Wyatt. "Did you find anything on your way to the bathroom?"

"I didn't see a phone with a yellow polka-dot case, not

that I was looking for that, but I think it would have stood out. When I left you and Carter, he was being cooperative. That changed fast."

"It did," she said, as she got into the car. "As soon as Carter started talking about the FBI grilling him and wanting to search his apartment, he suddenly realized you'd been gone awhile, and it freaked him out. He's hiding something and acting crazy. One minute I think he's grief-stricken and the next minute I feel like he's just angry and pissed off that Noelle's death has inconvenienced his life. He says he loves her, but he wants nothing to do with her memorial. Before all this I thought he was stable and a little boring. I was wrong."

"From what I've heard you say about Noelle, it doesn't seem like they go together."

"She said he reminded her of me and that she needed someone to hold her feet to the ground. If she loved me for that, maybe she would love him for that, too."

"Was that really why she loved you? Because I think there was a lot more to your friendship than that. You weren't just her anchor—you were her friend. You believed in her. You cared about her. You wanted the best for her. You even went out of your way to get her a job after she'd cut all ties to you for years. Those kinds of friends don't come around very often, and I think Noelle knew that."

"Thanks," she said, feeling a little teary at his words. "For saying all that. I'd like to believe our friendship was real, but there's a part of me now that isn't sure Noelle didn't use me to get into Nova Star. Maybe I helped start this whole security breach. Anyway…Noelle had things at Carter's place. Anyone who was in contact with her probably would have known about their relationship. If whoever killed her is still looking for something she had, then why haven't they gone to Carter's home? Or do you think they just haven't gotten there yet? I don't know if he understood that he could be in real danger."

"If Carter is involved, then he would not have any reason

to run, Avery. And if he doesn't understand what danger he might be in, then he's not as smart as I think he is."

"I can't imagine Carter stabbing Noelle. That doesn't feel right."

"He didn't have to do it himself to be involved. It's also possible that he and Noelle were working together, and he had no idea she was going to be taken out. I think part of his anger was covering up fear."

"It could just be fear that he won't get his promotion," she said bitterly. "Who would be worried about that at a time like this?"

"His fear went deeper than that."

"Maybe. I keep hoping I'll get answers, and all I get are more questions."

"The answers are coming." He started the engine. "Let's go to work. I want to check Noelle's desk, and you said you had something to do, right?"

"Yes, I do. And I'm sure that the police or the FBI already looked in Noelle's desk."

"I'm sure, too," he agreed. "But we're going to be there anyway, so why not check it out?"

She let out a sigh, not sure how it was going to feel to see Noelle's empty chair and know she would never sit in it again. "I hope I can do this."

"You can," Wyatt said, drawing her gaze to his. "You're stronger than you think."

"I guess we're going to find out."

Thirteen

—➤➤❰❰◄—

When they entered the lobby of Nova Star on Sunday afternoon, Jed Collins, an older security guard with dark-gray hair and bright-blue eyes, gave them a welcoming smile from behind the front counter. Wyatt liked Jed. He was in his late sixties, but he was an ex-cop, who had a good eye for detail. They didn't work together often, since Wyatt spent most of his time on the fifth floor in the security center, and Jed was usually at one of the entrances.

"Ms. Caldwell, I'm very sorry for your loss," Jed said. "I know you and Ms. Price were friends. It's horrific what happened to her."

"Thank you, Jed. I appreciate that," Avery said, accepting Jed's warm hand clasp.

"I don't know if her family needs any help with expenses, but if they do, please let me know."

"I will do that. We're still trying to figure things out."

"It's shocking. Ms. Price was such a happy, outgoing person. She always stopped and said hello. Of course, most of the time, it was because she was looking for her badge in that big, messy bag of hers," he added with a sad smile. "But still, she was a sweetheart. She even brought me sunflowers to give my wife when she had her foot surgery."

"I didn't know that," Avery said.

"She said she loved working here, never felt more at home, like we were all family. I can't believe someone killed her. Do they know who did it?"

"Not yet," she said tightly.

"We should get going," he put in, sensing that Avery wasn't quite ready to hear a lot of condolences from well-meaning employees. "Everything quiet around here, Jed? The police or FBI been around?"

"Yesterday there was a lot of action. Haven't seen anyone today. Engineering is busy with the launch coming up, but the rest of the building is empty. I hope you two don't have to work too long today."

"Not too long," Avery said, handing over her bag as Jed waved her through the security X-ray scanner.

There were three scanners in the lobby as well as scanners at two other entrances to the large building. The engineering building and science labs were in an adjacent wing that had a separate entrance and additional security procedures for employees or guests to enter. But none of that security would make a difference if there was a mole inside the building.

Wyatt placed his phone and wallet in a small container and made his way through the scanner. Then they headed across the slick marble floors, past the display of model rockets that soared two stories high, the gift shop that was now closed, and the press room that would be filled with reporters starting tomorrow.

The entrance to the two-story auditorium where Avery ran her shows was located past the bank of elevators at the end of the first-floor hallway.

"Should we check Noelle's desk first?" he asked, as he punched the elevator button.

"Seems like the best place to start," she said, a heavy note in her voice.

"I can do it myself."

"No, you were right earlier. I need to see her desk today, when there aren't dozens of other people around, watching my reaction." She squared her shoulders and stepped into the elevator as if she were going off to do battle.

He knew what she was feeling. He'd lost more than a few friends to violence in his life, and the first few days and weeks were always rough.

"After we check Noelle's desk, I need to go to my office and then the auditorium," Avery added. "And I don't need you looking over my shoulder for all that."

"That's fine. I have some work to do, too."

"Really?" she asked with surprise. "I thought you'd put up a fight."

"You'll be safe in your office and in the auditorium."

They got off the elevator on the third floor where the business, legal, and accounting departments were located. Noelle had been assigned as an admin for all three departments and had sat with a dozen other admins in a room filled with large cubicles and the latest equipment with seated, standing, and treadmill desks as well as oversized monitors, printers, and small filing cabinets for storing duplicate copies of information stored on the company's web server.

A bank of windows threw some nice light over the area, and as they walked toward Noelle's desk, which was in the middle of the room, he made a mental note of the names listed on gold placards on the cubicle walls next to Noelle's desk. Kathryn Sams and Jaycee Lawrence were apparently Noelle's closest cubicle buddies, and it definitely might be worth having a conversation with both of them.

Avery stepped into Noelle's cubicle, her expression tense and wary, as if she was afraid of what they would find, although he didn't believe they'd find much. He knew the FBI had already swept her desk and cubicle, but he wanted to see it for himself, as did Avery.

There was a yellow polka-dot mug on the desk that immediately captured his attention. Apparently, Noelle really liked yellow. But the top of the desk was clear of any other items. He opened the drawers and found nothing more than blank notepads and pens.

"Avery?"

A woman's voice brought both their heads up.

"Kathryn," Avery said in surprise.

"I can't believe Noelle is dead," Kathryn said, shaking her head in disbelief

As the two women hugged for a long minute, he made note of the fact that the short brunette was the woman who sat next to Noelle. If anyone might have overheard something or been privy to Noelle's confidence, it might have been her. Although, he would have thought that Noelle would have shared more with Avery, given their long history. If she hadn't, it had to be because she didn't want Avery to know what she was up to.

"I keep hoping it's a dream," Kathryn added, her gaze moving toward Noelle's desk. "It's so neat," she added, a note of surprise in her voice. "Did you clean out her desk?"

"Not me," Avery replied. "The police and FBI were here yesterday."

"Oh, of course, that makes sense."

Wyatt couldn't help noting how Kathryn's gaze darted around Noelle's cubicle, as if she were looking for something. Finally, her gaze came to rest on him, and she started. "Sorry, I don't think we've met."

"Wyatt Tanner. I work upstairs in security."

"Yes, that's right. I've seen you around."

He wondered if that were true, since he didn't really wander around much, especially not on this floor.

"Are there any leads on who killed Noelle?" Kathryn asked him.

"No. Do you have any thoughts on the matter?"

"Me? No!" she said somewhat emphatically. "I don't

know anything."

Wyatt noticed Avery's gaze sharpen at Kathryn's denial.

"Noelle didn't mention she was in any kind of trouble?" Avery asked.

"Was she in trouble?" Kathryn countered.

Avery shrugged. "I don't know. It certainly feels that way now."

"But you were with her Friday night. If she did have a problem, she would have told you. She always said you were good friends." Kathryn licked her lips. "There was one odd thing."

"What's that?" he asked sharply, drawing her gaze back to his.

"Her boyfriend, Carter. He came by Noelle's desk Friday night, and he was going through her drawers. He seemed angry about something. I asked him if he needed help, and he said Noelle had called him and told him she'd left her phone here, and he was looking for it. I helped him search for it, but we didn't find it. He seemed really annoyed." She paused, licking her lips. "He's—he's not a suspect, is he? I heard something rumored to that effect."

"Everyone is a suspect," he replied. "Did you notice Noelle having a problem with anyone else? Did she go out with other people in the company besides Carter?"

"I don't think so. I mean, she was really pretty, and very popular, and there were always a lot of men coming around to say hello or ask for her help. But she seemed most interested in Carter, especially after she was assigned to the patent office for a few days. I remember when she came back, she said that she found the legal stuff really interesting, that it was amazing all the things the company was inventing. Not that she knew what any of them were. We used to laugh about how we rarely knew what we were writing letters or memos about," she said with a teary smile. "Noelle said she was really over her head when she helped out in Kyle Tremaine's office one day. She said the man was clearly brilliant, but she could barely understand a word he said."

As Kathryn rambled on, he thought about how much access Noelle had had to other departments, something he hadn't really considered before. He also hadn't known that she'd spent time in Kyle's office, which might have given her even greater access to proprietary information. But what was also interesting was Carter's search of Noelle's desk on Friday night.

Had Carter been looking for Noelle's second phone that he'd denied having any knowledge of? And why hadn't he mentioned that Noelle had left her phone at work and asked him to look for it? They'd specifically spoken about the phone. It was hardly something he would have forgotten.

Finally, Kathryn came to a stop. "Sorry, I'm chattering on. I'm a little rattled after what happened to Noelle. I heard she was stabbed. It sounds awful. And you found her, Avery? Was she alive? Did she say anything to you?"

"No, she didn't," Avery lied. "And she had her phone when she was with me. In fact, she texted me when she was running a few minutes late."

"Maybe she found it then. Anyway, I just stopped in to grab my work computer." She paused. "Oh, is there going to be a service, Avery? I'd like to go, and I'm happy to help with any plans. Just let me know."

"I'll keep you in the loop," Avery said, as Kathryn moved into her own cubicle.

They walked back to the elevators in silence, not saying a word until they stepped inside and the doors shut.

"Oh, my God," Avery said, her eyes lit up with excitement. "Carter was looking through Noelle's desk on Friday night. He lied to us about Noelle's phone. Maybe he is involved in her death."

"He's involved in something, but I don't know what."

"I'd like to go back and confront him."

"I want to gather more information before we do that, and you have work to do."

"That's true. I know I need to concentrate on that, but it won't be easy."

As the elevator doors opened on the second floor, he put a hand on her arm, staying close as they walked down the hall to her office.

Avery opened the door to her office and waved him inside. It wasn't a large room, but it was filled to the brim. Bookshelves lined two walls and were crammed with books, flyers, brochures, DVDs about space, and boxes of Nova Star swag: tote bags and key chains, journals and educational booklets for teachers and students. Clearly, Avery had had a hand in designing and providing information for everything.

She walked around her desk and opened her computer. While it was booting up, she looked back at him. "You can go now. I need about a half hour here, and then I have to take my computer down to the auditorium and run through the show. That could take another half hour. What are you going to do?"

"Check through the security camera footage and see what else Carter was up to on Friday night besides going through Noelle's desk. Lock this door after I leave and call me if anyone comes knocking. When you're ready to go to the auditorium, let me know, and I'll walk you there."

"Wyatt, you can't babysit me every second. Tomorrow I'm going to be back here doing my job and the day after that."

"I'm only interested in today. Call me when you're done."

"All right."

He walked outside and waited for her to lock the door, then headed upstairs to his office.

--->=<---

Security ran lean on the weekends, and instead of the usual dozen or so men and women who worked in security operations during the week, there were six people in today: three sitting in front of a bank of security cameras, two working on their computers, and the last person sitting at a desk very near to his own. That person was Lance Hughes, a forty-six-year-old, ex-Navy communications tech who monitored their server for any unauthorized access to their computer system.

Hamilton liked hiring ex-military. He said he knew he could count on soldiers to not only protect but also to fight. And he was probably right about that. But what he most valued in the security personnel working under his direction was intuition, attention to detail, and an instinct for anomalies. Lance had all those traits and had become one of the people he relied most upon.

It also helped that Lance wasn't competitive. He hadn't cared that Wyatt had come in over personnel who had been there years before him. Some of his coworkers had definitely not liked his sudden appearance a month ago, or his close relationship with Hamilton, who had stated on more than one occasion that Wyatt was his guy.

Lance gave him a nod, as he looked up from his computer. "I didn't know you were coming in today."

"How's it going around here?" Lance was one of the few people who knew that there had been a security breach several months earlier. He didn't know that Jonathan Tremaine might have been involved, but he'd been put on high alert weeks ago to watch for anything unusual.

"It's quiet for now." Lance folded his arms across his chest as he leaned back in his swivel chair.

"What do you know about the homicide involving Noelle Price?"

"Not much. I've spoken to the police and the FBI. They're digging into the case."

"I noticed you came in with Avery Caldwell. How's she doing?"

"Not very well. Hamilton has asked me to keep an eye on her. She went to Noelle's apartment yesterday morning and ran into a man with a gun. Luckily, she was unharmed, but there's concern she might be in danger."

"And this has to do with Nova Star?"

"Don't know yet. But I'm going to find out." He moved over to his desk and sat down in front of his computer. Within minutes, he'd pulled up the security camera footage from Friday afternoon. He flipped back and forth between cameras as he tried to zero in on the path to Noelle's desk.

When he got a clear shot of her desk, he backed up the footage until Noelle was on the frame. The time on the camera read five twenty. She pulled a phone out of her bag, and his pulse quickened as he saw the black case. She texted someone. He tried to zoom in, but the message was too grainy to read.

Five minutes later, she got up and tossed her phone into her bag and then said good-bye to Kathryn and walked out of her cubicle.

He watched her empty desk for another ten minutes, speeding up the footage until he saw Carter come into the frame. He pulled open Noelle's drawers with force and anger, not seeming to care who might be watching him. Kathryn got up and said something to him and then came around to help him in his search.

As Carter slammed a final drawer shut, he said something to Kathryn, and as she replied, she put her hand on his arm.

His gut tightened. Kathryn was more than a little friendly with Carter. The way she touched him, the way she leaned in, suggested they had an intimate relationship.

What the hell was going on?

A moment later, Carter left. Kathryn glanced around Noelle's cubicle for another minute and then went back to her own desk.

He forwarded through the footage again and saw Kathryn leaving ten minutes later. He kept the footage going until the room grew dark and then picked up again the next morning. But it was Saturday, and no one was working. The next person who appeared on the camera was Detective Larimer. An hour later, Joanna Davis and several FBI techs appeared.

His phone vibrated, and he saw a text from Avery. She was ready to head to the auditorium. He pushed back his chair and stood up.

"Are you leaving already?" Lance asked, giving him a curious look.

"Yeah, I need to take Avery to the auditorium."

"Take her?"

"Like I said, Hamilton wants me to keep her close."

"Rough job," Lance said with a knowing gleam in his eyes. "She's very attractive. Almost makes me wish I'd taken more science classes in school."

He smiled. "I know what you mean."

"Hey, before you go. I don't know if this is anything, but someone tried to use Kyle Tremaine's access code to get into his email file. The user was outside the company and after three unsuccessful tries, they gave up."

"And the ISP?"

"That's the interesting thing—the ISP address led me to Brett Caldwell's house."

"Avery's dad?"

"And Whitney Tremaine's boyfriend. Now, it's possible that Kyle was at the house and just forgot his new password. We've been requiring updates every week since the security breach."

"Thanks for letting me know."

As he left the security center, his mind spun with the latest leads. Kathryn and Carter were connected. Maybe Kyle and Brett were connected, too. He didn't know where the clues would take him, but at least they had more to follow than they'd had an hour ago.

Fourteen

—➤➤◄◄◄—

On his way to pick up Avery and escort her to the auditorium, he stopped by Noelle's desk again.

Kathryn was gone. He wondered why she'd really come into the office. *Had she wanted to take another look at Noelle's space? Or had she simply come in to get her computer as she had said?* He would have to catch up with her later.

He hurried up to Avery's office and knocked, saying his name as he did so. She flipped the locks and stepped out with her computer in hand. "That took you awhile."

"Sorry, I went back by Noelle's desk," he said, as they walked to the elevator.

"Why?"

"I'll tell you when we get in the auditorium," he replied, as they passed by another employee heading out of an office and into a nearby restroom.

Avery gave him a frustrated look but didn't ask any more questions until they entered the auditorium. She flipped on the lights and they walked down the aisle toward the center stage, a thousand seats rising up two stories around them.

"Okay, talk, Wyatt," she said, putting her computer on

the podium. "We're all alone here."

"I reviewed the security footage from Friday night. Carter arrived at Noelle's desk about ten minutes after she left, just as Kathryn said. He went through the drawers and seemed angry and irritated."

"He was looking for her phone."

"Here's the thing—before Noelle left, I could see her texting on a phone, and the phone appeared to be in a black case. She put that phone in her bag."

"That's the one she had at the pier."

"I'm guessing the person she texted was you."

"She said she was running late," Avery confirmed. "So, we still don't know where her other phone is."

"There was no sign of it on the footage I watched. There was one other interesting note. When Carter was about to leave, he and Kathryn had an intense moment together. She put her hand on his arm and looked into his eyes, like she knew him as more than a friend."

"Carter and Kathryn?" she asked in surprise. "He was cheating on Noelle?"

"I don't know if he was cheating. He could have had a relationship with Kathryn before Noelle got hired at Nova Star. But Kathryn definitely didn't share that piece of information with us. She acted like she barely knew Carter, like she was almost afraid of him."

"She did point a finger at him, almost as if she wanted to make him a target. Was that to throw attention off herself? Or maybe she wanted to get back at Carter for something—like choosing Noelle instead of her? We need to talk to her again."

"She's gone. That's why I went by Noelle's desk before I came to get you."

"We'll go to her house then."

"We need to do some digging first. We don't want to alert Kathryn to anything until we know more. This is too important to rush, Avery. We say the wrong thing to the wrong person, and all the rats will run for cover."

She blew out a breath. "You're right. I just want some answers."

"Well, there's someone else we need answers from," he said, knowing she wasn't going to like what was coming next.

"Who?"

"Your father."

"What?" she asked in confusion. "What does my father have to do with any of this?"

"One of my security team discovered an attempt to log in to Kyle Tremaine's email account from your father's house."

"Well, my dad lives with Whitney, and Kyle does visit. So, maybe it was Whitney, or Kyle was there and just forgot his password. Your team has us changing passwords every other second these days. My father wouldn't try to get into Kyle's account. He can barely get into his own account."

"It's probably nothing, but I'd like to ask Kyle about it tonight at dinner."

"This party is looking to be more fun by the minute," she said dryly. "Is that it?"

"Yes."

"Good. I need to focus and get this work done."

"While you do that, I'm going to call the FBI and see what they know."

"Really?" she asked in surprise. "Do you think they'll tell you anything?"

"Probably not much, but it's worth a shot."

"I thought Hamilton wanted to keep the bureau at a distance."

"He also wants to know what's going on. I know how to play it." As he left the auditorium, he didn't dial Joanna; he contacted Bree. Now that she was part of their group, he preferred talking to her over anyone else.

Avery's mind spun with Wyatt's recent revelations, but as

she opened her computer, she forced herself to concentrate on the task at hand. She had already sent the video file to the computer on stage, but she wanted to double-check that everything was working correctly and ready for the media at nine o'clock in the morning.

It actually felt good to think about work, because considering whether Carter had cheated on Noelle and whether or not her father had tried to log in to Kyle's email account was making her sick to her stomach. She wanted new leads, but each one that came seemed worse than the last.

Wyatt returned to the auditorium a few minutes later and seeing him stride toward the stage with confidence and strength made her feel better. She was fast becoming addicted to his handsome face, strong presence, and the sharp intelligence in his eyes. When he was with her, she felt like they might just get to the bottom of everything. She also felt like he was the only person who really understood what she was going through, but that was because she'd shown him her grief, her fear, her vulnerability. She'd let loose of her emotions in front of him and cried all over him, and he hadn't judged her; he'd held her.

Her body tingled as he drew closer, as his gaze met hers. It was scary how attracted she was to him. He'd only been gone a few minutes, but she'd actually missed him, and she felt an absurdly giddy feeling that he was back. Clearly, she was getting too involved. But she couldn't back away. There was too much at stake.

"What did the FBI say?" she asked, as he stepped onto the stage.

"Very little. I told them they should look more closely into Carter and Kathryn. They assured me they were on it."

"Do you think that's true?"

"Yes. They won't ignore solid leads, but they're frustrated with Hamilton's reluctance to give them unfettered access, so they weren't particularly interested in sharing information with me."

"Did you say anything about my father?"

"No."

She felt an unexpected wave of relief. It wasn't her job to protect her dad, but she was happy her father's name had not come up.

"Like you said, it could have been Whitney or Kyle," Wyatt added. "I can ask them tonight."

"I'd wait until after cocktails. Both Kyle and Whitney enjoy their wine."

"What about your father? Is he a drinker?"

"Not at all. He's cleansed his body of toxins the past few years."

Wyatt smiled. "I'm really looking forward to meeting him. He sounds very interesting."

"Then he'll like you, because he finds himself very interesting."

"Are you almost done?"

"I actually want to run through the show. It only takes fifteen minutes. What do you think? Feel like being my test audience?"

"Sure, why not? I've actually never seen any of your shows."

"What?" she asked in surprise. "It's supposed to be part of your orientation. Everyone sees the welcome to Nova Star video."

"Hamilton fast-tracked me through orientation."

"Then this will be good. You'll be a completely objective audience, like the reporters coming tomorrow. Take a seat in the first row. I'm going to turn off the lights and soon you will be taking an incredible journey through the universe."

He smiled. "This better live up to the hype."

"Space always lives up to the hype. I know you don't like to look up, but today you will, and I'll be surprised if you aren't amazed."

"So says the space geek," he teased.

She grinned back at him. "This is my world, Wyatt."

"I can't wait to see it."

Something passed between them that had nothing to do with Noelle or Carter. It was a personal, intimate moment that only they were sharing. Her lips tingled as she remembered the kiss they'd shared the night before and wondered if it would happen again

Wyatt cleared his throat, his gaze filling with shadows. "I better take my seat."

"Yes," she said, letting out her breath as she turned to her computer and got the show ready to go.

―➤➤◀◀―

Wyatt kicked back in the leather recliner in the first row, grateful when Avery turned off the lights. It gave him a chance to regroup. For a moment there, he'd been tempted to kiss her again, and he'd promised himself that wouldn't happen—*shouldn't* happen. But that had been close, too close.

Thankfully, his racing heart began to calm in the cool darkness, only a small light coming from the podium where Avery stood in the shadows.

A moment later, she walked down the steps and took a seat in the chair next to him.

Then she pressed the switch in her hand, and the massive ceiling turned into the night sky. A trillion stars appeared, pulsating music playing in the background, building an expectation for what was to come.

And then a voice came through the speakers, and his nerves tightened. It was Avery's voice—hushed, breathy, excited. He glanced over at her, seeing her smile at him in the shadows and light from the night sky.

"Look up," she said.

He didn't want to look up; he wanted to keep looking at her.

But as her voice rang out again, stirring his senses, his gaze moved to the sky overhead.

"*The universe is an endless, infinite space of immense distance and time. Where does it begin? Where does it end? What lies beyond what we've discovered so far? And who will lead the way to interplanetary travel? Who will be the first to defend space and protect it for all mankind?*"

Her questions were followed by a kaleidoscope of colors. Stars, and planets spun around above him, carrying him away in a manner he had not expected.

He'd been working at Nova Star for a month and hadn't really paid much attention to the space stuff. But now he was looking up in a way he hadn't before—at least not in a very long time.

The sky above was filled with possibilities, with hope, optimism, wonder at the unexplainable, inexplicable universe...and the men and women who wanted to understand it, wanted to explore it, wanted to explain it...

He'd never been that interested in the universe, but he had wanted to change the world. He'd wanted to leave his mark on Earth. He'd wanted to take down the dark and bring out the light, although he'd never put it in those terms.

He'd been working undercover for the bureau for almost six years. He'd played so many different parts. He'd caught bad guys, protected innocent people, saved a few lives.

But was it worth it? Could he live forever in the shadows, never being who he really was, never letting anyone really know him?

He'd thought he could. But lately, he'd been feeling restless, yearning for something he couldn't quite define, wanting what he couldn't have...

His gaze moved to the woman next to him. He couldn't really see her in the darkness, but he was acutely aware of her presence, of the faint hint of lavender that must come from her shampoo or her body lotion. And thinking about her body only made the ache in his gut worse. Her kiss had taken him on an adventure, too. That brief taste had whetted his appetite for more, and he'd spent half the night telling himself to let it go, think of her as a job, but none of those reminders had worked. As soon as he'd seen her again, he'd wanted her back in his arms.

She was such an intriguing blend of smart, sexy and sweet. She didn't just fill him with desire, she also filled him with affection. And she'd slid in past his defenses before he'd even realized she was there. He still couldn't believe he'd told her about his family. That story had brought them closer. He just wished he could tell her everything.

But that couldn't happen. He needed to rein in the reckless feelings.

Looking back up at the sky, he told himself he was just tired. He never took vacations between jobs, and he probably should. It had been a long time since he'd been able to let down his guard and just be himself—whoever that was. He was starting to forget, which was another disturbing feeling. Agents older than him had warned him about the dangers of staying out in the cold too long. But he'd always believed he could handle it, because he didn't want what other people wanted. His happy family illusions had shattered years ago. He didn't believe in love or happily ever after. He didn't think being a husband, a father, was in the cards. He didn't know if he had it in him to open himself up to all the possible pain again.

But being with Avery…made him think about he was missing in his life, made him want more than he had. *Were the possibilities for his life as endless and as dream-worthy as the sky above him?*

As Avery's captivating voice fell away on a lingering, magical-feeling kind of whisper, he thought maybe, just maybe, they were.

He drew in several deep breaths, needing to get back to reality fast.

He was only with Avery because she needed protection and because she might be able to help him with his assignment. He really couldn't forget that.

But as she turned on the lights and gazed at him with eager, expectant, and very beautiful brown eyes—that resolve went right out the window.

"Well, what did you think?" she asked impatiently.

He raised his recliner to an upright position. "That was amazing. You took me right out of this world."

Her happy smile almost undid him.

"I'm so glad," she said, delight in her gaze. "That show was designed for people who have had no interest in space until now. It's supposed to whet their appetite to want more."

"It definitely did that," he muttered. "You have a very mesmerizing voice. Your passion for space is...palpable. I almost felt like I was spinning through the heavens."

"That's what I wanted you to feel. I remember the first time I saw a show like this. It was at the Griffith Park Observatory, and I went with my dad. Selfish quirks aside, he's the person who taught me how to dream. I think I was about nine at the time, and I was mesmerized by all the planets beyond this one. After that, I wanted to learn everything I could about space. Birthdays and holidays, I asked for books and more trips to the observatory. My mom used to say, 'Brett, look what you started—our daughter is obsessed.'"

He smiled. "Your obsession looks good on you."

She grinned back at him. "You're nice to say that. Not all guys have felt the same."

"No?"

"No," she said with a shake of her head. "I was late to my boyfriend's birthday my senior year in high school because I was waiting for a comet to shoot through the sky. He got mad and ended up hooking up with Lorraine Hobbs. And that was the end of that. He couldn't believe I'd blown him off. But it was a comet, Wyatt. Do you know how rare it is to see something like that?"

"I'll take your word for it."

"I would have made it up to him if he hadn't cheated on

me so quickly."

"He wasn't worth your time."

"He wasn't. And I knew that even then, but you know how high school is. No one wants to be alone, even geeky science nerds."

"You had to be the most beautiful nerd at that school."

She flushed at his words. "That's a charming thing to say but not true. I was very awkward back then. I still am, if you want to know the truth. When I study data, I wear really ugly glasses with thick black frames."

"Sounds sexy," he said, not knowing why the thought of Avery in a pair of glasses got his motor running, but it had certainly done that.

"It's not, trust me. I'm a very single woman."

"Is that the way you like it?" he asked curiously.

She licked her lips as she pondered his question. "I'm not unhappy on my own. My obsession does take a lot of time, and I love to work. But sometimes it's a little lonely. It would be nice to share my life with someone—the right someone. He hasn't come along yet."

"Maybe he's waiting for you to come back to Earth," he teased.

She made a face at him. "That could be a long wait."

He laughed. "You know, I've worked here for a while, but I don't really think I thought about what's being done here."

"Our mission is about more than just sending ordinary people into space. The satellites bring back important data as well as power the internet, GPS, so many things from ordinary life that people don't even realize. And, of course, they can also be used for spying, for war, for destruction. I worry sometimes that the beautiful universe will become a war zone. It's already happening with space debris from previous tests gone awry. Where will all the junk go?"

"I don't know, but I do know that almost every amazing technological advance can also be used in the worst possible way."

"Yes. That's why we have to fight to protect the technology we're developing."

"And that's why Hamilton hired me. I appreciate you reminding me of what's at stake from a science perspective."

"I'm glad it helped. So, now you know what I dreamed about as a little girl. What about you? What did you want to be when you grew up? A soldier? A security guy?"

"None of those jobs were even on my radar when I was a kid."

"Then what?"

"Well, let's see. I thought I could be a professional baseball player for a while, until I realized I wasn't that good."

"When did that happen?"

"When I got to college and realized that everyone there had been the best player on their team. There was nothing that special about me. I certainly wasn't the fastest or the biggest."

"Did you play in college?"

"First two years. I hurt my arm, and during the time it took to rehab, I discovered there was another life off the baseball field, and unlike you, I did not find that life in the library or the classroom. I had way too much fun."

She smiled. "I bet you did. What was your major?"

"Economics. At the time, I thought I'd probably go into the family financial business. I had no idea what was to come. I was probably lucky to be born nine years after my brother. He was already entrenched when everything went bad."

"Nine years is a big gap."

"I was an *accident*. My parents had only wanted one kid, but they apparently went to Hawaii and had too many vodka tonics, and voila—I was on deck."

She laughed. "Well, at least you were conceived in fun."

"They were happy then," he admitted, barely remembering those days now. "At least, I thought they were. I second guess everything now."

"It's weird how similar our dads are. Even though my father has never broken the law, he does kind of sell snake oil. And it sounds like your father did the same." The smile on her face dimmed. "What you said earlier about a possible email hack coming from my dad's house—I don't think he would do that. He sells dreams, and maybe he gets paid for his bullshit, but he's not a criminal. And he barely knows how to send an attachment to an email; I can't see him trying to hack into Kyle's account. I also doubt he'd understand anything Kyle was talking about. I've had Kyle talk to science groups before, and even physicists were lost when he went off on one of his tangents."

"Now you sound like my mother defending my father for his sins," he said.

She frowned. "Do I? It's not like I don't see his flaws. But…"

"But you don't want him to be guilty of anything more."

"He can't be guilty of anything more, because if he was involved in this, then that would mean that he had something to do with Noelle's death and that man pulling a gun on me, and that could not be true," she said with pain in her voice.

"We don't know that it is true. We're still fact-finding."

She frowned. "I want to find the facts more quickly."

"It actually hasn't been that long. Things are moving fast."

"I guess. I'm usually better at being patient."

"Well, usually your life isn't on the line. I get that, Avery."

"I know you do." She paused. "Your life has been on the line before, hasn't it?"

"Many times."

"How did you get from college fun to the Marines?"

"It was the fastest way to change my life after everything that happened with my dad," he said, hating that he had to keep playing with the truth and also annoyed that by telling her some of the truth about his life, he'd opened himself up to this line of questioning.

"And you couldn't just move to another city? You had to go risk your life?"

"I had to do something worthwhile, something to balance things out." He was talking about why he'd gone into the FBI, but in this instance, the reason worked for both his real life and his cover.

"Pay for your father's sins?" she questioned.

"Not exactly. But it turned out to be a good move."

"And now you're in security."

"Not quite the clear-cut route that you took toward a career, but I'm happy with where I am."

"I'm happy with where you are, too." She took a breath. "I'm kind of getting used to having you around, Wyatt."

"I'm not a pain in the ass, huh?"

"Well, I wouldn't go that far."

"Fair enough," he said with a grin.

"I do appreciate everything you've done to keep me safe."

"That's my job," he said, reminding himself not to forget that.

"And you do it well. I have no idea what's going to happen next, and that's scary for me. I like to know what's around the corner before I make the turn but being with you makes the unexpected easier to handle."

"Well...good," he said somewhat tersely, her faith in him starting to make him feel like the worst kind of person.

"Wait. What did I say? You're suddenly annoyed." Her brows drew together in a frown.

"I'm not annoyed. You feel safe with me. That's great. That's what you're supposed to feel."

"It's *not* the only thing I feel, Wyatt. You know that." Her gaze connected with his. "There's an electricity between us. I can feel the pull right now. I think you can, too. But we said we shouldn't do anything about it, right?"

It was the hesitancy in her question that made him lean across the armrest and answer her with the kiss he'd been thinking about since the last one they'd shared. He gripped her arms and covered her mouth with his, savoring the sweet heat of her lips, the passion that was so uniquely Avery, a mix of innocence and desire that was as out of this world as she was.

She'd stoked the fire between them with her show, with her hushed voice spinning tales of dreams and impossibilities.

She was absolutely an impossibility for him, but he wanted her anyway. He wanted what little he could get. Actually, he wanted as much as he could get, so he deepened the kiss, sliding his tongue into her mouth, savoring the soft moan that escaped her lips.

It just wasn't enough.

He wanted more.

So much more.

Too much more.

He broke the kiss, then framed her face with his hands as he gazed into her brown eyes that were lit with desire. "Beautiful," he whispered.

She put her hands on his face and smiled. "So handsome. Even with this scar," she added, tracing the thin line that ran across his jaw. "How did you get this?"

"I don't remember."

They stared at each other for a long minute, and he had the crazy feeling he could look at her for the rest of his life and never want to look away.

Her gaze grew serious. "What are we doing, Wyatt?" she murmured.

It was a good question.

And he had no *good* answer.

He wasn't supposed to be messing around with Avery. He was on a job. Hell, he was lying to her, and when she realized that, she'd be hurt and angry.

But they wouldn't have time to fight about it, because he'd be moving on to the next job, and she'd find out that he was just another man who had let her down.

He really didn't want to be that man.

Avery was too sweet, too open, too honest. He couldn't be the one to hurt her. He had to put on the brakes.

"Wyatt?" she pressed. "There's an awful lot going on in your eyes."

"Well, there's a lot going on in both our lives right now. And this should probably not be part of that." He let go of her and stood up, breaking the connection between them. "We should get back to business."

"Yes, I guess we should," she said, getting to her feet, a troubled look in her gaze.

"If you're done here, why don't we go back to the hotel?"

"That's a good idea. I want to change clothes before the party."

"Is this dinner formal?"

"Not formal, but I'm going to put on a dress. Men will be in slacks, nice shirts, but no coats or ties required."

He was relieved to hear that. "I can do that."

She nodded and then let out a sigh.

"What was that for?" he asked.

"I just have a feeling you're going to look really good, Wyatt, and I'm going to want to kiss you again—business or no business."

He smiled at her candor. "You're going to look good, too, Avery. We're screwed."

"So, I'm not in this alone."

"You're not, but..." He forced himself to say the words. "This isn't a good time for our own personal trip to another galaxy. It's not that I don't want to, because I do. Believe me, I do."

She smiled back at him. "You talk like that, and you're going to make it harder for this space geek to resist you. But you're right. There's a better time."

He grinned. "I'll keep that in mind...when we find our better time."

Fifteen

She was right. Wyatt looked deliciously sexy after he'd showered and put on gray slacks and a light-blue dress shirt. His hair was thick and wavy, his cheeks freshly shaven, and he smelled like musk and man, and it was all Avery could do not to throw herself into his arms and find that *better time* right now.

Despite the immediate guilty feeling that followed, a part of her wondered why they should wait?

Life was ridiculously short. Noelle had been eating cotton candy one minute and dying of a stab wound the next.

Maybe she should start living like there might not be a tomorrow, especially in view of how much danger she was currently in.

But there was no time to act on her reckless thoughts. They would be late for dinner and this dinner was turning out to be about more than her dad's fifty-sixth birthday. Still, she couldn't help smiling under Wyatt's appreciative gaze. "What?" she asked, sensing he wanted to say something, or maybe she just wanted him to say it.

"You look beautiful, Avery."

She smoothed down the sides of her short, clingy black

dress, glad she'd put on high heels and had a chance to pull herself together. Wyatt had seen her at her worst so far. This might not be her best, but it was quite an improvement. She'd left her hair down, put on some makeup, even spritzed herself with some perfume, and Wyatt's words made her feel even better about herself. "Thanks. You clean up well, too."

His eyes sparkled with warm humor. "Glad you think so."

She really did, and a gnawing hunger in her gut had nothing to do with the fact that she hadn't eaten in hours. It was all about this man who had appeared out of nowhere and had somehow become her constant companion. But they were in dangerous territory, alone in this hotel room, and she couldn't handle any more danger, no matter how sexy it might be.

"We should go," she said. "Whitney hates when people are late. Not that she's ever on time."

"One-way street, huh?"

"That's Whitney." She put a silky wrap around her shoulders that would do little to keep her warm, but the only jacket she had in her suitcase had Noelle's blood on it, and that wasn't going to work.

Within minutes, they were in the car and on their way to her father's house in Calabasas, an upscale suburb north of Los Angeles, on the other side of the Malibu Canyon. He'd purchased the house a few months ago when he and Whitney had moved in together, choosing the location because all the Tremaines had homes in the area and the hillside community offered views of the mountains and the beach.

Opting to avoid the freeways, Wyatt took the northern beach route, heading up the Pacific Coast Highway, turning off just past Malibu to drive through the Santa Monica Mountains to Calabasas.

"I am not looking forward to this," she muttered as Wyatt weaved his way through the unusually heavy traffic. Apparently, a lot of beachgoers had decided to take this route as well.

"I can understand that."

"On my best day, a dinner like this would not be high on my list of things to do, and this is nowhere near to my best day. But it is my dad's birthday, so I really can't skip it."

"It might be a good distraction."

"I doubt that, although it will give you an opportunity to get up close and personal with the Tremaines."

"I'm looking forward to that. I've had brief conversations with Jonathan and Kyle, but I've never spoken to Whitney. I did see her at Hamilton's house once, but she didn't come in to say hello."

"You were at Hamilton's house?" she asked with surprise. "He doesn't invite many employees to his home. It took me a year to get an invite. You seem awfully close to Hamilton for someone who has only worked at the company for a month. Did you bond over Marine stories?"

"We did, but our connection actually started when I saved Hamilton from being robbed and carjacked."

"What? When did that happen?"

"Right before I was hired. It was at the beach. Hamilton likes to surf in the mornings. I happened to be walking by when two thugs attacked him."

"His driver wasn't around?"

"He'd gone to get coffee. Anyway, Hamilton was grateful. We got to talking, and eventually he offered me a job. He's a good man—much more down-to-earth than I would have expected from a billionaire."

"Hamilton is very generous, and he talks to everyone. He's not class-conscious."

"That was one of the first things I noticed about him."

"Whitney, on the other hand, is very class-conscious. When you were describing your mother to me earlier, she reminded me of Whitney. My father's girlfriend is very into her women's groups and her charities. She dresses extremely well, always has her makeup on, her hair done, and she spends a lot of time working out."

"You don't like her," he said, shooting her a look. "Just because of her relationship with your dad?"

"Well, I don't love that, but even before they got involved, I wasn't a fan, and Whitney has never cared for me. She doesn't like Hamilton's friendship with me, or that we share a common love of astronomy. It seems to make her jealous in some way. But since she started seeing my father, she pretends to like me. It's not genuine, but that's fine. We do not have to be friends."

"Does your father want you to be friends?" Wyatt asked, as he turned off the highway and headed into the hills where there was a lot less traffic.

"Yes. He keeps telling me that Whitney has changed since she took his class on living your best life. She's now in tune with her emotions and is seeking peace instead of material goods and personal recognition. I don't believe that for one second. But I want my father to be happy. And I know how much Hamilton cares about Whitney's happiness, so I try to be friendly."

"It's a tangled web."

She blew out a breath, twisting her fingers together. "Yes. And if there's some kind of conspiracy going on at Nova Star that involves one of the Tremaines, I think things are going to get more complicated."

"You mentioned that you and your father reconnected several months ago?" Wyatt asked.

She frowned, having a feeling she knew where he was going. "Yes."

Wyatt glanced over at her. "Don't want to talk about it?"

He'd obviously heard the restraint in her voice. "I know what you're going to suggest—that my father reaching out to me to put him right into the Tremaine inner circle."

"Well, it did, didn't it?"

"Yes, but that was all by chance."

"Was it?" Wyatt countered. "You're a scientist, Avery. Is

that what the data tells you?"

"Don't play the science card. We're talking about my father." She settled back in her seat as Wyatt concentrated on the traffic. She didn't want to consider the fact that her dad could be involved in anything, because that seemed completely unbelievable. "My dad wouldn't have access to proprietary material. It's not like Whitney works at the company. She's rarely even at Nova Star."

"You're probably right."

She wondered if he really believed that. Despite the fact that they'd gotten closer, there was a part of Wyatt that she couldn't quite read. Even when he seemed to be in a sharing mood, he still held back. She was quite certain that there were things he knew that she didn't. But she believed he wanted to find Noelle's killer. And at the moment, that was the most important thing.

Twenty minutes later, Wyatt stopped at the guard house for the gated community her father lived in. She leaned over and gave her name to the female guard, Jessica, who she'd seen several times before. "Hi," she said. "Family dinner."

"I heard," Jessica replied. "Have fun."

The guard gate went up, and they drove into the complex and up several hilly streets before reaching her dad's home. They snagged a spot in the driveway and then made their way to the front door.

"This is nice," Wyatt said, his gaze scanning the house and surrounding area. While there were nearby neighbors, tall trees and shrubs prevented them from being seen. "It's not quite as large as Hamilton's home, but it's very luxurious."

"My father likes luxury. And even when he didn't have as much money as he does now, he wanted to appear successful. We always rented nice homes and my dad wore expensive suits, even when he was just job hunting. He said success breeds success, and I can't say he's wrong. He turned a book without a particularly original idea into a huge motivational enterprise. People actually use him to improve their lives."

She shook her head in bemusement, still not clear on how her dad had made that happen.

"People will believe anything if you hit them at their weak spot. We're all just looking for the secret to life, right?"

She gave him a thoughtful look. "Are you looking for a secret?"

"No, not me. I've already found it," he said lightly.

"You have? Please share."

"The secret is there is no secret. You live your life as best you can, enjoy what makes you happy, and that's it."

"Sounds very simple."

"Isn't it?"

"Peace and happiness seem much more complex to me. But I tend to make things more difficult than they are. At least, that's what Noelle used to say." She drew in a breath. "She keeps coming into my head."

"That's normal. She's on your mind. You don't want to let her go."

"I know I have to let her go. Maybe it will be easier once we know what really happened to her."

"I hope so," Wyatt said somberly, as he reached for the bell. "Ready?"

"Or not—here we come," she murmured.

Brett Caldwell looked exactly like the cover of his book jacket, Wyatt thought. He was tall and attractive, with dark-brown hair and eyes, and a charming, boyish smile that inspired trust. But Wyatt knew too much about him to be sucked in.

Brett gave Avery a smile and a hug. "I'm so glad you came, Avery. I know this is a terrible time for you and the last thing you want to do is come to a party."

"Well, I wouldn't miss your birthday, Dad."

"I appreciate that. I've been worried about you. I've sent

you several texts. When you didn't answer, I even called your mother to see if you were all right and caught her on the beach in Maui. I guess if you weren't all right, she wouldn't have gone on her trip."

"I'm doing okay, hanging in there as best I can. Sorry about the messages. I just haven't felt like talking to anyone."

"I understand. Your mother said that Kari can't pay for Noelle's funeral. If you need financial help, I'm happy to contribute."

"I'll figure it out." She stepped back from her dad. "This is Wyatt Tanner. I hope you don't mind an extra guest for dinner."

Brett's gaze swung to his, becoming suddenly sharper and more assessing. "Of course not. Nice to meet you, Mr. Tanner."

"Happy birthday, Mr. Caldwell."

"Are you and Avery—"

"We're friends," Avery said quickly, before he could offer an explanation for his presence. "Wyatt works in security at Nova Star. He's been very supportive since Noelle was killed. And he's staying on top of the investigation."

"Good," Brett said with a nod. "We need some answers. Noelle was a sweetheart. What happened to her is tragic."

"I completely agree," he said.

"Avery," a woman said, appearing behind Brett.

"Hi, Whitney," Avery said, giving the other woman an impersonal hug and an air kiss. "It's good to see you."

Whitney sidled up closer to Brett, as if needing to remind Avery that she and her father were together. They did make a striking couple. Whitney had straight blonde hair and deep blue eyes with an hourglass figure that probably had had some help from a plastic surgeon at some point.

"I've been thinking about you a lot since Friday night," Whitney said. "If there's anything I can do, I hope you'll let me know."

"Thanks. I appreciate that," Avery said politely.

"Mr. Tanner," Whitney said, turning to him with a speculative gleam in her eyes. "I saw you at my father's house a couple of weeks ago. I didn't want to interrupt your meeting. It appears that you're his new favorite friend at the company."

She didn't make that sound like a compliment. "I like and respect your father a great deal. And it's nice to finally meet you. I've heard a lot about you."

"I sincerely doubt my father has told you a lot about me," she said, an edge to her voice. "But come in, come in. We are having drinks out on the terrace. My father is already here with Larry Bickmore and his wife, Karen, and Tawny Spellman and her very boring husband, Walter. Oh, and another old friend of Dad's is here, whose name I forget."

"Are your brothers coming?" Avery asked.

"They're supposed to be. Jonathan is coming solo. He and Stephanie are having a few problems, not that they've publicly stated that, but she seems to come down with a headache or some other germ every time we get together," Whitney said. "Kyle and Liz will be here, as far as I know."

"Any friends of yours, Dad?" Avery asked Brett, as Whitney moved ahead to speak to one of the caterers.

"It's a Nova Star and Tremaine night tonight," he said with a smile. "Family time."

Wyatt had a feeling that Avery was biting back a reply that had something to do with the fact that the Tremaines weren't his family, but she remained silent.

As they walked through the house, he made note of the expensive furniture, paintings, and carefully designed décor, all in keeping with what Avery had told him earlier about her dad's taste for the finer things in life. But it was the spectacular floor-to-ceiling windows and the deck off the living room that really impressed. Not only did Brett's home offer a stunning view of the hills they'd just driven through, but also the Pacific Ocean in the distance.

They followed Brett out to the terrace where a bartender

was serving drinks, and a server was offering appetizers to the group of men and women.

He had previously met both Larry Bickmore, senior counsel, and Tawny Spellman, senior vice-president of manufacturing and production, but neither meeting had gone beyond perfunctory conversation and brief security updates. While he knew little about them personally, professionally they were well-respected by their employees and colleagues. They were both also very close to Hamilton.

Larry's spouse Karen wore a very low cut, clingy dress, showing off her breasts. She already seemed to be well into cocktail hour. Tawny's husband Walter was a balding, older man, who looked like he'd rather be anywhere else.

While Avery said hello to Tawny and Walter, he snagged a crab puff off a silver tray, he had to admit this undercover gig was certainly better than most of his jobs. Usually, he was inserted into some drug dealing cartel. But his good feeling vanished when he saw the man standing closest to Hamilton Tremaine.

It was Vincent Rowland, a former FBI agent, the father of his friend Jamie, who had died during a training assignment at Quantico, a man who knew exactly who he was and what he did for a living.

He drew in a sharp breath, hoping Vincent wouldn't blow his cover. He would soon find out.

But it wasn't Vincent who greeted him first; it was Hamilton, whose bright-blue eyes seemed to have dimmed the past few days.

"Wyatt," Hamilton said, coming forward to shake his hand. "It's good to see you. I'm glad Avery brought you. I hope we can find a few moments together."

"Of course."

"Daddy, this isn't the time for business with your favorite security guy," Whitney interrupted, as she joined them. "It's Brett's party."

"Just a little business," Hamilton said, giving his

daughter an apologetic smile. "It won't take long. You don't mind, do you, Brett?" he asked, giving Avery's father a questioning glance.

"It's fine with me," Brett said, waving them off.

Hamilton turned to Vincent, who was regarding them with a contemplative expression. "Vincent—I want you to meet Wyatt Tanner. He's running my security team now. Wyatt, this is Vincent Rowland, former FBI, long-time friend."

As he stepped forward to shake Vincent's hand, he couldn't help thinking that the last time they'd exchanged a handshake had been at Jamie's memorial celebration in New York a few months ago.

Vincent looked better tonight, wearing black slacks and a sport jacket, his black hair neatly styled. He was in his mid-sixties and had an air of wealth and sophistication about him, which made sense, since he was moving in the same circle as a billionaire and a celebrity writer.

"Mr. Tanner," Vincent said, a gleam in his eyes. "You must have a busy schedule these days."

"I do," he said, happy that Vincent was protecting his cover.

"Wyatt and I need to have a few words," Hamilton added. "We'll be back soon."

"Take your time," Vincent said.

As Hamilton motioned him toward the house, he glanced over at Avery, who gave him an uneasy nod, before turning back to her conversation.

Hamilton had clearly been in the home numerous times, as he confidently made his way through the living room and dining room, where a long table was laid out with fine china and expensive crystal, down a long hallway to a dark-paneled study at the back of the house that was clearly Brett's office.

A massive mahogany desk and leather armchair was placed in front of the window. On the desk was keyboard in front of a large monitor as well as several journals and a couple of framed photographs. On one wall were framed book covers and travel photos. On the other wall, a floor-to-ceiling bookcase held numerous hardcovers and paperbacks. Avery might not have a lot in common with her father, but they both certainly liked books.

"Well, what can you tell me?" Hamilton asked, as he shut the door behind them. "Do you have any more leads into who killed Ms. Price? Is it tied to my company?"

"Yes. I believe her death is tied to Nova Star."

"Damn. I did not want you to say that. Please don't tell me Jonathan is the best suspect."

"Not yet, but that will change when the FBI figures out that Jonathan met with Ms. Price two days before her murder."

"You haven't told them that, have you?"

"No, but we need to head this off. Have you spoken to Jonathan?"

"Briefly. He brushed me off. He said he ran into her at the restaurant, and her date had bailed on her, so they had a drink."

"That's not what happened."

Hamilton gave him a pained look. "Jonathan likes women, and I know his marriage is not as happy as it could be, but he's not a murderer. Nor, is he a thief. He was just in the wrong place at the wrong time."

"Twice," Wyatt pointed out. "Right before Jia Lin was killed and now Noelle."

"It's a coincidence. And you need to prove that, Wyatt."

"Which is why I intend to speak to Jonathan tonight. He needs to know how high the stakes are."

"If he doesn't know that, he's a fool," Hamilton said. He might be loyal to his son, but he also had little patience for bad behavior. "What else have you learned?"

"Carter Hayes, Noelle's boyfriend, went through Noelle's desk after she left work Friday night. He was definitely looking for something, and it appears that Noelle might have had two phones, one of which is missing."

"And that's what everyone is looking for?"

"Possibly. Carter has been interrogated by the FBI with more interviews on tap. Carter works in Larry's department."

"Larry mentioned that. It does concern me since legal obviously has access to our patent information. But Larry assured me that Carter is a stand-up guy and a loyal employee, and Larry has always been a good judge of character. Anything else?"

"There was an email hack attempt made on Kyle's work email, and the ISP was tracked to this house." His gaze traveled to the computer on Brett's desk.

"What?" Hamilton asked, surprise in his eyes. "You're saying someone in this house tried to get into Kyle's email? Then you're talking about Brett or Whitney."

"Or perhaps Kyle was here."

"He never comes over here unless there's a mandated event, like tonight's party." Hamilton paced around the room. "No. This is just a continuation of someone's plan to target my family and set them up for whatever crimes are going down. First, Jonathan, now Whitney or Brett. We have to figure this out fast."

"Agreed." He could see the agitation building in Hamilton's eyes, and he hadn't yet dealt the biggest blow. "I also wanted to let you know that the man who broke into Noelle's apartment yesterday was found dead this morning— executed."

Hamilton sucked in a breath, his skin turning as white as his hair. "This gets worse and worse."

"I think you should postpone the launch on Tuesday."

"That's asking a lot. There are so many moving parts, Wyatt."

"I believe the launch is a target. It's a big risk to move forward with all of this going on."

Hamilton shook his head in frustration and anger. "It takes years to get to where we are right now. It wouldn't be like postponing it for a week—it could be a month or more before we could get back to a good date. We'd have to wait for the right weather conditions, and we'd have to run through all the tests and pre-checks again."

"Better to wait than to lose your satellite or more lives," he said bluntly. "There's too much we don't know."

"How do you know about the man who was found dead today?"

"I have a friend in the police department," he lied, needing to keep his connection to the bureau a secret. If he blew his cover now that he'd given Hamilton even more to worry about when it came to his family, he'd be out the door faster than he could turn around.

"But the FBI took over the case."

"They're still sharing intel with the police. You might want to reconsider your stance on the feds. Maybe working with the bureau would be helpful."

"No. We need to keep this in-house. Hell, it could be someone from the FBI trying to frame my sons."

"But you brought an ex-FBI agent to this party. I'm curious as to why."

"Oh, Vincent is an old friend," he said, waving a dismissive hand. "And he's been out of the bureau for ten years."

"Have you spoken to him about what's going on?"

"A little. He supported maintaining my own investigation, so I need you to keep doing what you're doing but do it faster. We should get back to the party. This is Brett's night, and Whitney will have a fit if we mess it up."

"What do you think of Brett?" he asked, his gaze moving toward the desk where a photograph had caught his eye. It was a picture of Brett and an elderly Chinese man standing in front of the Temple of Heaven in Beijing.

"Brett knows how to make the most of what he has. He spent a year traveling the world. China was one of his favorite places. According to him, what he learned there changed him forever."

"Interesting that he was in China."

"He went other places as well," Hamilton said, a tight note in his voice, as he read Wyatt's thoughts. He waved his hand toward the photographs on the wall. "There he is in front of the Taj Mahal in India, Buckingham Palace in London, Moscow's Red Square. Because a man is well-traveled doesn't mean he's guilty of anything. Brett can't be involved in this. I've welcomed the man into my family. He wouldn't betray me. Hell, he's Avery's father, and she loves the company as much as I do."

Wyatt waited for Hamilton to run out of steam. He didn't want Brett Caldwell to be involved in anything, either, because no matter how complicated Avery's relationship was with her father, she loved the man even more than she loved Nova Star. And the last thing he wanted to do was bring Avery more pain. She'd just lost her best friend; she couldn't lose her father, too.

"Whitney is crazy about Brett," Hamilton added. "I haven't seen her this happy since before her mother died last year. Brett brings out the best in her. She'd gotten so bitter, so angry all the time. I sometimes felt like she blamed me for not saving her mother. But I got the best doctors. We tried every experimental opportunity we could. It just wasn't enough." He cleared his throat. "Let's go back to the party. This conversation is pointless. Noelle's murderer is not part of my family circle."

He nodded, following Hamilton out of the room. He would go back to the party, but he was not going to let Brett Caldwell off the hook just yet. The timing of his entrance back into Avery's life, his fast-moving relationship with Whitney, and the fact that he'd been in both Russia and China in the past year made him a very good suspect for something…

Sixteen

━━➤➤✖◀◀━━

Avery rested her forearms on the rail and stared out at the view. After exchanging small talk with the Nova Star executives and their spouses as well as Hamilton's friend, Vincent Rowland, she moved across the terrace to take a moment for herself. Whitney was checking on dinner, and her dad had disappeared somewhere, and she just didn't have it in her to exchange party talk when her head was filled with questions and her heart was still breaking over Noelle's death.

Plus, she couldn't stop wondering what Hamilton and Wyatt were talking about. They'd been gone a long time.

"Avery? Drink?"

She glanced at her dad as he joined her at the rail. She was about to say no when she realized he was holding a lemonade mixed with iced tea.

"Your favorite," he said with a smile.

"You made me my first Arnold Palmer when I was about eleven. I've been hooked ever since." She accepted the glass and took a sip. "Perfect."

"I know this is difficult for you, honey. If you want to leave, I would understand."

"I want to stay, but I might make a quick exit after

dinner."

"Whatever you want. Jonathan just arrived. Kyle and Liz are on their way, so we'll be eating shortly."

She had been wondering where the Tremaine sons were.

As she glanced past her father, she saw Jonathan having what appeared to be a heated conversation with Whitney. "Is something going on with Jonathan and Whitney?" she asked.

Her father turned his head, following her gaze. "Sibling rivalry, probably. Whitney is very competitive when it comes to her brothers. She can't stand it if they get something she doesn't."

"What did Jonathan get that she didn't?"

"I have no idea, but she keeps track of every little thing that Hamilton does for Jonathan or Kyle and doesn't do for her."

"Like..."

"You want an example?" he asked, a curious note in his eyes.

"I'm being nosy, I know. It's just nice not to talk about anything serious or depressing."

"I can understand that. Well, Whitney got pretty ticked off when her father gave Jonathan his Porsche."

"I remember that. Kyle wasn't too happy, either."

"No, but Kyle is the one pushing Nova Star forward with his new technology, so he's getting lots of attention from his father for that. Let's face it, Whitney, Jonathan and Hamilton are just along for the ride when it comes to what's really happening at the company. It's Kyle's work that drives the business."

She thought her father was along for the ride, too, but she wasn't going to get into that with him on his birthday. She sipped her drink. "This is good."

"I wish I could do more than just give you a drink—and one without alcohol at that."

"The last thing I want is alcohol right now. I need to keep my wits about me."

His gaze narrowed. "There's something you're not telling me. What is it?"

"It's nothing. I'm just shaken after what happened to Noelle."

"From what I hear, it doesn't appear to have been a random attack. Do you think it was her boyfriend?"

"I honestly don't know, Dad."

"Well, it wouldn't totally shock me if Noelle had gotten herself into some trouble. She was no stranger to crossing a line she shouldn't cross."

"She didn't like rules, but she wasn't a criminal. She didn't break the law."

Her father didn't appear totally convinced. "I hope not."

"Now I feel like you know something I don't," she said suspiciously.

"I ran into Noelle a couple of weeks ago when Whitney and I stopped by Nova Star to drop something off at Kyle's office. I was out in the hall, because it takes like ten badges to get into Kyle's office, and I personally don't find him to be particularly interesting or friendly. He doesn't like that I'm with his sister."

"Okay. Where does Noelle figure into this story?"

"She came out of some back hallway, and when she saw me, she gave me a shocked look, like I'd just caught her doing something she shouldn't have been doing."

"She was in the engineering building?"

"Wherever Kyle works. I lose track of what's what."

"Did you talk to her?"

"For a minute. She said how grateful she was to you for getting her into the company and that she wanted to make you proud of her. But she was fidgety and acted like she couldn't wait to get away. I asked her if she was okay, and she gave me a look that took me back to when she was a little kid and she'd done something wrong but didn't want to own up to it."

Her stomach twisted at her father's words. "She didn't say anything else?"

"Well, it didn't make sense to me, but she said she was fine and that she'd finally figured out she didn't always have to pick the bad boy or the wrong path; she could use her power for good. It was just a matter of choosing which side to be on. I didn't know what she was talking about, but then someone came down the hall, and she took off."

"Why didn't you tell me this before?"

"When would I tell you? We don't speak all that often, Avery," he reminded her. "And I still don't know what she meant. Do you?"

"Not really. Her boyfriend was different than anyone else she'd ever dated. He certainly wouldn't be considered a bad boy; maybe she was talking about him."

"I haven't helped, have I? I've made things worse."

"You couldn't make things worse, Dad. But I have to know why Noelle died the way she did. She's not here to fight for herself, so I have to fight for her."

"I can understand that. But be careful. I don't like that you were with her Friday night and that her killer is still at large. Someone could think you had seen something or heard something from Noelle. Is this man you brought tonight acting as a bodyguard?"

"Of sorts," she said. "Not that I need one. But Hamilton asked Wyatt to keep an eye on me, and he's been willing to do that. Let's talk about something else. It's your birthday. And Whitney has obviously gone to a lot of trouble."

"She's been great. I know you don't like to hear it, but it's true."

"Well, that's fine. As long as you're both happy."

"I'm crazy about Whitney. She's smart and strong and a little ruthless. I like that fire in her."

"You like that she's ruthless?" she asked doubtfully.

"Let's just say I like how she goes after what she wants. She's a firecracker. Your mom was—"

"I don't want to talk about Mom," she said cutting him off.

"I know you feel like you had to take her side."

"You left. There was only one side to take."

"I left because I was searching for something missing in my life. Your mom and I were eighteen when we met—childhood sweethearts. We grew up and we grew apart. I don't know who was right and who was wrong anymore, but I've learned a lot about myself in the past several years, and I know now that I wasn't mature enough to be in a relationship with your mom."

"I'm sure she'd agree with that. I have to admit, Dad, since we're being honest, that I'm less confused about who was right and who was wrong than you are."

"I know I disappointed you. I let you down."

"You did. Many times."

"But I want to make all that up to you now. We can't change the past; we can only move forward. Are you willing to try?"

"If I wasn't, I wouldn't be here."

"Good." Relief appeared in his eyes. "I'd like to believe I'm a better person now than I used to be, but you'll have to judge that for yourself."

His words reminded her of what Noelle had said to her on Friday night, that she was trying to be a better person. *Why was she always surrounded by people who were trying to be someone else? Why couldn't they already be good?*

"What are you two talking about so seriously?" Whitney asked, interrupting their conversation with a speculative smile.

"The past," her father replied.

"Well, since it's all ancient history, maybe we should focus on right now. It's your birthday. I'm sure Avery wants you to enjoy it."

There was a challenge in the look that Whitney gave her, and she had no choice but to respond. "I do. It's all good."

"Glad to hear it. Kyle just got here," Whitney added, glancing at Brett. "He said he has something for you, for your special day, and he wants to give it to you inside. He sounded rather mysterious. Do you know what he's talking about?"

"I don't, but I'm going to find out," Brett said.

"Do it now. We're almost ready to eat. He's in the house."

As her father left, Avery was hoping that Whitney would follow, but she lingered behind.

"Are you all right, Avery?"

"I'm still a little rattled," she admitted.

"That's understandable. I know that woman was your friend. She seemed very nice."

"You met her?" she asked in surprise.

"Yes, Brett introduced her to me a couple of weeks ago. We ran into her in the cafeteria at Nova Star. She was quite beautiful, very bright."

"She was."

"Although, I guess she had some financial problems."

"How did you hear that?"

"Brett said she told him she needed to make more money and she might need to get a second job."

"Really? He never mentioned that to me." Her father had just related his conversation with Noelle to her, so was Whitney embellishing? Or had her father left something out?

"I probably shouldn't have said anything. I know he offered to help her, and I think she said she might take him up on it. Your father is a very generous man, sometimes too generous. I hate to see people take advantage of him. Anyway, can I get you a drink, maybe something stronger than that lemonade?" Whitney asked.

"No, this is fine."

"I'm going to check on dinner."

"Sure," she said, happy to see Wyatt return to the patio with Hamilton.

As Whitney left, Wyatt moved across the terrace to join her.

"How did your conversation with Hamilton go?" she asked. "Anything new?"

"Not really. Just giving him the update. I don't think I made his night any better. I noticed your father and Kyle going upstairs, deep in conversation. I wonder what that was about."

"Whitney told my dad that Kyle wanted to give him something for his birthday."

"Interesting."

"Is it?" she challenged. "Or is it just ordinary birthday party stuff, and we're both being paranoid?"

He shot her a quick look. "What are you being paranoid about?"

She hesitated. "My dad told me he ran into Noelle at Nova Star, in the engineering wing, and she looked startled and guilty when she saw him. But maybe she was just surprised to see my dad there."

"It sounds like your dad and Kyle have more interactions than we would have thought."

"I don't know. He said he went to Nova Star with Whitney who was dropping something off with her brother. He waited in the hall for her. That's where he ran into Noelle." She sipped her drink, feeling parched and tense. "This party was a bad idea. Everyone is looking like a villain. I don't know who to trust."

"Good. Because right now, you really can't trust anyone. Why don't you go inside, see if you can find a bathroom, maybe one on the second floor?"

She stared back at him, pondering the sudden change in conversation. "You want me to spy on my father and Kyle?"

"If you happen to overhear anything… But if you'd rather not…"

"I could do that. I could go upstairs. No one would think anything."

"Exactly." He nodded. "I'm going to talk to Jonathan. We'll meet up in a bit."

"Okay." As Wyatt headed in Jonathan's direction, she walked into the house relieved to see no one near the staircase. She headed up the stairs and down the hall until she heard voices.

Her father and Kyle were speaking in the upstairs family room, and the door was ajar. She looked over her shoulder to make sure she was alone and then moved down the hall, her nerves tightening with every step. Hopefully, someone wouldn't suddenly come down the hall or out of a bedroom and catch her spying on an obviously private conversation.

"Dammit, Kyle, this is not going to work," her father said. "I don't care about your excuses. You told me what you were going to do, and you didn't do it."

Her eyes widened at her father's words. *What had Kyle said he would do that he didn't do? And what did that have to do with her father?* She didn't even know that they had a friendship, much less anything they were working on.

Kyle said something in return, but she couldn't hear him.

What she did hear were footsteps coming up the stairs. She whirled around and got herself as far as the bathroom door when Whitney reached the landing.

Whitney gave her a look of surprise. "Problem, Avery?"

"No, the bathroom downstairs was being used. I hope you don't mind."

"Of course not. I was just looking for your dad. Dinner is ready."

The door to the upstairs family room opened and her father and Kyle walked out.

"There he is," she said, waving her hand toward her dad.

"Dinner is ready," Whitney told Brett.

"Great, I'm starving," Brett said with a smile. "You coming, Avery?"

"In a second. I was just going to use the bathroom."

"See you down there," Brett said, as he put his arm around Whitney's shoulders.

Kyle gave her an odd look. "Avery."

"Kyle," she returned. "It's nice to see you. Is Liz with you?"

"She's downstairs." He paused, an awkward expression on his face. "Sorry about your friend."

He didn't sound sorry, but then she'd never heard Kyle express any kind of emotion. He was a short, heavily bearded man with dark hair and dark eyes that were always guarded. He never had much to say at family gatherings, usually letting one of his more outgoing siblings, his father, or his wife take the lead.

"Thanks," she said. "Did you know her—Noelle?"

"No," he said, a brief hesitation before his response. "I never met her. But it's tragic."

"I thought she might have done some work in your department."

"I don't think so, but I suppose it's possible. We have over eighty people in the department. Sometimes the admins bring in outside help."

"That's true. It's hard to keep track of everyone. Is everything all right with you and my father?"

"I was giving him his birthday present."

"What was that?"

"Oh. It was tickets to the Lakers. I got courtside seats for him for a game against the Warriors."

"I'm sure he'll love that."

"I'll see you downstairs," Kyle said.

"Yes," she said, slipping into the bathroom, as he continued down the hall. She stared at herself in the mirror. Her eyes were way too bright, and she looked guilty as hell. She really made a terrible spy. *And what had she even learned?* That her father was angry with Kyle about something he'd promised to do but hadn't done. And that Kyle claimed he'd never met Noelle, but had backtracked rather hastily, as if he'd realized he'd just told a lie he could be caught in.

But what did any of that mean?

Hopefully, Wyatt was doing a better job at getting information.

Seventeen

---><>><<<---

Wyatt found Jonathan sneaking a smoke on a side patio, which was absolutely perfect for a private conversation. Hamilton's oldest son had turned forty a few weeks earlier and had silvery strands of gray in his dark hair. But he appeared lean and fit in his dark slacks and dress shirt.

Jonathan flashed him a guilty look as he took another hit, and then flicked the ashes into an outdoor planter. "I thought you were my sister for a second. Whitney doesn't like smoking around her house, but it has been a stressful weekend."

He nodded. "Yes, it has. Your wife isn't here?"

"No, she had a headache. She gets a lot of headaches these days," he muttered.

As suspicious as Jonathan's behavior had been the last few months, the number of times his name seemed to come up with security breaches or homicides, there was something about the man that didn't make him a good suspect. Just mentioning dryly that his wife got a lot of headaches was a little too forthcoming for someone who might have a lot to hide. He'd want to keep up the illusion of the happy marriage, the great life.

"Sorry to hear that," he said.

Jonathan shrugged. "It's fine. Whitney and Steph don't get along that well, and Steph thinks it's absolutely creepy that Whitney is sleeping with a man old enough to be her father."

"They seem to be in love."

"Whatever that is," Jonathan said cynically. "I'm surprised to see you here, although I shouldn't be. My father likes you a lot. Probably more than his own sons."

"I doubt that."

"He likes talking to you. You're a soldier. He respects you. Last thing I would ever want to be is a military man."

"Well, you seem to have a good career going."

"Courtesy of dear old Dad." He blew out a swirl of smoke. "Whitney says you came with Avery."

"I'm keeping an eye on her since the murder of her friend, Noelle Price."

Jonathan took another puff of his cigarette. "That's nasty business. I need to offer my condolences to Avery. Is there going to be a memorial?"

"Avery is working on that, but I haven't heard any details. Did you know Noelle?"

Jonathan's gaze sharpened. "Since my father already spoke to me, I know you're aware I had a drink with her last Wednesday. Apparently, you saw us together. Quite a coincidence. Were you following me?"

"It doesn't matter. What matters is that the FBI will be knocking on your door soon, and if you want me to help you, you need to be honest with me."

"Why would I need your help?"

"Because you're in trouble. Noelle is dead. Jia Lin is dead. And both women met with you shortly before they were killed."

Jonathan stared back at him and then stubbed his cigarette out on the stone planter and tossed it into the dirt. "I'm being set up."

"Help me prove that."

"Why would I trust you? You show up out of nowhere a month ago, and suddenly you're running our entire security operation? Men my father trusted for years have been relegated to lower positions since you came on board."

"Because I'm experienced in foreign and industrial espionage. You don't have to trust me, you just have to work with me. Your father wants me to protect you. I'd like to try."

Jonathan's lips tightened and then he gave a resigned shrug. "Fine. I didn't just run into Noelle. I asked her to have a drink with me, and she said yes."

"But she has a boyfriend."

"And I have a wife—so what? We weren't having sex; we were having a drink."

"How did you meet her?"

"At work. Noelle was friendly, funny. She smiled at me, which was a nice change from the glaring, irritated looks I get at home. It felt good to relax and talk to someone who didn't have any expectations."

"Are you sure she didn't want something from you? I hear she needed money."

"Yeah, she told me that. Her mom had financial trouble, and she was trying to help her. She said she was interested in working her way up at the company and wanted to know if I could give her any tips on how to get promoted. I told her to let me know if she saw any openings that she thought she might be qualified for, and I'd try to help her."

"Why would she ask you and not Avery?"

"She said Avery had a rather low opinion of her, and rightfully so. She admitted to leading a wild, irresponsible life. I liked that she was honest. Most people aren't. I guess she didn't want Avery to know that the job she'd helped her get wasn't quite enough."

Jonathan's story was so basic it actually seemed plausible. "What about Noelle's boyfriend, Carter Hayes? Do you know him?"

"Barely. I've seen him with Larry. Frankly, he didn't seem like someone Noelle would be with, but she said she was trying to make better choices in her life."

That resonated with what Avery had said.

"So, what do I need to do?" Jonathan asked.

"Do you have an alibi for Friday night?"

"Not really. I was at home alone. My wife was out with her friends."

"Well, if the FBI questions you, don't lie. Tell them what you just told me. Noelle wanted to talk to you about a job transfer. That's it."

"All right."

"Anything else you want to share? Now is the time."

"Whatever I say stays between us, right?"

"It stays between us," he lied.

"I've been thinking about why I'm on the hot seat when it should be Kyle."

"Why Kyle?"

"He asked me to take the meeting with Jia Lin when I was on my way to San Francisco. I don't normally meet with engineering candidates, but he wanted to know what I thought of her as a potential employee." Jonathan paused. "And when I first met Noelle at work, she made a point of telling me that Kyle had suggested she talk to me about a job. That's when I asked her to get a drink."

"You're saying your brother put you at both meetings?"

"Yes. But I don't think he's selling secrets or trying to sabotage the company. Why would he? This satellite is his baby. He's going to make my father proud. He's the star of the family. He wouldn't have any motive to try to take Nova Star down."

"Maybe he just wants to take you down," he said bluntly.

"Believe me, Kyle does not look at me as competition," Jonathan said, a bitter note in his voice. "He's always been the smartest one in the family. I'm the one who gets by on charm and connections."

"What about Whitney? Where does she fit?"

"Daddy's little princess. But she doesn't care about Nova Star. She's consumed with love these days and improving her spiritual life." Jonathan drew in a breath. "I know it's a big coincidence that I met with both Noelle and Jia, but they were innocent meetings. Someone is setting me up, and it's not one of my siblings. We don't sell secrets and we don't kill women. So, do what my father pays you to do, and find the real killer before someone else pays with their life."

On that note, Jonathan pushed past him, almost slamming into Avery as she came around the corner.

"Sorry, Avery," he muttered. "Didn't see you."

"No problem. Is everything all right?" Avery asked.

"Great. Dinner ready?"

"Yes, Whitney sent me to look for you guys."

"We better not keep her waiting," Jonathan said, moving quickly away.

"He seems angry," Avery said.

"We had an interesting talk. But I'm not sure we have time to rehash it now."

"We don't. Whitney is getting antsy. But can you give me the highlights?"

"Jonathan says Kyle put him at both meetings. Kyle asked him to meet with Jia and also told Noelle that she should talk to Jonathan about a job promotion."

"Kyle told me he didn't know Noelle," Avery said, her brows knitting together. "Although, he was quick to prevaricate that it was possible he'd met her but didn't remember."

"That's curious. Did you pick up on anything in the conversation between him and your dad?"

"Only that my dad was angry about something he'd asked Kyle to do. I have no idea what that was about. Whitney came down the hall, so that's all I heard, before they ended their conversation. We better go in to dinner."

As he followed Avery into the house, he thought about

what he'd learned. Kyle was becoming more interesting by the minute. Unfortunately, so was Avery's father.

—➤➤◀◀—

Dinner felt interminably long, Avery thought an hour later, as she sat at a very long table in the dining room, eating pretentious food and having meaningless conversation with Karen Bickmore, wife of Nova Star's senior counsel. Across from her, Wyatt had been squeezed in between Kyle's wife Liz and Tawny's husband Walter.

Whitney had deliberately put her at the complete opposite end of the table from her father and from Hamilton, but since she wasn't really in the mood for the party at all, she didn't much care. If Whitney needed to be by her father's side, that was fine with her. She was definitely playing the role of supportive girlfriend, chatting on about Brett's newest book, bragging about how great it was going to be.

Maybe this was what her father had needed all along, she couldn't help thinking—a relentless cheerleader. Whitney had time to cheer him on, because she didn't have to work, didn't have to raise a kid as her mother had. And all her father had to worry about was himself.

As she glanced down the table, he gave her a smile, and for just that brief moment, she thought maybe he did remember that she was there, that they had a relationship that preceded all of this.

Or did she just want to believe that? Did they even have a real relationship? Or had he used her to get to this table?

She was the one who had introduced him to the Tremaines, to Whitney, who had brought him into the inner circle, which made what she'd heard upstairs very disturbing. On the other hand, it seemed ludicrous to think that her father could be involved in espionage. *He wouldn't betray the very people sitting at this table? He wouldn't betray her, would he?*

She rolled her neck around on her shoulders, thankful when Whitney finally got up to check on the cake.

Smaller conversations broke out around the table now that Whitney had stopped holding court. A few of the men got up and wandered outside, including Wyatt and Hamilton.

"Well, that seemed endless, didn't it?" Karen murmured, as she finished what had to be her third glass of wine. "We should get some more wine. Larry, can you pass that bottle?" she asked her husband, who was sitting on the other side of her.

"I think you've had enough," he said tersely. "Excuse me for a moment."

As her husband left the table, Karen grabbed the bottle and refilled her glass. "Want some, Avery?"

She shook her head. "No, thanks."

"More for me," Karen said with a bleary smile. "Larry is always so controlled, so proper. Sometimes I wonder why I ever married him. But then we've been married a long time, almost ten years. Maybe he would have loosened up if we'd had kids. But it wasn't meant to be."

"Sorry."

"I'm sorry for you," Karen returned. "About your friend, Carter's girlfriend. It's so sad."

Her gaze narrowed at Karen's words. "You know Carter?"

"Sure. He's been to our house a few times. He's trying awfully hard to impress Larry—works late, volunteers for whatever is needed. It's a little much sometimes, but I get it. Carter wants to get ahead. I can't blame him for that. Plus, he's very attractive. That doesn't hurt."

Avery's stomach turned over at the look in Karen's eyes. "Did Carter ever bring Noelle to your house?"

"No. He didn't bring any woman. He didn't have to. If he wanted entertainment..." She paused as she gulped down more wine, then she giggled, licking her lips. "I shouldn't have said that. No one knows. It's a secret." Karen put a finger to her lips. "Sh-sh."

"When did it happen?" she asked quietly, not that anyone was listening to their conversation.

"A couple of weeks ago."

"When he was with my friend?"

Karen looked startled, as if she suddenly realized what she'd said. "I—I don't know if he was with her then. I think it was before."

Avery didn't believe her for a second. "Carter was cheating on my friend, wasn't he?"

"Well, I suppose he was, but he didn't really want to. He wanted me to get some files for him so that he could impress Larry. I told him there was a price, and he was happy to pay it."

Karen was so lit, she had no idea what she was saying.

"You gave Carter files from Larry's office?"

"They weren't important. Just small cases. Nothing big. He keeps the big stuff in his safe, and I cannot get in there. Sometimes, I wonder what else he has in that safe. He won't even tell me the combi—nation," she said, stumbling over her word with another giggle. "Where's the cake?"

"I think it's coming soon."

Karen's wine sloshed over her glass as she took another drink.

"Karen," Larry said sharply, as he returned to the table. "It's time for us to go."

"We haven't had cake yet," Karen complained. "I'm hungry. Did we eat dinner?"

"We did." He put a firm hand around his wife's arm and pulled her to her feet. "We have to leave now."

"But, I don't want to go," Karen protested.

"We're all leaving," Avery put in, wanting to make it a little easier for Larry, who was clearly embarrassed, now that some of the other guests had returned to the table and were watching the interaction.

"Oh, we are?" Karen asked.

Avery helped Larry get his wife out of the dining room and to the front door.

He paused, as Karen went stumbling down the front steps but somehow managed to stay on her feet. "I'm sorry about this. She's been having some hard times."

"Take care of her," she said, shutting the door behind him.

As she made her way back to the dining room, she wondered where Wyatt was. Hamilton had come back to the table, but Wyatt was still absent.

"Come sit next to me," her dad said, patting Whitney's empty chair. "Until Whitney comes back."

She almost refused that invitation, thinking how sad it was that he only wanted her next to him until his girlfriend returned, but it was his birthday, so she did as he asked.

"Larry's wife had a few too many," he commented. "That seems to be happening quite often."

"She does seem to have a problem," she admitted. "Whitney is taking a long time with the cake."

"She likes everything to be perfect. Do you want to leave?"

"I'll wait until the cake is served." She didn't really have a choice. She needed Wyatt to go with her, and he was nowhere in sight.

"I'm glad we have a minute," Vincent Rowland said, offering Wyatt a brief smile, as they moved into the shadows at the far side of the terrace. "I bet you were surprised to see me."

"I was. Thanks for the cover."

"Reminded me of the old days," Vincent said. "You're looking into the security leak?"

"Did Hamilton tell you about that? Or was it Joanna Davis?"

"They both did, as a matter of fact. But I didn't share my conversation with Joanna with Hamilton, if that's what you're wondering. Are you getting close to a breakthrough?"

"I have some new leads, but I'm not sure where they'll go yet."

Vincent nodded. "You've always had good intuitive instincts and the ability to slip into any persona at any moment. I was never good at that. I could never be someone else quite so easily." He paused. "I think Jamie would have been good at it, though. He could charm anyone."

His gut tightened at the mention of his friend. "I'm sure he would have been great. I heard Cassie is getting married."

"Yes. She had a big engagement party last night. That's why I'm in town. I stopped in at the office earlier today, and I saw Bree. She looks good. I hear she has a new man in her life."

There was a definite edge to Vincent's voice now. Maybe Bree was right. Maybe he never had liked her and always thought she was somehow responsible for Jamie's distraction, his death. But Vincent couldn't have been more wrong.

However, as much as he wanted to defend Bree, this was not the time or the place. Anyone could walk out at any moment. He cleared his throat. "How long will you be in town?"

"A few days." Vincent glanced around to make sure they were still alone. "What's your relationship with Avery Caldwell?"

"I'm watching out for her."

"Seems like there's some interest between you two."

He shrugged. "She's a job."

"Well, it's good that she's not more than that."

"Why is it good?"

"Because I'm concerned about her father. Ever since Hamilton told me about the problems he's having, I wondered if he wasn't looking past what was right in front of him: a man who has traveled the world, has many friends in China,

Russia, and elsewhere, and made a surprising entrance into his family, into his company, into his daughter's life."

"It would be difficult for Brett to get access to the kind of information that's already been shared."

"Maybe—maybe not. I would just caution you not to be blinded by the brunette with the pretty brown eyes, who would probably not want you to go after her father."

"We should get back to the party," he said, not really caring for the conversation. He didn't need Vincent to tell him how to do his job, that Brett was a good suspect, or that Avery would hate him if he revealed her father to be a part of whatever criminal conspiracy was going on.

"I'll be in shortly. I have to make a call," Vincent said.

He walked around the corner and ran into Avery.

"There you are," she said. "Who were you talking to?"

"Hamilton's friend. Did Whitney bring the cake out?"

"Finally. She sent me to find you."

"Here I am."

"I have a lot to tell you when we're done with this party."

"I have a lot to tell you, too," he said.

"I wonder if it's going to be about the same person," she murmured.

As he took her back into the dining room, he wondered that, too. But, somehow, he didn't think that Avery would have come to the conclusion that her father was a traitor and maybe a murderer.

Eighteen

—➤➤➤◄◄◄—

Despite wanting to leave right after the cake had been served, it was another half hour before they were able to get out the door.

As Avery slid into the passenger seat just after eleven, she let out a sigh of relief. "That took forever. Can you turn the heat on?"

"Sure. You should have brought something warmer than that wrap, as pretty as it is."

"I was going to, but I realized the only coat I packed was the one that has Noelle's blood on it." She glanced out at the starry night sky as they drove away from her father's house and said, "Maybe I should go up in a rocket. Another galaxy is looking pretty good right now. But I know I can't run away from reality, as much as I want to." She turned her head toward Wyatt. "Did you learn anything else at dinner or afterwards?"

"Not really. What about you?"

"Karen Bickmore told me in a drunken ramble that she was sleeping with Carter."

"What?" he asked in surprise.

"She said Carter is very ambitious and came out to the

house a few times and even asked her to get something out of Larry's desk, but she didn't say what."

"That's new."

"I just don't know if she was telling the truth. She was wasted."

"It doesn't seem like something she'd make up. This is good, Avery."

"Really? I feel like it's all just random pieces of information. Nothing goes together."

"Not yet, but we're getting closer."

"Or farther away." She paused as Wyatt took a turn, heading into the canyon that would lead them back to the beach and to their hotel. "Did you ever ask Kyle about the email hack?"

"I did. He said he hadn't attempted to access his email from Whitney's house. He was going to speak to Whitney and Brett about it."

She glanced at Wyatt. "You don't think my father is involved in this, do you? He's a lot of things, but he's not a killer. He's not violent. Words are his weapon."

"He has spent time in China and Russia."

She frowned, wishing Wyatt had given her a different answer. "So have millions of people. And his contacts are spiritual advisers. They're not tech people."

"Your dad is probably completely innocent. I'm just curious about his conversation with Kyle, what he wanted Kyle to do that didn't happen."

"I should have asked my dad; I just didn't want him to know I was eavesdropping."

"It's best that you didn't. You don't want to show your hand."

"Not that I have any good cards," she countered. "I'm not a very good detective or spy."

He flashed her a smile. "You're doing very well, Avery. Answers can take time."

"I feel that might be time we don't have."

"We're working as quickly as we can."

As they drove through the dark canyon roads, the headlights from the car were the only light they had. It felt a little eerie, and she kind of wished they'd gone around to the freeway instead of cutting through the hills. But that was silly. No one else was even on the road.

No sooner had that thought crossed her mind when she saw a light in the side-view mirror.

She shifted in her seat and glanced over her shoulder.

"It's fine," Wyatt said, but she could hear a tension in his voice.

"Is it?"

Wyatt didn't reply, his gaze darting from the road to the mirror as the lights behind them got brighter. He pressed his foot down hard on the gas, taking the next turn at a fast rate of speed.

She looked over her shoulder, hoping to see that the other vehicle had fallen back, but it was drawing closer. It looked to be a large SUV of some sort.

"Hang on," Wyatt said.

"What are you going to do?"

"Outrun him."

Despite his promise, their car was bumped from behind a moment later. They swerved toward the hillside, but Wyatt quickly brought the vehicle back under control. Swearing under his breath, he pushed the car to the limit, but the vehicle behind them had more power and was soon within inches of their bumper.

The road grew narrow, twisting and turning through the hills—nowhere to turn, nowhere to escape.

She grabbed onto the armrest, biting down on her lip, wanting to close her eyes, but afraid to stop looking ahead in case she could help Wyatt in some way. They were coming out of the canyon. Maybe once they reached the Pacific Coast Highway, the person would back off.

If they didn't, she really didn't want to think about the

fact that going south on the highway, they'd also be on the ocean side of the road, and at some points that road went along a very high bluff over the ocean.

Her heart thundered against her chest as the car hit them hard from behind once again.

Wyatt hung on to the wheel as the back end of the car fishtailed for a moment, sending up dirt and rocks in their wake. And then Wyatt sped ahead once more.

They came out on the highway. She searched the road for somewhere to hide or run...

"Around the next curve," she said, remembering a spa she'd once gone to that was hidden away down a narrow road behind a wall of trees. "There's a road to the left. It comes up fast."

"Got it," he said in clipped tones.

She held on tight as Wyatt pushed the car as fast as it could go. The other car fell back.

They flew around the curve. Wyatt saw the road and took it on two wheels, turning off the lights as they disappeared into the trees. She knew he didn't want to hit the brakes, didn't want any light to show, but they were going too fast; another curve was coming up, and she held her breath, hoping this escape wasn't going to end in a fiery crash.

Finally, he slammed on the brakes as they went around another corner, and the side of the car skimmed off two trees, sending branches across the windshield, but, thankfully, the glass didn't break. They came to a halt. Her heart was pounding so loud, she couldn't hear anything else.

Wyatt turned in his seat. She did the same, as they both looked behind them. The road was empty, but she didn't know if they were safe or not.

Once the other car realized that they'd turned off the highway, they'd be back.

Wyatt must have had the same thought. "Where does this road go?" he asked.

"To a spa. It's a dead end." She really wished she hadn't

used the word *dead*.

Wyatt threw the car into reverse.

"What are you doing?" she asked in alarm.

"Getting out of here."

"What if they're waiting for us on the highway?"

"That's why we have to move now."

He turned around and then went back the way they'd come, keeping the lights off, which made the journey even more harrowing as there were so many trees, so many shadows. When they got back to the highway, he looked in both directions. There was a small coupe coming from the north, definitely not the car that had been behind them, and nothing from the south.

Wyatt pulled out onto the road heading north. He drove two miles and then turned in to the parking lot of a twenty-four-hour supermarket. Parking between two trucks, he cut the motor and the lights. From their position, they could see the entrance to the lot, and they watched for several tense minutes as cars passed by on the highway, with a minivan turning in, followed by a sedan. A woman and an older teenager stepped out of the van, while a young couple exited the other car.

"Do you think we lost them?" she asked.

"I think so. But we can't stay here. And we can't go back to the hotel."

"Why not? They followed us from my dad's house, not from the hotel. They might not know where we're staying."

"I'm not taking that chance." He pulled out his phone.

"What are you doing?"

"Calling for a ride."

"We're leaving the car here?"

"Yeah. We'll get it later." He paused. "There's a driver two minutes away."

"Where are we going to go, Wyatt?"

"We'll find another hotel. But right now, I just want to get us out of this car and on our way to another location."

She liked the idea of switching cars, although she wouldn't have thought of it. But Wyatt had. He'd driven through the canyon like a race car driver, never panicking, never losing control. He'd kept his head, and he'd probably saved her life—again.

She pulled out her phone and searched for a hotel. "What city do you want to go to?"

"Let's get into a more populated area."

She looked through the hotel listings. "There are a bunch of hotels by the airport."

"Perfect. Pick one, and I'll put in our destination."

She picked the hotel that was located between two others, thinking maybe it would be safer, although she had no idea why that would be. She gave him the address.

Wyatt tapped in the address and they waited in silence until their ride turned into the lot.

They got out of the car and met their driver in front of the market. He was a college kid driving a small black Hyundai. She kind of wished they'd gotten a ride in a more substantial vehicle, although maybe this was less obvious.

She wanted to talk to Wyatt but didn't want to say anything in front of the driver, although the young male was rocking out to a rap song blasting out of the radio and not paying them a bit of attention.

It took twenty minutes to get to the airport hotel, and she felt like she was holding her breath the entire time. When they got to the hotel, they made their way quickly inside. Wyatt checked them in, using a credit card, which worried her, but she didn't say anything until they were on their way upstairs in the elevator.

"Can't someone track us through your credit card?" she asked.

"Don't worry about it," he said vaguely.

She frowned at that answer, once again thinking that no matter how much she liked Wyatt and had come to depend on him, he still seemed to have his own secrets. But she still stayed close to him as they walked down the hall and entered their room—one room, she couldn't help noticing, although there were two beds.

"It's all they had left," Wyatt said, reading her mind. "You can trust me, Avery."

"I'm not worried about sharing a room with you. But tell me about the credit card. Can't someone trace it to us?"

He stared back at her. "I told you I changed my name."

"Yes."

"Well, I didn't change all my cards."

"It still seems like it could be tracked to you."

"It would take some work and some time. We'll be gone by then."

"Will we?" she asked, wandering around the modest, impersonal hotel room. "What happens next? I have to go to work tomorrow. The reporters are coming in for the show. I'm sure you have things to do."

"We'll figure it out, Avery."

She stared back at him, feeling wired and terrified and restless. "Someone tried to kill us just now. They tried to run us off the road. We could be dead."

"But we're not. We're very much alive."

"Why aren't you having a reaction?" she demanded, annoyed with his calm demeanor.

"I feel like there's no good answer to that question," he said carefully. "Do you want some water?"

"No, I don't want some water," she said with irritation. "I want you to feel the way I do. I want you to be normal, to be afraid, to be human, instead of like some ice-cold, superhero."

He walked across the room and put his hands on her shoulders. "I'm not a superhero."

"The way you drove tonight, you could have fooled me."

"It's over now, Avery. We're okay for tonight. We'll be safe here. You can breathe again."

She stared back at him, really wanting to believe him. "Do you think they were waiting outside my dad's house?"

"I'm guessing they picked us up after we drove through the guard gate. I didn't see anyone until we hit the canyon, but they were probably hanging back."

"Do you think it was the man with the tattoo again?" Something shifted in Wyatt's gaze. "What? What aren't you telling me?"

"That man is dead, Avery."

"Seriously?" she asked in surprise. "How do you know that?"

"I followed up with the FBI earlier."

"When we were at Nova Star?"

He hesitated. "Yes."

"But why didn't you tell me, Wyatt? Didn't you think I'd be relieved to know he was dead?" She paused. "Wait a second. Who killed him?"

"All I was told was that it looked like a hit."

"Like a hit? What does that mean?"

"Someone took him out, Avery. Maybe whoever he was working for knew we could identify him. He became a loose end."

"So, they just killed him? Just like that? What kind of world is this?"

"Not a world you should be living in," he said tersely. "I need to get you out of it."

"But I am living in it. And I'm still in danger. *We're* in danger."

"Until we figure out who is responsible, yes."

She paced around the room, wishing she could be happy that the man who had pulled a gun on her was now dead, but it just seemed to make things worse.

Wyatt sat down on the bed and took off his shoes. The casual gesture startled her.

"What are you doing?" she asked.

"Getting more comfortable. Why don't you try it?"

"I'm too tense. I can't just sit down and relax."

"Then pace it out. I wouldn't try the screaming exercise

here," he said. "Or security will come running."

"You're joking right now?"

"Just trying to lighten the mood. Sit down, Avery. Take a breath."

She made three more trips back and forth across the room before she moved to the bed and sat down on the mattress across from him. After a moment, she kicked off her high heels.

"That wasn't so hard, was it?" he asked.

"Yes, it was," she said. "How do you handle it all so well, Wyatt? You don't seem bothered by what happened."

"I'm concentrating on the positive. We survived. We're safe. I'm staying in the moment, Avery. It's all we can do."

"Is it all we can do? I'm thinking we should call someone—the police or the FBI. You said you spoke to an FBI agent earlier today. You must have a number. We should tell someone that we were almost killed tonight. Maybe they can do something."

"There's nothing anyone can do tonight. I couldn't identify the car, other than that it was a large, black SUV. I didn't catch the license plate. I couldn't even tell you how many people were in the car."

"I couldn't say that, either," she admitted.

"We can touch base with the bureau in the morning. It's almost midnight. I think we should get a few hours of sleep. We'll go into work tomorrow. While you handle your show and the media tour, I'll call the agent I spoke to today, let them know what happened and see what I can find out."

His logic was difficult to argue with, and as the minutes ticked by, she found her panic beginning to subside. Wyatt was right. They were safe for now. And with no information to go on, no one was going to be able to catch whoever had been following them anyway.

Wyatt took off his suit jacket and tossed it on the end of the bed. Then he leaned against the pillows, his legs stretched out in front of him. "This bed isn't too bad," he said. "You want to turn on the TV?"

"This is so weird," she said, with a shake of her head. "You're trying to be normal, but this is not normal."

He smiled. "What is normal anyway?"

"Well, it's not this."

"So, no TV then. What do you want to do?"

She stared back at him, and suddenly her tension shifted. *What did she want to do?* What she *should not* do!

Wyatt's mouth tightened, and he gave a subtle shake of his head. "Forget I asked that."

"Why?"

"Because what you're thinking is a bad idea."

"How do you know what I'm thinking?" she challenged.

"Your eyes are glittering. Your face has new color in it. And you're looking at me like a woman feeling incredibly reckless."

"I do feel reckless," she admitted. "We almost died today. Hell, we almost died yesterday. Who knows what's going to happen tomorrow?"

"We're not going to die."

"You can't promise me that."

His jaw tightened, and his gaze filled with shadows. "You're right. I can't promise you that, but I can tell you I'll do everything in my power to protect you."

"Why? Because Hamilton asked you to?"

Her simple question hung in the air for a long minute.

"Because I care about you," he said slowly.

Her whole body tingled at his words. "I thought I was just a job."

"I've been trying to keep you in that category, but I can't. You're a beautiful woman, Avery, not just on the outside. You're kindhearted, generous, and fiercely loyal, putting your own life at risk to get justice for Noelle. And you're a dreamer. Earlier today, you made me look up at the stars, and I haven't done that in a really long time. You made me think about possibilities." He paused, meeting her gaze. "It's hard to be cynical around you."

His words pulled at her heart. "Really? I feel so pessimistic right now."

"That's not pessimism; that's fear. But you're fighting. You haven't given up. You haven't thrown in the towel. You have courage."

"I don't have courage. I'm terrified."

"But when you act in the face of fear, that's bravery. It doesn't matter if you're scared. It only matters what you do."

"Is that what they taught you in the Marines?"

"It's what I've learned over my lifetime. I've been in some bad situations. As long as you don't give up, you can always find a way out. So, we're not going to give up."

"No, we're not," she agreed. "Wyatt...what you just said—it was really nice. If you were trying to make me like you less, it didn't work."

His lips curved into a sexy smile and her breath caught in her chest.

"Wrong tactic, huh?" he drawled.

She nodded. "That connection I was talking about before—it's even stronger now. I've never felt like this before, and it's not just because you're protecting me. It's because I can talk to you. I can be my complete and utter self and know you're not going to judge."

"I'm the last person who should judge anyone. There's a lot you don't know about me, Avery."

There was a warning note in his voice, but she blasted right through it. "There's a lot you don't know about me, too. But isn't part of the fun finding out what we don't know?"

He cleared his throat. "Where's that TV remote?"

She gave him a knowing smile. "Now, who's getting scared?" she teased.

"I'm trying to be professional, Avery."

"You don't have to be professional after midnight." She checked her watch. "And it's two minutes after." She got up from the bed and breached the distance between them, sitting down next to him and putting her hand on his very hard, masculine chest.

"Avery, stop," he said, covering her hand with his. "We can't do this."

"Why not?"

"You're too vulnerable. This isn't what you want. I'm not *who* you want."

"Yes, you are."

"There's too much you don't know, Avery."

"The only thing I need to know right now is whether you want me, too."

Shadows flew across his face. There was a fight going on in his eyes, and she didn't know why. "I've never really had to talk anyone into taking me to bed before," she murmured. "Have I misread this? Do you not feel the same way?" Doubt suddenly ran through her. "Am I embarrassing myself?"

She tried to pull her hand away, but now he was holding on to her instead of pushing her away.

"You aren't misreading anything. I want you, too—in every possible way."

"Then why are you saying no? Why aren't you following your philosophy to live in the moment?"

"I don't want to hurt you."

"I've been hurt a lot already. I don't think tonight is going to be about that."

"Tomorrow might be."

She smiled at his cynicism. "Hey, look up, remember," she said, squeezing his fingers. "See the possibilities, not the improbabilities. I borrowed that from Hamilton, by the way."

"It's a good line," he said. "But not as good as this." He pulled her forward, so close she could feel the heat of his breath, but still he hesitated. "I know we should not do this."

"And I know we should. No regrets," she whispered. "Just you, me, tonight…that's all we can count on. All we need." And with that, she put her mouth on his.

All hesitation, reluctance, restraint, worries about doing

the right thing, vanished with their first kiss.

It didn't just feel good—it felt right...*perfect*.

She couldn't get enough of Wyatt's mouth, his taste, the slide of his tongue against hers, his warm, sexy heat. Pleasure spread through her, tingling every nerve. She wanted to touch him, and the buttons of his shirt were right in front of her.

She flicked them open, one by one and then pressed her palm against his skin, running her fingers through the smattering of brown hair. She pressed her mouth against his chest and took delight in the groan that escaped his lips.

She lifted her head and smiled into his eyes. "You like that?"

"I like you." He ran his hand through her hair, pulling her down for a kiss.

And then he turned the tables on her, switching positions, tumbling her onto her back. She sank into the soft mattress as he covered her body with his.

He ran his thumb across her mouth, following that gesture with his lips, and she drank him in like a long, cool drink on the hottest day imaginable.

His hand ran up her thigh under her dress, and she shivered with anticipation, wanting him to touch her there and everywhere.

"You're so amazing, Avery," he breathed, lifting his head to gaze at her. "I want to take my time but damn...the way you kiss..."

Her heart pounded against her chest at the hungry look in his eyes.

"The way *we* kiss," she breathed. "The way *we* touch. It's not me or you—it's us."

"Hell, yes, it's us," he said, pulling back so that he could take off his shirt.

She caught her breath once more at the sight of him. Wyatt was in incredible shape. He actually had a six-pack, and his well-defined abs, muscular arms, and broad shoulders all made her mouth water. If anyone was amazing, it was him.

She almost felt a little self-conscious at her soft, not-at-all-defined muscles, but she didn't have time to think about it as Wyatt took off his pants.

"Wow," she muttered.

He smiled. "Your turn, babe."

She sat up and pulled her dress over her head, glad she'd worn a lacy black bra and matching thong. She'd always had full breasts, and Wyatt's appreciative gaze made her feel beautiful, feminine, wanted... But as he came in for another kiss, the sane part of her brain made one last gasping attempt to make her think.

"Wait," she said.

His gaze darkened. "Second thoughts?"

"Condom. I don't have any with me."

"Right." He reached back for his pants and pulled out his wallet and a foil package.

"Always prepared."

"Since I met you," he said.

She didn't really believe that, but she pulled him down on top of her. "Thank God you sometimes think ahead and don't always live in the moment."

"Thank God," he echoed, as he lowered his head and kissed her again. And then he dropped his mouth to her breasts, his fingers slicing underneath the lace of her bra, teasing her nipples into tight points of pleasure. She ached with need, running her hands over his back as they moved together, kissing, touching, and loving each other in all the ways she'd ever imagined...

Nineteen

—➤➤◄◄◄—

Wyatt tightened his arms around Avery as he woke up just before five. The room was still dark, and the air had chilled considerably since their fevered lovemaking of the past few hours. He didn't know when they'd finally fallen asleep. Maybe an hour ago?

He pulled the covers up and over them. Avery snuggled closer to him, her face just inches away from his own. He smiled to himself, feeling ridiculously…what was the word…oh, yeah—happy. He felt happy, and he couldn't really remember when he'd felt this happy. It wasn't just the sex that had been spectacular. It was Avery. She'd blown him away even before they'd gotten naked together, but tonight…

He didn't even know how to describe it. But for the first time in a long time, he felt himself, which was crazy, because he was still living a lie. But for a few hours, he hadn't been undercover, he hadn't been an FBI agent, he hadn't even been the guy who'd watched his father and brother go to prison. He'd just been himself—the person he'd thought he'd lost, forgotten, or maybe just put away.

He frowned at the direction of his thoughts. Talk about losing the happy mojo as fast as possible. He needed to keep hanging onto the moment, because he was pragmatic enough to know that this moment wasn't going to last forever, or even for very much longer. The light was coming, and he wished he could hold it off, let Avery relax and sleep in blissful oblivion for a while longer.

He'd told her he would do everything he could to protect her, and he believed he could keep her out of physical danger, but emotional danger…that was another story. His gut was telling him that whoever had killed Noelle, whoever had gone after them last night, was probably someone Avery knew, maybe even someone she cared about. He really hoped it wasn't her father. She could probably handle betrayal from the Tremaines, but her dad—that would devastate her.

"You're crushing me," Avery said, blinking her eyes open.

"Sorry." His grip on her had obviously gotten tighter as his thoughts had gone to a dark place.

"What time is it?"

"Five-ish," he said. "You can go back to sleep."

"But you can't," she said, making it a statement and not a question.

"I don't think so. My brain has fired up."

"Come to any answers?"

"Unfortunately, no, but we have a lot of leads to follow. Hopefully, one of them will take us somewhere."

"Somewhere that doesn't involve my dad," she said.

He stroked the soft skin of her back. "That would be my preference as well. I just wish he hadn't spent time in Russia and China."

"The Tremaines have traveled there as well, and my dad has no motivation to spy on Nova Star."

"Money is always a motivation."

"He's already rich. It's not him. He's not a criminal, even if he's not the greatest father or even person."

"Okay," he said, seeing the agitation in her eyes.

"You don't believe me," she said with annoyance.

"I just remember saying the same thing about my father at first. I couldn't believe the evidence that was in front of my eyes. Eventually, I had to acknowledge that I was wrong, that I couldn't defend him."

"This situation isn't the same, Wyatt. And I'm not wrong."

"All right. We'll work all the other angles and leave your father out of it."

"Thank you. There are certainly a lot of other people with more to gain. We should make a list. I like lists. They keep me organized."

He smiled. "I bet they do, but we can do that later," he said, kissing her forehead.

The smile returned to her eyes. "Really? You have something else you want to do now?"

"I do actually."

"So, do I."

"I like how we're on the same page."

"I like a lot of things about us," she murmured. "Kiss me already."

His lips had barely touched hers when a loud bell went off in the hallway.

"Is that the fire alarm?" she asked.

He jumped out of bed and began collecting their clothes. "Get dressed," he said, as the bells continued to ring.

"Maybe it's a false alarm," she said, as he handed her dress to her.

Or maybe it wasn't a fire but a way to get them out of the hotel.

He threw on his clothes at record speed. He could hear doors opening and closing, people talking in the hallway, and his gut told him this was bad—very bad.

The phone by the bed rang, and he grabbed it as Avery put on her dress and slid into her heels, shaking out her tangled hair with her hands.

The call was recorded, alerting them to the need for them

to evacuate their room as calmly and as quickly as possible, using the closest stairwell.

"What did they say?" Avery asked, as she picked up her bag.

"To leave our room in an orderly manner." He put on his jacket and made a quick check of the room. They hadn't brought anything with them, so there were no bags to worry about, and Avery already had the strap of her purse over her shoulder.

They walked to the door, and he took a quick peek outside before he opened it.

"Are you checking for fire?" Avery asked, her hand on his back.

"Yeah," he said shortly. But he was more worried that someone had followed them to the hotel than that there was a fire. Although, that was probably shortsighted, considering what had happened to Noelle's apartment building.

He opened the door. An elderly couple was making their way down the hallway, the man grumbling about the damned fire alarm. He didn't smell smoke, but that didn't necessarily mean anything. They followed their fellow guests to the stairwell, making their way down six flights of stairs. He grabbed Avery's hand as they neared the first floor and the emergency exit.

He leaned in and whispered, "Stay close to me. If I say run—run."

She glanced back at him, her eyes widening as she realized he was concerned about more than a fire. But he saw the gleam of determination enter her gaze.

"Got it," she said.

The emergency exit led them out the back of the hotel, and they were quickly pushed along with the others into the parking lot. While they were surrounded by people, he still felt exposed. He saw no flames, and while there appeared to be fire engines in front of the hotel, he still wasn't convinced there was a fire.

Unfortunately, they couldn't go back inside, nor could they easily leave. It was five o'clock in the morning and they didn't have a car. Calling a cab or a rideshare service was going to take a few minutes.

"What do you think?" Avery asked, huddling close to him as he held tight to her hand.

"I don't like it."

"Should we try to go somewhere else?"

"Yeah, let's move toward the front of the hotel where there are more people. The group they'd been in was quickly dispersing. They'd no sooner taken a step when he felt something whiz by his ear and the front window of a nearby car shattered. A moment later, another window blew out.

Someone yelled, "Shooter."

He broke into a run, pulling Avery along with him, as they dodged between cars in the huge parking lot, glass being broken every few seconds.

Thankfully, there were probably fifty or sixty cars, not only in the hotel lot, but in the rental car parking lot next door. Plus, there were now a lot of people running, so they weren't as noticeable.

He tried to get them away from the lights, into the darker corner of the lot, relieved when he heard more sirens.

He started flipping car door handles, until one opened. It was a rental car sedan. As Avery got in the passenger side, he ran around the car and got behind the wheel, slamming the door fast so there was no light.

Avery stared back at him with terror in her eyes and she slinked down in her seat. "Now what? Are we sitting ducks?"

"No." He pulled a set of keys out of the console.

"No way," she breathed.

"Must be our lucky day." He started the car and backed out of the spot, heading toward the exit. There were other cars leaving the area as well. He didn't know if any of those held the shooter or if they were filled with people trying to escape, but hopefully they would blend in.

When he got onto the street, he sped up, then maneuvered his way through the city by taking side streets and making unexpected turns to make sure no one was on their tail.

They'd gone about five miles when he started to breathe a little easier.

"I think we're okay," he said, looking over at Avery.

The sun was starting to come up, and he could see her face better now. She was pale but stoic, no sign of tears or panic. Considering this was the second time in less than twelve hours that they'd had to run for their lives, she was holding up amazingly well. He turned at the next corner and pulled into a parking lot behind a trio of retail shops. He turned off the lights but kept the engine on in case they had to make a quick exit.

"Why are we stopping, Wyatt?"

"I'm trying to figure out where to go," he admitted. "I'm also trying to figure out how they found us at the hotel."

"The fire alarm—it was just to get us out of the hotel."

"Yeah. I had a bad feeling about it. We probably should have stayed put."

"I don't understand how they found us."

"Maybe they traced the rideshare pickups in that area."

"Wouldn't that take some kind of police warrant? Would the people following us have that capability?"

"I don't know, but they found us, so they did something." His gaze fell to the handbag on Avery's lap. "Let me see your bag."

"Why?"

"Just let me take a look."

She handed her bag over, and he searched through it, pulling out her wallet, a brush, a couple of lipsticks, sunglasses, and a compact. For a woman's purse, it was fairly tidy—typical Avery, he thought. But there was something loose at the bottom. He pulled out what looked like a bead from a necklace and held it up to Avery. "Recognize this?"

"No. What is it?"

"It's a GPS tracker. Someone put it in your purse."

"Oh, my God, they could be right behind us."

"Not for long." He checked to make sure there was nothing else in her bag, then tossed the bead out the window and peeled out of the lot.

He got on the nearby freeway and drove south for several miles, then exited and drove city streets, carefully checking his mirrors for a tail. The sun was coming up higher in the sky and the neighborhoods were starting to wake up.

As he stopped at a light, he looked over at Avery. "Are you okay?"

"Yes. But do you have a plan beyond just driving around?"

"We need to kill an hour. We can go to Nova Star at seven. That's when all the security will be coming in, setting up for the day, checking the offices, the building, in preparation for the media."

"All right. I guess we can just drive around—" She stopped abruptly, her gaze dropping to his chest. "Oh, my God, Wyatt, you're bleeding."

"What?" he asked in bemusement.

"Your side. There's blood all over your shirt. You were hit."

"I don't feel anything," he said. But as he looked down, he could see blood all over the bottom half of his shirt. As the light changed, he pulled over to the side of the road. Then he pulled up his shirt, revealing a slice wound across his side. "It's not a big deal," he said, the pain starting to come now that he was coming down off the adrenaline high. "It's just a graze."

"It's still bleeding," she said with concern. "And that's a big deal. You need to have that cleaned, maybe stitched. We have to go to the hospital."

"No. They'll find us there. If they think they hit one of us, that's the first place they'll check."

"Well, we can't just sit here while you bleed."

No, they couldn't. He needed to get Avery somewhere safe, and right now there was only one person he could trust. Luckily, she lived about ten minutes away. He didn't want to bring danger to her, but if anyone could handle it, it was Bree.

He pulled out his phone and sent her a quick text, hoping she'd answer by the time he got to her house.

"Who did you contact?" Avery asked.

"A friend. We'll go to her house."

"I don't think we should bring anyone else into this."

"She can handle it."

"She?" Avery echoed.

He didn't answer as his phone buzzed. He glanced down at the text. Bree had sent him her address and told him to park in the driveway. "It's going to be fine," he told Avery.

"Why don't I drive?"

"I can make it," he said, forcing the lightheaded feeling out of his head. He powered down his phone, then turned to Avery, realizing he should have gotten rid of the phones at the same time he got rid of the tracker, but, clearly, he wasn't thinking as well as he should be. "Give me your phone."

"My phone?" she asked unhappily. "I have everything on my phone."

"It's backed up, right?"

"Yes."

"Then you don't need this one." He turned it off and then drove down the alley and tossed both phones into a nearby dumpster.

With the pain starting to increase in his side, he drove as quickly as he could to Bree's house.

She met them at the door. "Come in," she said. "What happened?"

"We got shot at," he said, his words starting to slur.

"Wyatt got hit," Avery put in, her arm sliding around him.

"It's nothing. I just need to sit down," he said.

Bree put her arm around his other side, and the two women helped him to the couch. Then Bree ran into the nearby bathroom and came back with some towels.

"Put pressure on the wound," she said to Avery, handing her a towel. "I'm Bree, by the way."

"I'm Avery."

"I know," Bree said. "I'll be right back with my first aid kit."

Avery helped him off with his jacket and then pressed the towel against his wound. "Sorry if I'm hurting you."

"It's okay. This is nothing. I've been hurt a lot worse."

"I really think you need a doctor."

"Bree can fix it up."

"She can?" Avery asked with a raised brow. "Is she a doctor?"

"No, I'm not a doctor," Bree said, returning with her kit. "But I think I can take care of this. Do you mind?"

Avery didn't look too convinced, but she moved to the other side of the couch, still staying close to him.

Bree handed him three pills and a glass of water. "Start with these."

He tossed them down his throat as Bree opened up his shirt.

"Probably going to scar," she said, as she cleaned the wound.

"That will just make me hotter, right?" He tried to smile at Avery, but she was staring back at him with worry and a bit of wariness. He probably shouldn't have brought her here, but he'd had to go somewhere, and Bree was his best option.

"Please don't agree with him," Bree said to Avery. "Wyatt's ego is already too big."

"Where do you two know each other from?" Avery asked.

Bree remained silent, letting him come up with the answer. "We met a while ago, in class," he said vaguely, hoping Avery would think he was talking about college.

"This might hurt," Bree said, as she cleaned his wound.

Avery slipped her hand into his. "Hang on to me," she said, holding his gaze. "You can break my fingers if you need to."

"I'd never want to do that." He winced as pain rocketed through him. Fortunately, Bree worked quickly.

"I'm just going to butterfly this," Bree said, putting bandage strips over his wound. "You could probably use a stitch or two."

"This will be fine," he said, as she finished.

"So, what happened?" Bree asked, getting up from where she'd been kneeling on the ground and perching on the edge of the coffee table in front of him. She wore leggings and a long T-shirt and, clearly, she'd been in bed when he'd called.

"We were staying at a hotel—someone pulled the fire alarm. When we got outside, shots were fired." He knew Bree would read between the lines.

"How did you get away?" she asked.

"That was luck. Hotel was next to a rental car agency. Found a car in the lot with the keys in the console."

"That is lucky. You really do have nine lives, Wyatt," Bree said. "Although, you have used up a few of them."

He could see Avery's interested gaze following their conversation. He turned to her. "Do you think you could get me a glass of water?"

"Of course. But this is Bree's house. Maybe she should do it. Unless you want to talk to her without me? If that's the case, I'm going to use the restroom."

"It's down the hall on the right," Bree said, as Avery got to her feet.

"Thanks. I'll bring you some water when I come back."

Wyatt waited until he heard the bathroom door close. He just hoped Avery had actually gone inside the bathroom before closing the door and wasn't listening in the hallway.

"Here's the deal," he said. "We went to Avery's father's house for dinner. Someone followed us through the Santa

Monica Mountains, almost ran us off the road. We switched cars, went to a different hotel, but I didn't find out until a brief while ago that someone had put a GPS tracker in Avery's bag. I got rid of it, as well as our phones, right after I texted you. Hopefully, no one knows we're here, but I can't promise anything."

"I'm sure you were careful. Someone put the tracker in Avery's bag while you were at the party?"

"I think so. She put it down by the front door when we walked in, although we were at Nova Star earlier in the day."

"Who was at the party?"

"Almost everyone who's a suspect. But if someone at that party was responsible for everything that came after that...it's someone Avery knows, someone I know." He paused. "I'm worried it's her father. He spent a lot of time in China. He likes money. He showed up at Avery's door several months ago. He's now practically engaged to a Tremaine heiress..."

"I'll look into that angle." She paused as Avery came back into the room. "Why don't I make you both some coffee, maybe breakfast?"

"I would love coffee," he said. "Avery?"

"Sure, why not?" she said, a hard note in her voice. "And then, maybe you can tell me who you are to each other."

"I told you we're friends," he said.

"We really are just friends," Bree added, with a reassuring smile. "I have a boyfriend—actually, a fiancé. He's just out of town today."

"I'm not jealous," Avery said, folding her arms in front of her. "I'm suspicious." She glanced at Bree. "You know how to take care of a gunshot wound. You were willing to open up your door at six o'clock in the morning and not ask any questions about how Wyatt got shot. I don't think you're just a friend." Her gaze moved to Wyatt. "But I don't want to hear the story from her. I want to hear it from you. Start talking, Wyatt."

He could see the determined glint in her eyes and knew

he had no choice but to give her the truth. "Okay. I'll tell you who Bree is."

"I'm going to take a shower and then make some coffee," Bree said, giving him a commiserating smile. "Good luck, Wyatt."

After Bree left, Avery sat down on the couch, keeping more distance between them. It was hard to believe now how close they'd been only a few hours ago.

Drawing in a breath, he said, "Remember when I told you that you didn't really know who I was?"

"Yes. So, who are you? And who is Bree?"

"Bree is an FBI agent." He paused. "And so am I."

Twenty

$\rightarrow$ ⇒ ⇐ ←

Avery sucked in a breath at his words. She didn't know what she'd been expecting Wyatt to say, but it wasn't that. As soon as he'd contacted Bree, as soon as they'd stepped into this house, she'd known something was off. Watching Bree take care of his wound in such a professional manner for a non-medical person had only reinforced that idea.

But now...now she had to deal with a truth she wasn't ready for, and that truth was that Wyatt had been lying to her.

"You're working for the FBI?" she said slowly.

"Undercover."

"So, Hamilton doesn't know—"

"No one at Nova Star knows—except you."

"And I only know because we're here. You weren't going to tell me, were you?"

"Not while the job was on," he admitted.

She thought for a moment, still trying to process his words. "I don't understand. If you're a federal agent, why did you sneak into Hamilton's company?"

"Because he shut the FBI out. Because Nova Star's new satellite defense system has far-reaching implications, and if anyone steals it or sabotages it, the country as a whole could suffer serious consequences. The bureau could not make Hamilton understand that. Actually, that's not true. He understood. He just wanted to protect his family and try to handle things himself."

His words made sense, but as she thought about everything he'd told her, she realized just how underhanded he'd been. "You said that you saved Hamilton from a carjacking, and that's how you met him, how you got the job. That's a big coincidence."

"It was a set-up. The two men who attempted to rob Hamilton were FBI."

"So, you were never in any danger when you saved his life?"

"No. It was my way in. And it didn't start there. We made sure that Hamilton's former security director won an unexpected lottery prize and suddenly had the money to retire with his wife. Then we made plans on how to insert me into his operation. He obviously wasn't looking to hire a stranger off the street. I had to make him trust me. Then when Hamilton saw my Marine-issued duffel bag, we bonded as former soldiers. He wanted to reward me for saving him. I said I didn't want charity, and after some discussion, he gave me a job in security. Once there, I showed him I could be of help to him, and he handed me more responsibilities. He told me about the security breach, the FBI, and his concern for Jonathan. I've been working on finding the truth from the inside. It actually worked out well, because Hamilton did want someone looking into the breach; he just wanted to protect his family at the same time."

His words were delivered in a pragmatic, and non-emotional tone. There was no regret in his voice, no guilt about the secrecy, the lies.

She twisted her fingers together. "Were you even a Marine?"

"No, I wasn't."

"But you have the tattoo on your wrist."

"It's fake."

She let out a breath. "Wow, I really don't know you."

His hard gaze met hers. "I didn't lie about everything, Avery."

"You didn't? Because it sure seems like you did."

"What I told you about my family—that was all true. It happened. My father and brother went to jail. I lived through that. It's part of my real life, a part that very few people know about."

"A life you lived under another name, which I still don't know." She shook her head in bewilderment. "How does that make this better?"

"I don't know about better, but I wanted you to know that not everything I told you was a lie."

He grimaced as he shifted position, and her heart tweaked a little, knowing he'd just taken a bullet for her. But she was still angry, still hurt, and she needed to stop letting her emotions rule her decisions.

"Let's get back to your cover. Hamilton doesn't know you're on the inside, but you're not really on the opposite side. He wants to find the mole and so do you."

"Yes, which has made it easier. But Hamilton was still reluctant to give me real access to his sons until Noelle was killed. He'd convinced himself that Jia Lin's death was one isolated incident and that whoever had stolen the classified information had either gone underground or no longer had access to anything with our new enhanced security procedures. Noelle's death changed that."

"Why didn't you just tell me this before, Wyatt? Maybe not right away, but what about yesterday? What about last night? We escaped with our lives twice. Couldn't you trust me with the truth?"

"I'm trusting you now."

"It's a little late, Wyatt."

He frowned. "I know. We shouldn't have slept together."

"This isn't about that."

He gave her a long look. "Isn't it partly about that, Avery?" He paused, waiting for her answer, but she didn't feel like providing one. Then he continued. "In my defense—"

"You have a defense?" she asked, cutting him off.

"Last night, I told you there was a lot about me you didn't know. You said you wanted to live in the moment, that you didn't care," he reminded her.

"But I didn't know what I didn't know," she protested, wishing she had a stronger leg to stand on. But he was right. She had ignored the fact that they didn't know each other well. She'd wanted him, and she'd acted on it.

"And I said that you'd regret it, that you wouldn't want me if you knew me better, and you told me not to tell you what you wanted."

"I know what I said," she said, getting to her feet and looking out the window as the sun rose higher in the sky.

"I'm sorry," Wyatt said. "For what it's worth."

She turned around. "For what exactly?"

"For not being able to tell you the truth. I do trust you, Avery. That's why I brought you here, why I let you meet Bree, why I'm telling you all this now." He let that sink in, and then added, "And why I have to ask you to keep my cover. Someone is trying to kill you, and we need to deal with that before we deal with the rest."

"Kill me or kill you?" she wondered, returning to the couch. "It occurs to me that I've been in more danger since I've been with you."

"It's possible they're after both of us," he conceded.

"Because we can identify a dead man? That doesn't make sense anymore, Wyatt. The man is dead. What does it matter if we can put him in Noelle's apartment after the murder? He's not going to jail. He's not going to tell us what's really going on." She stopped abruptly. "Wait, let's back up. When we went to the police station together—"

"I called the bureau and asked them to get there first," he

said, obviously reading her question before she could spit it
out. "They needed to take over the case, so we could keep the
police away from my cover and out of our investigation."

"When you say it like that, it feels like Noelle's murder
was of lesser importance."

"It wasn't," he said forcefully. "But it was a piece in a
bigger puzzle. I'm part of a specialized task force that has
been running data and financials and tracking people at Nova
Star for the last few months."

"But with all that, you haven't found the leak."

"We didn't have a lot to go on until Noelle was killed.
Now we have more."

"And my friend is dead." She paused.

"I would have saved Noelle if I could. I hope you can
believe that, even if you can't believe anything else."

She did believe that, because the Wyatt she knew
wouldn't have walked away from an injured person. *On the
other hand, was she being a fool to think she knew anything
about this man?*

"So, what do we do now?" she asked, knowing she
couldn't deal with the emotional fall-out from Wyatt's lives
right this minute. It was just too much.

"We keep looking for the traitor."

"How? You're hurt. You should be at the hospital right
now."

"I'm fine, although I might need a new shirt before we go
in to Nova Star."

"Are we going in to work like nothing is happening?"
That idea seemed completely ridiculous.

"Right now, it might be the safest place."

"Even though all the suspects work for the company?"
she countered.

"Yes. And you can't blow my cover, Avery. If you do, it
will set everything back. Hamilton will lock all the doors
behind me, and not just me—probably you, too, maybe this
entire investigation. You have to stay silent."

"You're very persuasive when it comes to protecting yourself."

"This isn't about protecting me. You can trust me on that."

"I can't trust you at all," she snapped. "So, stop talking about trust. If I keep your cover, it's because I want to find who killed Noelle and who has been trying to kill me."

"I understand."

"Do you?" she challenged, really hating the calm expression on his face, even though she should have learned by now that Wyatt did not show his emotions. "I thought you were different, Wyatt. I thought you were a man of substance. Someone I could count on. I trusted what I saw when I looked at you, when I spoke to you, even when I made love to you. But you're a chameleon. You change yourself into whoever you need to be to fit in. You lie so easily and so well. God, you're just like my father. You're a ghost. You have no substance. I can touch you, but I can't really touch you, because the real you isn't there."

"I was there last night."

"Were you?" she asked, searching the face she had come to love and now felt she would have to hate.

"I was myself with you. I couldn't be anyone else. You brought me out of the shadows, and even though I knew it was wrong, I wanted to be with you. If we could only have one night, I selfishly wanted that night."

"I don't know what to think," she said, completely bewildered. "You're a liar. It's what you do for a living."

"It is what I do," he admitted. "I lie to gain trust. That gives me access to information I wouldn't be able to get otherwise. Then I take criminals down."

"But I'm not a criminal. So, what am I? Collateral damage?"

"I don't want you to be damaged," he said, an intensity in his gaze now. "I don't want you to be hurt at all. I've been trying to protect you, and I'm going to keep doing that no matter how much you may dislike me."

"You just can't protect me from you," she said, feeling an immense wave of sadness.

His lips tightened, but there was no defense he could offer.

"You know who you're also like?" she asked. "*Your* father. He was a con man, too."

"Yes. It was a skill I inherited from the old man," he said with a bitter nod. "Don't think I haven't thought that before, because I have. And you might not want to believe this, but you're the only person outside of a few close friends in the FBI that I've ever told about my father."

"That doesn't matter now." She drew in a breath and let it out. "I don't want to talk about us anymore, because there is no us. I want to focus on how we're going to catch the person who's trying to kill us."

"So do I."

Bree cleared her throat as she came into the room, wearing tight black jeans and a cream-colored blouse. "Sorry to interrupt."

"It's fine," she said, getting to her feet. "Wyatt and I are done."

"The coffee is ready in the kitchen. I'll make us some breakfast," Bree said.

"I don't need anything." She walked through the double doors leading out to the balcony and stood at the rail. Maybe it was dangerous to stand in plain view, but there was no one in sight, and she really just needed a minute to process everything.

Her mind was spinning with all that had happened. There was a part of her that was deeply hurt, and those emotions kept wanting to come out, pushing moisture into her eyes, sobs rising up in her throat. She had totally bared herself to Wyatt in so many ways, not just physically but emotionally. And to know that he'd been lying to her the whole time…it made her wonder if anyone would ever love her with any kind of honesty, and if she could ever trust her instincts.

She brushed her hair off her face as the wind picked up. She couldn't let herself cry. She couldn't let the emotion overwhelm her. Later...she could give in. But now she had to pull herself together and think. The sun was rising, the minutes were ticking forward, and somewhere out there was someone who wanted to kill her.

How was she going to figure out who was after her? And what was she going to do if she found out it was someone she knew? If it was her father...she felt like she just might break.

How many betrayals could one person take?

* * *

Wyatt changed into one of Nathan's shirts and then returned to the living room. He could see Avery still standing out on the deck and as much as it pained him to see her making herself so vulnerable, he knew he had to give her a few minutes, so he moved into the kitchen.

Bree poured him a mug of coffee. "I've been keeping an eye on her."

"Is she crying?"

"Maybe on the inside." She stirred some eggs in a pan on the stove. "I've got bacon cooking and some toast. I hope you'll both eat something."

"Thanks—for everything. I didn't know where else to go."

"You can always come to me. You know that." She paused, giving him a thoughtful glance. "You like her, don't you?"

He sipped his coffee. "Maybe."

"No maybe about it. And she has a thing for you."

"If she did, it's gone now," he said tersely. "But it doesn't matter. We need to figure out what's going on."

"Any leads from the party?"

"A few. Larry Bickmore, senior counsel for Nova Star

was there. His wife drank too much and told Avery that Larry and Carter were working on something together that required Carter to come to his house. It sounded interesting enough to follow up."

Bree slid the eggs onto a plate. "I agree."

His gaze shifted back to Avery. "Do you think you could get her to come back in here? I don't like her out there."

Bree smiled. "You think she'll listen to me over you? She didn't seem too friendly."

"She's very friendly; she's just upset."

"I'll give it a shot."

As Bree walked out of the kitchen, the bread popped up from the toaster. He smeared it with butter and put it on a plate as Bree returned with Avery in tow.

"I'll take some coffee," Avery said.

He was happy she was speaking to him, even if it was an unfriendly order. He filled her a mug and then helped Bree take the plates to the table.

While Avery at first seemed reluctant to join in, she eventually ate some eggs and bacon.

"Wyatt and I went to Quantico together," Bree said, breaking into the tense silence that accompanied their meal. "In case you were wondering how we met, Avery. We were put together in a group of six people. We spent most of our training together, working through mission assignments, stripping down each other's barriers, interrogating, grilling, competing with each other and learning how to watch each other's backs." Bree cleared her throat. "We were all really close, and then one of us was killed in one of our last assignments. We all blamed ourselves for not saving Jamie."

"Jamie?" Avery cut in, her gaze narrowing. "Last night at the party, I spoke to Hamilton's friend, Vincent Rowland, and he mentioned that he was in town for his daughter's engagement party and that he was happy for her but sad that her brother Jamie would not be there. Is that the same Jamie?"

"Vincent was at the party?" Bree asked in surprise,

turning her gaze to his.

"Yes. He's apparently friends with Hamilton. Fortunately, he realized I was undercover and didn't say anything."

"Why would he have been at the party?" Bree asked. "There's something going on with him, Wyatt. I don't know what it is, but something is off."

"I know he wasn't particularly friendly to you when you ran into him the other day, Bree, but—"

"No, it's not that. It's that he's always showing up or being involved in some way in our cases."

"What do you mean?"

"Think about it. When you were in New York, your cover was blown with the Venturi family, Alan was killed, and Damon and Sophie were running for their lives, and Vincent was right in the middle of that."

"I wouldn't say he was in the middle."

"Damon and Sophie hid out at his house. Sophie communicated with Cassie, his daughter, while they were on the run."

"I don't know where you're going with this," he said with a frown.

"I don't know, either, but something has been bugging me since everything went down in Chicago on my last case. Someone lured me to Chicago, someone who knew my past, and I never really figured out who."

"I thought it was that serial kidnapper."

"It appeared that way, but I'm not sure. And then my FBI file showed up in the kidnapper's house. How did it get there? We assumed that the crooked cop got the file from one of his contacts, but he died, so I couldn't ask him. I always felt like something was off in the way everything wrapped up, but I let it go." She paused. "Now Vincent shows up in the middle of your case. He's friends with your mark. He's suddenly interested in what you're doing. He's retired, for God's sake. Why the hell is he always around?"

"I think it's a coincidence."

"Since when do you believe in coincidences?" Bree challenged. "And let's not forget he met with Joanna before he went to your party."

"Because he was in town and they're friends. I don't see a connection here. Sorry, Bree."

"Maybe you're right. Maybe I'm just imagining things because his negative attitude toward me always bugs me."

"Why doesn't Mr. Rowland like you?" Avery cut in, interest in her eyes.

"I dated Jamie for a short time. I broke up with him before he died, and Vincent acts like I broke his son's heart and maybe that's why Jamie was distracted and lost his life."

"That's a lot to put on you," Avery said.

"It could just be that it's painful for Vincent to see you because he remembers when Jamie was happy and in love with you."

"You're probably right, and we are getting way off track," Bree said. "I'm sorry about all this. We need to get back to the case."

"Are you on the case?" Avery asked curiously.

"I came on board after your friend was killed."

"So, you know everything that's going on?"

"Pretty much. You should be aware that you're going to see me again later this morning. I'll be attending the press briefing as a reporter for the *LA Star*. I'd like to know that I can count on you not to blow my cover."

"I'm not going to blow anyone's cover," Avery said, tucking a strand of hair behind her ear. "I know what's at stake here."

He was happy to hear that. "Thanks, Avery."

She shot him a dark look. "I'm not doing it for either of you; I'm doing it for Noelle and for me. I need to stop at the hotel in Santa Monica on the way to Nova Star. I have to change clothes, and I have some things there I need for my work day."

"I don't like that idea," he said.

"Well, it has to happen."

"Why don't I go pick up your things?" Bree suggested. "I'll bring everything back here."

Avery glanced at her watch. "I need to be at work in an hour."

"Then I better go now," Bree said, getting to her feet.

Wyatt handed her the hotel key. "Room 423, Hotel Royale, Santa Monica. Bree, the rental car I pinched—"

"I'll ditch it," she said, taking the key from his hand.

"You're a lifesaver."

She smiled. "I'll be back soon. You can use my computer if you want to check in with Flynn." She paused, looking back at Avery. "Maybe you two can talk things out while I'm gone."

When Bree left the room, the tension between him and Avery went up a notch. There were things he wanted to say to her, but he doubted she wanted to hear them. Their gazes clung together for a long moment, and then Avery got up and took her plate to the sink.

They did the dishes and cleaned up the kitchen in a very awkward and uncomfortable silence, and then Avery went into the bathroom to freshen up. He doubted she was going to come out any time soon.

He sat down at the dining room table and jumped onto Bree's computer. He sent Flynn a long message, updating him on what had happened since he'd last spoken to him. There were a lot of leads to follow, and he needed Flynn and the IT guys to run some of them down, starting with whoever had shot at them. Maybe they could pull some footage from the hotel cams.

When that was done, he got up and walked to the window, looking out at the water. He'd crossed a line he shouldn't have crossed last night.

But he couldn't take it back. *He didn't want to take it back.*

He wished he could make it up to Avery, but he didn't think that was possible. But at the very least he would keep her safe. That was all that really mattered.

Twenty-One

—→∙⋙⋘∙←—

Bree came back to the house with their belongings and the keys to a small brown Toyota pickup truck. Avery didn't ask where she'd gotten the car and neither did Wyatt. She was more interested in changing her clothes and getting in to work. Even though it seemed surreal to be thinking about having a normal workday, she was actually eager to feel the familiarity that would come with being at Nova Star, doing her job, and having a chance to look up at the magnificent sky instead of at all the danger and uncertainty swirling around her.

"We don't have to talk," Wyatt said as he drove to Nova Star. "But we need to stay in communication, and we need to stay close. Just because you've discovered I'm an FBI agent doesn't change the fact that you're still in danger."

"I know," she said, wrapping her arms around her waist. She'd put on dark jeans and a long-sleeve lacy white knit top. Wyatt was still wearing Nathan's shirt, and she'd seen him wince as he got into the car, but of course he'd refused to let her drive. She was actually fine with that. She was operating on little sleep and too much adrenaline.

"How long will you be involved with the media?"

"About an hour."

"We'll touch base after that, figure out our next move."

"Sure, whatever," she said, too confused to imagine what their next move could be.

Several minutes later, Wyatt turned in to the employee parking lot at Nova Star, flashing his badge to the guard at the gate and exchanging a quick hello. He had apparently made it a mission to know every guard's first name and personal story. Obviously, he'd gotten very deep into his role as Hamilton's top security guy.

It was still mind-boggling to think that he'd set up a carjacking as a ruse to get into Hamilton's good graces and into his company. And Hamilton was crazy about Wyatt. She'd seen his respect firsthand. He was in for a big surprise.

Although, she couldn't totally blame the FBI for inserting Wyatt into the company. If Hamilton was being blind when it came to his family members, and the safety of their technology was in jeopardy and could possibly be used by a foreign power, what other choice had the bureau had?

But she wasn't going to tell Wyatt that. She was still feeling hurt and betrayed on a personal level, and she was not ready to let that go. It was that anger that was keeping the memories at bay. She couldn't let herself remember how good it had been between them, because whatever they'd had—the crazy connection, the ridiculous chemistry, the talks that had felt so honest, so real—was all gone now, part of an illusion, a cover.

Wyatt parked the car, and she grabbed her bag from behind the seat, wanting to keep it with her, not sure where the day would go or where she'd end up spending the night.

It felt good to walk into Nova Star, the building where she'd spent so much of her time the last three years. Even though there could be a spy, or more than one, somewhere in the building, this was her turf, and she felt more in control once she'd made it through security.

Wyatt walked her up to her office. She didn't bother

arguing with him. There was no point.

Two women were waiting outside her door: Beth Meeks, a forty-year-old, ex-schoolteacher, who usually worked on school programs, and Kim Walton, the thirty-two-year-old director of media relations.

Seeing that she was in good company, Wyatt tipped his head and headed upstairs to his office.

She rolled her suitcase into the office as the women crowded inside, both giving her very curious looks.

"So, you and the hunky security guy—what's going on there?" Kim asked with a sparkle in her blue eyes. A single woman, Kim loved to talk about men. She'd joined Avery and Noelle at a few lunches and discussing hot guys at the company was always Kim's favorite topic.

"Wyatt was just helping me with my suitcase," she said.

"Why do you have your suitcase? Are you going out to the desert tonight? I didn't think you were going to the launch," Beth said.

"I'm not sure," she said, happy that Beth had actually given her a good excuse for having her bag.

"What's Wyatt like?" Kim asked. "He's so sexy. Does he have a girlfriend?"

"I don't know. Let's talk about the show, about today's events," she said, desperately needing to change the topic.

Thankfully, Beth took the hint and they got down to business.

After reviewing the schedule and their various responsibilities, they made their way down to the first-floor auditorium. Avery stepped up to the stage, made sure everything was ready to go and then asked the ushers to let the media in. She saw Bree in the first group of people. She took a seat in the second row, offering Avery a warm smile.

She didn't really know what to think about Bree. Clearly, she and Wyatt were the best of friends, and while she'd said earlier she wasn't jealous, maybe she was—a little. Maybe because Bree seemed to know the real Wyatt, and she didn't.

But she couldn't think about Wyatt now, and she was happy to have Bree in the crowd.

Nothing was going to happen here. She was in the middle of a huge crowd, but she felt a little safer knowing there was an FBI agent nearby.

* * *

Wyatt checked in with his security team when he arrived at the command center. All the monitors were up. There were extra personnel on site, both at the exits and entrances but also walking the halls. Some of that security would leave at the end of the day and make the ninety-minute drive to the desert facility where Nova Star would launch their new satellite early tomorrow morning.

It would be a big day for the company, an important step forward in the space race. But someone was determined to mess with that. He just wished he knew what the end game was. Did they want to stop the launch, steal the defensive technology, destroy the satellite, shoot down some other country's satellite? There were many possible scenarios, but the one that seemed most likely involved destroying the satellite itself, proving that the technology didn't work, which would send Hamilton and Nova Star from the top of the race to the back of the line.

He'd thought the threat was coming from China because of the connection to Jia Lin. Now, he wondered about the Russians. But the Russians and the Americans had worked together in space for a long time. It was China who had been the odd man out, who was desperate to get in the race. So where was the tie between a Russian thug and the Chinese government? There had to be a connection somewhere.

He grabbed his second work phone out of his desk and went up to the sixth-floor rooftop deck to call Flynn. Hopefully, the team had come up with something based on the information he'd sent earlier.

"What have you got for me?" he asked.

"We pulled footage from the hotel security camera where you stayed last night," Flynn replied. "We got a few images of the shooter from the roof of the hotel restaurant. Facial ID identified him as Ran Ding, a former soldier for the PLA."

Wyatt sucked in a breath. *There was his China connection.* The PLA stood for the People's Liberation Army of China. "Do you have him yet?"

"No. But I can tell you that he arrived in LA four days ago and was staying at a downtown hotel until yesterday. We're searching for him, but he could be anywhere."

"Has he had any contact with our persons of interest?"

"Still looking into that. We also ran financials on Larry Bickmore. He has a tremendous amount of debt, underwater on a couple of real-estate deals, living way beyond his means. His wife also did a stint in a very expensive rehab center about six months ago."

"That clearly didn't work. She was very drunk last night." He could hardly believe it had been just last night that he'd been sitting at a dinner party with whoever might have ordered someone to take him and Avery out.

"Unfortunately, we found no evidence that he has come into any money recently. He could be keeping it off the books or it's buried somewhere we haven't discovered yet."

"What about Carter Hayes?"

"Joanna wants to handle Hayes. She said she'd talk to him today."

"It had better be today. We're running out of time. But I'd rather we were doing the questioning."

"So, would I, but Joanna was pulling rank on me, and she was asking a lot of odd questions about you. Something is going on with her. I don't have a good feeling about it."

"What kind of questions about me?"

"Like whether you were checking in with me regularly. Was I concerned you might be getting into bed with Avery Caldwell? Were you following up on her father, whose ties to

China are worrisome?"

"I'm doing my job. That's all she needs to know."

"I agree, but I wanted to give you a heads up. The woman does not like you. Where are you now?"

"At Nova Star."

"And Avery?"

"She's putting on a show for the press." He hadn't told Flynn that he'd broken his cover for Avery. It was a calculated risk, but he didn't believe Flynn needed to know, and it would only complicate matters. "I'll talk to you soon."

As he put his phone into his pocket, he checked his watch. It was almost eleven. Avery's show would be letting out soon, and he wanted to be in the lobby when she came out of the auditorium, but he had time to stop by Carter's desk on his way downstairs. Joanna might want to lead that interrogation, but he was on site, and if he could get any information out of Carter now, that could only be helpful. If anyone was going to break, it would probably be Carter.

Unfortunately, when he reached the legal offices, Carter's desk was empty, and an admin told him that Carter had called in sick for the day, which, of course, was completely understandable considering the fact that he'd just lost his girlfriend.

He didn't doubt that Carter was heartsick; he just didn't know if it was for Noelle or for whatever part of the mess he was involved in.

He got back on the elevator and went down to the first floor, eager to see Avery again. Even though she was perfectly safe in the auditorium, he felt a little lost without her, and that was a feeling he didn't want to examine too closely.

When he reached the lobby, there were dozens of people milling around the display cases and the gift shop. The show had obviously just let out, and there was a buzz of excitement in the building. He could practically feel the sizzle in the air. It would be even greater tomorrow on launch day, not that the launch would happen here, but there would be a viewing in the auditorium again for members of the press and also VIP guests who would not be making it out to the desert.

As he neared the auditorium doors, he saw Avery come out. She was speaking to a man wearing a press badge, and they were having quite an animated conversation.

His gut tightened as she smiled, then laughed, and the other man touched her on the shoulder with some gesture of affection.

Did she know this guy? Were they friends? And why the hell did it bother him?

Frowning, he pushed the unexpected wave of jealousy down. It was ridiculous. She could laugh and smile with someone else. And she probably would—lots of times. They were done, and he couldn't be surprised. He'd always known as soon as he told her the truth that she would feel betrayed and hurt, which was exactly why he shouldn't have gotten involved with her. He could have kept his foot on the brake. He just hadn't wanted to.

But he couldn't take back the last few days, and if he had nothing else, at least he had some hellishly good memories.

His job had gotten in his way before with women, but not like this. He'd never fallen for anyone while he was undercover. He'd had to play a role on occasion but what he'd felt for Avery was real. Unfortunately, she would never be able to believe that.

He saw Bree hanging behind Avery. She gave him a subtle nod and a somewhat knowing smile. He had a feeling too much was written across his face.

Avery gave the man a hug as they said good-bye. Then her gaze moved to his. They were standing at least twenty feet apart and there were dozens of people around, but all he saw was her. And there was something in her eyes that made him question if it was really over. Maybe there was some chance they could get past the lies. Or was he just being a fool?

A commotion at the front entrance broke their connection.

He swung around, his instincts back on high alert, shocked to see Joanna Davis and two male FBI agents, all wearing FBI jackets, walk into the lobby.

Had something happened that he didn't know about?

He started forward, planning to play the scene out in his role as security director, and Joanna immediately zeroed in on him.

She stopped in front of him and gave him a hard, cold look that he couldn't begin to interpret. "I'm glad you saved us the trouble of coming to look for you," she said.

"What's going on?"

"Wyatt Tanner, you're under arrest," she said.

"Are you serious?" He could not fathom what was happening, but the two agents flanking Joanna were now closing in on him.

He heard someone let out a shocked gasp, and he suspected it was Avery, but he couldn't turn around to look. As his gaze met Joanna's, he felt a chill run through him. This wasn't out of the playbook.

"Hold on. What's this about?" he asked, trying not to blow his cover but unsure where this was going. He told himself he had to trust she was doing this for a reason. *But why hadn't she informed him that she was going to make a very public arrest?*

"It's about national security, Mr. Tanner," Joanna said. "You're going to need to come with us."

As one of the agents cuffed his wrists, he glanced over his shoulder, seeing a troubled look on Bree's face. He didn't think she knew what was going on, either.

Avery also looked confused and worried.

But it was Hamilton Tremaine striding across the lobby who really caught his attention.

"What's going on?" Hamilton demanded.

He didn't know where Hamilton had come from, and he

wasn't sure if the presence of the billionaire owner of Nova Star was a good thing or a bad thing. *Probably bad,* he thought, as camera lights flashed in his face. The media was all over the lobby, and his arrest would be on the news before he left the building.

"Mr. Tremaine," Joanna said, intercepting Hamilton. "I need to speak to you in private."

"Where are you taking Wyatt? He's my top security guy. You can't just come in here and arrest him without explanation."

"That's what I'm going to talk to you about—but not here," she said pointedly.

"Wyatt?" Hamilton asked, giving him a confused look. "Do you know what this is about?"

"I don't," he said honestly. "But I'll get it straightened out. Don't worry."

As Hamilton and Joanna walked away, the agents escorted him out of the building and into a dark SUV. He didn't know these men, and neither one was inclined to speak to him.

What the hell had just happened?

He wasn't worried so much about his arrest, but by the fact that Avery was now cut off from him. She might not want him in her life, but he needed to be there to protect her. His only hope was that Bree could step in for him until he could figure out why Joanna had made this abrupt and bewildering move.

Twenty-Two

"What's happening?" Avery asked Bree.

"Take me to your office," Bree said, an urgent note in her voice.

As she and Bree entered the elevator, they were followed by a half-dozen people, several of whom were muttering about what had just happened. Wyatt's arrest had certainly been dramatic, and she had no idea what was going on.

How could he be arrested by the agency that he worked for? It didn't make sense. *Was it part of the game, some part no one had prepped her for?*

When they got to her floor, she led Bree down the hall, smiling and giving quick, positive answers as some of her colleagues asked her how the event had gone. Apparently, news of the drama that had occurred downstairs had not made its way to her floor yet.

When she got into her office, she closed the door behind Bree and said, "I didn't think there was anything else that could surprise me, but I was wrong."

Bree nodded as she finished tapping in a text on her phone.

"Who are you talking to?" she asked.

"Hopefully someone who can find out what's going on," Bree returned, a clipped, worried note in her voice.

"Does that mean you don't know?"

Bree raised her gaze to meet Avery's. "I don't."

"But I thought Wyatt works for the FBI. Why would that woman arrest him?"

"Wyatt is part of a special task force, separate from Agent Davis's department. But she's very aware of his role in this operation. I can't imagine why she would pull him out of his job in such a public way. It doesn't make sense."

A cold chill ran through her. "She said something about national security. Does she think Wyatt is..." She couldn't even get the word out.

"She knows what Wyatt came here to do," Bree said shortly, glancing back at her phone.

Whatever text had just come in obviously disturbed her, lines creasing her forehead as she frowned.

"What did they say?" she asked.

Bree looked back at her. "I need to go down to the field office, so I can get more information." She paused. "But I'm reluctant to leave you here alone. I know Wyatt would want me to stay with you."

"I'm not alone. I'm in a building filled with people. And I think Wyatt needs your help more than I do right now. You don't believe he's a traitor or a double agent, do you?"

"No possible way. Wyatt could never be bought."

She liked Bree's definitive answer. "I didn't think so."

"Good," Bree said sharply. "I don't know what went down with you two, but I know this—Wyatt is a good man. And he cares about you."

"Because I'm his job."

"No, because he has feelings for you. I've seen him on the job before. I know how he acts. He's not acting with you. He probably should have been, but somewhere along the way, he stopped."

"He told me about his parents," she said. "His father and

brother going to jail."

Bree's surprised reaction told her that story was true. "He doesn't tell just anyone that story."

"That's what he said, but I don't know what to believe. He also told me he was a Marine."

"That was his way in to Hamilton's circle. But the other story is true. Wyatt hated the spotlight of his father's criminal activities. I don't know if he told you, but the media were relentless in writing stories about his family's downfall. Wyatt couldn't walk down the street without someone snapping a photo of him. He needed to get away from all that. He also wanted to right the wrongs in some way. That's why he came to the bureau, why he likes to work in the shadows, why he is devoted to taking down criminals, who never see him coming."

"To do penance for his father," she murmured.

"And because he hates when the wrong people have power. He's one of the best people I've ever known, Avery. He would literally lay down his life for you."

"You don't have to tell me that."

"I just want you to know that he's an amazing guy, and I consider him to be a great friend."

"Then go and help him," she said. "I'll be fine here."

"Are you sure?"

"Positive."

"I'll check back in with you. Give me your number."

"Wyatt threw my personal phone away, but I have a work phone." She walked around her desk and pulled her other phone out of the drawer. She'd had all her business calls forwarded to her other phone, so she wouldn't have to carry two phones around, but she could change that. She gave Bree her number and then said, "Tell Wyatt...Just tell him not to worry about me. Tell him to take care of himself."

"I will do that. Stay here in your office. Don't go outside, Avery. There's a chance that this happened to separate you and Wyatt."

"And they were able to use the FBI to do that? Who is this person?"

"That's what I'm going to find out."

* * *

Wyatt had been released from his cuffs but locked in an interrogation room at the FBI field office for almost thirty minutes before Joanna Davis came in.

Finally, he would get some answers.

She sat down across from him and gave him a smug smile. "Hello, Wyatt."

"Why am I here? Why did you arrest me that way?"

"I had to." She took a file out of her bag and put it on the desk between them.

"What's this?"

"Bank records from an offshore account in your name."

"I don't have any offshore accounts."

"Take a look," she said.

He opened the file, his gaze running down a statement from a bank in the Cayman Islands that did bear his name, along with a series of deposits dating back two months. "This is fake."

"It's not fake. The money is there. The account is in your name. Your signature matches the one we have on file for you. But that's not all. Read the second page."

He did as she asked, trepidation growing inside of him. Someone had gone to a lot of trouble to set him up, and he didn't think they had started just yesterday.

"The deposits were made in the form of wire transfers from a company by the name of Walken Industries," she continued.

"I've never heard of that company."

"Well, it's a shell corporation with ties to the Chinese government. They've been paying you to act as a double agent, to protect their theft of secrets from Nova Star, to implicate Jonathan Tremaine as a traitor and a spy, and to infiltrate Hamilton Tremaine's inner circle to gain more access to proprietary information."

"This is all doctored." He closed the file and gave Joanna a hard look. "You have to know that, Joanna. This is just an attempt to discredit me and probably to separate me from Avery."

"I also know that you've provided very little information back to the task force," she said, her gaze unwavering.

"I've provided everything I had. Where's Flynn? Why isn't he here?"

"I assume he's now being informed of your arrest, probably by Bree. I hope you didn't get her involved, too. When she asked to move to your task force, I almost refused. I hate to see good female agents go down the wrong path, but I could see she was bored with her current duties, so I said yes."

"I had nothing to do with Bree's request to join the task force, and I don't know what she's doing with Flynn. I've been a little busy running for my life." He pulled up his shirt, revealing his bandaged wound. "I was shot this morning outside of a hotel by the airport. I barely got Avery to safety. I could have been killed. You think that's part of my cover?"

"I think that if someone wanted you dead, you'd be dead," she said pointedly. "It's rather convenient for a sniper to miss."

Her comments made him very uneasy. For the first time, he felt real alarm. "Come on, Joanna, you know me. You know Flynn. These bank statements are manufactured."

"I don't think I know you at all, Wyatt. I might have known you, if you'd let me get close to you, but you were never interested enough in me to realize I could be of real help to you. You were always so tight with your group of friends at Quantico. You thought you all could rule the world. Little did you know that you would have had a lot more power if you'd worked with me."

"This is about payback," he said slowly. "I'm disappointed, Joanna. I thought you were better than that. Someone is using you. How can you not see that?"

A frown drew her brows together. "I'm not being used. I'm investigating the information I received."

"Who gave you the information?"

"An anonymous source."

He sat back in his chair and shook his head. "Unbelievable. You pulled me out of an undercover operation based on an anonymous source."

"As you can see, the information is very credible, and I have to protect the bureau's reputation. If there's any chance you're working both sides, you could be a threat to national security."

"Keeping me here is a threat to national security," he snapped back.

"I don't think so. You need to start being honest, Wyatt. If you went rogue, or if Flynn's operation was always on the wrong side of the law, you need to come clean now and try to save yourself. Why don't you think about that? And get comfortable. You're not going anywhere."

"You're leaving Avery unprotected. Someone is after her."

"I'm sure someone else on the task force can watch out for her."

"She won't trust anyone else. You have to let me go."

"I don't have to do anything." She pushed back her chair and stood up. "I'll be back."

"I want to call my lawyer."

"Sure," she said with a smooth smile. "We'll make that happen—at some point."

"This is crazy. You know that."

"You know what is really crazy—secret task forces," she returned. "I've never found the need for them. They almost always have an agenda and they're usually run by people who cut corners, who don't like to play by the rules. We do better as an agency when we run clean operations, not secret ones."

"That's bullshit. We had to be covert. Hamilton Tremaine wouldn't let you into his company, but I got inside."

"But now we have the question of whether you're on his side or ours. Until I know for sure, you're staying here."

The door closed on her revenge-filled smile, and he ran a hand through his hair in anger and frustration. Someone had set him up.

Was it Joanna working on her own? Had she been bought off by the same people who had stolen secrets, killed Noelle? Or was she simply a pawn?

If she was a pawn, then it seemed as if someone would know that Joanna didn't like him, that she might be receptive to an attack against him. *Who would know that? Someone else in the FBI?*

Bree's words from earlier that day came into his head. She'd asked him why Vincent Rowland was at the Tremaine house. She'd suggested that Vincent had been close by during all recent cases involving members of Jamie's former team. She'd even suggested that someone in the FBI had given her file to the ex-con who had tried to kill her, and she'd never been able to figure out who in the bureau would have done that. He'd dismissed Bree's words as pure conjecture, that she was just imagining that Vincent had something against her, because of her relationship with Jamie. But it did seem that their group of five was running into some unusual problems, often within the bureau itself, and who better to influence the agency then an ex-agent?

But did that really make sense?

It seemed more likely that one of the Tremaines or Carter or someone else at Nova Star had thought he was getting too close to the truth, too close to Avery, maybe even too close to Hamilton and decided to get him out of the picture.

Hell, maybe it was Hamilton himself.

That would be quite a twist—if Hamilton had figured out he was FBI all along and decided to use that to his advantage.

But that didn't seem logical, either, because ultimately someone was out to destroy Nova Star. And that wouldn't be Hamilton. It wouldn't be Rowland, either.

He shifted in his seat, feeling pain through his abdomen, reminding him of the wound that should probably be cleaned and re-bandaged at some point, not that Joanna had been impressed with his battle scars or his ability to dodge bullets.

Rolling his neck around on his shoulders, he considered the doctored bank statements. Was there really money sitting in that bank account or were the statements provided fake?

If there was real cash, then that meant someone with money had been willing to pay to set him up, because that account would be frozen by the FBI. He almost had to admire the move.

It was clever, and while it wouldn't work for long, because eventually the FBI would figure out he was innocent, it might work just long enough to keep him out of the way.

What he didn't understand was Joanna's motive for treating him like a criminal. She might have been forced to act on the intel, but she didn't have to act like this. She could have let him call a lawyer. She could have tried to work with him.

Was it just revenge because he'd turned her down years ago?

That seemed petty, even for her. As she'd said, this was about national security, and if he wasn't a double agent, then someone was still out there, someone probably about to sabotage the satellite, and he wasn't going to be able to do one damn thing to stop them.

And then there was Avery.

Putting him here had effectively isolated him from Avery. He had to hope Bree would stay with her. But Avery might send Bree away, too. She might think that he was guilty, that this was just one more lie he'd told her. *And how could he blame her?*

He slammed his fist hard against the desk. He needed to

get out of here, but he was going to need some help to do that. Maybe Flynn would realize it was a setup. Or it was possible that Flynn might be coming into the room in handcuffs next. Joanna might try to take down the whole operation. And Bree—she was on Joanna's hit list now, too, since she'd joined up with Flynn.

He needed a friend on the inside, but he didn't have one. He was going to have to figure a way out of this on his own.

* * *

Avery had been trying to work for over an hour, but it was a futile effort. Her mind was spinning, playing Wyatt's shocking arrest over and over again in her head.

She didn't believe that Wyatt was a double agent. It didn't make sense. He'd almost gotten killed several times; she'd been right beside him on all of those occasions. Just this morning, he had taken a bullet for her. It was only his quick thinking that had saved both their lives.

But the FBI had to have something on him to arrest him, especially since she'd recently learned he was also an agent. Going against one of their own people had to require some substantial evidence. *What on earth could that possibly be?*

Groaning, she pressed her fingers to her temples, feeling a blazing headache coming on. She was glad the media tour was over. The rest of her day was pretty open, since her part in the launch was done. She'd really like to take a nap at some point.

Closing her eyes for just a moment, she tried to breathe through the panic and anxiety. She'd already had a lot to worry about with someone trying to kill her, but now she had to worry about Wyatt, too. Clearly, someone had set Wyatt up, and she didn't know what was coming next.

She could hardly believe how quickly everything kept changing. It was difficult to keep up. Her emotions felt like they were on a spin cycle. Every time the clock turned, she was hit with something new. The only steady person in her life the past few days had been Wyatt, and last night had provided a glorious few hours of happiness. She should regret making love to him now that she knew he'd lied to her about so many things, but she couldn't seem to drag up the anger.

Maybe last night was the only time they would ever have together. If so, at least she had those memories. And for a moment, she let her mind go back in time, let herself feel his kiss, his hands on her body, his breath against her face, his husky voice murmuring words of pleasure. The way he'd said her name, with so much passion, so much need, sent a deep yearning ache through her body.

She missed him. It was incredible how close they'd gotten so quickly. And it hadn't just been physical. Their talks had been deeply personal. They'd shared and shown their true selves to each other. She'd admitted fears to him she'd never told anyone about, and he'd told her about his family, about how it had felt to see his father go from a great guy to a criminal.

While her father had never fallen that far, she'd understood the disappointment he'd felt. It had been another connection between them. She'd felt the same kind of love and conflict when it came to her dad. And Wyatt had made her feel like that was okay. Love and respect didn't always go together, especially when it came to parents.

She'd like to believe she'd had an impact on him, too. She thought about the expression in his eyes when she'd played the show for him in the auditorium yesterday, when he'd looked up after years of looking down, when he'd seen hope and possibility, when he'd perhaps lost just a touch of the cynicism he'd probably gained not only from his family circumstances but from his job. That had been a special moment, too.

She wanted more of those moments. She wanted a chance to get to know him—really know him. Because while it probably should be over between them, it wasn't—at least, not for her.

A knock came at her door, interrupting her reverie. Her eyes flew open, and she jumped to her feet.

Should she open it?

Bree had made sure she'd locked it earlier, but it wasn't much of a lock if someone really wanted to get in. She told herself not to get paranoid. Her office was in the middle of a very busy building, with thousands on staff, with security cameras in every hallway.

"Avery? Are you in there?"

Her tension eased at the sound of her father's voice, and she quickly crossed the room and unlocked the door.

"Dad," she said, surprised to see him there. He rarely visited her at work. "What are you doing here?"

He walked into her office. "I got a call from Hamilton earlier. He said Wyatt was arrested. Is that true?"

"Yes, but it's a mistake."

Her father gave her a speculative look. "Is it a mistake? Hamilton doesn't seem to think so. He's beside himself. He can't believe he might have hired a traitor, and not just hired him but made him a friend, invited him into his inner circle, entrusted him with your care."

She shook her head, hating that Hamilton was getting sucked in. "Wyatt isn't guilty of anything."

"How do you know?"

"I just know. My gut tells me he's being set up."

"Is that your gut or your heart?" he asked gently. "I know you don't think I know you anymore, Avery, but I always knew when your heart was breaking."

She didn't even think that was true, but his kind words made her tear up anyway. "It is breaking," she whispered.

"You care about him."

"I do," she admitted. "I know Wyatt is a good man. This is a mistake. He was getting too close to something and someone got nervous and turned the tables on him."

"I don't like any of this, especially the part where you're

in danger."

A part of her wanted to tell him just how much danger she'd been in since she'd left his house last night, but what would that accomplish? Instead, she said, "I have to admit I'm scared. I don't know what to do next. Wyatt was my touchstone. When he was around, I knew I was okay."

"Making you feel safe used to be my job."

She heard a sad note in her father's voice. "We have a lot of history between us. I don't want to get into any of that now."

"I understand. I can't change the past—who I was, how I acted—but I can be there for you now. What are you doing the rest of the day?"

"I'm not even sure. I've been trying to work, but I'm incredibly distracted."

"Not even stars and planets and galaxies can ease your mind, huh?" he said with an affectionate, knowing smile.

"No. Not even space can do it for me today."

"Here's what I'm thinking. Tonight, Hamilton is having his kids over for a private dinner in honor of tomorrow's launch, which is also the one-year anniversary of his late wife's death. Since I never met Whitney's mother, I'm not going to be a part of that."

"Whitney didn't want you to go?"

"I think it was more Hamilton. I understand why he didn't want me there. Whitney and I are not married, and I didn't know her mother, and there will be a lot of shared stories and probably some tears, and it's best I'm not there." He paused. "Did you know Hamilton's wife, Margery?"

"Yes, I spent a fair amount of time at their house when she was sick. It was really sad when she died. I can't believe it's been a year. I know Hamilton wanted to launch on the anniversary of her death as a tribute to her. She was his partner in all this."

"Well, it will be a nice time for Hamilton and his kids to spend together. So, why don't you come back to the house with me? Whitney is spending the afternoon at the spa and then going straight to her dad's. It will just be the two of us— like old times. I even gave Lois the night off, so she can watch her grandson," he added, referring to his housekeeper. "We can pick up some Tommy's Burgers on the way home and sit by the pool, and you can just relax."

"Now you're pulling out all the stops. Tommy's Burgers were always my favorite, although I have not had one of those incredibly delicious and really fattening chili cheeseburgers in a long time."

"Then you should have one now. Come on, Avery. You're not in any mental condition to work today. Let me take care of you for a few hours."

"Maybe just until tonight." It might be a bad idea, but this was her father. He had let her down before, but he wouldn't hurt her. He'd pushed her on the swings. He'd taught her to love the night sky. He'd bought her a gallon of ice cream after her first boyfriend had broken up with her. And she really didn't want to sit in her office all day. Her coworkers would start to wonder why her door was locked. People would be asking her about Noelle and the memorial she had yet to think about. She really did need to just escape for a few hours. And without Wyatt or Bree, her dad seemed like the best option, especially since Whitney would not be there.

She walked around her desk, pulled out her suitcase and pushed the roller bag in his direction. "Can you take this for me?"

"You always keep a suitcase in your office?" he asked with surprise.

"I haven't been staying at home since Noelle was killed."

He gave her a somber look. "There's quite a lot you haven't told me, isn't there?"

"We'll talk about it all after you buy me a cheeseburger. I'm holding you to that."

"You got it."

As they walked out of her office, a warning voice begged her to reconsider. But it was too late. She just hoped that she could trust her dad.

Once again, Noelle's voice rang through her head...*I trusted the wrong person.*

Noelle would have trusted her father, too.

Uneasiness ran down her spine. She didn't want any more horrifying surprises, but she had a feeling that it didn't really matter what she wanted.

Twenty-Three

—➤≫◄◄◄—

Wyatt had been brought in after eleven and almost five hours had passed since he'd been seated in an interrogation room at the LA field office. Although, he'd been shown an arrest warrant, he had not been photographed, fingerprinted, or given an opportunity to call an attorney. He had been offered water, coffee, a day-old muffin, and a bathroom break in between questioning by two male agents he had never met before.

He'd answered some of their questions, while continuing to take every opportunity he could to request a call with his attorney.

He'd been told numerous times he would be able to make that call soon, but *soon* never came. Now, he was alone again, and had been tapping his fingers against the table top for the last thirty minutes. He was also getting damned tired of looking at his reflection in the two-way mirror on the opposite wall. He wondered if Joanna had been watching his interview. He found it oddly curious that she had not come in to speak to him personally.

Flynn had not shown up, either. He didn't know if Flynn had also been detained in some other room or what had happened to the rest of the team, including Bree.

He hoped Bree had found a way to stay with Avery. Because every minute that passed increased his tension and worry. The launch was less than twenty-four hours away. Time was running out, and if someone was going after Avery again, it would happen today, while he was stuck here answering ridiculous questions and trying to defend himself against bogus charges.

The door opened, and he straightened in his chair as Bree walked in.

"I hope you have good news," he said.

"Come with me," she said in a short, brisk voice.

She didn't have to ask him twice. He followed her to the door, thrilled to see the hallway outside the room devoid of security guards. Bree swiped her security card, opening the door, and then led him down another corridor before finally taking him down to the parking garage. She flipped the locks on a gray sedan, and he got into the passenger seat, not speaking until they reached the street.

"How did that happen?" he asked finally.

"Joanna left the office, and I still have enough rank to call shots." She flashed him a smile. "Sorry, it took me so long. I had to wait for my opportunity."

"You could lose your job, Bree."

"I could," she agreed. "But I don't want to work for an agency that doesn't support its people, and acts on bogus evidence. I saw the bank statements Joanna showed you. While they were good; they weren't that good. I know they're fake, but I couldn't get Joanna to listen to me. She was quite gleeful about taking you out. Apparently, her dislike of you has overridden her intelligence. At any rate, I sent the information to Flynn. He's working on getting you cleared, but he had to move locations, so Joanna couldn't shut him down, too.

"Where's Avery?"

"I told her to stay at Nova Star, but I haven't talked to her in a few hours. I've been busy trying to figure out how to get you out of there before Joanna had you transferred to a real jail cell."

"You are a badass, Bree. I can't thank you enough."

"You'd do the same for me. Who do you think set you up?"

"Probably the real traitor at Nova Star. Although, I have to admit I started thinking about what you said about Vincent Rowland. Whoever set me up certainly had the ability to get the information to the right person at the FBI, someone who was willing to do the most damage to my game."

"I agree, but I could be wrong about Vincent. My feelings could be colored by his attitude toward me. I don't want to be like Joanna. I don't want to let my emotions cloud my brain."

"Well, it's something to keep in mind. While he might hate me, I don't see him selling out his friend's company. He also doesn't have access to proprietary information. But at the moment, who set me up is the least of my concerns." He paused. "Where are we going?"

"There's a rental car place near here. You're going to need some wheels."

"I need to get to Avery."

"And I need you to let me do that. You won't be able to get anywhere near Nova Star, Wyatt."

As much as it pained him not to rush to Avery's side immediately, he knew she was right. "True."

"You should meet up with Flynn. I have his new address." She handed him a prepaid phone. "I put it on here as well as a new number for me."

"All right, but I'm going to make a stop on the way."

"Why? You need to stay out of sight."

"There aren't any cameras where I'm going. I want to talk to Carter Hayes. I tried to get in to see him earlier today at Nova Star, but he'd taken the day off."

"He's a minor player at best. Why waste time on him?"

"Because he's panicked, hanging on by his fingertips. I'm going to remind him that it's always the little fish who get caught up in the net first. With the launch tomorrow, Carter is our best chance to break open a lead."

"Joanna was going to speak to him, too. I hope you don't run into her." She pulled over to the side of the road, just down the block from the rental agency.

"I hope not, either." He put his hand on the door, then paused. "Take care of Avery, Bree. She's...special."

She gave him a knowing smile. "I know. And, by the way, she likes you, too."

"I sincerely doubt that."

"Have I ever lied to you?"

He shut the door on Bree's question, because he couldn't let himself hope that he might get another chance with Avery. That would only set him up for another fall.

* * *

After picking up the cheapest rental car he could find, Wyatt drove to Carter's apartment. He parked at the end of the block behind a large van and barely in sight of the townhouse and took his time making his way to the front door. It was quite possible that the building was under FBI surveillance, but he didn't see any of the usual signs, no cars with random people sitting inside, no dog walkers strolling the street, no repair vans used in stakeouts.

It was a risk going out in the open. The last thing he wanted to do was end up back in the interrogation room or in jail. But he had to find a way to crack open the case before it was too late.

He stepped under the overhang by Carter's front door, but as he reached for the bell, he saw that the lock had been broken.

He heard a thud and pushed the door open, readying his gun for whatever he might be facing. Carter was on the floor, writhing in pain, and an Asian man with a gun was standing by the balcony.

The next shot came in his direction, but he was able to jump out of the way. When he moved back to take his own shot, the man was already vaulting over the balcony railing. He ran across the room and out onto the deck, seeing the man disappear around the corner of the next building. There was no way he was going to catch him.

Going back inside, he grabbed a sweatshirt off the couch and knelt down by Carter, who had been shot in the right side of his chest.

He pressed the towel against his wound. "Who was that?"

"I don't know," Carter moaned, practically crying.

"You do know. Why did he shoot you?"

"Gotta call 911, man," Carter pleaded.

"As soon as you tell me what's going on." Judging by the location of Carter's wound, he didn't believe the wound was fatal, but Carter didn't know that. "Unless you want to die. Who are you working with?"

"Bickmore. He said I could get a promotion, money. All I had to do was pass some things along."

"What kind of things?"

"Envelopes, flash drives, money, whatever. Didn't always know. Dropped them at the funhouse."

Another piece of the puzzle clicked into place. "Did Noelle make the drop for you on Friday?"

"Supposed to be Saturday. I didn't realize Noelle knew anything, but she must have been watching me. Asked me some weird questions about Bickmore. Must have been on to him. Must have figured out how I set the meet and moved it up. Didn't know she'd stolen the drive from me until that night."

Was that what Carter had been looking for in Noelle's desk? "Why did she take the drive? Why cut you out?"

"Needed money for her mom, I guess. But she didn't give them the drive. Told them it was over. Said she turned the information over to Hamilton, and they needed to leave me alone. They stabbed her to death." He groaned. "I can't do this. Help me. I'll tell you everything later."

"Who would you meet in the funhouse?" he said, ignoring Carter's plea, but he did keep pressure on the wound.

"Different guys, never the same one, mostly Asian men."

"Noelle didn't give Hamilton anything. Was she bluffing?"

"Yes. Bickmore says Hamilton knows nothing. Thinks Avery has it. Wasn't at Noelle's place," he gasped.

"Who else is working with Bickmore? Is he the top?"

"No. One of the Tremaine kids, I think."

"Why would they sell out their own company?"

"No idea, but Bickmore said everything is out of control." He sucked in a breath, beads of sweat appearing on his forehead. "God, I think I'm dying."

"You're not dying. Keep pressure on this," he said, putting Carter's left hand on the towel, as he pulled out his phone. He punched in 911 but before he connected the call, he said, "You're going to say you've been shot and give them your address. You speak my name, and I'll kill you before anyone gets here. Understand?"

Carter gave a weak nod.

Wyatt punched in the numbers and held the phone near Carter's mouth.

"Help," Carter said, "I've been shot. 442 Trenton Way." He paused as the dispatcher asked him if the shooter was still in the house. "He's gone. I'm alone. Please hurry."

Wyatt hung up the call as the dispatcher asked for more info. "Do you know who set me up?"

"Set you up?" Carter echoed in confusion. "What are you talking about?"

"Bank accounts—Caymans."

Carter gave him a blank look. "Don't know."

"What about Noelle's missing phone? What's the story? Where is it?"

"Don't know. It's not here. But it doesn't matter. Everything is on the drive."

"Okay. Listen up. I was never here. You understand me, Carter? I'm your best chance at surviving this, but not if you talk."

"Won't talk. Need a guard. They'll come back to kill me."

"You'll get one at the hospital. No one is coming back now."

He got to his feet, looking around Carter's apartment, making sure he wasn't leaving any sign of his presence behind, but he hadn't touched anything but the now bloody sweatshirt.

He quickly left the townhome, staying in the shadows as he made his way down the long block to his car. As he started the engine, an ambulance came racing down the street, stopping in front of Carter's home. A police car arrived a second later. A couple of neighbors came outside at the commotion. He waited until the responders had gone inside, then pulled into a driveway, turned around and went in the opposite direction.

Carter would survive this, but Avery was still in danger. Whoever had tried to take Carter out would be going after her next—if he hadn't done so already.

That terrifying thought sent him straight to his phone. He punched in Bree's number.

"I was just going to call you," she said.

His heart stopped. "What's wrong? Do you have Avery?"

"No. She's not at work. Her coworker told me that she left the building with her father a few hours ago."

His gut twisted as he remembered Carter saying Bickmore was working with someone big, possibly one of the Tremaines. Brett Caldwell wasn't a Tremaine, but he had access to the inner family circle and he also had connections with China.

Avery couldn't be in danger from her own dad, could she?

"Where would he take her?" Bree asked.

"I'm guessing his house in Calabasas. But I'm shocked she left work."

"She was shaken after your arrest. I'm sorry I left her hanging. I was working on getting you out."

"It's not your fault."

"She's with her dad. He's not going to hurt her."

He knew Bree wanted her words to be comforting, but they'd both seen parents do terrible things to their kids. "I hope not."

"What happened with Carter?"

"I got there just in time. He took a shot in the chest, not life-threatening. The shooter got away—Asian man in his early thirties. I'm guessing it's the same man who shot at me from the hotel restaurant roof—Ran Ding. He's probably for hire. You need to get Flynn and the team down to the hospital. Carter needs a guard and I'm sure he has more information to give. He was working for Bickmore, making drops at the funhouse on a regular basis. He said Noelle must have gotten wind of the operation. She stole a flash drive from him and changed the time of the meet. But she didn't hand over the drive and was stabbed to death."

"So, everyone is looking for the drive."

"And killing anyone who knows about it." He got on the freeway as he ended that sentence, heading for Calabasas. "I'm going to get Avery."

"I'll take care of everything else."

He set his phone down, as he pressed his foot on the gas. He wanted to gun it. He wanted to drive as fast as possible to Caldwell's house, but he couldn't risk getting pulled over by the cops. He just had to hope that Avery would be safe with her father.

Twenty-Four

→⇒⇐←

"You slept for a long time," her father commented as Avery walked into his study a little past six in the evening. It was already dark outside, and the warm light from the desk lamp lit the room.

"I didn't intend to," she said, giving him a still tired smile. "I guess everything just caught up to me."

After leaving Nova Star, they'd stopped at Tommy's Burgers on the way to Calabasas and then eaten their chili cheeseburgers and fries by the pool. Then she'd gone upstairs to freshen up in one of the guestrooms. After changing out of her work clothes, she'd put on comfy leggings and a long-sleeve T-shirt, stretched out on the bed for a second and had fallen asleep. That had been hours ago.

"Are you writing?" she asked, taking a seat in the chair in front of his desk. He had his monitor on, and she could see text on the screen.

"Playing around with my next book idea."

"What's it going to be about?"

"Not sure yet."

"You never like to talk about your books while you're

writing them."

"Because they can always change."

"But you discuss them with Whitney. She was going on about your new project at dinner the other night."

"She only knows the general topic. She brags too much about me."

She smiled at that self-deprecating comment. "Come on, you like it."

He returned her smile. "Well, perhaps a little bit." He sat back in his chair, pressing his fingers together as he gave her a thoughtful glance. "You look better. Coming here was a good idea, wasn't it? Sometimes you can let your dear old dad take care of you."

She could have said it had never been her choice for him to stop taking care of her, but she didn't want to mess up the peace between them. Plus, he was right. She did feel better. But now that her brain was starting to work again, she realized she'd disappeared on Bree and she hadn't checked her phone since she'd left Nova Star.

"I should get my phone," she said. "I must have left it upstairs."

"Hang on," her dad said, before she could get up. "Talk to me, Avery. Tell me what's happening. I only have bits and pieces, and I think there is a lot going on I don't know about."

"There's probably a lot going on neither one of us knows about."

"Like what?"

"I think Noelle was involved in some sort of conspiracy at Nova Star. I'm not sure what her role was or who else is involved."

"And this conspiracy is about what?"

"Secrets, technology, proprietary information. It's possible someone is trying to sabotage the launch or the satellite itself."

"Then why hasn't Hamilton shut down the launch?"

"Because he thinks he has the situation under control. Or

at least he thought that yesterday. I don't know what he thinks now since Wyatt was arrested. Have you spoken to him?"

"Not since I saw him earlier. I have talked to Whitney. She said her father is livid, that he thinks Wyatt betrayed him, that he came into the company under the guise of helping to find a traitor when he was there to steal from the inside."

She wondered if Hamilton had figured out that Wyatt was FBI or if he just believed he was a spy.

"I have to say, Avery," her father continued. "The FBI must have had some damning evidence on Wyatt to arrest him the day before the launch. He's Nova Star's top security guy. They left the company scrambling."

"I know. I've been thinking the same thing, but Wyatt isn't guilty. He's not a thief or a traitor."

"How do you know?"

It was a simple question, and, in reality, there was a simple answer. "Because I know what kind of person he is. I trust him." She realized how true the words were as soon as they came out of her mouth.

"Do you also love him?"

She hesitated at the blunt question. "Does love feel terrifying and wonderful at the same time?"

He gave her a faint smile. "That's a good description of it."

"I've always been a little afraid to love. When it ends, it hurts so much. I've wondered if it's worth the pain."

Shadows crossed his face. "That's because of me. I let you down. I hurt you."

"You did," she agreed, too tired not to be honest. "But it wasn't just that you left. It was that you and Mom were so happy together and then you weren't. I didn't know how you went from love to hate so quickly. How could I trust that my feelings about someone or their feelings for me wouldn't change just as fast?"

"Love and hate are two sides of the same coin," he said quietly. "Sometimes the love you have for someone doesn't last forever. That's not the fairy tale, but it's real life."

"Do you love Whitney? Will she last forever?"

He sucked in a breath. "I don't know, Avery. I don't have a crystal ball."

"But you have experience, and you know how you feel."

"I do love Whitney. She's more like me than anyone I've ever met. We understand each other."

She tilted her head, wondering about the odd note in his voice. "It sounds like there's a *but* coming..."

"But," he said with a smile. "I'm a lot older than her. She might wake up and wonder what she's doing with an old man when she could have a young stud."

"The age difference doesn't seem to bother her."

"I just hope she isn't using me to fill the hole in her heart."

"What do you mean?" she asked, surprised by his words.

"She adored her mother and her loss a year ago still haunts Whitney. She's not as close with her dad as she was with her mother. I think she often feels like the odd man out in the family, because she doesn't work at the company, isn't caught up in the space race as her father and brothers are. She only went to her dad's house tonight, because it's a celebration of her mother's life. She couldn't care less about the launch tomorrow."

"I guess I can understand that."

"I want to give Whitney what she needs. I'm happy to fill the empty places in her heart; I just don't want to heal her and then watch her walk away."

"It's a risk," she agreed, thinking that even when her dad was being open and honest, his ego still showed through. He had spoken of healing Whitney, as if he alone had that power, but that wasn't the way it worked. "I don't think you can give Whitney the peace she needs. Ultimately, that has to come from herself. Isn't that what you teach in your books and your seminars?"

"Some version of that," he admitted. "Have you read any

of my books?"

"I might have skimmed through one," she admitted.

He smiled. "Good to know. I like that you wrote a book, too. I like to believe you got something from me."

"I guess I did."

His expression changed, his eyes turning somber. He looked like he wanted to say something else but couldn't quite get the words out.

"What?" she asked. "What are you thinking?"

"That I wish I hadn't waited so long to come back into your life."

"Me, too," she said. "But as you said earlier, we can't change the past."

"I'm glad we're speaking freely now. I know that you don't love that I'm involved with Whitney and the Tremaines. This was your world, and I broke right into the middle of it."

"It has been awkward."

"I probably should have backed off in the beginning."

"But you didn't, because you wanted in with the Tremaines."

He looked a little surprised by her candor. "Is that what you think?"

"Yes," she said, not backing down. "I sometimes wonder if you reconnected with me just because you realized I could get you into their world."

"You think I'm a gold-digger, Avery? I have made quite a bit of my own money."

"I know that, but you like to live in luxury. Maybe you didn't come to see me with any kind of hidden motive, but when you saw an opportunity to get in with the Tremaines, you took it."

"Well, I guess I know what you really think now," he said, disappointment in his voice.

"I guess you do," she said wearily. "This wasn't a good idea. I'm going to leave. I'll get my things and call a cab." She got to her feet. She had no idea where she was going to go, but anywhere else seemed like a good idea. Maybe she'd call Bree and see what she knew.

"You don't have to leave, Avery," her father said, as he rose. "Let's keep talking. Let's hash it all out."

"It's pretty much all out, Dad."

"Is it? Are you sure?"

As he came around the desk, he knocked over a framed photo. She instinctively reached for it. It was a photo of her father in front of a Chinese temple, another reminder that her dad had had a life she didn't really know much about. But her father wasn't hiding the fact that he'd been in China. *Was that because he was clever or because his trips there were completely innocent of what was going on at Nova Star?*

"Thanks," he said, as she handed him the frame, and he set it on his desk. "Now, are you sure there isn't something else you want to talk about? Believe it or not, I want to have a relationship with you, Avery."

She looked into his warm, familiar brown eyes and wanted more than anything to believe him. "We've said enough for now."

"Well, I don't want you to leave. Stay and have some birthday cake. We have a lot left over from last night, and Whitney won't be home for hours."

She brushed her hair off her face, feeling incredibly weary despite her long nap. The constant stress and uncertainty about everyone in her life was starting to get to her. "I suppose I could have a piece of cake, but I'm going to get my things together. I can't spend the night here."

"I understand. I'll drive you wherever you want to go. But I don't want you to be alone. Can I take you to a friend's house?"

"I'll figure it out. First, I'm going to take a shower and change clothes. Then we can have some cake."

"Sounds good," he said, relief in his eyes. "Take your time."

As she left the study, she walked toward the stairs. She

had only gone up a few steps when she heard her father's voice. That gave her pause. *Her dad was on the phone.*

"Yes, Avery is here," he said, then fell silent. "Sure, no problem."

Her heart skipped a beat. *Who was her dad talking to? Why had he said she was at the house?*

She tried not to jump to conclusions. He could just be talking to Whitney.

But what if he was talking to someone else?

She suddenly didn't feel safe at all anymore. She jogged up the stairs and ran into the guest room. She took her phone out of her bag and saw a bunch of texts from Bree, asking her to call her. She would call her back, but right now she needed to get out of the house.

Forget the shower. Forget the cake. She needed to find some place to hide where no one, not even her father, knew where she was. She might be completely paranoid, but every instinct she had was telling her to run.

She put on her shoes and grabbed her open suitcase from the floor, so she could put her work clothes in it. As she did so, her gaze caught on the sleeve of her short black leather coat, the one still stained with Noelle's blood.

So much had happened since Noelle had been killed, and yet she still didn't know who had murdered her best friend.

When she pulled the coat from the case, something fell out of the pocket. She leaned down to pick it up from the bed, realizing it was the charm bracelet she'd taken from Noelle's apartment.

An uneasy shiver ran down her spine.

She'd completely forgotten about the bracelet.

She'd stuffed it in her pocket when she'd seen the autographed book on the floor, and from then on it had been a race to stay ahead of Noelle's killer.

But was the bracelet important? It didn't seem like it could be.

Noelle's last words rang through her head: *Left*

something... apartment...you'll recognize it from when we were young. So innocent then.

She held it up to the light, the charms dangling in front of her. They were the charms of a young girl: a silver heart, a starfish, a guitar and a book. Her pulse beat faster.

She flipped open the corner of the book, remembering when they used to hide candy hearts inside the space. There was no candy heart today, but a tiny silver rectangle. She pulled it out with shaky fingers. A tiny button flipped open a flash drive.

"Oh, God!" she whispered. Her breath came fast as her fingers closed around the drive. *This has to be what everyone was looking for. She'd had it all along.*

"Avery."

She jumped as her father walked into the room.

His gaze narrowed as he looked at her. "What's wrong? You're white as a sheet."

"I—I..." She didn't know what to say.

"Honey, talk to me. Trust me."

Noelle's words rang through her head again...*I trusted the wrong person.*

Her fingers tightened around the drive. "I have to go."

"Not like this. You're upset. What changed? You weren't this distraught a few minutes ago." His gaze dropped to her closed hand. "What do you have in your hand?"

When she didn't answer, he looked disappointed. "You really don't trust me, do you?"

"I don't. I can't."

"Why not?"

"Because you were just on the phone telling someone I was here. And last night you had a cryptic conversation with Kyle about asking him to do something for you. Then Wyatt and I were followed when we left here, almost run off the road and later we were shot at..." The words poured out of her.

Her father looked at her in stunned amazement. "I have

no idea what you're talking about Avery. Whitney called just
now, and I told her you were here, and she didn't have to
hurry home. We were catching up with each other. As for
Kyle last night, I had asked him to help Whitney get into a
country club she's on the waiting list for, but he keeps
stalling. I was annoyed with him. I reminded him that
Whitney does a lot for him."

"But someone tried to get into Kyle's email from this
house. Was that you? Whitney?"

"I don't know. It wasn't me. It was probably Kyle. Did
you say you were shot at?"

"Yes. Wyatt saved my life—not just once, but three
times."

He stared back at her. "You need protection, Avery. I
need to hire you a bodyguard or two."

"I wouldn't be able to trust whoever you hired. The
danger is coming from someone close to me. The only person
I know I can count on is Wyatt."

"You can count on me."

Before she could reply, she heard a noise from outside
the room. "Who's here?"

"No one is here," he said with a frown. "It's just the two
of us."

Her heart started pounding as she heard another subtle
noise. This time her father heard it, too, his gaze moving
toward the open door.

"He's here," she whispered, knowing in her gut that time
had just run out.

"Who?"

"Whoever killed Noelle. Whoever wants me dead."

His face paled, but his eyes filled with determination.
"We have to get out of here. Come on. We'll go down the
back stairs."

She was afraid to leave the room and terrified to stay.
They had no weapons, nothing with which to defend
themselves, so they might as well try to make a run for it.

Luckily, the room she'd chosen was closer to the back stairs than the front.

Her dad went out the door first, checking the landing, then motioning her forward. She came into the hall and her father gently pushed her toward the back staircase, staying behind her, as they crept down the hall. Despite their efforts to remain quiet, they were making too much noise, she realized, as hard footsteps came after them.

She picked up the pace. It was now or never. They couldn't stop. They hit the ground-floor hallway, and she saw the front door wide open. She made a run for it, her dad on her heels.

And then she heard her father yell out. She whirled around as he crumpled to the floor, grabbing his left arm in pain. A stone-cold, dark-haired Asian man in a black T-shirt and black jeans pointed his gun at her.

"Where is it?" he demanded.

She realized she had the drive still clasped in her hand. If she handed it over, he'd kill her. If she didn't hand it over, he'd kill her.

She looked at her dad, saw anguish in his eyes.

The man saw her indecision and pointed his weapon at her father. "Him or the drive."

"You're going to kill us anyway."

"I just want the drive."

She didn't believe him for a second, but what choice did she have? "All right."

Before she could open her hand, a blast rang out from behind her, deafening her, terrifying her. She dropped to her knees as the Asian fell backward, a bullet hole ripping through his chest.

And then, miraculously, Wyatt was there.

"Avery, are you all right?" He came towards her, gun in hand, fear in his eyes.

"I'm okay. But Dad—" She moved toward her father. "We'll get help," she promised him. "Hang in there."

Wyatt took off his belt and strapped it around her father's arms as he propped her dad up against the wall. "That should stop the bleeding."

"Don't worry about me. Get Avery out of here in case there are more coming," her dad said.

"I'm not leaving you," she said, realizing he'd saved her life by making her go down the stairs first.

"My phone is in my pocket," her dad said, trying to reach into his pocket with his good hand. "I'll call 911 after you're gone."

"Here it is," Wyatt said, helping her father get his phone out.

"Get her out of here, Wyatt. I expect you to protect her with your life."

The two men exchanged a pointed look.

"I will," Wyatt promised.

Despite their agreement, she shook her head when he motioned her toward the door. "Not until I know help is here. I have to wait. He's defenseless."

"Give me the guy's gun," her dad said, as he got off the phone with 911. "I can take care of myself."

Wyatt walked over and picked up the gun. He also took a moment to go through the man's pockets, pulling out a cell phone and a wallet. He glanced at the ID, then he returned to her father and handed him the weapon, putting the other items in his pocket.

"Get the hell out of here, Avery," her father commanded. "Now."

With both men adamant on her leaving, she gave in, and followed Wyatt out the kitchen door. He grabbed her hand and took her through the backyard, past the pool and the gardens, and down a long hill that led to a tall fence and a secondary gate to the property. The gate was propped open with a stick. Clearly Wyatt had used the gate to come in without anyone seeing him.

When they came through the gate, they jogged down

another street and another. Wyatt seemed to have a clear-minded vision of where they were going, but she didn't understand why he had parked so far away.

She heard sirens in the distance and was relieved that help was coming. But along with that relief came fear.

"Are you still in trouble?" she asked.

"Yes," he said, his fingers squeezing hers. "But I'm not guilty."

She met his gaze. "I know."

His eyes brightened. "I'm glad. I had to park outside the development. Couldn't risk the guard turning me in."

"I understand."

They didn't speak again for several more minutes as Wyatt took her down a side yard, over a low fence and down another more rugged hillside to a parked car.

Her pulse was still racing, as he turned on the engine and pulled away from the curb. She was afraid to go through the canyon roads again, but Wyatt turned away at the last minute, heading onto the crowded freeway.

There was a lot of traffic, which slowed their escape, but she also felt more hidden amidst all the cars.

A few exits later, Wyatt pulled off the freeway and turned into a crowded parking lot by a fashion center mall. While the lot was well-lit, he picked a spot in the shadows, then turned off engine and lights and then shifted in his seat to look at her.

"Are you all right, Avery?"

"You saved my life—again."

"Third time was the charm."

"That was actually the fourth time."

"But who's counting," he said lightly.

She shook her head, feeling overwhelmed with emotion. "God, Wyatt, how are you always there when I need you?"

"I was afraid I wouldn't get there in time."

"But you did."

"And that guy won't be coming after you again."

"I just hope my dad—"

"He's going to be all right, Avery."

"Are you sure?"

"Yes."

It was ironic that the one person who had lied to her the most was the one person she absolutely trusted to tell her the truth now.

"I'm sorry I was gone all day, Avery," he continued. "I wish you hadn't had to go through that. I've been trying to get back to you for hours."

"What happened?"

"Someone set me up to look like a double agent."

"Who?"

"I don't know. Bree broke me out of there."

"What?" she asked in astonishment. "Bree broke you out of jail?"

"Not jail, just a holding room at the FBI field office. She knew I needed to fight for you, and I needed to be able to defend myself against the bogus charges. I wasn't going to be able to do that from the office."

She was amazed by Bree's actions. "Won't Bree be in a lot of trouble?"

"She could lose everything," he said tightly. "But that's what we do for each other."

"I can't imagine that kind of loyalty. Actually, that's not true. I can imagine it. Because you've shown it to me."

His gaze met hers. "There are a lot of things I want to say to you."

"I know, but now isn't the time. Who was that man in the house?"

"Ran Ding, a hired gun, tied to the Chinese PLA. He shot Carter before he got to you."

"Is Carter dead?"

"No, he's going to live. Carter told me Bickmore was using him to make drops at the funhouse. He was the go-between."

"Are you serious? He admitted that?"

"He thought he was dying. He said Noelle must have caught on to what he was doing. She apparently stole the flash drive he was supposed to deliver and set up her own meet. He thought she wanted the money to help her mom. But he said she didn't hand over the drive. She told the person at the meet that the game was over, that everything on the drive had been handed over to Hamilton, that she'd come to tell them it was done."

"And they stabbed her. Why would she do that? Why didn't she just turn the drive over and not show up?"

"I don't know. Hopefully, we can fill in a few more blanks when Carter gets medical attention. At any rate, they didn't believe she'd given the drive to Hamilton, because Bickmore knew that Hamilton didn't have it and was going about his business as usual. So, they went looking for the drive. Carter told them that you had to have it, because he didn't. Or it was lost in the fire."

"I do have it." She opened her left palm.

Wyatt's eyes widened in surprise. "Where did you get that?"

"It was in the charm bracelet I took from Noelle's place the morning after her murder."

"You never said you took a bracelet."

"I honestly forgot all about it. When I got to her apartment that day, everything was such a mess. I was just wandering around, looking for some clue to jump out at me. I saw the bracelet and a heart necklace in her jewelry box, and I wanted to keep them to remember her by. I picked them up and put them in the pocket of my coat." She paused, trying to remember her exact movements. "And then I saw the book on the floor, and I grabbed it. After that, everything went crazy. When we got back to my place, I put the coat in the suitcase when I packed my bag, and I haven't worn it since then because there is blood on the sleeve."

"But tonight..."

"I was repacking my clothes and I pulled out the coat, and the bracelet fell out. This was hidden inside the book charm." She held up the drive. "What do you think is on it?"

"Hell if I know, but we're going to find out."

"I left my computer at my dad's house. Should we go to Bree's?"

"No time." He glanced at the front door of the mall. "Looks like I picked the right place to park. I'm betting there's an electronics store inside."

"I'll go. You need to stay out of sight."

He didn't look like he wanted to agree, but what choice did he have. He was a wanted man. "All right." He took out his wallet. "You can use this card."

She took it out of his hand. "I won't be long."

He put a hand on her leg. "Avery…I'm glad you're okay."

"I'm glad you're okay," she said, feeling a rush of love that wanted to bring tears to her eyes.

Wyatt leaned over and kissed her, a warm, tender, promising kiss that she wished she could savor and revel in and keep on going forever. For just a moment, she closed her eyes and breathed him in, feeling warmth and pleasure wash over her. There were still so many questions, so much fear, but for this moment, everything felt—perfect.

Wyatt finally pulled away, as if it was the most difficult thing he'd ever had to do. "We'll talk more later."

She smiled. "Sure. I can't wait for more *talking.*"

He smiled back. "I can't believe you can joke right now. You're a lot tougher than you think, Avery."

"I'm actually beginning to think I'm pretty tough, too. I'll be right back."

Twenty-Five

Every minute that Avery was gone felt like an hour. He tapped his fingers restlessly on his thigh, wishing he hadn't had to send her into the mall alone. But he told himself that the immediate danger had been crushed with Ran Ding's death. It would take time for whoever had hired him to know he had failed.

At least, he'd taken care of one contract player, but there would be more until they figured out what was on the drive and who was really behind the killings. While he was waiting, he got on the phone to Bree.

"Wyatt," she said. "Tell me Avery is all right."

"She's fine. I got there just in time. Ran Ding is dead. Avery's father was shot in the arm, and he's on his way to the hospital."

"Where are you?"

"Sitting in a car at the mall," he said.

"Well, I didn't expect to hear you say that."

"Avery found the missing drive. She had it all along. It

was hidden away in a charm bracelet. She went into the mall to get a computer."

"Why not just come here?"

"I need to look at that drive now, so I know what we're dealing with. It will take too long to get across town. I'll forward the contents as soon as I can."

"You still have the encrypted email?"

"I've got it. What's happening there? How's Carter?"

"He's in surgery, but it looks like he should survive. Unfortunately, we haven't been able to speak to him since he arrived at the hospital. Both Flynn and Joanna have agents down there, ready to interrogate him as soon as he's able to speak."

"Flynn and Joanna are working together?"

"They are now. Flynn was able to track down the bank account in the Caymans," she replied. "It doesn't actually exist. All the records were fake. There is no cash despite what Joanna thought."

"I'm not surprised."

"We sent the evidence both to Joanna and to her boss, so she couldn't bury it. She's livid that I helped you get away and even more furious that she was played. She's going to go to the ends of the earth to determine who used her—at least that's her story."

"How much trouble are you in for breaking me out?"

"There will be a lot of discussions for both of us after this is all over," she said. "But you're in the clear, and right now the focus is on Nova Star and the launch tomorrow. Call me back as soon as you know anything."

"I will. Can you also check on Avery's father? I'm not sure what hospital they would have taken him, too, probably whatever is closest to his house."

"Will do."

As he ended the call, Avery returned to the car with a triumphant gleam in her eyes. "I found a computer that still has a USB port to open the drive."

"That's great. Let's see what we've got." As Avery tore open the packaging, he added, "I asked Bree to check on your dad."

She paused to look at him. "What else did Bree say? I assume she's not under arrest since she reached you."

"No. In fact, my team leader has managed to find information to clear my name."

"Thank God for that." Avery tore open the packaging and turned on the computer. "Looks like we have enough juice to see what's on the drive," she said, as she inserted it into the USB port.

He leaned over the console as they both watched the screen light up. For a moment, he worried that the computer light was making them too visible, but he didn't want to waste time moving to another location.

"This better give us some answers," Avery murmured.

"I think it will." His instincts told him that whatever was on this drive would finally fill in the remaining puzzle pieces.

There was only one folder on the drive. It included several files. Avery clicked on the first one, revealing pages and pages of computer code. Another file contained specs and technical drawings of the satellite. The third file appeared to hold test reports and analyses, some with handwritten notes. Every page was stamped with a Nova Star watermark.

"Can you tell what these are about?" he asked.

"They're about the new defense system on the satellite," she replied, as she skimmed through the open pages, pausing every and now and then. "It's a bit too technical for me, but this information is clearly about the satellite. The test results look odd," she added, studying one page for another minute. "These results show more failures than previously noted."

"Maybe the system doesn't work and the reports you saw earlier didn't contain accurate information."

"Or these reports are wrong. Either way, there's a good chance there's a problem with the satellite." She gazed back at him. "We need to get this information to Hamilton. He has to stop the launch."

"He's been unwilling to do that."

"This should convince him." She frowned. "This information had to come from Kyle's division of the company. Not that it necessarily means he stole it."

"Nor does it mean that he didn't. Carter told me Bickmore is working for someone higher up, one of the Tremaines. We don't have a lot of choices."

"Would he really sabotage his own company?" she asked. "We're still missing something."

"Motivation," he agreed. "Maybe we'll find it when we show the family what we have."

"They're all together at Hamilton's house." She paused. "I should call Whitney and tell her about my dad."

"You can't do that yet. You'll tip our hand."

"My father might have called her from the ambulance."

"I'm going to hope he didn't. I want to send this file to Bree, but I need an internet connection."

Avery tipped her head to a nearby coffee house. "We can probably do it from there."

He nodded. "Let me drive closer. You might not even need to go inside." He started the car and moved it into a spot out the café.

"Got it," Avery said.

He took the computer out of her hand and went on the net, sending Bree the file through an encrypted email server. When that was done, he handed the laptop back to Avery.

As she put it by her feet, she said, "Did you check the phone you took from the gunman?"

"No, dammit." He reached into his pocket for the other phone, unable to believe he'd forgotten to do that.

"Is it locked?" Avery asked.

"It's actually not," he said. "It's obviously a burner phone and not meant to be kept for long." He opened up the messages and skimmed through them.

"What do the texts say?" Avery asked impatiently.

"There are two addresses, one for Carter's house and one for your dad's house."

"He was hired to kill us."

"Yes," he said shortly, moving from the texts to the voicemail. There was one number that he didn't recognize, but he pushed play and put the message on speaker, so Avery could hear it.

A familiar voice came across the line, and a shiver ran down his spine.

"This is your last chance. Avery has to die tonight. Call me when it's done."

"Oh, my God," Avery breathed, shock in her eyes. "Is that who I think it is?"

"Yes," he said grimly, thanking God again that he'd gotten to her in time.

"I can't believe it."

He revved the engine and pulled out of the lot. "Looks like Hamilton's private family party is going to get a little bigger." As he pulled onto the road, he handed her his phone. "Text Bree the latest. She'll send backup."

"If it's not there by the time we get to Hamilton's house, I'm not waiting," Avery declared, her fear turning to fury.

"Neither am I," he swore, impatient to end this once and for all.

* * *

Hamilton lived in a mansion in Calabasas, in a separate development from that of Brett and Whitney, but only a few miles away from where they'd just come from.

Avery's stomach churned as Wyatt sped down the freeway. She couldn't believe what she'd just heard. Betrayal, anger, hurt—so many emotions were running through her. She'd been targeted for death by someone she knew. She could hardly believe it.

"No guard gate here," Wyatt muttered. "Your father has

more security than Hamilton."

"Hamilton always says he's not a man to hide behind gates," she muttered.

"One less problem for us."

When Wyatt pulled up in the circular drive in front of the three-story home, Avery jumped out of the car as it came to a rolling stop. Wyatt was right behind her.

She rang the bell twice, impatient to get inside, to face the person who'd killed Noelle, who'd shot Carter and her father, who'd wanted her dead.

Wyatt had his gun at the ready, but she didn't think they were going to need it. Someone who paid others to do the dirty work was a coward.

Hamilton's housekeeper, Rena Khouri, opened the door. She was an older Indian woman who had been working for Hamilton for almost twenty years.

"Avery," she said with surprise. "I didn't think you were coming tonight."

"I had a change of plans," she said, pushing past Rena. "Where is everyone?"

"They're in the living room, but this is a very emotional evening," Rena said, giving her and Wyatt a worried look. "I just took them champagne to toast sweet Margery."

"This can't wait," she said, storming across the marbled floor of the entry, pushing open the double doors that led into the luxurious living room.

They were all there: Hamilton, Kyle, Jonathan, and Whitney.

Hamilton stood up at their abrupt entrance, surprise and wariness in his gaze.

"What's going on, Avery?" Hamilton demanded. "What's he doing here?"

"Wyatt is with me." She saw worry and even a little fear on the faces of Hamilton's three adult children.

"You bring a traitor into my house?" Hamilton asked in amazement, sending Wyatt a burning look. "I'm calling the

FBI."

"Don't bother," she said sharply, happy to take charge, because she was full of steam, and she was ready to blow it out. "There is a traitor in your house, but it's not Wyatt. The past few days, since my best friend died, someone has been trying to kill me—someone in this room."

Whitney let out a gasp, putting a hand to her heart. "Don't be ridiculous, Avery. That's absurd."

"It's not absurd. I was in your house when a hit man came in. He shot my dad."

"What?" Whitney jumped to her feet. "Is Brett all right?"

There appeared to be genuine panic in Whitney's eyes, but at this point, Avery didn't really trust anyone. She didn't know if one of them was involved or all of them. "My father was shot in the arm. He's on his way to the hospital."

"I have to go see him," Whitney said.

"Sit down," Wyatt ordered. "You're not going anywhere. Brett will be fine. It was not a life-threatening wound. He's being taken care of, and none of you are going anywhere until we sort all this out."

"The gunman is dead by the way," Avery continued. "Wyatt killed him." She held up a phone. "But he left this phone behind. It has an interesting voicemail on it. I think you should all hear it."

She pushed play, and Kyle's voice rang out in the room.

Kyle jumped to his feet and rushed toward her.

But Wyatt was too quick, grabbing Kyle by the shoulders and slamming him into the wall by the fireplace, pinning him there, a gun at his head. "I don't think so," Wyatt said. "Your father needs to hear the whole message. Play it again, Avery."

She did as he asked.

"What did you do, Kyle?" Hamilton asked in shock, staring at his middle child.

"Yeah. What the hell did you do?" Jonathan demanded, also rising. "You're the one who's been setting me up? My own brother?"

Wyatt let go of Kyle but kept the gun on him. "You're not going anywhere, Kyle. It's over. Start talking."

"I have nothing to say," Kyle bit out.

"Not good enough," Wyatt said, slamming a fist into Kyle's stomach.

The man doubled over, gasping for breath.

"Try again," Wyatt ordered.

"I—" Kyle couldn't get the words out.

Hamilton moved forward, shaking his head in bewilderment. "You wanted to kill Avery? She's been a friend to you. She's part of the family. Why would you do that?"

"Because I have a flash drive that Noelle took from Carter," Avery replied when Kyle gave his father a helpless shrug. "I didn't actually know I had it until tonight, but it contains information about the satellite. It's apparently one of several drives that Larry Bickmore asked Carter Hayes to hand over to a third party. But all that was done at the request of Kyle."

"You sold our technology?" Hamilton asked in astonishment. "Why? So much of it was your work. This was our dream—our family dream. Your mother…she would be so disappointed in you."

"Don't talk about my mother," Kyle said bitterly. "You're the reason she's dead."

"What are you talking about?" Whitney interrupted. "Dad didn't kill Mom."

"He did," Kyle said, fury raging in his eyes now that he realized he had no defense and his secrets were all coming out. "He kept pouring money into the space program instead of medical research. Billions of dollars went into putting rockets into space, all in the hopes of landing people on Mars. All that cash could have gone into finding a cure for Mom's cancer. She could still be alive if he wasn't so obsessed with space."

Hamilton turned white at his son's accusations. "I did everything I could for your mother."

"You didn't do enough. She didn't care about space. She just loved you with a blindness that never allowed her to see you for the selfish person that you are," Kyle ranted. "After she died, I was angry, so damned angry. And I wasn't alone. Larry felt the same way."

"Larry?" Hamilton echoed. "My best friend, Larry?"

"Who loved Mom as much as you did," Kyle reminded him. "Larry said that he never would have let her die, that with the kind of money you have, you could have hired a team of researchers the minute she was diagnosed. You could have thrown all your money into the drug trials. But no, you just wanted to go to space."

"The cancer was too widespread," Hamilton said, pain in his eyes. "I loved your mother. She was my life. I would have done anything to save her."

"You didn't do anything. That was the point. I was going to quit Nova Star after she died. I was done. And then Larry introduced me to a woman—Jia Lin."

Avery shot Wyatt a quick look at the mention of the Chinese woman's name.

"She was very sweet, very smart, very kind," Kyle continued, seemingly resigned now to telling the entire story. Or maybe he just wanted his father to know the hatred burning in his heart. "Jia helped me through my pain. She helped me see that there was a way to get revenge and get myself out from under your thumb. She said I was the brains behind Nova Star. Why shouldn't I make more money, be the man on the magazine covers, be the one to pioneer space? Why give you all the glory? Her friends ran a private aerospace company in Beijing. They offered me money and a chance to be part of something that didn't belong to you. I thought what better way to take you down than to give my technology to a competitor, to a foreign country, one you believed would never make a dent in the space race."

"I can't believe this," Whitney said. "You sound insane right now, Kyle."

"I'm not the one who's crazy—it's him." Kyle tipped his head in Hamilton's direction.

"No, it's you," Jonathan said. "You're rewriting history. Mom wanted Nova Star to succeed as much as Dad did, and she didn't want extraordinary measures used to keep her alive."

"That's because she didn't want to take money away from Dad's dream when she was dying," Kyle shouted.

"What happened to Jia?" Wyatt interjected. "Who killed her and why?"

"She was killed because I started getting cold feet," Kyle admitted. "I was getting my head back together, and I wanted to back out. I realized what I really wanted to do was get out of the space race entirely, but I was in too deep. They killed Jia as a warning to me. And then they blackmailed me with recordings of all my conversations with her. If I didn't do what they said, they would kill me, too. I was trapped."

"You sent me to talk to that woman," Jonathan said, giving his brother a bewildered look. "You set me up, Kyle."

"I couldn't go myself. I was surprised she asked for me to come to San Francisco. She didn't realize she was being set up, that the information she'd been told to bring to me would actually be found in her car. Her employers wanted you to know there was a mole in your company, that it might be your son," Kyle added, looking at his father. "Just not the son you thought it was."

"I never believed it was Jonathan, but I also never could have imagined it would be you," Hamilton said, sitting down on the couch, suddenly looking every one of his sixty-eight years.

Avery felt sorry for Hamilton, but right now her attention was on Kyle. "Why did the Chinese, I assume it was the Chinese, want Hamilton to know there was a spy in the company?"

"They thought it would put pressure on me, and, yes, it's a Chinese company secretly funded by the state.

"How did Noelle get involved?" she asked.

"She was working in my department for a while. Larry was using Carter as a go-between. I guess Noelle got suspicious as to why Carter was in my wing of the building so often. I don't know. I asked him about it, and he said she must have figured out that he was selling secrets to secure a promotion from Larry. She had money problems of her own, so she took the drive that he was supposed to turn over on Saturday night and set up her own meet. But I guess she had second thoughts and didn't hand over the drive. My associates don't tolerate disloyalty, so she was killed." Kyle's gaze bored into hers. "I knew you had it, Avery. Where was it?"

"It isn't important where it was. You ordered me to be killed. This wasn't just about selling secrets; this was about murder. People died because of you, Kyle."

"I had no choice. I got caught up in a situation that went really bad. They put out the contract on you; I was just supposed to help them locate you, but Wyatt kept saving you. We were desperate. The launch is tomorrow. That's why I said it had to be done tonight, or it would all be over."

She couldn't believe how calmly he was talking about working with a hit man, about plotting out her death. "You put the GPS tracker in my bag at the birthday party, didn't you?"

"That was easy. You left it in the living room."

"I thought of you as a brother, Kyle," she murmured.

"Yeah, you wanted to be in the family so bad, and Dad wanted you in our family, too, because you shared his dreams," Kyle said bitterly. "You were part of the problem. You encouraged him to go for everything he wanted. You became the voice in his head."

"What's supposed to happen at the launch tomorrow?" Wyatt interrupted.

Kyle hesitated, then shrugged, as if realizing it was truly over. "The satellite will destroy itself after it separates from the rocket. The Chinese company is already building a satellite defense system that will work, based on my engineering. Nova Star won't be able to regroup fast enough to beat them. It's the end of the race, Dad," he added, looking back Hamilton. "You're not going to beat anyone to Mars. You're going to be human, and you're going to die on Earth just like Mom did."

As Kyle stopped talking, they heard a pounding on the front door, a ringing of the bell, followed by shouts of, "FBI."

Rena threw open the door and a dozen agents swarmed into the house.

Wyatt put away his gun, grabbed Kyle's arm and turned him over to one of the agents.

Avery didn't recognize any of the men, but Bree and the woman who had arrested Wyatt earlier were front and center. She was surprised to see the other agent there. She'd thought Bree and Flynn would bring their own team, and she really hoped Wyatt wasn't going to be arrested again, too. She felt like she was on the very edge of a breakdown, overwhelmed by emotion, and she couldn't lose Wyatt for a second time that day.

She instinctively took a step toward him.

Wyatt gave her a reassuring look. "It's fine," he said.

Hamilton was back on his feet now. "Agent Davis," he said to the blonde woman. "It turns out you were right. One of my sons was working with a foreign government to sabotage my company. But it wasn't Jonathan."

"I've been read in on everything," Joanna said, in a crisp, cold tone. "We also have agents arresting Larry Bickmore as we speak. We would like you to call off the launch tomorrow. That's not really a request, by the way. This is a matter of national security."

"I understand," Hamilton said, a weary note in his voice. "I'll make the call."

"We're going to need to interview each and every one of you as well as numerous individuals at Nova Star," Joanna continued. "Special Agents Adams and MacKenzie will take your initial statements now. This is just the beginning of a long investigation. But it will not be conducted by me. Agents from New York and DC will be in town tomorrow." Her gaze moved to Wyatt. "You have friends in high places, Wyatt. But someday you and I will finish our unfinished business."

That sounded ominous, Avery thought, wondering why the agent seemed so personally angered by Wyatt. Maybe she was just embarrassed that she'd been used as a pawn in the game.

Joanna walked out of the room, followed by all the agents, except two people in plain clothes: Bree and an attractive man who had to be Flynn, the leader of Wyatt's task force.

"I need to get to my boyfriend," Whitney said to Bree. "He's been shot. I don't know anything about any of this."

"We'll start with a few basic questions and then you can be on your way," Bree said, leading Whitney to another corner of the room, while Flynn isolated Jonathan.

That left Hamilton standing with her and Wyatt.

"Who are you?" Hamilton asked Wyatt.

"I'm FBI. I was inserted into your company by a secret task force after you refused to cooperate with the FBI. My mission was to find the traitor in your company."

"Even if it was one of my children."

"Yes," Wyatt replied, meeting Hamilton's gaze. "You didn't want the bureau in your business, but the stakes are too high when it comes to a foreign government and national security."

"You were very good. Very convincing. Are you even an ex-Marine?"

"No, but I knew you had a soft spot for fellow soldiers."

A growing awareness spread through Hamilton's gaze. "The carjacking—the robbery—"

"A set-up," Wyatt admitted. "Your former security director also won a lottery prize courtesy of the bureau."

"Which allowed him to move up his retirement. You

thought of everything." Hamilton's gaze moved to her. "You knew all this, Avery?"

"Not until this morning," she said, hardly able to believe it had only been that morning. So much had happened in the intervening hours.

"So, he lied to you, too? But it looks like you've forgiven him."

"How could I not? He saved my life three times. And Wyatt is a good man. He was working to find the mole in your company. He was working to prevent a national security disaster. You might hate him for lying to you, but you can't deny that without Wyatt, you might be launching a defective satellite tomorrow, destroying your company and everything you have worked for."

Hamilton gave her a thoughtful look. "That's quite an impassioned response."

"I'm just telling the truth. I know you feel betrayed—"

"You have no idea how I feel," he said bitterly. "But most of those emotions are directed at my son."

"I'm sorry about Kyle," she couldn't help saying. "I didn't want it to be anyone in the family. I didn't want to believe that someone at the dinner table last night was plotting to kill me."

"And I'm sorry that you had to go through all this," Hamilton said. "You lost your friend. And you almost lost your life. I had no idea Kyle felt the way he did about his mother's illness and her death. Margery and I were a team. I begged her to let me get her the most experimental treatment in the world. I would have spent my entire fortune to save her life, but there was nothing that could be done, and she didn't want any of that. She wanted to spend her last days with her family."

"I believe you," she said, seeing the pain in his eyes.

"Kyle was very close to his mother. I should realized he was more deeply affected than the others, but he always keeps everything inside of himself. As for the security breach, I honestly didn't think anyone was conspiring with the

Chinese to sell our technology, especially not Kyle. He was the brains behind the business, and I always gave him credit for that. I thought we had a shared dream, but I was wrong. I don't even know my own son." He paused, his eyes turning even more embittered. "And Larry—my best friend. He was conspiring against me, too. What's that old saying—it's always the person closest to you who carries the knife? I should have remembered that sooner."

"Larry has a lot of debts, from what I understand," she said.

"And a drunk for a wife," Hamilton added. "I've been bailing him out for years. I was happy to do it. I thought that's what friends did for each other." He let out a heavy breath. "I need to call the launch team, scrub the mission."

"You're not going to give up, are you?" she asked. "You can reschedule once everything is back on course."

"I don't know, Avery," he said with sad eyes. "Maybe this dream has run its course."

"Or maybe it just needs to be rethought."

He gave her a small smile. "I know you love space as much as I do. We might be the only ones."

"We're not the only ones. There are thousands of people at Nova Star alone who believe in your vision. You can come back from this."

"Thank you, Avery." He glanced at Wyatt. "And what will you do now, Mr. Tanner? Move on to the next case?"

"Eventually."

"You were a good undercover agent," Hamilton said with a note of admiration in his eyes. "You knew exactly what I needed, and you gave it to me."

"I doubt you'll believe this, but I actually enjoyed getting to know you, and I didn't want any of your children to be guilty."

"Well, you didn't make Kyle do what he did. That's on him. He's going to pay a heavy price, won't he?"

Wyatt nodded. "A very heavy price."

"I still want to protect him. How ridiculous is that?"

"It's not ridiculous. You're his father," Wyatt replied.

Hamilton looked back at her. "Is Brett going to be all right, Avery?"

"He will be. He put himself between me and a bullet. I don't think I ever expected he would do that."

"Funny. I would have never expected anything less. If I could take a bullet for Kyle, I would it in a heartbeat. You love your kids even when you shouldn't—even when they hate you.

As Hamilton walked away, she blew out a breath, then turned to Wyatt. She wanted to throw herself into his arms, but she hesitated, thinking not here—not with so many people around.

But Wyatt had no such concern. He pulled her against his chest and gave her a kiss. "It's over, Avery. You're safe now."

She closed her eyes, believing every word. Not just because Kyle was on his way to jail and the contract killer was dead, but because she was back in Wyatt's arms, and that's where she wanted to stay."

Twenty-Six

—➤➤◄◄◄—

Wyatt drove Avery and Whitney to the hospital, leaving Bree and Flynn to finish up with Jonathan and Hamilton. He didn't know what was in store for his future career, but based on Joanna's cryptic comment, someone high up had come to his defense. He wondered who that could possibly be. He didn't know that many people in the upper echelons of the bureau. He also still wanted to know who had taken the time to frame him.

Maybe Kyle had done that, too, just to separate him from Avery.

But that was a problem for another day.

Both Avery and Whitney were quiet on the drive. He would have expected Whitney to be filled with questions, but since she'd gotten into the back of the car ten minutes ago, she hadn't said a word.

Avery shifted in her seat, glancing at him, and then over her shoulder at Whitney. "Are you all right?"

"I don't think so," Whitney said, a lost note in her voice. "I can't believe what Kyle did, how many people he hurt, how many lies he told. He even set Jonathan up. He would have sold his own brother if he had to. He probably would have sold me out, too, if I'd had anything to do with Nova Star." She paused. "I really need to see Brett. I need to talk to him. He'll know what to say, how to make me feel better." She took another breath. "That sounded selfish, didn't it? That's me, always thinking of myself. I want Brett to be okay. I need him to be all right. He's everything to me."

"We'll be there soon," Avery said, not commenting on whether or not she believed Whitney was selfish.

"I know you don't like me," Whitney said. "Or at least you don't like me with your father. Oh, hell, maybe you just don't like me. But you have to know that I am crazy about Brett. He's the best thing that ever happened to me. I love him like mad. And, surprisingly, he seems to love me, too."

"He does love you," Avery said. "He told me that earlier tonight. He said the only thing he was afraid of was that you'd suddenly realize he wasn't that young."

"I don't care about his age. He gets me. You know how rare it is to feel free to be yourself with someone?"

"I do know," Avery said, her gaze moving to him. "It's very rare."

He gave her a smile, really wanting to get her alone, so he could tell her how he felt about her. Her defense of him at Hamilton's house had given him hope that they might be able to get past the lies he'd told her. He really hoped so. But he couldn't go there now. They still needed to tie up some loose ends, and one of those ends was her dad. Avery wouldn't be able to really relax until she saw that her father was all right.

A few minutes later, he dropped Avery and Whitney at the front door, then parked the car in the lot and headed inside. He found both women in Brett's room on the fourth floor. Whitney sat on the bed next to Brett, who was propped up against the pillows, pale but smiling, while Avery was in an adjacent chair, watching the two of them. She seemed to appreciate their loving reunion.

After undergoing minor surgery, Brett's arm had been bandaged and was now encased in a sling. He was apparently going to spend the night just to make sure there were no complications.

"Thanks for bringing these very special women to me," Brett told him, as he moved into the room. "And thank you for showing up at the house when you did. Avery and I owe you both our lives."

"I'm happy I arrived in time."

"I can't believe it was Kyle behind all of this madness," Brett added. "Avery was just filling me in. Hamilton must be beside himself."

"He's going to need some time to work it out," he said.

"My brother is truly crazy," Whitney put in. "I never had any idea he blamed my father for my mother's death. My dad really did try to save her life. But my mom didn't want experimental treatments. She just wanted to live while she could. I thought Kyle knew that."

"It sounds like he was blinded by grief," Brett told Whitney.

"We were all grief-stricken; he wasn't the only one. I was incredibly sad."

"But you're stronger than Kyle," Brett told Whitney. "And you'll have to use that strength to help Jonathan and your dad get through all this."

Wyatt saw Whitney respond to Brett's words like a flower opening up to the sun. She soaked it all in and somehow became a better person.

Avery got to her feet. "I'm going to leave you two alone. Dad, I'll call you tomorrow."

"Where are you going now?" Brett asked.

She hesitated. "I guess I'm going home."

"You're really safe?"

"I am, Dad. It's all over."

"Maybe you could still keep an eye on her," Brett told Wyatt.

"I am absolutely going to do that," he said, opening the door for Avery.

As they stepped into the hall, she said, "I still have my bag at my dad's house, but I don't want to go back there right now. I don't know what happened to that man's body, and I really don't want to see him again."

"You don't want to go back there anyway. The police and FBI are probably at your dad's house. It's a crime scene."

"Well, I don't need to break into any more crime scenes," she said lightly, reminding him of when they'd first met.

"That's a good idea," he said, as they walked out to the car. "You can pick up your things later. But you're not going home, Avery."

She frowned at his words. "My home is safe now."

"It is safe, but I'm fairly certain that your apartment was trashed at some point since we left on Saturday, and I don't think you should deal with that tonight. I want to take you to a nice hotel by the beach. We'll get a room with a balcony and a view, so you can take a look at the stars before you go to sleep."

She gave him a smile. "That does sound nice. I'm exhausted, but I don't really feel sleepy."

"You're still coming off the adrenaline."

"That must be it."

Silence fell between them for a few moments, as they got into the car, and he maneuvered his way out of the parking lot.

"I want to stay with you at the hotel," he added, just so there was no confusion. "I'll sleep in a separate bed. I just need to be near to you." He turned his head when she didn't reply and saw her heart in her eyes. "Is that okay?"

"More than okay. I need to be near you, too, Wyatt."

"I know that you're still angry about the lies I told you."

"Honestly, right now I'm all out of anger. I'm tired of being afraid, worried, suspicious, or angry. I just want to breathe and be grateful that we're both alive, and my dad is alive, and we're going to get justice for Noelle. Although, I still don't really know what her motivation was. She kept telling me that night at the pier that she'd finally decided to do the right thing, be a better person, so why did she steal the drive but then not go through with the hand off? Why leave her bracelet in her apartment? It's really a miracle that I found it."

"Well, Carter is going to survive his wounds. He may be able to tell us more when he's not fighting for his life. My gut tells me that Noelle first saw the opportunity to make some quick cash, but then she saw a chance to make a big play, to save Nova Star, the company she was coming to love, and maybe to impress you. I'm sure she thought the foreign agent would believe that the game was over, since Hamilton had the information, and that she could walk away, but that was naïve. She was in over her head."

"Noelle always leapt before she looked."

"Whoever stabbed Noelle probably consulted with Kyle right after her death. Kyle must have confirmed that his father was in the dark and that the drive was still missing."

"So they went to her apartment and then came after me. I wish she would have just talked to me, told me what she'd discovered. There were a few moments that Friday night when I thought she wanted to say something, but she didn't."

"I don't know why she didn't, Avery. Unless she was embarrassed that her new boyfriend was a thief and a traitor."

"Maybe it was that," she said. "I guess I just have to hang on to the fact that as misguided as her actions might have been, her heart was in the right place. And that's actually how Noelle always was—a good person, who didn't always make the best decisions. I'm going to miss her. I might have held her feet to the ground, but she always pushed me to let go, step out of my comfort zone." She paused. "I wish you could have known her."

"I feel like I know her through you."

"I still have to plan her memorial."

"You'll get to all that, but not tonight."

"Definitely not tonight."

Fifteen minutes later, he pulled up in front of the valet at a five-star beachfront hotel, hoping they could get a room. Since it was a Monday night in December, he was hopeful.

Their luck held out, and they were given an oceanfront room with a balcony.

"This is going to cost a fortune," Avery said, as he unlocked the door and ushered her inside.

"I've still got the two thousand dollars from the contract killer's wallet," he said lightly.

"Let's use that," she said with a reckless smile. "Although, it's probably against the rules, isn't it?"

He shrugged. "Since it was money toward killing you, I think if anyone deserves it, it's you."

"Me, too." She walked through the bedroom to the balcony doors and opened them.

He followed her onto the dark deck. The night was clear but cold, with a brisk wind coming off the water.

Avery looked up at the sky and let out a sigh that was more pleasure than weariness. "It's beautiful, isn't it? The stars are so bright tonight."

Gazing at her beautiful profile, amazed that there could still be wonder in her eyes after everything that had happened, he thought she was far more beautiful than the night sky."

She glanced over at him. "You're not looking up, Wyatt."

"No. I'm looking at you, Avery."

"And what do you see?"

"The brightest star…the one that can lead me home."

"Where is home?" she asked, a hushed note in her voice.

"I'm pretty sure it's wherever you are," he confessed.

Her eyes widened. "Really, Wyatt? That might be the best line I've ever heard."

"It's not a line, Avery." He put his hands on her shoulders, turning her to face him. "I'm being honest. I know that might seem ironic, because I've spent a lot of time lying to you. But that ends now."

"I was really angry at first. I felt betrayed…confused. But I've had a little time to think, and I know it was the job, Wyatt. You had to protect your cover. You didn't know who I was in the beginning. And even then, you couldn't really trust me because of my father." She paused. "I know you had doubts about him. I actually had a few myself."

"I didn't want him to be guilty. I'm glad he wasn't."

"Me, too."

"I hated lying to you, Avery. It's usually not a problem for me. When I go undercover, I'm normally infiltrating criminal organizations where everyone is bad, everyone is a liar. It was different being at Nova Star, getting caught up in Hamilton's dreams, and in yours. I'm not sure I could have kept up the pretense much longer, especially not with you."

"Your job sounds dangerous."

"It can be," he admitted.

"Do you always work undercover?"

"I have for the last five years, but I don't know what's next."

"Because you don't have another assignment…"

"Because for the first time in my career, I don't want to disappear into some other world. I don't want to become someone else." He paused. "I've been in the shadows a long time. I liked it a lot at first. I'd wanted to disappear from my own life, and this job was the perfect way to do that. But as the years have passed, I've started to feel like I'm missing something. I've sometimes wondered if I'm forgetting who I really am. When I met you, something inside me snapped. I didn't want to keep my walls up. I didn't want to look down; I wanted to look up. You didn't just show me the universe, you showed me myself."

"I'm so glad," she whispered, her heart in her eyes.

"I know I saved your life."

"Multiple times," she put in.

"But you saved me, too. And no matter what happens, I'm never going to forget you."

"What you should never forget is yourself," she said.

"I'm going to try to hang on to that, too," he admitted.

"Could you work for the FBI and not go undercover, Wyatt?"

"Yes, I could. But I don't know how good of an agent I would be. I'm better on my own. No rules. No politics."

"Then maybe you should keep doing what you're doing."

"Or maybe it's time for a change, but a lot of that is dependent on what happens with any internal investigations the bureau decides to conduct regarding my behavior and Bree's."

"I hope she won't get into any trouble."

"I'm going to do everything I can to make sure she doesn't pay for my sins."

Avery gave him a questioning look. "That blonde agent who arrested you…"

"Joanna?"

"She has something against you, doesn't she? When she looked at you at Hamilton's house, it felt personal."

"I don't know exactly what her deal is, but she asked me out years ago when we were at Quantico, and I said no. She was one of the instructors, and she's ten years older than me. I thought it was inappropriate."

"Ah, a scorned woman. You do leave broken hearts behind you, don't you?"

"Her heart was not broken. We never went out." He paused. "I don't care about Joanna, and I will figure out who set me up, but that's for tomorrow or the next day."

"Are we back to living in the moment?" she asked wrapping her arms around his waist.

He smiled down at her and couldn't help but steal a kiss before he answered. "I definitely want to live in the moment with you again…I just want there to be a lot more moments in our future. I don't know what I want in my career, what will work for me, but I do know that I want a life that's more than my career. And I want you in it."

"You do?" she asked, uncertainty in her eyes. "Are you sure when all this excitement wears off, you won't find me incredibly boring?"

He laughed. "Never."

"I can be boring, Wyatt. The last few days aren't me. You know how you said everyone has a secret...well, I do have one."

"What's that?"

"When you turn off the lights in my bedroom apartment, the ceiling turns into the night sky. Yes. I am that crazy about space."

He laughed. "I can live with that. But I'm not trying to rush you into anything. I just want you to know that this is me, the real me. There are no more secrets. Everything I told you about my past was true. And the way I feel about you is true. I hope you can believe that."

"I do believe it. I trust you, Wyatt. And I want to get to know you. I want to hear all your stories. I want to meet your friends."

"I want to hear your stories and meet your friends, too." He paused. "But mostly I just want to show you that I'm not going to be like your dad. I'm not going to change into someone else and disappear on you. My professional life is not my personal life."

"I know that, Wyatt. I admit that at first, when I heard about your disguise, I thought that I'd been taken in again, but now after everything that's happened, I realize how wrong I was. When I made love to you last night, I told you I knew who you were, and I did, and I do. It doesn't matter what your name is. I know your heart." She put her hand on his chest and gave him a smile that nearly undid him.

"You are something else, Avery. You have knocked me off my feet. You have spun me around and turned me upside down. You have made me look at the world, at myself, in a different way."

"That wasn't all me."

"It was you," he said, pressing his lips against her soft cheek. "Last night was the most amazing night of my life."

"I hope you're talking about the hours when we weren't running for our lives."

"I am."

She smiled up at him. "Let's see if we can top it. You like a challenge, don't you?"

"Always," he said, as he slid his hands through her hair, trapping her face for another long, tender, promising kiss.

"Then take me to bed, Wyatt."

"I thought you'd never ask."

Epilogue

Six days later, on a beautiful but cold Sunday afternoon, Avery stood on the same beach where she'd let herself scream into the wind only a week earlier. But she wasn't crying this time. She was with Wyatt as well as friends and family who were coming together to celebrate Noelle's life.

Having finally decided that the last thing Noelle would want was a funeral, she had thrown together a gourmet picnic. There were a couple of coolers filled with drinks, and a dozen colorful blankets spread across the sand. Tomorrow, she and Wyatt would hire a boat to take them out on the ocean, so they could toss Noelle's ashes at sea, but today was to laugh and smile and live life the way Noelle always had.

"You did a great job," Wyatt told her, as he joined her at the water's edge.

"Thanks. I think Noelle would like it." She smiled at Wyatt, feeling her heart flip over just from gazing into his sexy brown eyes. They'd spent every night together, and most days, of the past week, sorting out their lives, cleaning up their ransacked apartments, and dealing with the fallout from everything that had happened.

Wyatt had spent long hours with the FBI, following up

all aspects of the conspiracy case, interrogating Carter and Bickmore and even tracking down the Chinese company involved and rounding up a few other people from Kyle's department who had been complicit in small ways.

After Hamilton had canceled the launch, she'd been kept busy at work, dealing with endless questions about Nova Star's future as well as keeping the daily programs going.

But every day, life had started to make a little more sense. And a lot of that had to do with Wyatt. She was getting to know the real him, and she was falling more in love each day.

She thought Noelle would like that, too. She'd always said that falling in love was the best feeling you could ever have, which was why she liked to do it so often.

"Hello there," Whitney said with a wave, coming across the sand with Avery's father.

"Thanks for coming," she said, giving both her dad and Whitney a hug. She was starting to like Whitney more, too, finally believing in the love she had for Brett. "I do have to warn you, Dad, that Mom will also be here."

"I can handle seeing your mother," her dad said easily. "And this isn't about us; it's about Noelle. What about Kari?"

"She's not going to make it. I sent her some money to help her out with her immediate bills and told her I would take care of everything here."

Her father gave her an approving nod. "You always do the right thing."

"I try."

"It's nice to see you as well," her father told Wyatt.

"You, too. Happy to see you got the sling off."

"Everything is healing well. I'm back to writing, too. The past few weeks have inspired me to dig a little deeper into family relationships."

She gave him a smile that held no more bitterness. Her dad might always be an opportunist, but he was still a good person.

"My father will be here, too," Whitney said.

She was surprised. She'd given Hamilton an invite but hadn't thought he would come with all the turmoil going on in his life.

"I'm so glad," she said.

"There he is now," Whitney said, tipping her head toward the path.

"I'm going to say hello," she said. "Make yourselves comfortable. Get food. Get drinks."

"We'll be fine," her dad said.

"I'll take care of them," Wyatt added.

She walked across the beach and gave him a big smile. "Hamilton."

"Avery," he returned, giving her a warm hug.

"I really appreciate you being here."

"Noelle was part of our Nova Star family. And since Kyle was also responsible for her death, I wanted to pay my respects."

"Thank you. How are you doing?"

"Well, the past week has been filled with revelations, most bewildering and disappointing. But I'm starting to see a path to the stars again."

She liked the gleam in his eyes. "Really? You're not going to shut down the company?"

"No. Kyle's actions have definitely set us back, but he wasn't the only engineer working on our technology. And I feel like I owe it to everyone at the company to keep things going. I also believe my wife would have wanted that. She did believe in this dream, Avery. And I did do everything I could to save her."

"I know that, Hamilton. I know you loved her. She was a special woman."

"I don't know what's going to happen to Kyle. He doesn't want to speak to me, and maybe that's just as well. There's really nothing to say. His actions are indefensible. Even if he believed I let his mother die, he shouldn't have done what he did. He left death and injury in his wake."

"I know it's complicated, though. As you said, he's your child."

"He is. And I'm going to make sure he has a good attorney. Other than that, he'll fight his own battles." His gaze moved past her. "I see that Wyatt is still here. The two of you are together, aren't you?"

"We are. I'm in love with Wyatt."

"It doesn't bother you how easily he became someone else?"

"No. I know who he is. And he's a good man. The two of you were actually on the same side. You both wanted the truth."

"But I didn't want it enough to risk my son's life. I thought I was protecting Jonathan. And there was even a point when I thought Whitney might be involved. She's always complaining about being left out. Kyle was my last choice. In fact, he wasn't even on the radar. I guess that's why you shouldn't investigate yourself."

"Probably not. Can I get you a drink?"

"I'll help myself. Go visit with your friends."

"Whitney and my dad are here."

"I see them. You really don't have to worry about me, Avery, but I appreciate your concern."

As Hamilton wandered off, she saw Wyatt talking to Bree. She thought about joining them, but her mom was coming down the path, followed by her boyfriend, Don. Her mom was not going to love the fact that she'd been shot at while she was gone, but she'd probably be happy to know she'd met the man of her dreams. The definitely had a lot to talk about.

* * *

"What are you going to do, Wyatt?" Bree asked. "Now that you've been completely reinstated, and your slate has been wiped clean?"

"I'm not entirely sure. Flynn might be moving on to another case."

"You're going to stick with Flynn."

"That depends."

"On Avery?"

"Yes," he admitted.

Bree smiled. "You finally found the woman who made you want to come out of the shadows."

"I did. And I'm not sure I want to go back under."

"There are jobs you can do that don't require that."

"I'm looking into all that. By the way, I still don't know who set me up. I've gone through the players involved, and no one seems to be a good choice for Joanna's anonymous source."

"Well, it looks like my instincts about Vincent Rowland were wrong."

"Why do you say that?" he asked sharply.

"Because I found out from Joanna that Vincent was the one who made calls on your behalf to the top people in the bureau. He basically saved your ass."

He thought about that, wondering why Vincent had gone to the trouble. "It would be an interesting play to throw me into the fire and then save me."

She gave him a doubtful look. "Now you sound like the one who's paranoid about Vincent."

"It just doesn't quite add up. And I trust your instincts, Bree."

"We should have a group chat one day soon—get Damon, Parisa, and Diego in on a call."

"We should definitely warn them to watch their backs, especially Parisa and Diego. If Vincent was part of what happened in New York, then he already messed with Damon. But we don't need to talk about that now." His gaze wandered to Avery, who was talking to her mother.

"Is that Avery's mom?" Bree asked.

"I think so. I've only seen her picture until now."

"So, you're going to meet her today," Bree said with a gleam in her eyes. "I know you can blend into any group, any situation, but how good are you with mothers?"

"I've never met one before now," he admitted. "Never got close to anyone to meet their family, to be my real self."

"She's going to love you, Wyatt."

"For saving her daughter?"

"And for loving her daughter. You do love Avery, don't you?"

"More than I thought possible. I feel like I've been punched in the gut and I can't quite catch my breath."

"Yep, that's love," she said with a laugh.

"Speaking of love, where's your significant other?"

"Nathan is coming back to town tonight. Maybe we can double date one day next week."

"That sounds almost…normal," he said with a laugh.

"Well, I wouldn't get used to it. Our lives don't stay normal for long. You think Avery is up for it?"

"Most definitely," he said, as Avery joined them.

"Am I up for what?" she asked, having heard Bree's question.

"Loving an FBI agent," Bree said.

Avery's gaze met his. "Most definitely," she said, echoing his answer.

Bree laughed. "You two are too much. I'm going to get some food."

"I hope Bree didn't bring bad news," Avery said, linking her hands with his as she faced him.

"All good. I have a clean slate. I can do whatever I want to do next."

"What's that going to be?"

"I have no idea," he said with a laugh. "We'll figure it out together. As long as you're in my life, I honestly could do anything."

"I feel the same way. We make a good team."

"We do." He gazed deep into her eyes. "I love you, Avery. You have my heart. It's a little battered, but it's all yours."

Her gaze softened with tenderness. "And you have mine."

THE END

Want more
OFF THE GRID: FBI Series?

Available in 2019
Elusive Promise (#4)
Dangerous Choice (#5)

Continue reading for an excerpt from
Barbara Freethy's NYT Bestselling Book

TAKEN

Excerpt from
TAKEN

—➤➤◄◄◄—

Kayla Sheridan had longed for love, marriage and a family. Now, after a miraculous whirlwind courtship with the man of her dreams, she is his wife. But on their wedding night, he vanishes, leaving Kayla with the bitter realization that her desire has made her an easy mark for deception.

Nick Granville has an ingrained sense of honor and an intense desire to succeed in building the world's most challenging high-tech bridges. But when he crosses paths with a ruthless con man, he's robbed of everything he values, including his identity. With nothing left to lose, he'll risk any danger to clear his name and reclaim his life.

Thrown together by fate, Kayla and Nick embark on a desperate journey toward the truth -- to uncover the mysterious motives of an ingenious and seductive stranger who boasts he can't be caught ... and to reveal the shocking secrets of their own shattered pasts.

Prologue

"To my wife." Nick Granville gave Kayla Sheridan a dazzling smile as he raised his champagne glass to hers.

Kayla tapped her glass against his. As she looked into the gorgeous blue eyes of the man she had married, she felt a rush of pure joy. She could hardly believe she was married, but an hour ago she'd vowed to love this man above all others. He'd put a ring on her finger and a diamond necklace around her neck and he'd promised to stay forever, which was really all she'd ever wanted. A child of divorce, she'd split her time between two houses, two sets of parents, two cities, and she'd said more than her share of good-byes. That was over now. She was Mrs. Nicholas Granville, and she would make her marriage stick.

The champagne tickled her throat. She felt almost dizzy with delight. "I can't believe how happy I am," she murmured. "My head is spinning."

"I like it when you're off balance," he said.

"I've been that way since the first second we met," she confessed. "Marrying you tonight is the most impulsive, reckless thing I have ever done in my life." She glanced down at the two-carat diamond ring on her finger. It was huge, dramatic, and wildly expensive. It wasn't the kind of ring she'd imagined wearing. She'd thought she'd have something set in an old-fashioned silver band, and in her wildest dreams the stone had never been this big; she was an incredibly lucky woman. And Nick was a very generous man. He'd been spoiling her rotten since their first date.

"You do impulsive well," Nick commented. "Better than I would have thought when we first met."

"Because you're a bad influence," she teased.

His grin broadened. "I've been told that before. Life is supposed to be fun. You are having fun, aren't you?"

"Absolutely. This day has been perfect. The chapel was lovely. The minister made a nice speech about love and marriage. I was afraid it would feel like a quickie wedding, but it didn't. And this hotel room -- it's incredible." She waved her hand in the air as she glanced around their honeymoon suite. Nick had ordered in scented candles that bathed the room in a soft light, riotous colorful wildflowers on every table, rose petals lining a romantic path to the bedroom, and silver trays with chocolate-covered strawberries, her favorite dessert. She couldn't have asked for a more romantic setting in which to begin her new life. "You've made me so happy, Nick. You've given me exactly what I wanted."

He nodded. "I feel the same way." He leaned forward and kissed her softly on the mouth, a promise of what was to come. "I'm going to get some ice." He sent her a meaningful look. "I think we'll want some cold champagne...later."

A tingle of anticipation ran down her spine. "Don't be long."

He picked up the ice bucket and headed for the door. Once there, he paused and pulled out the antique pocket watch she'd given him as a wedding present a few minutes earlier. "Thanks again for this," he said. "It means a lot to me."

"My grandmother told me I should give it to the man I love. And that's you."

Kayla wanted him to say he loved her, too, but he simply smiled and gave her a little wave as he left the room. It didn't matter that he hadn't said the words. He'd married her. That was what was important. She'd spent most of her twenties with a commitment-phobic boyfriend who couldn't bring himself to pop the question. Nick had told her almost immediately that he intended to be her husband. She'd been swept away by his love and his confidence that they were perfect for each other. Now, only three weeks since that first date, she was his wife. She could hardly believe it. Three weeks! This was definitely the craziest thing she'd ever done.

Well, so what? She'd been responsible and cautious her entire life. She was almost thirty years old. It was about time she took a chance.

Too restless to sit, Kayla got up to look out the window. Their luxurious honeymoon suite was on the hotel's twenty-fifth floor and offered a spectacular view of Lake Tahoe and the surrounding Sierra Nevada mountains. She was only four hours from her home in the San Francisco Bay Area, but it felt like a million miles. Her entire life had changed during a simple wedding ceremony that had been witnessed by only two strangers. It was her one regret that neither her family nor Nick's had attended the wedding. But the past was behind her. Tonight was a new beginning.

Turning away from the window, she entered the bedroom. She took off her dress and slipped on a scarlet see-through silk teddy that left nothing to the imagination. Then she drew a brush through her long, thick, curly brown hair that fell past her shoulders and never seemed to do exactly what she wanted. Her best friend, Samantha, had told her that the messy, curly look was coming back in, so maybe for the first time in her life, Kayla's hair was actually in style.

A flash of insecurity made her wonder if the hot-red teddy was too much or if she should have gone with elegant white silk. But the sophisticated white lingerie she'd considered purchasing had reminded her of something her mother would wear, and she was definitely not her mother.

Smiling at that thought, Kayla couldn't help but be pleased by her reflection in the mirror. There was a sparkle in her brown eyes, a rosy glow in her cheeks. She looked like a woman in love. And that was exactly what she was. She'd made the right decision, she told herself again, trying to ignore the niggling little doubt that wouldn't seem to go away.

The quiet in the room made the voices in her head grow louder. She could hear her mother's shocked and disgusted words: *"Kayla, have you lost your mind? You can't marry a man you've known for three weeks. It's foolish. You'll regret this."* And her friend Samantha had pleaded with her. *"Just wait until I get back from London. You need to think, Kayla. How much do you really know about this man?"*

She knew enough, Kayla told herself firmly. And this marriage was between her and Nick, no one else. Turning away from the mirror, she sprayed some perfume in the air and walked through it. Debating whether or not she should wait for Nick in bed, she tried out several sexy poses on the satiny duvet. She felt completely ridiculous and chided herself for being nervous. It wasn't as if they hadn't had sex. And it had been good. It would be even better tonight because they were married, they were in love, and they were committed.

As she stood up, the suite seemed too quiet. She wondered what was taking Nick so long. The ice machine was only a short distance from the room, and he had left at least fifteen minutes ago. He must have decided to run downstairs and pick up another special dessert or more champagne. She smiled at the thought. Nick was so romantic. He always knew just how to make her feel loved and cherished.

She walked into the living room and sat down on the couch to wait. She flipped on the television and ran through the channels. The minutes continued to tick by. Glancing at her watch, she realized an hour had passed. An uneasy feeling swept through her body. She got up and paced. Within seconds the room grew too small for her growing agitation. She had a terrible feeling something was wrong.

Returning to the bedroom, she slipped out of her lingerie and dug through her suitcase for a pair of jeans and a T-shirt. All the while she kept hoping to hear Nick's footsteps or his voice.

Nothing. Silence.

She grabbed the key and left the suite, heading to the nearest ice machine. Nick wasn't there. She tried the other end of the hall, the next floor up, the next floor down. Her heart began to race. She checked the room again, then took the elevator down to the lobby, searching the casino, the shops, the restaurants and bars, and even the parking lot, where Nick's Porsche was parked right where they'd left it. She stopped by the phone bank in the lobby and called the room again. There was still no answer.

Kayla didn't know she was crying until an older woman stopped her by the elevator and asked her if everything was all right.

"My husband. I can't find my husband," she muttered.

The woman gave her a pitying smile. "Story of my life. He'll come back when he runs out of money, honey. They all do."

"He's not gambling. It's our wedding night. He went to get ice." Kayla entered the next elevator, leaving the woman and her disbelieving expression behind. She didn't care what that woman thought. Kayla knew Nick wouldn't gamble away their wedding night. He wouldn't do that to her. But when she returned to her room, it was as empty as when she'd left it.

She didn't know what to do. She sat back down to wait.

When the clock struck midnight, and Nick had been gone for almost five hours, Kayla called the front desk and told them her husband was missing. The hotel sent up George

Benedict, an older man who worked for hotel security. After discussing her situation, he assured her they would look for Nick, but there was something in his expression that told her they wouldn't look too hard. It was obvious to Kayla that Mr. Benedict thought Nick was either downstairs gambling and had lost track of time or he had skipped out on her, plain and simple. Neither explanation made sense to her.

Kayla didn't sleep all night. In her mind she ran through a dozen possible scenarios of what could have happened to Nick. Maybe he'd been robbed, hit over the head, knocked unconscious. Maybe he was sitting in a hospital right now with amnesia, not knowing who he was. She hoped to God it wasn't worse than that. No news had to be good news, right?

Finally, she curled up in a chair by the window, watching the moon go down and the sun come up over the lake.

It was the longest night of her life.

A knock came at the door just before nine o'clock in the morning. She ran to open it, hoping she'd see Nick in the hallway, wearing a sheepish smile, offering some crazy explanation.

It wasn't Nick. It was the security guy from the night before, George Benedict. His expression was serious, his eyes somber.

Putting a hand to her suddenly racing heart, she said, "What's happened?"

He held up a black tuxedo jacket. A now limp and wilted red rose boutonniere hung from the lapel. "We found this in a men's room off the lobby. Is it your husband's jacket?"

"I...I think so. I don't understand. Where's Nick?"

"We don't know yet, but this was in the pocket." He held out his hand, a solid gold wedding band in his palm.

She took the ring from him, terrified when she read the simple inscription on the inside of the band, FOREVER LOVE, the same words that were engraved on her wedding ring. She couldn't breathe, couldn't speak.

This was Nick's ring, the one she'd slipped on his finger

when she'd vowed to spend the rest of her life with him. "No," she breathed.

"I've seen it happen before," the older man said gently. "A hasty marriage in a casino chapel, second thoughts..."

She saw the pity in his eyes, and she couldn't accept it. "You're wrong. You have to be wrong. Nick loved me. He wanted to get married. It was his idea. *His* idea," she repeated desperately.

She closed her hand around the ring, her fingers tightening into a fist. Her husband had not run out on her... had he?

Chapter One

Two weeks later

Nick Granville was happy to be home. He hadn't left his heart in San Francisco, as the song went, but he had missed the city of narrow, steep streets and sweeping bay vistas. As he set down his suitcases on the gleaming hardwood floor in the living room of his two-story house, he drew in a deep breath and slowly let it out. While the past three months spent in the jungles of Africa had been spectacular, engineering bridges in remote parts of the world had taught him to appreciate the simple pleasures in life, like a hot shower, a good cup of coffee, and a soft bed. He intended to enjoy all three as soon as possible.

He walked across the room to throw open the windows. He was surprised to find the blinds open. The cleaning service must have forgotten to close them. He'd hired a service to come in once a month while he was gone to keep the dust under control. They'd obviously done a good job. The air didn't smell nearly as musty as he'd anticipated, but he opened a window just the same, allowing the cool March breezes to blow through the room.

He'd chosen this small house because it overlooked the

Marina Green, the bay, the Marin Headlands, and most important, the Golden Gate Bridge. Bridges were his passion. He was an admitted junkie. His living room walls were covered with photographs of his favorite bridges, a few he'd had a hand in building. There was something about the massive structures that made his blood stir. He'd decided to become an engineer before he graduated from high school, and he'd gone after that career with single-minded determination. It hadn't been easy. He'd had a lot of other distractions and responsibilities, which he'd acquired when his father had run out on the family, but that was water under the proverbial bridge, he thought with a small smile. He had the life he wanted now. That was all that mattered.

Turning away from the view, he caught sight of his telephone answering machine. The red light was blinking. He pushed the button on the machine and listened as the first message played back. A woman's voice came out of the speaker.

"Nick, it's Kayla. Where are you? Please call me as soon as you can."

Kayla? Who the hell was Kayla? The machine beeped.

"Nick, it's Kayla again. I don't know what to do. The security guard found your coat and wedding ring in a men's room at the hotel. I'm really worried. If you wanted out, you should have told me. Please call me."

His coat and his wedding ring? He sure as hell didn't have a wedding ring. She obviously had the wrong number and the wrong Nick.

"Me again," she said, her voice filled with panic. "I don't know why I keep calling, except I don't know what else to do. The police say they can't help me because there's no evidence anything happened to you. They think you ran out on me. I guess that's what you did. Don't you think you owe me at least an explanation? I love you, Nick." Her voice caught on a sob. "I thought you loved me, too. It was your idea to get married so fast."

Nick shut off the machine, reluctant to hear more of her desperate pleas. He felt as if he had stepped into the middle of someone else's life, and his relief at being home was tempered by the sense that something was very wrong. As he looked around the room, his uneasiness grew. Small things began to stand out: the celebrity magazines on the coffee table, the wilted roses in a vase by the window, the empty coffee mug on a side table, the throw blanket that he usually kept on his bed now resting on the arm of his brown leather couch.

Unsettled, Nick walked into the kitchen and found a box of Lucky Charms on the counter, the kind of sugared cereal he'd never eaten in his life. In the refrigerator there was a half-open bottle of chardonnay and a carton of milk that had expired a month ago. His stomach began to churn as he considered the possibilities. Obviously, someone had been in his home. The only people who had keys were his mother and the cleaning service. His mother would never leave sour milk in the refrigerator.

His nerves began to tingle. The air was filled with vague scents he couldn't quite place -- a man's cologne or a woman's perfume? The silence felt thick and tense. He turned around, feeling as if someone were standing behind him, but there was no one there.

He picked up the phone and called the cleaning service. "This is Nick Granville," he told the woman who answered. "I'd like to speak to the person who has been cleaning my house for the last three months."

He heard the flip of papers, and then she said, "That would be Joanne. She's not in right now. Can I have her call you?"

"Yes, I need to speak to her as soon as possible. It's urgent." He ended the call and punched in his mother's number. She didn't answer. Not wanting to leave a long message on her machine, he simply told her he was home and asked her to call him back as soon as possible.

He moved across the living room and up the stairs. The master bedroom was the first door on the right. He paused just inside the room. The cream-colored down comforter on his bed was pulled back, the sheets and blankets tangled, as if someone had recently gotten up. A couple of towels from his bathroom lay in a heap on the floor. An empty wineglass sat on the bedside table.

Every detail made his blood pressure rise. What kind of thief slept in his bed, took a shower in his bathroom, and kept food in his kitchen?

The phone rang and he grabbed the extension by the bed, hoping for some answers. It was Joanne from the cleaning service.

"Is something wrong, Mr. Granville?" she asked. "Laurie told me I needed to call you right away."

"Yes, there's something wrong," he snapped. "This place is a mess. There's crap everywhere, towels on the floor, and the bed is unmade. What the hell has been going on in my home?"

"Excuse me? I don't understand," she said, obvious confusion in her voice.

"What don't you understand? I've been out of the country. The only person to have access to my house is your cleaning service."

"But you were home a few weeks ago," she said. "I ran into you right before Valentine's Day. Don't you remember? We spoke about how funny it was that we were finally meeting face-to-face."

"What are you talking about? I haven't been home in three months, so you couldn't possibly have spoken to me." Nick's mind raced. Joanne had spoken to someone—who? Obviously, it had been a man, and that man had told her that he was Nick Granville. Who would do that? Nick didn't have any brothers, no friends who would play that kind of a joke on him.

The silence on the phone lengthened. Finally, Joanne

said, "I don't know what to say, Mr. Granville. Perhaps you've forgotten. You should ask the woman you were with."

The woman? He was reminded of the pleading, desperate voice from the answering machine.

"You said you were getting married that weekend," Joanne continued. "You both looked incredibly happy. I thought it was so romantic that you were going to have a Valentine's Day wedding."

He couldn't believe what he was hearing. "That wasn't me. You didn't talk to me."

"The man I spoke to said he was Nick Granville," Joanne stated. "I didn't imagine it."

"I'm sure you spoke to someone, but it wasn't me. I'll need to talk to you further about what these people look like. First I'm going to call the police."

"I'll do whatever I can to help," Joanne replied, a nervous note in her voice. "But I swear I thought the man was you."

"I'm sure you did." Nick hung up the phone, feeling completely rocked by the conversation. He'd always prided himself on being able to roll with the punches, adapt to any situation, no matter how dangerous or bizarre. But this invasion of his home, his privacy, his life, disturbed him more than he wanted to admit. As he gazed around the room, he saw his computer on the desk. The monitor was dark, but the light on the hard drive was on. Someone had been on his computer. He cursed himself for never setting a password, but he'd put it off. No one used the computer but him. Now he realized whoever had been in his home could have accessed his bank accounts, his credit cards, and God knew what else. It occurred to him that he hadn't looked at a bank statement in a very long time. He hadn't felt the need. His income far outstripped his living expenses, especially when he was working in the field. He could have been ripped off in a big way.

He rushed across the room to check the computer. The

machine whirred and whirred. It must have frozen. *Damn.* He turned it off, then back on. While he was waiting for it to boot up, he returned downstairs to the living room and replayed the messages on the answering machine.

"Nick, it's Kayla...."

Kayla. She had to be involved. How the hell was he going to find her?

❖

END OF EXCERPT

About The Author

Barbara Freethy is a #1 New York Times Bestselling Author of 67 novels ranging from contemporary romance to romantic suspense and women's fiction. Traditionally published for many years, Barbara opened her own publishing company in 2011 and has since sold over 7 million books! Twenty of her titles have appeared on the New York Times and USA Today Bestseller Lists.

Known for her emotional and compelling stories of love, family, mystery and romance, Barbara enjoys writing about ordinary people caught up in extraordinary adventures. Barbara's books have won numerous awards. She is a six-time finalist for the RITA for best contemporary romance from Romance Writers of America and a two-time winner for DANIEL'S GIFT and THE WAY BACK HOME.

Barbara has lived all over the state of California and currently resides in Northern California where she draws much of her inspiration from the beautiful bay area.

For a complete listing of books, as well as excerpts and contests, and to connect with Barbara:

Visit Barbara's Website:
www.barbarafreethy.com

Join Barbara on Facebook:
www.facebook.com/barbarafreethybooks

Follow Barbara on Twitter:
www.twitter.com/barbarafreethy